"Did Lulu hire you to find her?"

"No."

"She was just handing out pictures to strangers when you happened by?"

"Has anyone ever told you you suck at sarcasm?"

"No."

Yeah, that was probably true. "You know what?" I said, "I don't have to tell you anything, but here's the truth. I'm out. Good luck finding Lulu and Rheesha. I want nothing to do with it." I held the photo out for him again. He kept his hands firmly in his pockets.

"It's too late for that," he said.

"For what?"

"Backing out. You're a part of this, Beckstrom."

"Really? Since when?"

"Since you touched that photo. They're looking for you now. And they'll find you."

Then the bastard turned around and started walking away.

—From "The Sweet Smell of Cherries"
by Devon Monk

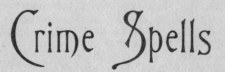

Crime Spells

Also Available from DAW Books:

Blood Bank, by Tanya Huff
Tanya Huff's *Blood* books centered around three main characters, Vicki Nelson, a homicide cop turned private detective, her former partner Mike Celluci, and vampire Henry Fitzroy, who is the illegitimate son of Henry VIII. Not only are the three of them caught in a love triangle, but they are, time and again, involved in mysteries with a supernatural slant from demons, to werewolves, to mummies. Here are all the short stories featuring Henry, Vicki, and Mike, and as an added bonus for fans of the TV series, *Blood Bank* includes the actual screenplay for "Stone Cold," the episode Tanya herself wrote for the *Blood Ties* series, along with a special introduction by Tanya, detailing her own experiences with the show.

Enchantment Place, edited by Denise Little
A new mall is always worth a visit, especially if it's filled with one-of-a-kind specialty stores. And the shops in Enchantment Place couldn't be more special. For Enchantment Place lives up to its name, catering to a rather unique clientele, ranging from vampires and were-creatures, to wizards and witches, elves and unicorns. In short, anyone with shopping needs not likely to be met in the chain stores. With stories by Mary Jo Putney, Peter Morwood, Diane Duane, Laura Resnick, Esther Friesner, Sarah A. Hoyt, and others.

Witch High, edited by Denise Little
There are high schools attended by students with special talents, like music and art, or science and mathematics. But what if there was a school that catered to those rarest of students—people with the talent to perform actual magic? The fourteen original tales included in *Witch High* explore the challenges that students of the magical arts may face in a high school of their very own. If you think chemistry is difficult, try studying alchemy. If you ever fell victim to a school bully, how would you deal with a bully gifted with powerful magic? If you ever wished for extra time to study for those exams, could the right spell give you all the time you could possibly need? These are just a few of the magical adventures that will await you when you enter Salem Township Public High School #4, a place where Harry Potter and his friends would feel right at home.

Crime Spells

edited by
Martin H. Greenberg
and Loren L. Coleman

DAW BOOKS, INC.
DONALD A. WOLLHEIM, FOUNDER
375 Hudson Street, New York, NY 10014

ELIZABETH R. WOLLHEIM
SHEILA E. GILBERT
PUBLISHERS
http://www.dawbooks.com

First Printing, February 2009
1 2 3 4 5 6 7 8 9

Acknowledgments

Table of Contents

vii

Foreword

Loren L. Coleman

I've always been fascinated with the idea, apparently shared by so many people, that magic—if it does or could exist—would somehow make everything easier.

That you *can* get something for nothing.

You hear it in conversations all the time. After something happens that was easier than it should have been, someone will shrug and say, "Must have been magic." Searching for the solution to a hard problem is described as "needing some magic." And a windfall, a bonus, a lucky occurrence: "magical."

I suppose the quick and easy answer for this is to blame some of the old fables. Aladdin and his magic lamp, for instance. On the surface, it sounds like such a great deal. Three wishes, no waiting. Don't need a permit, no license, and the IRS doesn't even have a check-off box for the value returned from the djinn. There is no downside. Right?

Ahh, but the fine print. That's what everyone tends to forget when reminiscing about the "grand olde days," when magic was real and talking fishes still granted wishes for the low, low price of being returned to the water. Even in the Disney animated flick, Aladdin's wishes don't bring him the happiness he thought he would receive. No sudden drop-off on Easy Street for him. In the end, he's lucky enough just to break even.

If you think about it, he was fortunate to even make that.

Because there has never been an invention or discovery for which someone did not pay a price. Often a heavy price. And right on the heels of implementation often follows the disreputable element. The shady side of the street. You know:

Crime.

Feats of skill led to gambling. Corporate espionage is only a shade younger than corporations. And nothing revitalized the porn industry like the internet.

Which is what made me wonder about the shadier side of all this magic for which everyone yearns. Would the IRS (or someone) try to collect their due from chiseling wishmongers? What happens when magic is used to handicap the ponies? What kind of people are going to step forward to save us from all this "easy living?"

And once magic is outlawed, will only outlaws have magic?

Reading this anthology, you may begin to find answers to some of these questions. We'll scratch the surface, certainly. Poke at some of the softer bits you've been hiding. In the end, though, I think you'll find that this is only the beginning. The start of the path—one filled with many twists, turns, and pitfalls—but worth taking regardless. That you knew all along that you could not get something for nothing.

Because nothing is free.

Not even magic . . .

Web Ginn House: A Zoë Martinique Investigation

Phaedra M. Weldon

A toaster spun across the room straight for my head.

Luckily I was out-of-body (OOB to the initiated), so the blasted thing drove right *through* me and into the ceramic clown behind me. Crash!

I hate clowns.

But then again, how rude! I didn't feel the solid object, but I sure as hell was going to remember it later as a migraine on the physical plane. Oh, I could *choose* to go through things, like doors and walls, but when I did that, I was prepared. Nothing like walking down Peachtree Street and having some very angry spirit bean you with a kitchen appliance.

Though I'm not sure which is worse—the flying ginzu knives or the hideous furniture flashback to 1964, complete with plastic couch cover.

Whoa! Look out—a juicer!

Oh, speaking of rude, let me introduce myself. Name's Zoë Martinique. Long *e* sound. Not like toe. I'm not a ghost or anything—not even a distant relation to Danny Phantom (but it'd be cool to have his white hair)—but a living, breathing (and ever curious) Latino Irish American who just happens to travel out of body.

Sounds weird, huh?

Yeah, most people hear Latino and Irish, and before they see me, they think, "She either looks like Jennifer Lopez or Opie Griffith."

Hell, you think if I looked like JLo, I'd be incorporeal in north Georgia dodging toasters? Nope. I'd be making me some sexy music videos and racking up husband number two.

I'm a stick with mounds of brown hair, brown eyes, and freckles.

Ack! This time a Betty Crocker cookbook spun at me, hard cover open, pages flapping in the wind. I moved to the side and did a nice duck behind the sofa. The book dented the wall behind me, just missing—I stopped and glared at the garish figurines on the shelf—what were those things? *Gah*—ceramic harlequins.

Hideous.

Mental note: I *really* hate clowns.

If I could, I'd let loose with some rather colorful metaphors about now, but even incorporeal, the SPRITE equipment set up throughout the two story house would hear me on tape. And that just wouldn't do.

Oh, yeah, SPRITE stands for Southeast Paranormal Research Investigators for Tactical Extermination. Uh-huh. What killed me was their obnoxious little logo of a fairy holding a ghost around the neck.

Sick, sick, sick.

But with that kind of publicity, I'd rather not be noticed by them. I might be invisible to the naked eye, and I'm not that sure I won't show up on film, but for some strange reason I can be heard. Learned that the hard way once and nearly gave one of my targets a heart attack.

Let me set the stage here so it doesn't seem like I'm babbling.

I learned I could go out of body six years ago, and once I got past that whole adolescent need to spy on people (like boyfriends, hussies who stole my boyfriends, cheating boyfriends), I learned I could make money with this little talent and have for the last two years. I rent out my services for information gathering. Well, okay, I snoop. The code word is Traveler—I'm a Traveler for their information needs.

Don't try this at home, kiddies.

I've also learned the more under-the-table it sounds, the more money customers are willing to pay. People prefer to dish out high dollar for something they think is illegal—and I have a mortgage that keeps a roof over my physical body, which is at present resting comfortably in my condo near Piedmont Park.

I sell my services on eBay. I know, odd modus operandi (I love using those words), I admit, but as I said before, I Travel for people, and my friend and Magical MacGuyver of all things spooky, Rhonda Orly, handles the business end of things. eBay was her idea.

And as of two days ago, three days before Halloween—which is tomorrow—I received a request from a repeating client. I never know their names or their locations, just their e-mail addresses. This guy's handle was maharba@maharba.com. Did a good bit of odd Traveling for him these past two years.

Paid good too. His requests were pretty straightforward. Snoop on this meeting, report back in detail. Watch this couple, report back. Watch this building, tell me what happened between yadda time and yadda time. My information wasn't admissible in court—I had no physical proof (as an incorporeal entity I couldn't lift anything solid, so no takey evidence from the scene). I couldn't even take pictures like a private investigator.

But the clients didn't seem to care. They trusted me, and I enjoyed the work. I often thought they'd find my methods a bit . . . questionable. And if not the methods, then maybe my attire. I usually went out in black leggings, black turtleneck, and black bunny slippers. They were so cute with their nylon whiskers and pink ears. I could honestly say I loved my job.

Except when it put me in front of hurling objects.

My instructions sent me to Web Ginn House Road in downtown Lawrenceville, Georgia. I live in Atlanta. The assignment was to investigate a haunted house, though my client neglected to tell me I'd be sharing space with a spook team. Oh, I believed in ghosts. Trust me. My mom has a couple living at her house—and I don't mean one or two ghosts, I mean a couple as in they're *together*. Tim and Steve. Quite a pair. She lives in Little Five Points—the artsy part of Atlanta.

But as for actually seeing ghosts other than those two—nope. This was a new experience for me. And it was just classic that I was doing it the night before Halloween.

Yay. Go me.

This time I wasn't paying attention when two of the members of SPRITE meandered into the room. The hurling of dangerous objects immediately ceased when they stepped in with their equipment held out in front of them and flashlights fixed to their foreheads.

"Randall, look over there!" the thinner of the two men said in an excited whisper. He was pointing in my direction, so I exited stage right, out of the line of fire of whatever electronic ghost snooping gadgetry they had in their hands.

"How the hell did these kitchen appliances get into the living room?" Randall, the wider of the two, with less hair, stopped looking down at his display and looked at the ceramic mess to the right of the couch. He had a light strapped to his forehead, and he shined the beam onto the floor.

"I told you I heard something in here," the thinner one said. I thought his name was Herb, though I wasn't sure. "I hope the cameras caught this on tape."

"Oh, hell. Clowns," muttered Randall. "I *hate* clowns. Menacing alien creatures."

I liked him.

"Well, you know what this proves, don't you?"

"What, Herb? That ghosts hate clowns?"

I slapped my hand over my mouth. Nearly chuckled out loud on that one.

"No, that poltergeists aren't always phenomena attached to teenagers entering puberty. No kids live here."

Poltergeist?

Interesting. Maharba never mentioned anything about poltergeists.

I felt a slight vibration then, something racing up my back. It was the same feeling I'd had right before the first object sailed through me. Martinique Spidey-sense.

Yep! And there it was! I didn't actually see what the flying object was at first because this one came from the living room and not the kitchen. I did feel it as it passed through my chest—a sort of odd pressure.

There was a moment of dizziness as I moved back to see a clock smash against the wall beside the ceramic mess. Whatever this thing was, I got the impression it was targeting me.

Oh joy.

"You see that? The clock's still plugged in." Herb moved over the broken ceramic toward me.

Still plugged in? Electricity. Was that why I felt like I'd been zapped? Might be—I'd always heard that electronic equipment went fritzy around electromagnetic entities (or so Rhonda had said on occasion). So why shouldn't they have the same effect on out-of-body girlies like me?

"Herb . . . rewind the thermal imager . . ."

That's when I saw the first of what looked like a whitish tentacle ooze its way around the feet of the couch. I stepped back and stared at it with mounting fear as it wound itself around the stubby couch leg on the front right. Another appeared from beneath, a soft white iridescent squidlike arm, and wrapped itself around the front left.

"Oh geez. . . ." Randall said. "Do you *see* that?"

"Oh, the fuck I do!" I blurted out and moved out

of the way just before the entire couch launched itself into the air and came at me. I had just enough time to duck down the hall to my left as the yellow-with-pink-flowers piece of furniture bounced into the wall and landed on top of the floor-model television.

Sorry about the furniture, but *what the hell was that?* I ran down the hall and circled around to the den, avoiding the kitchen and its whirling appliances altogether. I was getting winded, which in Traveling speak meant I'd been out of body a good while. Four hours appeared to be my limit before all sorts of nasty afflictions screwed up my physical self.

Headache (migraines), lethargy, upset stomach, dark circles under the eyes—not attractive to the opposite sex.

I stopped in my astral tracks once I entered the den.

It was there, standing in the center of the room, all glowy and horror-movie-of-the-week.

A giant squid. And I mean a *giant* freakin' squid. The thing looked as if it were made out of smoke and ash. A monochromatic nightmare of infinite proportions.

This thing made clowns seem normal.

Well—maybe not.

And the mother was staring right at me.

Oh, no way!

The tentacles were stretched out all over the house, but here in the den was where the body was. I'd overheard the SPRITE team talking about the upstairs bedroom being the central area where most of the activity was centered, not the den.

So, how come no one told this wacko sea animal he was in the wrong room?

Astral wind picked up, and I actually felt my incorporeal hair stand on end. Two of the tentacles lashed out at me, and I screamed as I watched them try to wind their way around my ankles.

Try being the key word here.

They melted right through me. Coiled and then oozed away.

It never touched me.

Well, not completely true. Something happened, because I was abruptly cold. While Traveling, I never experienced the elements. I could actually step out of my body naked (which had been my first one or two full experiences) and not feel a thing.

But my teeth were chattering. My ankles were the coldest, and they were knocking together. Ah! Even my bunny slippers had frost on their nylon whiskers.

Yikes!

"There it is again!" Herb shouted from the end of the hall. The two SPRITE members had moved to the start of the hallway where I had backed into.

Thunder vibrated within the house. Two more members of the team bounded down the stairs from the bedrooms, their little devices up and ready as they descended.

"Oh, Jesus, what happened here?" came a female voice. That would be the one called Boo. The one that looked most like Rhonda, with black hair and pink eyeshadow.

"Boo," Herb said in a whisper. "You and Ron circle back around to the den and get a shot of this thing."

Yeah, I thought. Shoot it. The giant squid looked as if it were listening—it wasn't making any more attempts at snagging me, or at throwing anything. I stood rooted to the spot in the hall—not because I was scared stiff, but because my legs weren't working. I jerked at them a few times, but I was locked in place!

What is up with this?!

"What is it you see?" Boo said and I heard her moving in the house.

"It looks like . . ."

A giant freakin' squid. A huge, bulbous octopus with more than eight tentacles. A larger than life Cousteau nightmare. A—

"It looks like a woman."

Blink. *No—it looks like a—*

Oh, no. I turned my upper body since my lower half wasn't budging. It felt as though I had ice shackles around my ankles. Herb and Randall were looking at the monitor and then up at me.

At *me!*

"It *is* a woman," Randall said in voice full of excitement. "And she's wearing . . . bunny slippers?"

Damnit.

Boo and her partner appeared at the opposite end of the hall near the front door. The light from her monitor illuminated her face, exaggerating her features. "Where is this woman ghost?"

"Right there," Randall pointed directly at me. "You can't see her?"

Boo looked up from her monitor and squinted down the hall. "No. She's not showing up on the camera."

Well, thank goodness for small favors. I was already panicked enough to know I showed up on the thermal imager.

I paused in my erratic thoughts as Randall and Herb started a rather hesitant walk down the hall in my direction. If I'm incorporeal, which means I'm without a warm body, how is it I show up on a thermal imager? Do I look all blue?

"What is it doing?" Herb said. "It looks like it's . . . *looking* at us."

"Nah," Randall said in a soft voice. "It doesn't even know we're here."

A movement in the den caught my eye, and I looked back at Squidward long enough to see several tentacles slither out down the hall in either direction toward the ghost hunters.

I watched in morbid fascination (while trying to make my legs move) as the glowing, whitish limbs wound down the hall toward the unsuspecting and evidently unseeing people. One tentacle reached out for Randall's monitor.

"Look out!" I shouted.

Well, he heard me, but not fast enough to prevent the monitor from bashing up into his face. I heard a crunch and knew the force had done some damage to his nose. He fell back against the wall and was on the floor in seconds.

I heard a yell to my left and turned in time to see Boo's camera fly out of her hands and bean her partner in the side of his head.

"Ron! I'm so sorry, that wasn't me. It was that ghost woman." Boo yelled out.

Me? I did *not* do that. And I could argue this out loud with both her and Randall. But at that moment I felt as well as heard a low growl. It seemed to come from the floor and up through my ankles.

I looked back into the den door in front of me. The huge squid was gone, and I got the distinct impression it was *below* me now.

And coming up through the floor under my feet. Now, I didn't know if this was a bad thing, but it couldn't be good. If the tentacles around my ankles had had such a nasty effect, I did not want to stick around and see what the entirety of the creature did if its body swallowed my incorporeal one.

So I did the only thing any respectable astral presence would do.

I got the hell out of there.

In truth, I concentrated on my silver cord, the one that anchored my spirit to my body, and I followed it back, leaving the squid, and SPRITE, far behind.

What I didn't mention was what a really bad idea this little trick was.

Traveling back into my body this way, instead of easing back as I normally did, caused a great deal of stress on the physical. Meaning when I slammed back into my body (there's an interesting velocity that picks up along the silver cord), it *hurts*.

Mom said it looked as though I'd been shocked with

a couple of those paddle things the doctors use to restart the heart. It actually felt a lot worse than it looked. The only way I can describe it from a physical standpoint is to imagine your blood replaced with liquid fire.

Acid. Everything burns.

The immediate reaction lasts maybe about two minutes, and then I'm usually a jelly lump on the floor catching my breath. The burning—that lasts a *lot* longer. Ouch.

I managed to stay on top of the little single bed I'd set up in my office for my traveling jaunts. Usually I fell off when I used my cord. I opened my eyes. I focused on my ceiling and concentrated on my breathing.

In. Out. In. Out.

Ow, ow, ow.

I could imagine my blood as the sparkling, crackling fire, and my veins were the fuse melting away as it grew closer to my heart.

The pain subsided, and a dull ache in the back of my head surged forward. I groaned out loud and lay very still for a while. I caught the front LCD face of the clock beside my desktop computer. Three seventeen in the morning.

Time for a nice glass of water, vitamins and—

Holy Mary Mother Of God!

I'd sat up slowly, and my black leggings had pulled up to my knees as well. My ankles were black and blue. Literally, black and blue! It looked as if someone had hammered on them with a meat mallet. I touched them tenderly (ouch!) and sucked air in between my teeth.

So—could I stand on them?

I tried and promptly landed on the Pergo floor, knees and elbows first. It wasn't that I couldn't put weight on them—well, okay, I couldn't. It hurt too much, and tears instantly sprang to my eyes. I am not afraid of crying. At least not by myself.

This was the first physical manifestation I'd seen of something that happened while I was traveling, and I didn't know if I'd done something permanent.

My purse lay in a heap on the floor a few inches away, and I reached in for my cell. No bars left. Curse me and my inability to remember to plug the damned thing in.

Well, to find out what I could about the present owners of that house, the Brentwoods, I simply learned what SPRITE knew—which was plastered all over the article in *Creative Loafing* the next morning. Elderly couple, just moved here from Florida, escaping the hurricanes, wanting to find a place to retire and make a life after spending years traveling. No children. All their money was tied up in the house.

And the previous owners? Now, that's the strange part. The Smiths had a single child, a daughter, who now was an almost grandmother. Daughter was born in 1960. But if she'd created a poltergeist back in her puberty years, would it have lived this long?

Something in my gut told me not so. According to what Rhonda had told me on my newly charged phone, these things remained, but without something feeding it, the thing would linger in a weakened state. So why was it so absolutely all-fired creepy now?

There was a gear missing in this mechanism for disaster, and me with my hobbled ankles wasn't sure what it was, or how to find it, or even how to fix it once I did. I'd spent the entire afternoon on the couch surfing the web and Googling all over the place.

I set my iBook on the coffee table and decided it was time to test my ankles and the just-over-the-top lovely braces my mom had brought over at lunch. Time because hydraulic pressure was going to pop my bladder and send me shooting straight up into the cat lady's condo above me.

I scooted forward, put my feet beneath me, and with a deep breath, stood straight up—and stayed there.

Interesting. Pursing my lips, I took a few steps away from my couch around my coffee table. I could feel the bruises on my ankles, but they didn't hurt. Not like they had earlier. Was I already healed? Wow . . . was this a super new power?

"What the hell are you doing?"

YOW!! I nearly shot out of my body right then, my mom scared me so bad. I turned and nearly fell over. "Geesus, would you not *do* that?"

She came from the kitchen (I had no idea she was still in there) and stood behind the couch. "Zoë, those braces aren't meant to be walked on."

"Well, duh—I know that. But look." I pointed down at my feet. "I can walk!"

"Because the braces are supporting you." She put her hands on her amble hips. "Try it without the braces."

I did.

I fell down.

"I have to pee," I said from the floor.

Mom towered over me. "Then I'll help you. I used to change your diapers, you know."

Ugh.

Rhonda was in the living room holding the remote and flipping channels when we came back in. She must have entered while I was in the bathroom. She'd put on nice pants, a white shirt, and a black blazer. Only the black lipstick, nails, and spiked bracelets gave her true nature away. Oh, that and the flat black matte Betty Page coiffure.

Two clicks to Channel Two Action News. "Check this out."

I looked at the clock over the television. It was after five. Wow, where was the afternoon?

". . . . as promised . . . a very startling . . . and creepy . . . Halloween event."

The screen broke from the anchor to the Smith house, where I'd been last night. Only it was a night shot, and the wind around the autumn trees did look spooky. Jump photography, two flashes of special effects lightning, and we were in the house with a guide.

Randall. Only he looked awful. The monitor had broken his nose, and his eyes were bruised. The man looked like a raccoon.

I listened with interest as the SPRITE member showed the camera crew the mess and then gave an account of what they saw, and then to my surprise, they played the video they'd taken of me.

"Nice profile," Rhonda said.

And it was, but just not something I wanted filmed. Not that I thought anyone was going to recognize me in the shot.

"We're not sure if this is the entity causing the nightmares the Smiths have been through these past few weeks since buying the house," Randall was saying. "We did catch her voice on tape."

The image changed to a voice image with a straight line and then a squiggle. Then I heard my voice say, "Look out!" as white letters clarified it for the television audience.

Oh, greeeeeat.

If there was one thing distinctive about me, it was my voice. Gravely. Rough. Deep. Kinda manly.

"Sounds as if she was warning you," the reporter commented as they stood in the living room carnage.

Randall nodded. "Yeah, yeah. And she did, because right after that is when the camera and monitors we were holding jumped out of our hands."

"So you're saying maybe she's more of a guardian angel?"

Randall smiled. "Right now, I don't know what to believe. We hope to make contact again tonight."

Rhonda switched off the television. "You know what this means?"

I was still on Guardian Angel. Aw. How sweet. "Randall looks like a raccoon?"

"It means the whole area's going to be crawling with people. Kids trying to get in to see the ghost.

Freaks. Groups singing outside in midnight vigils to stop the evil."

In a word, mob.

"You need to get in, find that fetter keeping that thing anchored to that house, destroy it, and get out. You don't need SPRITE taping you anymore." She tilted her head to the side, almost resting it on her shoulder. "And please . . . please . . . keep your mouth shut. If you don't I'll kick your damaged ankles."

Mental note: Rhonda is mean.

Goth chick wasn't kidding when she said mob.

Circus might have been more appropriate, though. There were indeed prayer groups with heads bowed, people with signs saying "Ghosts have rights too," and even a few men in white collars preaching the dangers of doing God's work.

Wasn't even a full moon tonight and the crazies were there for their Halloween fix.

The SPRITE van was in the driveway, their little fairy logo incongruent with the kids in sheets and black robes. Several news vans were there as well. Must not be much happening on this Thursday night.

Rhonda stayed in the background, blending in (LOL!) as I made my way past the cameras and reporters to the back of the house. There I found an open door and slipped inside, happy I wouldn't have to sieve through the wood. I can do it, but I don't like to. Especially not glass. Too cold.

I stopped in the kitchen. There was equipment everywhere. Camera lenses pointed at me from every angle. Luckily none of them were turned on and running.

Yay.

I moved to the hallway and the den. Fewer cameras here, and none of them looked like thermal imagers. My guess was they'd keep those in their hands, as they had the night before.

I stood in the room's center. The television in the

corner was dark, the books on the shelf all in place. My guess was that since the thing had been centered in here, maybe the fetter was too.

So, what would it look like? Would it glow? Jump up and down?

Sing?

I wanted to shout out, call to it. But not if they could actually record me. Think, think, think.

What had SPRITE done to provoke it the night before?

"Randall we can't work with all those people outside." That was Herb, and he didn't sound happy. "I told you not to do that interview—not till we were done."

They stopped right outside the den, in the hallway, where I'd been stuck the night before.

"I thought it needed to be shown that we're not crazy people." Randall said.

"I know we're not crazy, and so do you. Why should it matter who else does?"

"But we actually have proof, Herb. We need to show it around."

Did something just vibrate on that shelf?

"Randall, just because we got something on tape doesn't mean people will believe. Hell, someone could say that was Boo we caught on the imager."

Yep, something was definitely vibrating over there.

"That was not Boo," Randall said a bit louder, and I wouldn't have been too shocked to see him stomp his foot. "I know what I saw."

A book sailed across the room. I ducked, and it slammed into the two-person sofa.

"Randall, we both saw it, and we heard it too. There's something in this house."

"Then why are you ashamed of it?"

Another book flew across the room, followed by a trophy. I ducked both of them and then looked at the two SPRITE members. Uh, hello? Moving objects?

"I am not ashamed of it, Randall. Geez." Herb put

his hands in the air. "We just didn't need that circus outside."

This time the television actually lifted in the air and sailed at the door.

Right at them.

"Move, you idiots!" Okay, so I think my outburst then was justified, right?

Randall and Herb both looked in time to see the television hurtling at them. A few girlie screams, but the two ducked out of the way.

That's when the giant squid sort of appeared. It didn't take a rocket scientist, or even a Wall Street tycoon, to realize what I did at that moment. The poltergeist activity from last night wasn't fed from the Smiths, but from SPRITE. Point of sale: Randall.

Some unresolved issues there. A little frustration and anger?

"Christ! Get the cameras rolling! We have activity in the den!"

I moved to the side, behind what looked like the eye of the squid. It continued to grab up random objects with its tentacles and toss them at the doorway. Keeping quiet while it was busy, I looked for the fetter. Anything that might work.

A fetter was a leash of sorts. So, it'd have to be somehow connected to old Squidward here, right? Not around his neck because he didn't seem to have one. So—where?

Randall and Herb arrived then, as well as Ron, who sported a nasty bruise on his right cheek. Randall had the thermal imager in hand and was getting it geared up to point in the room. I moved to the side, out of the way and hopefully still out of sight of the poltergeist.

"Anything?" Herb said.

"No . . . wait. What the hell is that?"

I moved up behind them, slipping in between the two so I could look at the imager's screen. Had they seen the squid?

"I—that's weird," Randall looked at the monitor and then up into the room. "What's so hot?"

Ah ha! There was a hot thing in there. The fetter? I moved in a little bit closer and saw it. Some orange and red spot in the far corner of the room.

Wait . . . wasn't that—

"Is that the camera?" Herb asked as he squinted into the room.

"Yeah," Ron said. "What camera is that? I don't recognize it."

"It's one the Smiths found when they moved in," Randall said.

Everyone looked at him. He shrugged. "It's a classic Polaroid, and Mr. Smith said I could have it."

"Why is it hot?" Herb said.

Old camera . . . I moved away from the trio and eased to the left of the room around the squid. It'd been busy extending its tentacles through the house again, and it hadn't seen me.

Yet.

So the fetter was a camera. I guess cameras could be a source of frustration. Especially if they'd been used in some oogy way. Like for porno? For taking pictures that shouldn't be taken?

Somehow I needed to convince them to destroy it— and from the sound of admiration in Randall's voice, that wasn't going to be easy.

"There she is," Randall said. "Just to the left in the room. See her?"

"Wow . . . you weren't kidding," Ron said.

I turned and glared at them. They needed to stop focusing on me and focus on the squid. Why couldn't they see the squid? Didn't make any sense to me— not that I understood any of this.

"Why'd she throw the television at us?" Herb said.

"Because she's a poltergeist." Randall said. He faced the room, with no idea he was less than two feet from a giant glowing squid. "We mean you no harm—why are you trying to kill us? Are you angry?

Did something really bad happen to you here?" He held something in his hand, and I realized it was an MP3 recorder.

Wow . . . I'd never been interviewed before.

Something rumbled under my feet. I turned and saw the squid had turned as well and was looking at me with its one good eye. Yikes!

Tentacles whipped out of every nook and cranny of the room and threw themselves at me. It looked like thousands of white ropes uncoiling my way—and I had nowhere to run!

Within seconds I was encased in them. They moved slowly through me as they had my ankles the night before, but as some fell away, they were quickly replaced by others.

I was trapped . . . and cold. Antarctica cold. My teeth rattled in my head, and I felt myself drop to my knees. I tried to concentrate on my cord, but I couldn't find it in all the tentacles encircling me.

"What's—" Randall said. "What's happening? She looks like she's sick."

"Randall . . . what are those snakelike things?"

I tried to concentrate on their voices to keep from disappearing into the ice surrounding my body. "Destroy . . . camera," I managed to say. But could they hear me through the sound of the wind in my ears?

Wind? There was wind?

"Ron, did you hear that too?"

"Yeah, yeah. Let me rewind." I heard my voice replayed again and again.

"Does it mean the new camera?" Herb said. Then he said louder. "Can you tell us why?"

"Killing . . . me," I managed to get out. "You . . . *geek.*"

Okay, so maybe I shouldn't have said that last part. But I was cold.

"Killing her," Ron muttered and even I could hear

the incredulousness in his voice. "How can it kill her if she's a ghost?"

"Randall." Herb's voice sounded a little high. I pushed and pressed on the tentacles encasing me, but they continued to pass through me and then replaced themselves. "Look at the monitor closer. There and there . . . what the hell are those?"

"Holy—" Randall said and his voice cracked. "They're strangling her!"

Finally! Hello? Geeks are slooooooowwww.

I saw Herb move past me, skirting the edge of the poltergeist's position, and grab for the camera. Two tentacles that oozed through me whipped out toward him—no—they whipped out ahead of him as if to grab the camera.

"Herb!" Randall called out before I could. "It's going for—"

It grabbed the camera before Herb could get to it and slammed it against the side of his face. I felt a slight warming around me and did my best to move away from the tentacles. My mind was racing ahead to my physical body—thinking of the bruises on my ankles from a single brush with its tentacles and terrified of what I'd find left in my bed after this little travel.

Herb went down, and Randall moved into action. He dropped the thermal imager on the floor and dove for the camera. It whipped about in the air. I screamed for him to watch his left, then his right, and then it moved through me—

And I was free.

Wha—?

I wasted no time in moving out of the way. I was free, and warm, and not rooted to the spot as I'd been the night before. I didn't know why that'd happened and in that instant I didn't care. I just knew I needed to somehow get that frackin' camera away from the poltergiesty squid.

Randall was still doing his jump and duck dance

about the den, Herb lay on the floor clutching his head but making a solid attempt to get up, and Ron—well, he was struck dumb at the door, probably freaked out by the levitating camera. I moved to the back, able to see what Randall couldn't.

If I looked carefully, the thing's tentacle arms moved as well as looked like a squid, so the lower parts attached to the body led the movement. I watched it for a few seconds to test my theory, and after two near misses at Randall's skull, I knew right where it would be next.

Yelling at Randall to go right and up, I gave a good ole Georgia Bulldog woof when he caught the thing like a football, intercepting a supernatural pass.

"Smash it!" Herb yelled.

"No," Randall said, scrambling to get out of the den and shoving Ron to the side. "It's an antique."

"It's a damned fetter!" I shouted and ran around the poltergeist, jumping over the tentacles and doing a limbo. "Destroy it."

"I—can't," Randall said.

And just when I thought I was going to have to do some serious tongue-lashing (damn, I wish I could move solid things!), Ron unfroze and grabbed the camera out of Randall's hand. He moved with it down the hall.

A tentacle followed, and so did I. As did Randall and a stumbling Herb.

I got there in time to see Ron set the camera on the counter. He grabbed a hammer from the junk drawer (isn't it interesting how every kitchen has one of those drawers, and they have hammers in them?), and opened a can of whup-ass on that piece of electronic equipment.

It was broken in two whacks, pulverized in four, and by the ninth hit, he was denting the white and gold-flecked formica counter.

Ohhh . . . Ron gets busy.

Randall grabbed Ron's raised hammer hand and put a finger to his own lips. Everyone stopped. The hum in the house was gone (not that I'd realized there was one till it was missing). Was it . . . ?

That's when hell broke loose.

Every thingie that carried a current of any kind sparked in the house at the same instant. I ducked, even though my hair wouldn't actually catch fire from the exploding microwave behind Herb. In fact, everyone was on the floor.

Once the fireworks stopped, I stood first and moved quickly back to the den. The poltergeist was gone. But was it really gone? As in dissolved into the abysmal plane?

I didn't know. Nor did I care. I just really didn't want anyone else hurt by it.

SPRITE's electronic equipment lay on the orange and turquoise blue rug in smoking heaps. Ooh, they were not going to be happy about that.

"Oh, hell," Randall said as he saw the mess. "Look what that ghost did."

"This is going to cost us a fortune." Herb still clutched at his head as he knelt down beside the sparking remains of the thermal imager. "And to think we helped her—and she does this to our equipment?"

Me? They thought *I* did this?

That's it.

I went home.

SPRITE did blame me, as I thought they would. All their equipment was destroyed, and in an odd twist of circumstance, the video they'd captured of me went missing. Even the copy Randall had kept was wiped clean.

I didn't know how, and I didn't care. The Smiths arranged for the house to be bulldozed and sold the property for more money than they paid. Bully for them. Woohoo.

It took me a week to get back on my feet, and I did come back to my body with a series of bruises over every inch of skin and muscle.

Ow, ow, and ow. Rest and plenty of Mom's cooking and I'd be okay. Maybe a few pounds heavier. A new job came in—a small case involving a dot com company—involving snooping on the owners while they watched *Chicago*.

Two weeks away, mid-November. Tuesday.

With Rhonda in tow, I tracked down the Brentwood daughter and learned the camera had been her father's. And it'd been used to do exactly what I was afraid of—to take pictures of her naked and prostrate.

But it hadn't been her father that did it. It'd been her uncle.

We were sitting in a Starbucks in Augusta, Georgia. The crisp turn of cold bit at my nose as we sat outside, enjoying the break from the south's cruel and soupy heat. It was nice now, but we all knew it'd be hot again in a day or so.

Pumpkins and corn stalks propped on hay bails still decorated the corner.

Rhonda sat forward. "Did your dad know?"

The daughter nodded. She was still a pretty woman at forty-five. Slim. Delicate. Careful. "I hid the camera, and my uncle accused my dad of taking it and keeping the pictures for himself. Dad found out what he'd been doing." She gave a half smile. "And I never saw my uncle again. Even to this day I don't know where he is. No one's seen him."

Rhonda and I looked at each other then, and I felt icy fingers move up along my spine to the base of my skull. I didn't want to think about it or even consider it. But it'd be interesting to see what sort of things happened in whatever building rose on Web Ginn House Road.

The Hex Is In:
A Harry the Book Story

Mike Resnick

So I am sitting there in the stands, and the Pittsburgh Pompadoodles are beating the Manhattan Misfits by a score of 63 to 10, which is not unexpected since the Misfits have not won a game since John Alden had a fling with Pocahontas, and I am silently cursing my luck, because the point spread is 46, and if the Misfits could have managed just one more touchdown, I would not have to pay off any bets to *either* side.

But it is the fourth quarter, and there are only twenty-two seconds left on the clock, and the Misfits are eighty-seven yards away from paydirt, and the Pompadoodles have been beating them like a drum all day. And then, suddenly, Godzilla Monsoon finds a hole off left tackle, and he races through it, and two of the Pompadoodles' defensive backs run into each other, and damned if he hasn't passed the midfield mark and is racing toward the end zone. Everyone is chasing him, but Godzilla's got a head of steam up, and no one gets close to him. Now he's at the forty-yard line, now he's at the thirty, now the twenty—and then, just as I'm counting my profits, a piano falls out of the sky on top of him, and the ref whistles the play dead on the eight-yard line.

Benny Fifth Street turns to me, a puzzled expression on his face. "You ever seen it rain pianos before?" he asks.

"Not that I can remember," I admit.

"I wonder if it was a Steinway," says Gently Gently Dawkins, who is sitting on the other side of me.

"What difference does it make?" I ask.

"Them Steinways are always a little flat in the upper scales," he says.

"You want to see flat, take a look at Godzilla Monsoon," offers Benny Fifth Street.

"You guys are getting off the point," I say.

"Was there one?" asks Gently Gently Dawkins.

"The subject was rain," answers Benny. "I suppose if it can rain cats and dogs, it can rain pianos every once in a while."

"The subject," I say, "is who wanted the Pompadoodles to beat the spread?"

"That should be easy enough," says Benny. "Who put some serious money on the Pompadoodles?"

"Everybody," says Gently Gently, chuckling in amusement. "The last time the Misfits won they were the New Amsterdam Misfits—and then they only won because the other team was attacked by Indians on the way to the game and never showed up."

I give what has occurred a little serious thought, and then I say, "You know, pianos hardly ever fall out of the sky on their own."

"Maybe it fell out of an airplane," says Gently Gently.

"Or maybe a roc was carrying it off to its nest," adds Benny.

"Rocks don't fly," protests Gently Gently. "They just lie there quietly, and sometimes they grow moss, which I figure is like a five o'clock shadow for inanimate objects."

"You guys are missing the point," I say. "Clearly the hex is in, and I paid my hex protection to Big-Hearted Milton. If the piano was going to fall on anyone, it should have fallen on the referee, who's been blowing calls all afternoon."

"Or the tuba player in the band," adds Benny. "He's always off key."

"So why didn't Milton stop it, or at least misdirect it?" I continue.

"Speaking of Milton, here," says Gently Gently, handing me five one-hundred-dollar bills.

"If *I* speak of Milton, will you lay another five C-notes on *me*?" asked Benny curiously.

"This is a bet," answers Gently Gently. "I forgot to give it to you."

"From Big-Hearted Milton?" I say, frowning.

"Right. He gave it to me at halftime."

"But Milton never bets," I say. "It's against the rules of the Mages Guild."

"I heard they tossed him out for nonpayment," says Benny.

"Which team did he bet on, as if I didn't know?" I ask.

"The Pompadoodles, of course," answers Gently Gently.

"Well, that explains why he didn't stop the piano," puts in Benny.

I get to my feet. "I'll see you guys later."

"Where are you going, Harry?" asks Benny.

"I got to pay off all the guys who bet on Pittsburgh, and then I have to have a talk with Milton."

"Where will you find him?"

"Same place as always," I reply.

So I do like I say, and pay Longshot Louie and Velma the Vamp and Hagridden Henry and all the others, and then I head over to Joey Chicago's Bar, where my office is the third booth on the left, and I toss my hat there and then go to men's room, where I find Big-Hearted Milton sitting on the tile floor as usual, surrounded by five candles and half-singing half-muttering some chant.

"Milton," I say, "we've got to talk."

"Why, Harry the Book—what a surprise," he says. "Wait'll I finish this spell." He goes back to chanting in a tongue so alien that it might very well be French. Finally he looks up. "Okay, I'm done. Did you bring my money?"

"That's what we have to talk about," I say.

"All right," he says, getting to his feet and snuffing out the candles with his shoe. "But I want you to know that I'm protected against spells, curses, betrayals, demonic visitations, and small nuclear devices."

"Are you protected against a punch in the nose?" I ask.

He frowns and looks worried. "No."

"Then let's talk."

"About my money?"

"About Godzilla Monsoon getting flattened by a piano."

"He'll be all right," says Milton. "It fell on his head. It's not as if it hit him in the knee or anything he ever uses."

"Why did it hit him at all?" I ask. "And just when he was about to wipe out the spread?"

"It wasn't my fault," whimpers Milton.

"Come on, Milton," I say. "The only time in five years you make a bet, and nine million pounds of music falls down on the guy who's about to make you lose?"

"I didn't do it."

"Maybe you didn't drop it," I say. "But I pay for hex protection, and you didn't stop it."

"It's too complicated to explain," says Milton. "Just give me my winnings and we'll agree never to discuss it again."

"Come on, Milton," I say. "You can tell me what's going on. We've known each other for fifteen years now."

"We've been friends for fifteen years?" he says, surprised. "How time flies."

"I didn't say we were friends. I said we've known each other. Now, what the hell is going on?"

He cups his hand to his ear. "They're calling you from the bar, Harry."

"The bar's empty, except for Joey Chicago, who was guzzling some Old Peculiar from the tap when I walked through."

He looks at his wrist. "Oh, my goodness, look at the time!" he exclaims. "I'm late for an appointment. I really must run."

"Milton, you're not wearing a watch," I point out.

"I pawned it," he says. "But I remember where the hands should be."

"Milton," I say, "I just want you to know that this hurts me more than it hurts you."

And with that, I haul off and punch him in the nose.

He hits the ground with a *thud!*, pulls out a handkerchief to try to push the blood back into his nostrils, and climbs slowly to his feet.

"You were wrong, Harry," he says reproachfully. "It hurts me *much* more than it hurt you."

"An honest mistake," I say. "And now, unless you tell me what's going on, I am going to make honest mistakes all over your face."

"All right, all right," he says. "But let's leave my office and go to yours. I feel the need of a drink."

We emerge from the men's room and walk over to my booth, where Milton orders us each an Old Washensox.

"My treat," he says. "Joey, put 'em on my tab."

"I been meaning to talk to you about your tab," says Joey.

"Holler when it hits fifty," says Milton.

"I been hollering since it hit twenty, for all the good it's done me," answers Joey.

Joey brings us our beers, mutters the usual about firing Milton and hiring Morris the Mage to protect the place, and goes back to the bar.

"All right," says Milton, "here's the situation. I find myself a little short for money this year"—which is not a surprise; Milton has been short for money since Teddy Roosevelt charged up San Juan Hill—"and suddenly someone throws a beautiful gift in my lap."

"What was her name?" asks Joey, who was listening from behind the bar.

"Opportunity," says Milton.

"Not much of a name," says Joey, making a face. "I prefer Bubbles, or maybe Fifi."

"So tell me about this opportunity," I say, as Joey leans forward to get her measurements.

"Gerhardt the Goblin—you know, that little green critter who's always screaming 'Down in front!' at Tasteful Teddy's 5-Star Burlesque Emporium—anyway, Gerhardt approaches me one day last week and tells me that he's got a client who wants to put five hundred down on the Pompadoodles, but doesn't want to do it himself, and that if I knew anyone who would act as a middleman, he'd get twenty percent of the winnings."

"And you don't know who you're working for?"

"I'm working for *me*," says Milton with dignity. "I don't know whose money I'm betting, but that's a whole different matter."

"Where can I find Gerhardt?" I ask.

"Beside Tasteful Teddy's?" says Milton. "He loves betting on the lady mud wrestlers over at Club Elegante." He lowered his voice confidentially. "They're the only wrestling matches in the whole city that aren't fixed."

"You know," I say, "I've been there a couple of times—just for the coffee, mind you; I paid no attention to the wrestlers at all—but I don't remember any of the matches having a winner."

"They don't."

"Then what's to bet on?"

"Which one gets naked first. How long before they're so covered with mud you can't tell 'em apart.

How many men say they just go there for the coffee. That kind of thing."

"Is there anything else you can tell me?" I ask.

"Not a thing."

"Okay, Milton," I say, getting up. "I'll see you soon."

"You're leaving?"

"Yes," I say.

"Where's my money?" he asks.

"Right here," I say, patting my vest pocket. "And it's *my* money."

"Aw, come on, Harry," he pleads. "Show a little charity."

"You insist?" I say.

"I do."

"Okay," I say. "Tomorrow I'll hunt up some charitable organization that repairs pianos."

Then, before he can say another word, I am out the door.

I stop by Club Elegante looking for Gerhardt the Goblin, grab a ringside table, and when he hasn't shown up by the seventh match, I decide to leave, especially because the next match features Botox Betty, who once broke her hand slapping my face over a friendly misunderstanding and a couple of intimate pinches, and Lizzie the Lizard, who shed her skin faster than French Fatima shed her clothes over at Tasteful Teddy's.

By the time I get to my apartment, Benny Fifth Street is already there, watching replays of the piano flattening Godzilla Monsoon just as he crosses the ten-yard line, followed by a hospital interview with Godzilla, who doesn't sound any more punch-drunk than usual, and finally a statement from the winning coach to all the young Pompadoodle fans out there that they should never neglect their music lessons because today clearly proves that music *is* important to their daily lives, and without music they might only have won by 46 points and disappointed all the big Pittsburgh plungers who bet on them to beat the spread.

Gently Gently Dawkins shows up just as we turn off the television—he was busy eating his fourth meal of the day, which puts him maybe two hours behind his normal schedule—and I tell them what Milton told me.

"Clearly, it's got to be some Pittsburgh fan," says Gently Gently.

"Why?" I reply. "You don't have to be a Pittsburgh fan to fix a game."

"You don't?" he ask, frowning, and I can see he's still a few thousand calories short of functioning on all cylinders.

"No," I say. "Maybe this isn't confined to Milton, or even to Manhattan. I mean, it's got to cost a lot of loot to get a wizard good enough to pull that stunt with the piano. Maybe we should see if anything like that has happened anywhere else."

"How should we go about it?" asks Benny.

"Start by calling Vegas. See if anything like today has happened when it looked like an underdog might win, or even just beat the spread."

"I'll do it," says Gently Gently.

"Are you sure?" asks Benny. "I don't mind making the call."

"No problem," says Gently Gently.

"Okay," I say. "The phone's in the next room."

"I know," he says, getting up. "So are the cookies."

"He eats three more cookies and a biscuit, and you won't need Milton to hex the bad guys," says Benny, as Gently Gently leaves the room. "Just have him breathe on 'em, or maybe step on their toes."

Gently Gently is back out in less than a minute.

"That was fast," I say.

"It was all negative," he replies. "No one's dropped a piano anywhere." He pauses. "Some Acme Movers dropped a pipe organ carrying it into a church out there, if that helps."

"Not a whole lot," says Benny.

"Anyway, our contact's sorry, but no pianos. The only weird thing they've had out there is the tidal wave."

"A tidal wave?" I repeat. "In *Las Vegas*?"

"Yeah," he says. "Funny, isn't it?"

"Tell me about it," I say.

"No one was hurt," says Gently Gently. "It comes from out of nowhere and practically drowns Nasty Nick Norris just when he's about to pull a 300-to-1 upset in their tennis tournament, and then as quick as it comes, it goes away. I think they would have been convinced it was a mass hallucination, except that they found half a dozen codfish and a sea urchin stuck in the net."

I pull out my abacus and dope out the odds that the tidal wave and the piano aren't related. Since the abacus can't compute any higher than a google-to-one, it melts.

"What have a Vegas tennis match and a New York football game got in common?" I muse.

Gently Gently raises his hand. "They're both sports?"

I ignore him and say, "We need to find the connection. Someone's paying a hell of an expensive wizard to rig these events, which means someone's making a bundle on them—someone who doesn't want his name to be known."

"That does not make a lot of sense," opines Benny. "So someone is paying a wizard. That doesn't mean he has to hide his own name. Anyone can lay a bet. Are you sure Milton wasn't holding something back?"

"Pretty sure," I say. "But even if he is, he knows that I am also holding something back from him"—I pat my wallet—"and we can trade whenever he wants."

"You mind if I turn on the TV?" asks Gently Gently.

"Trying to find out who's robbing us doesn't interest you enough?" asks Benny.

"It ain't that," explains Gently Gently. "But I got a sawbuck down on Loathesome Lortonoi in the seventh at Del Mar, and it's almost post time."

"You bet with some other totally illegal bookie?" demands Benny.

"It ain't ethical to bet with the illegal bookie I work for," responds Gently Gently. He searches for the right words. "It's a conscript of interns."

"Let him watch," I say. "It's easier than arguing with him."

The picture comes on, and the horses are already parading to the post.

"There's Loathesome Lortonoi!" says Gently Gently, pointing to a huge black horse who looks like he and his rider should be chasing Ichabod Crane around Sleepy Hollow. "They shipped him out there just for this race. It's a perfect spot for him."

There are six horses approaching the starting gate. Four of them look like close relatives of Loathesome Lortonoi. The sixth horse looks like he should be pulling a death cart in medieval Graustark, or maybe be spread throughout a few hundred cans of dog food. Even the flies avoid him. His jockey looks like he wishes he could wear a brown paper bag over his head. The tote board says he's 750-to-1.

"Is that Pondscum?" asks Benny.

"No, it's just a little smudge on the screen," says Gently Gently.

"I mean the horse."

Gently Gently pulls a *Racing Form* out of his pocket and looks at it. "Yes, it is. Have you seen him before?"

"He was losing races back when I was in grammar school," says Benny. "He was the slowest, ugliest horse in the world even then."

The horses enter the gate, and a few seconds later the doors spring open and Loathesome Lortonoi comes out of there like a bat out of hell, and before they hit the far turn he's fifteen lengths in front. The next four horses are spread out over another thirty lengths. Pondscum isn't even in the picture.

They hit the homestretch, and now Loathesome Lortonoi is twenty lengths in front—and suddenly the crowd starts screaming, and the announcer gets so excited he starts whistling and cheering and forgets to say what's happening, but he doesn't have to because in another two seconds Pondscum enters the picture. He is going maybe ninety miles an hour, and it seems like his feet are hardly touching the ground—and then I realize that his feet *are* hardly touching the ground, because somehow while rounding the far turn he has sprouted wings and is literally flying down the home stretch. He catches Loathesome Lortonoi with a sixteenth of a mile to go and wins by thirty lengths.

Gently Gently turns to me. "Is that fair?" he asks in hurt, puzzled tones.

"We'll know in a minute," I say. And sure enough, a minute later the result is official and Pondscum returns $1,578.20 for a two-dollar bet.

I turn to Benny. "Who do we know out there?"

Benny consults his little book. "The biggest bookie working Del Mar is No-Neck McGee."

"Give me his number," I say, and a moment later I dial it, and No-Neck McGee picks it up on the third ring.

"Hi, No-Neck," I say. "This is Harry the Book."

"Harry," he says. "Long time no see."

"No, I can see again," I tell him. "Wanda the Witch's spell only lasted a couple of weeks."

"So what can I do for you on this most terrible of days? Did you see what just happened in the seventh?"

"That's what I want to ask you about."

"I'm making a formal complaint to the Jockey Club."

"It'll never hold up," I say. "There's nothing in the rules that says a horse can't have wings."

"Just as there's nothing in the rules that says he

can't have blinkers, or shoes for that matter. I'm basing my case not on the fact that he had wings but that he didn't declare them prior to the race, the way you have to declare all other equipment. Is that what you're calling about? Did someone pull the same trick up at Belmont?"

"No," I say. "I just want to know if you had any big plungers on Pondscum?"

"I took just one bet on him," answers No-Neck. "Problem is, it was for six hundred dollars. That's why I've filed the complaint. Paying it off will break me."

"Who placed the bet?" I ask.

"An ex-jockey who hangs around the track all the time," says No-Neck. "Remember Charlie Romanoff?"

"Chinless Charlie?" I say. "Didn't he get ruled off the track for life?"

"Life or three hundred years, whichever comes first," answers No-Neck. "Anyway, he lays the bet, but he's never seen six hundred dollars at one time in his life, so I know he is someone else's stalking horse. Or is it stalking bettor?"

"Thanks, No-Neck," I say. "That's what I needed to know."

"Glad you called today," says No-Neck. "I have a feeling my phone will be disconnected by next week."

We hang up, and I turn back to Benny and Gently Gently. "I think I'm starting to see the light," I say.

"I don't know how you can," says Gently Gently. "It's almost nine o'clock at night."

"Give your *Form* to Benny and go into the next room for another cookie," I say, and he does so faster than Pondscum or even Godzilla Monsoon ever moved.

"I can tell by your face you got an idea," says Benny. "Or maybe it's just a sty in your eye. But it's *something*."

"It's an idea," I say. "It comes back to your question: Why would someone hide the fact that he was laying bets? After all, betting is legal at the track and in Vegas, and it's almost legal with bookies."

"I already asked that," says Benny.

"The logical answer is that the hex was in, and he didn't want people to know that he was the one who made the bet."

"Yes, that makes sense," says Benny. "But we already know the race and the game and the match were hexed."

"But we know something else," I say. "We know that the kind of wizard who can cause a tidal wave or do the other things does not come cheap. So the next thing to do is find out who can afford three such wizards on the same day."

"There's hundreds of guys with that kind of loot just in Manhattan," says Benny. "It's like finding a blonde in a haystack."

"Don't you mean a needle?" I ask.

"I found a needle in a haystack once," he answers. "I've never found a blonde."

I couldn't argue with that, so I went back to the subject at hand. "We can work it from either end," I say. "We can narrow it down by finding someone who could afford all three wizards, or we can narrow it down by finding out just which wizards have the power to pull these stunts off."

"Too many either way," says Benny, as Gently Gently comes back into the room. "There's a third way."

"Oh?" I say. "What it is?"

"Pound the hell out of Big-Hearted Milton until he tells you who gave him the money."

"It could have passed through four or five hands before it got to Milton," I say.

"That narrows it down," says Gently Gently. "Who do we know who has four or five hands?"

I send him out to a chili parlor.

"You know," I say when he is gone, "I think the money is the key to it all."

"Of course it is," agrees Benny. "No money, no hexes."

"No," I say. "I mean, I think you hit on something before. There are hundreds of possible plungers, and dozens of possible wizards, but there's only one pay-off, and that's the one I have to make to Milton."

"You're going to pay him?"

"Tomorrow," I say. "Tonight there's something I have to do. Get me Morris the Mage's phone number."

I talk to Morris, and we agree on a price, and he casts his spell and gives me the magic word, and the next morning I hunt up Milton in the men's room at Joey Chicago's, where he is sitting fully clothed on one of the toilets, his nose covered in bandages, reading an ancient book of magic.

"Good morning, Milton," I say pleasantly.

"I ab nod talkig to you," he says through the bandages.

"That's too bad," I say. "Because I have sought you out to pay my debt of honor."

I pull out the money and hand it to him.

He smiles, gets up, puts the money in a pocket, and walks to the door.

"Thag you, Harry," he says. "I god to deliver this. I'll see you lader."

He walks out of the men's room, through the tavern, and out the front door, and I go back to the apartment, where Benny and Gently Gently have spent the night. (Well, Benny spent the whole night; Gently Gently made four more trips out for nine-thousand-calorie snacks.)

"Is it accomplished?" asks Benny.

"Let's give it an hour," I say.

Benny spends the time staring at his watch and counting down minute by minute. Finally it is time.

"He's got to have delivered it by now," I say, "and whoever he's delivered it to hasn't had time to get to a bank. So let's make sure he thinks twice before trying to rob Harry the Book again." I pause for dramatic effect, and then say: "Abracadabra."

"That's it?" asks Benny. "Nothing's happened."

"It's not going to happen here," I say. "Turn on the news in another hour and we'll see if it worked."

Benny counts down from sixty to zero once more, and then turns on the television. The news is on all the channels: The estate of Mafia don Boom-Boom Machiavelli has spontaneously caught fire and burned to the ground.

"And that's that!" says Benny, rubbing his hands together gleefully.

"Not quite," I say.

"Oh?"

"Milton never used a bank or a safe in his life, which means his share caught fire in his pocket. Find out what hospital he's in and send him some flowers."

"Any note with it?" asks Benny.

"Yeah," I say. "Tell him that if God had meant pianos to fly, He'd have given them wings."

Gently Gently looks surprised. "You mean He didn't?"

If Vanity Doesn't Kill Me

Michael A. Stackpole

For a guy who squeezed into a rubber nun's habit before hanging himself in a dingy motel room closet, Robert Anderson didn't look so bad. Sure, his face was still livid, especially that purple ring right above the noose, and his neck had stretched a bit, but with his eyes closed you couldn't see the burst blood vessels. He looked peaceful.

I glanced back over my shoulder at Cate Chase, the Medical Examiner. "I've seen worse. Is that a good thing?"

"Let's not start comparing instances." With her red hair, blue eyes, and cream complexion, Cate should have been a heartbreaker. She would have been, save she was built like a legbreaker. One glance convinced most men that she could hurt them badly, and not in a good way. She jerked a thumb at the room's vanity table. "What do you think?"

I shrugged. Dragging it along had tipped over a can of soda, and a half-eaten sandwich had soaked most of it up. The Twinkie had resisted the soda, being stale enough you could have pounded nails with it. "Looks like he unscrewed it from the wall, shifted it so he could watch himself. Autoerotic asphyxiation?"

She nodded. "Suffocating as you climax is supposed

40

to take the orgasm off the charts. You pass out, you can strangle to death."

"Not my idea of fun."

"There go my plans for the rest of our afternoon." She flicked a finger at Anderson. "Take another *look*."

I caught her emphasis and breathed in. I closed my eyes for a second, then reopened them. I peered at him through magick. He was a silhouette, all black and drippy. Corpses tend to look like that. I'd seen it before.

"Something special I'm supposed to see?" I faced her as I asked the question, and magick rendered her in shades of red gold, much like her hair. It put color into everything, save for that Twinkie. It was neither alive nor dead.

Cate shook her head. "Something, I hoped. Anything."

I waited for her to expand on her comment, but she never got a chance.

Detective Inspector Winston Prout charged into the room and thrust a finger into my chest. "What the hell are you doing here, Molloy?"

"I invited him, Prout," Cate said.

I smiled. "Coffee date."

He glared at the both of us, about a heartbeat from arresting us for indecent urges. He was one of those skinny guys who'd look better as a corpse. He wouldn't have to keep his parts all puckered and pinched tight. He habitually dressed in white from head to toe, and he had exchanged his skimmer for a fedora after his recent promotion to Inspector.

"Civilians aren't allowed in a crime scene, Molloy."

"My prints, my DNA are on record. I haven't touched anything."

"If you don't have a connection to this case, get the hell out of here."

I hesitated just a second too long.

He raised an eyebrow. "You connected?"

"Maybe." I shrugged. "A little."

"Spill it."

"Your vic?" I nodded toward the man in the closet. "He's married to my mother."

That little revelation had Prout's eyes bugging out the way Anderson's must have at the end. I'd have enjoyed poking them back into his face, but he got control of himself pretty quickly. He was torn between wanting to arrest me right that second and fear that I'd already set a trap for him. He'd wanted a piece of me since before his stint in the Internal Affairs division. He saw it as a divine mission, and getting me tossed from the force for bribery hadn't been enough.

He punted the two of us, leaving a tech team to do the crime scene. Cate and I retreated through a hallway where painters were trying to cover years of grime in a jaunty yellow to a nearby coffee joint. We ordered in java-jerkese, then sat on the patio amid lunch-bunnies catching a post-Pilates, pre-spa jolt.

"You didn't know about Anderson, did you?"

Cate shook her head. "Should I say I'm sorry for your loss?"

"If it will make you feel better."

"I'm sorry."

"Don't be. He was a shit. He and my mother were very Christian, which meant they were usually anti-me."

Cate understood. Prejudice against those who are magically gifted isn't uncommon, especially with Fundies. It's that "thou shalt not suffer a witch to live" thing. Having a *talented* child is as bad as having a gay kid was late last century. My mom had compounded things by being the society girl who ran off with a working man—my father—then getting pregnant and actually delivering the child. My having talent was the last straw. She ditched my father, the

Church got the marriage annulled, and she made a proper society match with Anderson.

I blew on my coffee. "Why *did* you call me?"

Cate leaned forward, resting her forearms on the table. "Anderson's the fifth Brahmin who's died like that in the last two months. Very embarrassing circumstances. The deaths have been swept under the carpet."

She fished in her pocket, produced a PDA, and beamed case files into mine. I glanced at the names on each document. I knew them. I dimly recalled that they'd died, but I couldn't remember any details. I'd met three of them, liked one, but only because she didn't like my mother.

"How did Amanda Preakness die?"

"You won't want to look at the photos. She drowned. In her tub. In chocolate syrup."

"What?" She'd been slender enough to make Nancy Reagan look like a sumo wrestler. Tall and aristocratic, with a shock of white hair and a piercing stare, she could have dropped an enraged rhino with a glance. She always threw lavish parties but never ate more than a crumb. "Not possible."

"Not only did she drown in the syrup, but her belly was stuffed full of chocolate bars. Junk food everywhere at the scene, all washed down with cheap soda." Cate shook her head. "Nothing to suggest anything but an accidental death. Or suicide."

"Neither of which could be reported, so her society friends wouldn't snigger at her passing." I frowned. "No leads?"

"Plenty. Problem's no investigation. I pester Prout. He hears but doesn't listen."

"Which is odd since you suspect our killer is *talented*."

"Has to be. And strong."

Just being born with talent isn't enough. Talent needs a trigger, and not many folks find that trigger.

Mine's whiskey—I discovered it when I was four by sucking drops from my old man's shot glass after he passed out. The better the whiskey, the faster the power comes.

Once you find the trigger, you next have to learn your channel. For most folks it's the elements: earth, air, fire or water. A talented gardener with an earth channel is good; one who works with plants is better. Some channels are a bit more esoteric, like emotions. I even met a guy whose channel was death.

Not really a fun guy, that one.

If there was a killer, knowing his trigger and channel would be useful. I could guess on the channel being emotional or biological, but that didn't narrow things down much. More importantly, it really did nothing to figure out *why* the murders were taking place. Without a *why*, figuring out *who* was going to be tough.

I set the PDA down. "What's in this for me?"

Cate rocked back. "Stopping a murderer isn't enough?"

"Not like it's my hobby. I work mopping up puke in a strip club. I know where I stand in the world. I don't see this getting me ahead."

"Maybe it won't, Molloy, maybe it won't." Cate's eyes half lidded, and she gave me a pretty good Preakness-class glance. "Maybe it'll stop you from sinking any lower."

"Is that possible?"

"You're not there yet." Her expression hardened. "If you were, I'd ask if you had an alibi for when Anderson died."

I guess being a murderer would be a step down. Not that I minded Anderson being dead. Given the right circumstances I might even have killed him. Or, at least, let him die. A shrink would have said it because he was a surrogate for my mother and that secretly I was wishing her dead.

There wasn't any "secretly" about it. I knew I had

to start with her, so I reluctantly left Cate. The part I was resisting was that seeing her would prove she was still alive.

I tried to look on the bright side.

Maybe she was sick, really, really sick.

And not just in the head this time.

The Anderson Estate up in Union Heights was hard to miss. Fortune 500 companies had smaller corporate headquarters. The fence surrounding it had just enough juice flowing through it to stun you; then the dogs would gnaw on you for a good long time.

The gate was already open, and a squad car was parked there. The officers waved me past, but it wasn't any blue-brotherhood thing. I'd never known them when I was on the force. I'd just gotten their asses out of trouble at the strip club.

Took me two minutes to reach the front door. Would have been longer, but I cut straight across the lawn. Wilkerson, the chief of staff—which is how you now pronounce the word "butler"—opened the door before I'd hit the top step. "It will do no good to say the lady of the house does not wish to see you, correct?"

He didn't even wait for me to reply before he stepped aside. He looked me up and down once. He channeled my mother's mortification, then led the way up the grand staircase to my mother's dressing room. He hesitated for a moment and memorized the location of every item in the room, then reluctantly departed, confident the looting would begin once the door clicked shut.

The room was my mother: elegant, well appointed, tasteful, and traditional. I'm sure it was all "revival" something, but I couldn't tell what. Even though she'd made an attempt to "civilize" me in my teens, very little had stuck. I did know that if it looked old, it was *very* old, including some Byzantine icons in the corner with a candle glowing in front of them. In a world where even people were disposable, antiques held a certain charm.

Not so my mother.

She swept into the room wearing a dark blue dressing gown—clearly Anderson's—and dabbed at her eyes with a monogrammed handkerchief. Her eyes were puffy and rimmed with red. For a moment I believed she might have been crying for him, but grief I could have felt radiating out from her.

My mother doesn't radiate emotions. She sucks them in. Like a black hole. I think that's why her daughter is a nun in Nepal, I'm a waste of flesh, and my half-brother is the Prince of Darkness.

"There's nothing in his will for you, Patrick."

"Good to see you, too, Mother. I hope he spent it all on himself."

Her blue eyes tightened. "It's in a trust, all of it, save for a few charitable donations."

I chuckled. "That explains the tears. Hurts to still be on an allowance."

"Yours is done, Patrick. I know he used to give you money." She fingered the diamond-encrusted crucifix at her throat. "He was too softhearted."

"He gave me money *once*, and it wasn't Christian charity." I opened my hands. "I came from the crime scene . . ."

Her eyes widened. "You beast! If you breathe a word!" Tears flowed fast. "How much do you want?"

"I don't want anything." I shook my head. "Five people have died in the last two months, your husband included. All of them nasty. Sean Hogan, Amanda Preakness, Percival Kendall Ford, and Dorothy Kent."

"Dottie? They said it was a botox allergy."

"It doesn't matter what they said, Mother."

She blinked and quickly made the sign of the cross. "Are you confessing to me, Patrick? Have you done this? Have you come for me?"

"Stop!" I balled my fists and began to mutter. Like most folks, she bought into the Vatican version of the *talented*. She figured I was going sacrifice her to my Satanic Master, or at least turn her into a toad.

Tempting, so tempting.

She paled and then sat hard on a daybed. "I'll do anything you ask, Patrick. You don't want to hurt me, your mother."

I snorted. If she had enough presence of mind to invoke the maternal bond, she wasn't really shocked, just scheming. "How was Anderson hooked up with the others?"

"Hogan did the trust work, damn him. Everyone else we knew socially. The Club, of course, the Opera Society. Various nonprofit boards." She paused, her eyes sharpening. "Yes, this is all your fault."

"My fault?"

"Absolutely. They were all on the board of The Fellowship. All of them." Her accusing finger quivered. "I never wanted him to have anything to do with that place, but he did, because of you. And now he's dead."

"The Fellowship never killed anyone."

"They saved your life, Patrick. I know. He told me." Her eyes became arctic slits. "If they hadn't, if you were dead, my husband wouldn't be. Dear God, I wish it were so."

She burst into a series of sobs that were as piteous as they were fake, so I took my leave. It really hadn't been her best effort at emotional torture. Anderson's death had hurt her. Probably it was more than having a leash on her spending. I wondered how long it would be until she realized that herself.

From the Heights I descended back into my realm. People in my mother's class acknowledge it exists, but only just barely. It's where they go slumming when cheating at golf has lost its thrill. For the rest of us it's just a waiting room. Prison or death, those are your choices. Sure, you hear stories of someone making good and escaping. Never seems any of us down here knew them when; and they damned sure don't know any of us now.

Reverend Martha Raines could have made it out, but she stayed by choice. She was kind of the "after" picture of Amanda Preakness doing a chocolate diet for a decade or two; but her brown eyes had never narrowed in anger. Not that she couldn't be passionate. She could, and she often held forth at City Council meetings or prayer services. She kept her white hair long and wore it in a braid that she tied off with little beaded cords the children in her mission made for her.

She smiled broadly as I stepped through the door, and I couldn't help but mirror it. Even before we could speak, she caught me in a hug and held on tight, even when I was ready to let go. She whispered, "You need this, Patrick."

Maybe I did.

Finally she stepped back. "I'm so sorry for your loss."

"No loss."

She gave me a sidelong glance. "I seem to remember things a little bit differently."

"You always think the best of everyone."

"It's a skill you could acquire."

"I don't like being disappointed."

She slipped an arm around my waist and guided me into the mission. The Fellowship has built out through several warehouses and manufacturing buildings that, save for Martha's fiery oratory, would have long since been converted into lofts. The city wanted this end of town gentrified and envisioned galleries and bistros. Martha thought buildings should house people and proved convincing when she addressed the City Council.

Things had changed a lot since I'd done my time in the mission. The first hall still served as church and dining facility, but the stacks of mattresses that used to be piled in the corner had moved deeper into the complex. The far wall had been decorated with a huge mural that looked like a detail piece of da Vinci's *Last Supper*. Thirteen plates, each with a piece of bread on it; but one was already moldy. The style wasn't quite right for da Vinci—some of that stuff my mother had forced into my head was creeping back.

Martha smiled. "Our artist is very talented."

I raised an eyebrow. "Talented? Or *talented*?"

"She's a lot like you, Patrick." Martha just smiled. "You'll like her."

"I need to ask you some questions."

"About Bob Anderson?"

"About all of them."

She studied my face for a moment, then led me over to a table and pulled out two chairs. She sat facing me and took my hands in hers. "They were all lovely people, every one of them. I know many people said bad things about them; but they had seen the work we do here. They wanted to help. They did things for us. Projects. Fundraisers. What they gave wasn't much for them, but it was everything for us."

I nodded. "When they died, they left the mission money."

Martha drew back. "What are you suggesting?"

"There are idiots down here who figure that if you start making money, they want a piece. Criminals aren't bright; and you're a soft touch."

"True on both counts." She smiled. "But your stepfather and Sean Hogan were not stupid. Bequests go into a trust with a board of trustees who vote on capital expenses. I can't really touch that money. More to the point, no one has tried to extort money."

"No rivalries? No animosity on the committee?"

Martha smiled. "The meetings were all very pleasant."

That didn't surprise me. Martha had *talent*, though I wasn't sure she knew it. Somehow her positive nature was infectious. When she gave a sermon, people listened and her words got inside them. She always exhorted folks to be their best selves. It was like a round of applause accompanied by a boot in the ass that left you wanting more of each.

It was her inclination to think the best of folks that had her believing Anderson's death was a loss. She remembered he'd pulled me out of the mission and had given me money. She thought I'd been rescued. My mother, having taken to Christianity like a drunk to vodka, had tried to save me a couple times before, especially after my father went away. Martha thought this was another instance of maternal concern.

Truth was, Anderson had been fed up. He just wanted me to stop embarrassing my mother. He wanted me gone from the city. By giving me money he hoped I'd crawl into some motel room and die anonymously, pretty much the way he did.

What goes around, comes around.

"Who else was on the committee?"

"No one, per se. They'd lined up a number of people to make donations. Let me get you a list."

Martha left her chair, then waved a hand at a petite woman with white blonde hair and a pale complexion. She had freckles, but they were barely visible beneath a spattering of paint. "Leah, come here. I want you to meet Patrick Molloy. He used to live here, too."

Leah smiled at me, all the way up into her blue eyes. I started liking her right then, because a lot of beautiful women would have been mortified to be introduced wearing overalls thick with paint. She wiped her hand on a rag, then offered it to me, bespeckled and smeared. "I've heard a lot about you, Mr. Molloy."

"Trick." She had a firm handshake, warm and dry. My flesh tingled as we touched. It was more than attraction. She truly was *talented*, but I was liking what I was seeing normally so much that I didn't look at her through magick. That would have been an invasion of privacy—the last bastion of privacy in the mission.

I nodded toward the mural. "Nice work."

She smiled and reluctantly released my hand as Martha headed toward her office. "You recognize it as da Vinci, yes?"

"Not his style."

"True. I interpreted it through *vanitas*."

"Uh-huh."

Leah laughed delightfully. "Sixteenth- and seventeenth century painters in Flanders and the Netherlands popularized the style. It's still-life with decay. It's supposed to remind us that everything is fleeting and that we'll die some day. But you knew that."

It was my turn to laugh. "That's maybe the one bit of art knowledge that stuck. I was in my nihilistic teen phase when I was force-fed."

"I'm sorry."

"For?"

"Art is something that everyone should experience because it helps them grow. You got it as though you were a veal calf being fattened up. No wonder you didn't like it."

"I wouldn't say that."

"But you don't go to galleries or museums, do you?" She glanced down. "I used to, all the time. I'd sit and sketch. I'd see the work through the artist's eyes, and then I'd endure watching boorish people troop through, or school kids rushed through with only enough time to look at the back of the kid in front of them. They were walking through beauty and saw none of it. Yet the teachers and the parents all thought the kids were getting culture."

"They were, it was just the McRembrandt version of it."

She snorted out a little laugh but didn't look up. "I kind of lost it. Nervous breakdown. That's how I ended up here. Martha's very good at putting puzzles back together."

I nodded, reached up, and parted my hair. "You can't even see the joints anymore."

Leah laughed openly, warmly, and looked up again. "She said you could be cold, but I don't get that. And she said you could be trusted."

"She's right on both counts."

"I'm right? I guess my work here is done." Martha handed me a printout of the recent donors to the mission. "The initials after each name indicates the contact."

"Thanks." I wasn't sure what the list would get me, but if the Fellowship was the connection, it was a vector in. "I guess I have to go to work."

Martha smiled. "You go, but you're going to come back later. We'll be having a big crowd tonight, and I need an extra hand on the soup line."

Leah nodded. "You soup them, I'll bread them."

I studied her face, then smiled pretty much against my will. "I think I'd like that."

Back in the street, my phone rang.

Cate. "4721 Black Oak Road. You want to be here now."

"Who?"

"E. Theodore Carlson."

I glanced at the printout. "We have a winner."

"I'd hate to see what happened to the loser. Hurry, Trick. It's not pretty, and it isn't going to get any better with time."

Cate wasn't kidding. The corpse was ripe. He'd been dead a couple of days. Carlson had a reputation as a food critic and gourmand who got himself a cooking show and sold a lot of cookbooks and spices. While he liked exotic stuff, his critics claimed he simplified things for the common man. He took folks living hand to mouth and made them think they were mastering *haut cuisine*.

All while using hot dogs, ground chuck, catsup, and the secret ingredient.

Food lay all around in the kitchen, on presentation platters, but it had curdled or dried, crumbled or gotten covered in flies. He even had packaged cupcakes arranged on a set of stacked trays looking festive. They were the only things that hadn't gone bad yet, but that didn't soften the most gruesome aspect of the scene—aside from the corpse, that is.

On the granite countertop of the island, in a roasting pan surrounded by potatoes and carrots and chopped onions, lay a leg.

A human leg.

Carlson's leg.

He'd managed to hack it off at the knee, rub some salt on it, add pepper, before he collapsed and bled out on the floor. The butcher's knife lay half beneath him, covered in bloody prints. The angle of the cuts and the way the bone was sheared meant he'd taken the leg off with only a couple whacks.

I looked around. "What did Prout say? Carlson slipped?"

Cate shook her head. "He was gone before I got here. Manny said he covered his mouth with a handkerchief, then got that look on his face like he'd gotten an idea."

Manny, who was taking pictures of the scene, grunted. "I said he looked like he'd just dumped a load in his tighty-whities."

"Same thing when his brain has movement." My eyes tightened. "Time of death?"

"Two days, three."

I glanced at my PDA and the listing of case files. "Killer's on a tight cycle, and it's getting faster. Two days between Carlson and Anderson. Someone is going to die in the next twelve hours."

"No, they won't."

I spun. Prout had returned, with handkerchief in place. "We just arrested the murderer."

"What? Who?"

He lowered the handkerchief so I could see his sneer. "Martha Raines."

"Are you out of your mind?"

"Only if you are, Molloy." His beady eyes never wavered. "You followed the money. So did I. The Fellowship's made millions on these deaths. You didn't want to see it because you always were a lousy detective."

"Arresting Raines solves nothing."

"You trying to confess to being an accomplice? How much did she pay you?"

I glanced at Prout through magick. He looked almost as bad as the corpse, all mushroom gray and speckled with black. He had no *talent*—nor talent, for that matter—so one spell, just a tiny one, and his white suit would be sopping up blood as he thrashed on the floor.

Cate grabbed my shoulder. "Don't."

Prout gave her a hard stare. "I think you better escort your friend from my crime scene."

"He's going. He's got a friend in jail who could use a visit." She poked a finger into Prout's chest, leaving a single bloody fingerprint on his tie. It looked like a bullet hole, and I wished to God it were. "But this isn't *your* crime scene. It isn't even a crime until I says it is, Inspector. Right now, my running verdict is that he slipped. Death by misadventure, and unless you want to be doing all the paperwork and having all the hearings to change that, you'll be letting me finish this one fast."

Prout snorted. "Take your time."

Cate shook her head. "I don't have any. The killer's next vic will show up in another six hours, so time is not a luxury I enjoy."

I would have stayed, just to bask in the glory of that sour expression on Prout's face, but Manny got a shot of it. He gave me a wink. I'd be seeing it again. I wished he had a shot of the sneer too. I wanted it for reference. Next time I saw it I was going to realign the nose and jaw.

Cate had been right. Martha was in jail, and it wasn't for picketing some city office this time. She needed a friend. I owed her. I didn't think the bulls down in lockup would want to do her any harm, but they'd have to cage her with the hard cases. Still, a visit could get her out of a holding cell at least for a little bit.

I got down to the jail pretty quick. I only made one stop, at a drive-through liquor store. I bought a bottle of twelve-year-old Irish whiskey and took a long pull off it. Recorking it, I slid it under my seat. It burned down my throat and out into my veins. It made me feel more alive, and it prepped me to use magick, just in case.

I didn't need it. Hector Sands was working the desk, and he'd always believed I'd been framed for bribery. "You want to see Raines? Do you have to?"

"What am I not getting?"

Hector took me through into the holding area. Two big cells separated by a tiled corridor. Usually it was awash in profanity, urine, spittle, blood, and any other bodily fluid or solid that could be squirted, hurled or expelled. People didn't like being caged like animals; so they acted like animals in protest.

Not this time, though. Martha Raines sat on a cot, with all the other inmates sitting on the floor and the people across the corridor hanging onto the bars. And hanging onto her every word. She just spoke in low tones, so quiet I could barely hear her.

Maybe I couldn't. Maybe I was just remembering her calm voice and soft words. I heard her telling me that drinking myself to death wasn't going to solve problems. She told me I had something to live for. It really didn't matter what. I could change things from day to day. They were out there. I owed it to them and myself to straighten out.

"Been like that since we put her in the population. See why I don't want to take her out?"

"Yeah. You'll call me if there is trouble?"

Hector nodded. "I have to call Prout, too." He glanced up at the security cameras. "I wouldn't, but he wanted to know when you showed up, and he'll go through the tapes."

"Got it. Don't want you jammed up."

"I'll wait till the end of my shift, about an hour, to call, you know, if that will help."

I nodded, even though I didn't care. He'd call Prout. Prout would call me. I wouldn't answer. It didn't matter.

"Thanks." I left the jail armed with two things. The first was the list. The fact that Martha had given it to me without hesitation spoke against her guilt. If she were killing people, there's no reason she would hand me a list of her victims.

Unless she wanted to be stopped.

Serial killers feel compelled to kill, which is why they cycle faster and faster, their need pushing aside anything else. I wanted to dismiss the possibility of Martha's guilt outright, but I didn't know if she had alibis. I only had her word about how nicely things had gone. What if Anderson and Hogan set up the trusts for another reason, to deny her funding and to oust her? What if they were scheming to move the mission and profit from the location, using that project as some cornerstone to gentrify a swath of the city? Would that be enough to make her snap?

I crossed to a little bistro and ordered coffee. Martha was *talented*. She sat in that den of lions and made them into lambs. I'd felt it. I knew her power. I'd benefited from it. But that was the good side of it. Was there a dark side? Could she talk someone into hanging himself or chopping off his own leg?

And if she could do that, could she convince a jury—no matter how overwhelming the evidence—to let her go? If she could, there was no way she could ever be brought to justice. While the Fellowship was a noble undertaking, did its preservation justify murder?

Those were bigger questions than I could answer, so I did what I could do with the meager resources at hand. Starting at the top, I called down the donor list. I left messages—mostly with servants, since these sorts of folks like that personal touch—or talked to the donors directly. I told them there was a meeting of do-nors in the Diamond Room at the Ultra Hotel at nine. I told everyone to be there. I didn't so much care that it disrupted their evenings as much as I hoped it would disrupt the killer's pattern.

It took me two hours to go through the list. I spent a lot of time on hold or listening to bullshit excuses, so I used it to study those case files. Cate was right; I really didn't want to look at the Preakness photos. There was something there, though, in all of them, but I couldn't put my finger on it.

At the end of those two hours I was no closer to knowing who the next victim would be.

Then it came to me.

Prout.

He'd never called.

I drove to his home as fast as I could. Red lights and a fender bender let me double-check the full case packages Cate had sent me. I finally saw it. As far as a signature for a serial killer goes, this one was pretty subtle. Maybe there was part of me that didn't want to see it before, but there was no denying it now.

I rolled to a stop on the darkened street in front of the little house with the white picket fence. Figured. He probably owned a poodle. A sign in an upstairs window told firefighters there were two children in that room. I didn't even know he was married.

I fished the whiskey from beneath the seat and drank deep. I brought the bottle. Prout wouldn't have anything there, and if he did, he'd not offer.

That's okay. I don't like to impose.

I crossed the street and vaulted the fence. I could have boosted my leap with magick, but there was no reason to waste it.

And it didn't surprise me that the hand I'd put on the fencepost came away wet with white paint. Had my head not been full of whiskey vapors, I'd have smelled it. White footprints led up the steps and across the porch, hurried and urgent. The screen door had shut behind him, but the solid door remained ajar.

Beyond it, darkness and the flickering of candles. That wasn't right for the house. It should have been brightly lit, all Formica and white vinyl, with plastic couch-condoms covering every stick of furniture. Lace doilies, and white leather-bound editions of the Bible scattered about.

I toed the door open.

I got the last thing right. Bibles had been scattered, page by page. They littered the darkened living room. Across from the doorway sat a woman in a modest dress, and a little girl in a matching outfit. Both had been duct taped into spindly chairs, with a strip over their mouths to keep them quiet.

On the wall, where I guess once hung the slashed portrait of Jesus crumpled in the corner, someone had painted a pentagram in sloppy red strokes. A little boy hung upside down at the heart of it, from a hook to which his feet were bound. He'd been muted with duct tape too, and stared in horror at the center of the floor.

His father sat there, naked, in a circle of black candles. Thirteen of them. He'd cut himself on the neck and wrists—nothing life-threatening—and blood had run over his chest and been smeared over his belly. He clutched a long carving knife in two hands. He waved it through the air, closing one eye, measuring his son for strokes that would take him to pieces.

I took another drink, and not because I needed the magick.

Prout looked up at me. "Yes, Father Satan, I have serve thee well, and I now have this sacrifice for you."

I held a hand out. "Easy, Prout."

He wasn't listening. "You come to me in the shape of my enemy to mock me. I did harm to your pet. That opened my heart to you, didn't it?"

I had no idea what he was going on about, but talking was better than slashing. "You begin to see things, my son."

He nodded and studied his reflection in the blade.

I looked at him through magick. Prout had always been leopard-spotted, just full of weaknesses. That had changed. The spots had become long, oily rivers that ran up and down his body, like circulating currents. I'd never seen its like before, but it wasn't part of Prout. He had no talent.

I closed my fist and opened it again. A blue spark, invisible to Prout and his family, flew from my palm and drilled into his forehead. His stripes went jagged. He tried to rise, then toppled and fell, snuffing two of the candles against his belly.

I looked past him toward the kitchen. "Come on out, Leah. This ends here."

The young artist stepped from the darkened kitchen, glowing silver with magick. She'd streaked paint over her face and in her hair. It had to be her trigger—something in it, or the scent—and the glow made her very powerful. She opened her hands innocently and stared into my eyes.

"You don't know what he did, Trick."

"He arrested Martha for your murders."

"Not that." Her voice came soft and gentle, like a lover's whisper. "Before that, when he was investigating you. He knew you were set up. He had evidence to clear you. He didn't. You know why? Your mother is part of his church. You were an embarrassment for her. He wanted to make you go away."

I stared down at the man and suddenly found the knife in my hand. Prout *had* known I was innocent. He destroyed my life because magick was evil, and he couldn't abide it. He got me tossed from the force and hid behind being a good church-going man, an upstanding officer.

I weighed the knife in my hand. "Right. He's a hypocrite."

"Just like the others. They all pledged money, but only in trust, only upon death, for capital expenses, not operations." Leah's eyes narrowed. "They knew how tight things were for the mission. They helped Martha to expand until she couldn't keep the place going. They had their own plans. They'd move her out, revoke their gifts. They had to be stopped."

"You made them pay."

"I made them reveal themselves. They wallowed in their own vanity. They died embracing their inner reality."

"Why the staging? The rotten food from the *vanitas* paintings?"

"It was all a warning to others. They should have seen death coming."

"And the Twinkie. I saw one at each site."

Leah smiled coldly. "The promise of life everlasting. They never saw it."

"They never could have understood."

"But you do, Trick." Her eyes blazed. "You have to kill Prout. He betrayed you. Let him die here. Let everyone see how black his heart really is."

Argent arcane fire poured over me. Every moment of pain I'd felt exploded within. I'd made a good life. I'd had friends. I'd been respected, and Prout conspired with my mother and with criminals to smear me and destroy me. Leah's magick wrapped me up and bled down into the blade, tracing silver lightning bolts over the metal.

One second. A heartbeat. A quick stroke and Prout's blood would splash hot over me. I could revel in it. Victory, finally.

Then it was over.

I dropped the knife.

She stared at me. "How?"

"I've been where you've been, darlin'. As low as can be." I let blue energy gather in my palm. "No vanity. No illusion. I know exactly what I am."

The azure bolt caught her in the chest and smashed her back against the wall. Plasterboard cracked. She left a bloody smear as she sank to the floor.

In turn I used magick to put Prout's family out and

to let them forget. They'd have nightmares, but there was no reason to make them worse.

And it was going to get worse.

I'd been worried that Martha could have turned a jury with her *talent*. There's no juror in the world, much less jurist or lawyer, that isn't a little bit vain. I never figured the way Prout did, that being talented meant one was evil; but I knew better than to rule it out.

I had to deal with it.

I picked up the knife. I wrapped Prout's hand around it.

We went to work.

Cate found me on the hill overlooking Anderson's graveside service. Huge crowd, including Prout. He dressed properly. The only white on him was his shirt and bandages on his face. He stood beside my mother, steadying her, being stoic and heroic.

That was his right, after all, since he'd put an end to the Society Murderess.

"How can you watch this, Trick?"

"Only way I can make sure he's dead." I half-smiled. "Think my mother will throw herself on the casket?"

"Not her. Prout. Preening."

"Why shouldn't he? He's a hero. He killed a sociopath." I nodded toward him. "She put up a hell of a fight before he stabbed her through the heart. I heard his jaw was broken in two places."

"Three. Cracked orbit, busted nose."

"Whoda thunk she could hit that hard?"

"Never met her." Cate shook her head. "How's your hand?"

"Scrapes and bruises. I'll be more careful walking to the bathroom in the dark."

"You know, there were some anomalous fingerprints on the knife."

"Ever match 'em?"

"No. Was I wrong about you, Trick?"

"I don't think so, Cate." I met her stare openly. "They need their heroes. They need someone to fend off the things lurking beyond the firelight. Prout battled to save his family. Its best he never knows how much danger he was in. How much danger they were all in. All their fear and they couldn't even imagine."

"I don't think they really want to."

"You're probably right."

Down below, Martha Raines closed the prayer book and made a final comment. I didn't hear it. I didn't need to.

They did, and they looked peaceful.

Witness to the Fall

Jay Lake

The bottles shiver quietly in their rack on the kitchen windowsill. Wind gnaws at the house like a cat worrying a kill. Rafters creak the music of their years fighting gravity's claim. Outside a groaning window, trees dip in a dance likely to break a back and give me kindling for half a season.

Most strange is the sound. The weather hisses and spits, a long-drawn ess slithering from one horizon to the other. I can yet see the water-blue of the sky, furtive clouds hurrying along the wind's business. This will not bring rain, no relief of any kind. It is only the hands of angels pushing the house (and me) toward our eventual ashy dissolution.

Down in the town there has been a murder. People will say it was the blow, five days of wind so strong a man could not stand facing it. People will say it was an old love gone sour, the harder heart come back for one last stab at passion. People will say it was a baby, never an hour's rest since the poor squalling mite was first born into this world.

Me, I listen to the quiet clatter of the bottles, a tiny sound beneath the roaring lion of the air, and hear the song of death as clearly as if I'd played the tune myself on the old piano in the parlor.

Knowing the truth, I turn out my cloak, fetch my

bag and inkwells. Soon enough the preacher man or old Cromie will call for me to sit judgment. It has never hurt to be prepared, to remind them of their own belief that I can hear the hammers of their hearts.

That's not all true, but I never lost by letting them think such a thing.

I am surprised when Maybelle turns up for me. She is the preacher's daughter, a pretty peach borne off the withered branch that is Caleb Witherspoon. For every glint-eyed slight and patriarchal judgment out of him, she has a smile or a warm hand or a basket of eggs and carrots. Of such small economies are the life of a town made.

Still, she has not before called at my gate on business such as this. A Christmas pie, or a letter come by distant post over mountains and rivers, yes, but she has never come for blood or sorrow.

I open the front door before she can raise her hand to knock. "Hello, child," I say, though in truth I do not have even ten years on her new-grown womanhood.

The wind runs its fingers through her braids, sending hair flyaway around her in a pale brown halo. The hem of her dress whips wompered about her shins and calves. The practical countrywoman's boots beneath are scuffed and too solid to be pulled by air. There is a smile on her face, belied only by the worried set of her pale gray eyes.

"Master Thorne," she says, with a fumbled curtsy that is withdrawn before it can truly take hold. "Please, sir, the beadle and Mister Cromie have asked you come right quick."

I nod and step out on the porch, my cloak seized in the dry gale as soon as I pass the door. "Death's a sad business," I tell her, more loudly than it is my wont to speak, "but there's rarely a hurry once the thing is already done."

"Yes, but 'tis my daddy with blood under his nails

this day. We need a Foretelling." She holds her silence a breath, then two, before blurting, "I know he ain't done it."

Interesting. The bottles had not spoken clear, or I didn't listen well. I'd have thought it was a child died for love, not a preacher taking literally the murderous word of God. "All will be well."

My words are both a lie and a truth, depending on how far away from the moment one is willing to stand. Together we set out down the track amid summer's brambles and the wind-flattened heads of wild grass caught gold and sharp beneath the noonday sun.

Neverance is a town of small blessings. There is enough of a river to water the horses and fields in all seasons, though it will not sustain navigation from the metropolii far downstream. There are groves of chestnuts and hoary pear trees to lay forth autumn's windfall and provide children with ladders to the sky come spring. The first white men to settle here had possessed more ambition than sense and so laid strong foundations of stone quarried from the surrounding hills for the city that never came.

In sum, Neverance is a town typical of these mountains—nestled in a valley between tree-clad peaks, sheltered from winter's worst excesses, surrounded by bounteous fields bearing hay and corn and the small truck grown on hillsides by farm wives and those too old to harness a team to work the larger plantings. The cattle now standing with their faces away from the remorseless wind, clumped like crows on a kill, are symbols of sufficiency as surely as the great beeves of ancient myth.

Wealth, no, but neither is life is too difficult here. Some, especially women fallen on hard times, live at the edges. Most people in the valley show their faces in church on Sunday with a smile. A turnpike might come someday, or even a railroad ushering the restless through the ever-moving Western Gates, but for these years Neverance slumbers amid its quiet dreams of pumpkins and smokehouses and the peal of the school bell.

Not this day, though.

There is a crowd outside Haighsmith's Dairy. They huddle like the cattle against the wind. Despite the name, the dairy is a co-op serving farmers and townsmen alike. Maybelle leads me to the back of the kerfuffle, intent on pushing through the mass of shoulders to the door, but I tug at her elbow to halt our progress.

At my touch a spark passes between us with an audible crack, tiny lightning raised by the dry wind. Her face flickers with a fragment of pain as she turns toward me.

I cup my hand and speak close to her ear. "I should like to remain out here a few moments, to observe."

Maybelle scowls, an expression that suits her poorly, but she nods. Taking that as my permission, I study the people who crowd the door of the dairy.

Most are known to me. Farmers in their denims and roughspun blouses, townsmen wearing wool trousers and gartered cotton shirts, a scattering of women bustled and gowned for the sake of their appearance before one another. The wind has stolen a few hats and sent hair flying, so this assembly bears an unintentionally disrupted aspect, as if some tiny demon of disorder has descended upon Neverance's well-starched citizens.

What I do not see in evidence are firearms or ropes or shovels. This is not a lynching awaiting its moment. These people are worried, frightened even, but they have not turned to hunters of blood.

The bottles would have told me if they were.

I listen now for whispers in the windows, echoes of truth, but the wretched wind snatches so much away out here in the street. Instead I nod to Maybelle, and we push forward.

To my surprise the crowd parts like loose soil before a plow.

Thin as a fence rail and with a face just as weathered, Caleb Witherspoon sits upon a coffee-stained settee in the co-op manager's office. In here the howling wind is little more than a murmur, a substitute for the voice of the crowd waiting outside for justice, or at least law. The room reeks of male fear and rage mixed in a sour perfume all too familiar to me.

The manager has absented himself before the face of justice, but in his stead is Ellsworth Clanton, the elderly beadle from Neverance's sole church. Clanton stands shivering with age beside Witherspoon, hiding a hard smile that he cannot keep from lighting his eyes as he clamps a hand on the preacher's shoulder. Mister Cromie is also present, who would be municipal judge if Neverance had the formality of a city charter. Still, he wears black robes and mounts a bench to pronounce marriages, hear suits and sign the certificates of death. Though not smiling, he too seems strangely pleased for someone officiating over a murder.

I am witnessing the fall of a man.

Clearly it matters nothing what Caleb Witherspoon has actually done, whether Maybelle has the right of her father's innocence. His years of uncompromising rectitude have layered old scars in everyone around him, the memories of which still burn within angry hearts throughout Neverance.

Though I have not lived here so long, being one of the few immigrants in living memory, I know well enough for what sorts of sins these countrymen punish one another. They can be read so easily.

Clanton the beadle always craved the pulpit for himself. He nurses a coal of resentment in his heart for Witherspoon as the faith holder who took the word of God from his mouth. There is old blood between them, a thorn prick scarred by time and never healed.

Cromie rushes to judge lest he be judged himself. Of his misdeeds I hold more certain knowledge, having emptied the wombs of two of his daughters by the dark of the moon in my years here. Not long after my attentions, his Ellen Marie drowned herself in the mill pond. Jeanne Ann is long since married to Fred Sardo's son and lives at the high end of the valley, where they tend nut orchards and rarely come to town. I doubt Cromie will ever see his grandchildren except in church.

Caleb Witherspoon has measured all of these men time and again and found them wanting in his holy scales on each occasion. Now that the preacher is caught on the point of justice, they have no more mercy than ferrets on a rat.

Maybelle has requested a Foretelling. Even so, I know without asking that these men desire a Truthsaying, which they might use as a cloak for the vengeance each nurses in his heart.

"Do not tell me aught." I address Cromie, for he is the power in this room. "I know there has been a murder, and I know where the blood is found. Let me first do my work untrammeled by testimony, then we shall see what we shall see."

"He is guilty, Thorne." Cromie's voice is cold as a child's headstone. "There does not even need to be a trial, except for the form of the thing."

I meet Cromie's slate-gray eyes. "Then why did you trouble to send for me?"

"I did not."

Though I do not glance at Maybelle, I know she blushes like the fires of dawn. I ask the next question, the true question. "If I am unsent for, why did you await my coming?"

Though the words seem to choke him, Cromie manages to spit an answer. "I could do nothing else." This time *he* looks at the girl.

There is nothing more to be said. I shed my cloak, sweep the dairy's business journals off a small table, and set out my inkwells.

* * *

These are the essential inks with which I sketch the visions of my art. You will forgive me if I do not tell the precise secrets of their processes of creation.

Culpability—Made from lampblack and the ashes of a hanged man's hand. It smells of a last, choking breath.

Vision—Made from the humors of an eagle's eye and the juice of carrots, much reduced. A sharp scent of nature.

Realization—Made from photographer's chemicals and the bile of a dying child, strained through pages torn from Latin Bibles. Tingles the sinuses like an insult not yet forgotten.

Action—Made from paraffin and the crushed bodies of bluebottle wasps. Stings the nostrils as if to sneeze.

Regret—Made from grave dust, the tears of a nun, and the juice of winter apples. A musty odor that will close your throat if you are careless.

I tip them from their wells by drop and gill and mix them in proportion to the need that I have at the moment. A scrivener's greatest works are meant to be drawn on vellum scraped from the flayed skin of kings or presidents, but most purposes can be inked onto any paper at hand. Always, it must be something that I will eventually burn. Fresh wood, living skin, or stone are therefore not ideal.

All children draw, if the stick or coal or pencil is not snatched from their hand. All children represent the world they see in a language that reflects the essentials of their vision. For most, growing up means accepting the way the world is said to look. But a few cling to their craft. A few hang onto their lidless vision the way ants cling to a rotting apple.

Very few find their way to the essential inks.

Very, very few find their way to someone with the wit and craft to instruct them further.

Someone, at some time, must have been the original autodidact. There was a first teacher. Perhaps more than one. In the lands across the ocean where little yellow men write their thoughts in tiny pictures, mine is presumably a powerful art. Here on the country frontiers of America, where no one recalls that "A" stands for ox, the forms of the words themselves do not mean so very much.

Here is the trick to the craft: Consider that there is no present moment. We have anticipation, then we have memory. The present flees our grasp at least as fast as it arrives, slipping from future to past before we can take note. Everything we experience can only be a memory of what has come immediately before. Try to find the space between the earth and the sky— that is the present moment.

If you can see that space between earth and sky, if you can find that present moment, then you can craft a Foretelling, or a Truthsaying, or a Sending, or any of the dozens of forms it is given to me and my fellow scriveners to render.

Today I set to scribing a Passage. I spread out a sheet of birch bark pounded with quicklime and thrush's bile, anchoring the edges with my inkwells. I lay down the jade tortoise, which has come from the lands across the ocean. There I begin to mix my recipe in the shallow cup upon its head. As I pour, each tiny ring of glass on jade tells me something, in the manner of my art. Even while listening, I begin a speaking to Caleb Witherspoon. The truth is already with us, after all, waiting only to be discovered.

Three drops of *Regret*. I guard my breath.

"Have you ever wondered on the brown of May-belle's hair?" The floorboards settle as the dairy building shifts in the wind.

Three drops of *Realization*. The burn touches me deep within my face.

"Your child's eyes are most gray, though your own are oaken dark." Something rattles on the roof. A

few stray hailstones, perhaps, or the claws of a mighty
wingéd creature.

Caleb Witherspoon begins to shiver. Rage, fear, the
chill of mortality. Cromie stirs behind me.

"A prick of your finger, Mister Cromie." His breath
hisses his surprise. Amid a sweaty stink of fear, he
struggles to answer me. "I . . ."

Reaching out without looking, my fingers find the
judge's wrist limp and dangling. I tug him toward my
mixture and stab him carelessly with a silver needle.
This does not have to hurt, if I do it better than I
have bothered for him.

Three drops of an angry man's boiling blood, reeking hot and metallic.

"Caleb, where is her mother?" Though his long-lost
wife is said to have died in childbirth, this time the
preacher groans as though freshly stabbed.

A drop of *Vision*. A tiny gust of forest scent.

"Who cries on the wind?" I am answered only by
silence.

A drop of *Culpability*. Airs from the grave.

I dip my brush and begin to paint.

I know even before I begin that I will paint the portrait of a woman. I have already seen her on the wind.
She is not who I might have expected. Witherspoon's
reach was long.

The bones of her face, the curve of cheek and jaw,
are an older echo of Maybelle. Her hair falls differently, lighter in hue. This shows on the wet birch bark
even though I do not work in colors beyond what my
mixture gives me. Their hairline is not the same—
despite my speculations about the beadle, Maybelle's
is more the shape of Cromie's.

The eyes come to me, half-lidded and bright with
standing tears. The secret of portraits is in the eyes.
If people can see themselves and those they love peering back from the scribing, they will be convinced.

The outlines now, as if she is growing from a center. She becomes real. This has only taken minutes, with the passion and power that makes the room crackle as electric as the hot, hard wind outside.

It is about a woman. It is almost always about a woman.

"That is Alton Miller's widow Chastity," mutters the beadle behind me. "What lives up behind Corncrib Hill."

The words choke from Caleb Witherspoon's mouth as if dragged on chains. "She is my daughter's mother."

"No," Maybelle begins. She bites off whatever words were to come next.

Cromie's voice is bitter with hollow satisfaction. "*Was*. Now we know who Otis Blunt saw floating in the river today."

"You knew all along," Caleb Witherspoon says.

A woman no one would have mentioned had gone missing, even here in Neverance. Not their grass widow. Who would want to claim to have noticed her? I wonder whose back door the preacher had seen her stepping away from, checking the buttons of her dress.

Does it matter?

I finish the portrait of Maybelle's mother. Caleb Witherspoon's young love. Cromie's conquest, whom Alton Miller had taken as a castoff after she'd borne her child in secret. Well before my time here, but even I knew that the preacher put out that his absent wife had died while the daughter was being sent on to be raised by him. All these men should be in the picture, as well, staring over her shoulder, daring their neighbors to sin.

There must have been a ruse, a carriage or a rider in the dark, in the last moment of friendship between the preacher and the judge before the child took the stage at the center of their lives.

It is a hurt nearly two decades old now but never really done with. Especially not for Chastity Miller.

I look at Caleb Witherspoon. There is no need to ask him why. The reason has been written on his daughter's face every day of her life in the lines of another man's jaw and cheeks. Still, it does matter, I realize. If only for the sake of her memory, which no one wanted to account for now. "Why now?"

"The wind makes madmen of us all," he says.

"Hardly," mutters the beadle.

I think back on the song of the bottles, my vision of a crying baby. "You saw her hurrying, to Mister Cromie once more perhaps?"

Caleb Witherspoon clears his throat. "From Cromie's back step, actually." He turns his face away from Maybelle, whose breath hitches in her throat.

I have it right, I realize. This is a thing to be finished.

Cromie appears uncomfortable, as if he now wishes for silence.

"Was there to be another child?" I ask him. He does seem short on daughters these days, and the widow Miller was not so old.

"It doesn't matter now." The judge's voice is blurred with tears.

So there were two murders today. Did Witherspoon know? There is nothing else to say. The wind pushes at the building, sending dust spiraling down mote by mote from the grubby ceiling. I pack my inkwells one by one in my satchel, carefully avoiding Maybelle's distress.

"Mister Cromie?" It is Clanton, the beadle, practically creaking in his excitement. "Might be a good idea if I preach this Sunday's sermon, don't you think?"

I take my leave, wondering as I go where the river has taken Chastity Miller and her quickened child. Perhaps I should follow them away from this place. Beneath my arm, the bottles shiver a little hymn that I lack the wit or courage to understand.

The Best Defense

Kristine Kathryn Rusch

They tell me time has no meaning here. I sit in cross-legged in a glade, surrounded by willow trees and strong oak and all sorts of green plants I don't recognize. Flowers bloom out of season—roses next to tulips next to mums. The air is warm, the breeze is fresh, and I have never felt more trapped in my life.

Except when I was in law school.

Third year, sitting in my carrel in the law library, various teas stacked around the top, hiding me from the other students. I'd spend a few hours digging through some musty old tomes to find one little nugget of information that might help my hypothetical client or, failing that, impress some stupid professor, all the while wondering if I should just drop out.

Escape.

Pretend the past three years of Aristotelian logic and Socratic debate had never happened at all.

Now I have tea at my fingertips—all I have to do is snap them and some scantily clad nymph pours me a cup—and all the food I want (oh, yeah, that's the thing they don't tell you: never eat the food), and it doesn't matter.

I'm still digging through tomes, trying to find something to get my client off. He's not so hypothetical any more. Although I am going to have to impress a few people.

People I don't really want to impress.
People who may not be people at all.

I only caught the case because I didn't escape quickly
enough from Judge Lewandowski's courtroom. I'd
been there to argue against remand for a repeater,
even though I knew all of Chicagoland would be better off if he went to prison for life.

That's what I do. I defend the defenseless. At least,
that's what I tell the newspapers when they ask, or
that schmo at a cocktail party who thinks he'll get the
better of a seasoned public defender.

Mostly I do it because I like to argue, and I like to
win against impossible odds. I'm not one of the liberal-
hippie types who gravitates to the PD's office to save
the planet; I'm not even sure I believe everyone is
entitled to a fair trial.

What I do believe is that everyone is entitled to the
best defense I can provide—given that I have hundreds of other active cases, only twenty-four hours in
my day, and no real budget to hire a legal assistant.

Which was actually what I was thinking about as I
slipped into the bench two rows back from the defense
table to repack my briefcase before heading down to
the hot dog carts on California Avenue.

"John Lundgren."

Hearing my name intoned by the judge after my
case had already been gaveled closed was not a good
sign. I looked up so fast my notes almost slipped off
my lap. I caught them but lost the briefcase. It thud-
ded against the gray tile floor.

"Yes, Judge," I said, standing up, even though my
entire day's work was lying in a mess around me.

The judge was peering at me through her half-
glasses. She looked tired and disgusted all at the same
time. "You'll represent Mr. Palmer."

I glanced around, trying to figure out what I'd
missed. The courtroom was filled with attorneys waiting for their cases to be called, a few witnesses and

even fewer victims, and a couple of defendants who had probably made a previous case's bail.

"*Now*," the judge said.

The one place I hadn't looked was the defense table. A scruffy man with long black hair stood behind it, his shoulders hunched forward. He wore a trench coat covered with soot, burn marks, and not a few holes.

I slid out of my bench, leaving my briefcase on the floor and grabbing only a yellow legal pad, knowing that no one else would pick up my mess. Unlike TV lawyers, real lawyers are so overwhelmed they don't dig through each other's briefcases, hoping for the one nugget of information that will make or break the trial of the century.

Not that I'd ever handled a client involved in the trial of the century. Or even one involved in the trial of the year.

"You must be Mr. Palmer," I said as I dropped my legal pad on the defense table.

Palmer didn't even look at me. His face was covered in soot and a three-day beard. He smelled like gasoline and smoke.

I didn't even have to guess what he was charged with. It was as obvious as the stench of his clothes.

The prosecutor—some new twit who looked like he was wearing his father's suit—rustled his papers together. "Mr. Richard Palmer is charged with arson in the first degree, attempted arson in the second degree, and sixteen counts of murder in the first degree."

"Mr. Lundgren, how does your client plead?"

I looked at my client, but he didn't look at me. The smell was so overwhelming, my eyes were watering.

"Mr. Lundgren?"

"Mr. Palmer?" I said softly. "What do you want to plead?"

Palmer kept his head down.

"Mr. Lundgren," the judge said, "I asked you a question."

Well, Palmer wasn't talking. I wasn't even sure he

was present and accounted for. But if he was like 99.9% of my clients, his plea would be simple, no matter what the evidence against him.

"Not guilty, Your Honor," I said.

"See?" she muttered. "That wasn't hard, now was it? Bail, counselor?"

She was looking at the young prosecutor. His hands were shaking.

"Since Mr. Palmer is accused of burning down one of the largest mansions on the Gold Coast, your honor, and killing all sixteen people inside, we're asking for remand."

He made it sound like they'd ask for more if they could get it.

I opened my mouth, but the judge brought down her gavel so hard it sounded like a gunshot.

"Remand," she said. "Next case."

And with that, I became responsible for Richard Mark Harrison Palmer the Third.

Or at least, for his legal defense.

Every last bit of it.

It took hours before I could get to the Cook County Jail to see my brand-new client. By then, he was in prison blues. Someone had washed his face, and, surprisingly, there were no burns beneath all that soot.

I'd represented arsonists before, many of whom smelled just as Palmer had when he was brought to court, and they were always covered with burns or shiny puckered burn scars.

They were also bug-eyed crazy. Something about staring at fire made their eyes revolve in their skulls— rather like the eyes of someone who'd taken too much LSD over too long a period of time.

But this guy didn't look crazy. He didn't give off the crazy vibe either, the one that always made me stand near the door so that I could pound it for a guard and then get the hell out of the way if I needed to.

Palmer sat at the scratched table, his head down, his hands folded before him. His hair was wet and he smelled faintly of industrial soap.

"Mr. Palmer." I sat down across from him, set my briefcase on the table, and snapped the top open so that it stood like a shield between us. "I don't know if you remember me. I'm John Lundgren, your court-appointed public defender."

"I don't need you." His voice was deep, his accent so purely Chicago that the sentence sounded more like a mushy version of *I doon need yoo*.

"I'm afraid you do, Mr. Palmer. You charged with some serious capital crimes, and it was pretty clear that Judge Lewandowski doesn't believe you can handle it on your own. So she assigned me—"

"And I'm unassigning you. Go away." He looked up as he said that, and I was stunned to see intelligence in his blood-shot brown eyes.

I sighed. I always hated clients who argued with me, clients who believed they knew more about the legal system than I did.

Or worse, clients who somehow believed they could go up against Chicago's finest prosecutors all by themselves.

"I'm not charging you, Mr. Palmer," I said. "The county pays my salary to represent people who can't afford their own attorney."

"I don't want an attorney," he said.

I sighed again. It was always a nightmare to go before the judge—any judge—and say that my indigent client wants me off the case in favor of his own counsel. Usually I'd have to sit in anyway, advise the stupid client on matters of the law (or, as I'd privately say, matters on which he was screwing up royally).

"It's better to have one," I said, "especially when you're facing sixteen counts of premeditated murder. You want to tell me what happened?"

Usually that ploy worked. The client forgot his belligerence and wanted to brag. Or to defend himself. Or make excuses.

A lot of my colleagues never wanted to know what the client believed he did, but I always figured the more information I had, the better. That way, I wouldn't get blindsided by my own client's idiocy in the middle of trial.

"No, I don't want to tell you what happened," Palmer said. "I think it would be better if you leave."

I closed my briefcase. "You're not going to be rid of me that easily. I will remain your attorney until we can go to court to sever the relationship, and then the judge is going to want to know all kinds of things, like what kind of preparation you have to represent yourself. And frankly, Mr. Palmer, I'd be remiss if I didn't—"

"Tell me how stupid I'm being for taking this on alone, I know." He gave me half a smile. It was condescending. I'd never met an arsonist capable of being condescending before. "But you're the one who pleaded me not guilty."

"You weren't exactly talking," I said. "I even gave you a moment to give me some kind of response, and you didn't say a word. So I gave my standard answer. Not guilty. We can always modify the plea later. Do you have medical records that would show mental health treatments—"

"I wasn't going to plead out to a mental defect," he said.

My hand froze on top of the briefcase. "You were going to plead guilty? Why in the hell would you do that, Mr. Palmer?"

He shrugged. "It seemed like the only thing to do."

"Look, I don't know the details of your case, Mr. Palmer. The file hasn't come up to our offices yet. So I don't know what they have on you. But let me tell you, I've seen some supposedly tight police cases unravel in court. It might look hopeless now, but I can assure you that with good counsel we should be able to fight this. So let me—"

"I'm not suicidal or stupid," he said. "I have no defense."

I'd heard that before too, usually from guilty clients who felt remorse.

"I'll decide that," I said, and flicked the locks on the briefcase so the top popped open again. I pulled out the legal pad that had Palmer's name on it and *indictment* scrawled almost illegibly in my handwriting. "Just tell me your side of the events."

"The events, Mr. Lundgren?" He raised his eyebrows at me. I had a sense that I have had only rarely, that I was sitting across from someone with an intellect more formidable than mine.

"Where were you? What happened? What exactly are they accusing you of? That kind of thing."

"You heard what they're accusing me of. They think I burned down the Brickstone mansion and killed everyone inside."

I hadn't known it was the Brickstone mansion. When I was an undergrad at Northwestern, my buddies and I used to climb over the ivy-and-moss covered stone fence onto the three-block expanse of yard owned by the Brickstones. We'd walk to the edge of Lake Michigan, plop behind a group of giant rocks that blocked that section of the shore from the mansion proper, and proceed to get very drunk. We'd see who could drink the most and still be awake for sunrise.

Usually that would be me.

"The Brickstone mansion," I repeated, trying to put this together. "They say you burned it *down*?"

I expected him to tell me that was a figure of speech. In fact, so convinced was I that that was going to be his next sentence that I almost missed his actual one:

"To the ground." His tone was dry. "Nothing left but charred remains."

I frowned at him. That made no sense. The Brick-stone mansion was in Chicago's city limits—and any building in the city limits had to be made of stone. The famous Chicago Fire left its legacy: No building could be made of combustible materials.

And I'd seen the Brickstone mansion. It was well named. It was made of a kind of white stone you didn't find outside of the Midwest, but the wealthy in Chicago seemed to adore it. Each "brick" was the size of an armchair, and when I looked at them one drunken dawn, those giant stones gleamed whitely in the light of the rising sun.

"Did you see it?" I asked. "What was left?"

"Of course I saw it," he said. That look was making me uncomfortable. I was beginning to feel as if I truly was dumber than he was.

"And was it burned to the ground?"

"Nothing left except rubble," he said.

"You smelled of gasoline when I met you, Mr. Palmer," I said.

He shrugged.

"Gasoline fires burn hot."

He looked down.

"But they can't melt stone. You want to tell me what's going on?"

He lifted his head. His mouth was open slightly, as if he hadn't expected real thought from me. "I burned down the Brickstone mansion," he said. "Killing everyone inside."

I no longer believed him. "How?"

"What do you want me to do? Say I waved my magic wand, brought down lightning from the heavens into a puddle of magicked up gasoline, and caused the building to explode?"

It was my turn to shrug. "That's about the only thing that would reduce that white brick mansion to rubble."

"Well, then," he said, crossing his arms. "That's exactly what I did."

*   *   *

We left it at that. I couldn't get him to tell me anything else, and I didn't really try, because he seemed
to have dumped the idea of firing me. He didn't exactly say I could stay, but he nodded when I said I'd
be back after I had a chance to review the file.

I took that as a change of heart. We were now
attorney and client, whether either of us liked it or
not.

So I went back to the office in hopes of finding the
file. It was on my desk along with six other brand-
new case files, eight old case files, and the seven cases
I'd been trying desperately to plead out. My office was
a graveyard of active files. They trailed off my desk
to boxes on the floor, accordion files on my chair, and
half-opened file cabinet drawers beneath my window.

I wasn't exactly overworked. Overworked would
mean that I had some free time to look forward to.
My workload was impossible, which made it exactly
like everyone else's workload inside the Public Defender's office.

Which meant that the minute I saw all those piles
of paper, I should have forgotten about Palmer. But
I didn't. In fact, I grabbed his file first.

It was incomplete. A lot of the paperwork had little
typed notations TK which, oddly enough, meant "to
come" (I always thought: shouldn't that be TC? Probably too close to TLC, something the police department did not believe in.) A few sticky notes explained
that the documentation was being copied, and one
handwritten note said that the arson squad planned
to finish its investigation tomorrow and would have a
detailed report by the end of the week.

And pigs would fly out of my butt.

But I made do with what I had. I often got incomplete files, especially on cases as new as this one.
Sometimes the police department felt they'd done
enough and would "forget" to update me. So every
morning, I made a list of cases that needed additional

material, and I'd talk to a clerk, who'd talk to a squad leader, who'd talk to a detective, who would sigh and fill out the necessary paperwork.

The more times I had to do that, the more the detective got irritated at me, so that by the time we went to court, I was usually as big a bad guy in the detective's eyes as the person he arrested. Fortunately for me, detectives, while smart, aren't all that articulate, and I can—if I choose—slice one of them into tiny little pieces on the stand.

I don't always choose. Because if I do, that detective and his buddies'll be gunning for me on the next case. So I reserve such treatment for special cases.

I had a hunch this was one those.

Special. How I hated that word.

But I stopped feeling sorry for myself and started to make notes about all I could glean from the file.

At 12:13 A.M., neighbors near the Brickstone Mansion (and you'd have to be stretching it to call them neighbors, considering the three-block lawn, the half-mile driveway, and the large stone fence blocking the view) called 911 to report flames shooting into the sky "so high that it looked like the entire North Side is on fire." A few boats on Lake Michigan called in a massive fire as well.

The fire seemed localized around the Brickstone Mansion. Fire crews were called in. When they arrived, they realized the doors were all bolted shut on the outside. The building was "fully engaged." When they attempted to put out the fire, the entire place exploded.

Debris fell all over that massive yard, but somehow it managed to miss outbuildings, vehicles, and people. Fortunately, the flaming debris did not ignite secondary fires anywhere on the property or on nearby properties.

But the mansion itself was a total loss.

By six A.M., it was clear to fire investigators that at least sixteen people had died inside that building—all of them unidentified. An accurate body count was, according to the report, TK.

Investigators found my client hiding between the shrubs and the stone wall—on the inside of the Brickstone property. He smelled of gasoline, had soot marks on his hands, and "couldn't give a coherent account of where he had been or what had happened to him."

Finally, when pushed, he said, "I had to do it," and then clammed up.

The fire department called in the police, who arrested my client and brought him to the station.

I searched the file and found no mention of hospitals or trauma centers or counselors. I made a note of that too—because it was good for us.

Then I continued to read. At the police station, my client was offered breakfast, including coffee (they always make that sound like a service when, in fact, I think it part of the torture), which he declined. He was interrogated but refused to say much more than what he said to me, which was that no one would believe what actually happened.

Finally, the exasperated detectives figured they had enough to charge him and brought him into Judge Lewandowski, where the lucky defendant got introduced to me.

Which was going to make Mr. Palmer's day—or, rather, his tomorrow. Because I was filing a motion first thing to have his case immediately thrown out for lack of evidence. And for severe mistreatment on the part of the police and fire departments. The man was covered in soot and gasoline. He needed to go to a hospital. He was probably disoriented when they found him.

There was no proof that he wasn't in that house when it exploded and had somehow miraculously survived.

I was going to argue all of that in front of whatever

sympathetic judge I could find (adding, of course, as much legal mumbo jumbo as I could assemble by nine A.M.).

I was pretty good at putting together case dismissal arguments, so good I wouldn't need to do too much research on the case law. And I thought my client's appearance (I'd put him back in his street clothes for court), his nonconfession, and one or two well timed coughs on his part would be enough to get him off.

I was in a great mood as I outlined the argument on my trusty laptop—until I got the harebrained idea to look up Palmer himself.

Palmer is an old and venerable name in Chicago. During the last half of the nineteenth century, Potter Palmer and his wife Bertha remade Chicago into the city it is today. In addition to building the Palmer House Hotel, they donated their private art collection to the Art Institute (those Monets? Bertha's), redesigned downtown Chicago into the configuration it has today, and built the very first mansion on Chicago's Gold Coast.

In fact, it was their decision (rather, Bertha's) to move north that segregated the rich from the rest of the plebs in Chi-town. If there hadn't been Palmers in Chicago, there wouldn't have been a Brickstone mansion to burn down, over a century later.

Richard Mark Harrison Palmer the Third was related to those Palmers but not on the right side of the sheets. From what I could gather, the first Richard Mark Harrison Palmer was really Richard Mark Harrison until he got someone to admit something and prove that there was Palmer blood in the Harrison bloodline.

That didn't get Richard the First any money or any of the Palmer property (of which there is still a lot, at least according to city rumors), but it did give him some status among people who care about that kind of thing.

Which led to his son and his grandson getting the family name (and, apparently, the family snobbery), as well as inheriting the family business.

When Richard the First ran it, it was some kind of ghostly empire where a number of "real" mediums brought back the dead, if only for an evening and a bit of conversation. By the time Richard the Third inherited it, it had become a school for the psychic and those with magical abilities.

I didn't make a note of that or any of the rest of this, particularly the files I found all over the internet about Richard the Third being some kind of magical hero—a man with strong abilities who wasn't afraid to use them to fight the Forces of Darkness.

Stories like this—even though they came from places like the *Star* and the *National Enquirer*—would be enough to torpedo my case, if I couldn't get the damn thing dismissed. At the moment, it wouldn't negate my client's mistreatment at the hands of the authorities, although it would explain that mistreatment.

No one likes a nutcase. Particularly a nutcase with delusions of grandeur.

And sure enough, the following morning, the prosecution brought it all up while we stood in front of the judge, arguing for dismissal. Palmer stood on the other side of me, reeking in his gasoline- and smoke-damaged clothing.

When we met just before court, I told him to look as pathetic as he could, which really wasn't hard for him, considering the ill treatment he'd gotten in jail the night before. I'd also asked him to give me at least two deep tuberculoid coughs, one at the beginning of the hearing and the other somewhere in the middle.

His first cough, just after Judge Galica entered, was a tour-de-force of shudders and phlegm. It was so convincing that the judge himself asked Palmer if he needed water or a lozenge or—heaven forbid—a break. But Palmer managed to shake his head, and the prose-

cutor used that moment to shoot me an accusatory
glare as if I'd been the one to do the coughing.

This time, the prosecutor wasn't a baby. It was Rita
Varona, one of the office's very best. Normally she
made me nervous.

This morning, she didn't. They'd sent her because
of the judge we'd been assigned.

Judge Joseph Galica had gone from law school to
the Fair Housing Council and later became an advo-
cate for the homeless before getting appointed to the
bench. He was as liberal as possible, someone who
knew the excesses of the Chicago police (some say
because he was in the middle of the 1968 riots and
got teargassed), and who actually believed that all defendants should be treated with respect.

Yes, I milked Galica's attitude. But I did focus on
the legal argument as well. I was brilliant, and was
about to make my most important point when Palmer
interrupted me with another prolonged coughing
spell—this one requiring a glass of water from the
bailiff.

That spell got Varona to butt in, saying what a fake
Palmer was, both in his life and his profession, that
he had a hatred of the Brickstones, and he'd told a
number of people that the house on the coast was
"evil" and had to be destroyed.

I carefully did not look at my client while these
arguments were made. Varona talked a lot about my
client's beliefs, and finally she made the slip I was
hoping for.

"He claims he's a magician, Judge," she said. "Once
the arson squad's reports come back, we'll be able to
show that he used the wonders of science—chemistry
and physics—to explode that house as if he'd per-
formed a spell on it."

"Why would he do that?" I asked in my best
snide manner.

Varona gave me a sideways glance. She'd hoped for

that question. "To cement his claim that he's the best wizard in the city of Chicago. To get rid of a family that he considered to be his enemies and to increase his business traffic and visibility at the same time."

Then she launched into his family's history of quackery as if that were proof of his murderous tendencies.

I let her talk, even though the judge kept glancing at me, clearly wanting me to object.

Finally, the judge himself said in a blatant hint-hint, nudge-nudge kinda way, "Mr. Lundgren, what do you have to say about Ms. Varona's claims?"

I made sure I didn't grin. This was the moment I'd been waiting for.

"Simply this, Your Honor. If my client really were Chicagoland's best wizard, then he should have been able to get himself out of jail. In fact, he would have cast some kind of spell on the responding officers to leave him alone or on the fire investigators so that they wouldn't find him. Instead, he spent the night in lock-up and has the bruises to prove it."

"Your Honor," Varona said. "I never claimed he was a wizard. Just that he advertised himself to be one."

"And if he's not a wizard," I said over her, "then all you have to do is look at the family history that Ms. Varona outlined to see that there's a solid record of mental instability here. And the Chicago PD knows it. That's why they didn't take him to the hospital. That's why they conducted such a shoddy interrogation. And that's why the fire investigator's report doesn't record what my client actually said when they found him. Just that he—and I quote—'couldn't give a coherent account of where he had been or what had happened to him.' "

"He's clearly guilty, your honor," Varona said. "He was on the scene. He's wearing the same clothes he wore yesterday, and I'm sure you can tell from there that they stink of smoke and gasoline. He—"

"Gasoline?" I said, trying not to overplay my incredulousness. "Your Honor, Brickstone mansion was built of stone. Gasoline couldn't burn that place down. Nor could it cause an explosion of the magnitude described in the other reports. I got assigned this case while Mr. Palmer was standing alone in front of Judge Lewandowski. I didn't get the file until late last night. That's why we're here. If I'd had any of this information, I would have asked for dismissal then."

Varona rolled her eyes. "Your Honor, Mr. Palmer is a very dangerous man—"

"If that's true," the judge said, "you should have waited until you had a real case before charging him. I'm going to drop all the charges against this poor man, and I'm going to instruct his attorney to get him to the hospital immediately."

And the gavel came down.

Palmer turned to me. His mouth was open, and his eyes were wide. I'd never seen a man look so astonished.

"*That*," he said, "was pure magic. You're amazing."

I shrugged. It was less egotistical than agreeing. Then I touched his arm. "You heard the judge. I have to make sure you get medical treatment."

Palmer nodded. We walked out of the courtroom together, and I surreptitiously checked my watch. Another two hours before I had to be back. I actually could take the guy to get medical care.

Besides, the judge would probably check, so I wanted to be able to prove I'd followed instructions.

"You know," I said as we walked down the stairs, "you might want to pull every favor you have and hire a good attorney. Because the prosecutor's office will come after you again."

"I'm not worried," he said.

"Yesterday, you were ready to chuck it all."

He smiled. "Yesterday I had no idea what a good defense lawyer can do."

I permitted myself one small smile of satisfaction.

We walked in silence through the hallways that connected the courthouse with the Public Defender's office. Because Palmer reeked so bad, I stopped at a desk and asked for an official car to take us to the hospital. I didn't want Palmer in my used Lexus.

As we waited, Palmer turned to me. "You seem to love what you do."

"Yeah," I said.

"Because you appreciate the challenge." That sense I'd had of his intelligence came back. He'd seen through me faster than most did.

"Yes," I said.

"Would you consider continuing to defend me?"

"If they charge you again, you can come to me," I said, hoping it wouldn't come to that. Then I realized I already had a strategy in place. I'd work the evidence, and if that turned against us, then I'd get a few shrinks to examine the family history and Palmer himself and declare him mentally incompetent. He'd probably get time in a mental hospital or some outpatient counseling, but that wouldn't necessarily be bad—if all those articles on his past had even a smidgeon of truth.

"Good," he said. "Then you won't mind handling the most difficult part of the case."

And Lord help me, I thought he was still talking about the criminal case. Because egotistical me, I said, "The difficult part of any case is my favorite part."

Which is how I ended up here in this glade, surrounded by willow trees and strong oak and all sorts of green plants I don't recognize. A place where the breeze is warm and smells of roses, and the little creatures who bring me food and drink have human faces and multicolored wings.

You see, the most difficult part of the case is arguing to get Palmer's magic back. Apparently, the magical world has laws and rules and regulations just like ours.

And while there isn't jail per se, there are worse pun-
ishments, like taking away someone's magical abilities.

Palmer *is* Chicagoland's greatest wizard. He can
wave a wand and bring down lightning from the sky
to ignite a puddle of magically enhanced gasoline to
destroy a mansion made of stone. (And yes, I checked
just before I got whisked here. There was a lightning
storm that night.)

It seems no one here cares that Palmer destroyed
the house. They're not even that upset that he managed to kill the beings inside, which were—if the files
I have scattered across the grass are to be believed—
dragons that could assume human form.

Seems the dragons had a plan to steal every treasure
in the City of Chicago, starting with the contents of
the Art Institute but ending with very human treasure
like the Chicago Bears—the actual team members, not
the team ownership. When dragons steal a city's treasure, they don't move it. They just take over the city.
Chicago would have been a haven for evil—that's
what Palmer says—and after seeing the folks who run
the magical justice system, I'm inclined to believe him.

Not that I have to. I just have to defend him. I have
to make the case that even though he used his magic
injudiciously and caused sixteen deaths and—worse,
under magic laws—called attention to himself in the
nonmagical world, he was justified in doing so.

Palmer's right; this is the most difficult part of the
case. Not to make the argument—I'm great at argument. But to understand the stupid magical laws. I
have to know the system before I can beat it.

Which is why his magical friends dumped me here,
in this glade which is run by faeries. And what I didn't
know at first was these faeries are the kind Rip Van
Winkle ran into on his famous night of bowling and
carousing. These folks control time. They make it go
slow or they speed it up.

Palmer promises me I'll have all the time in the

world to do my research. I won't lose a day of my life. I'll be here, I'll make my arguments, I'll win my case (I'd better, considering what these people can do), and then I'll go home as if nothing's happened.

Of course, I'll be a little older, a little grayer, a little paunchier. They can't completely negate the effects of time on a human being.

But, as Palmer says, now at least I'll know how people seem to age overnight.

As if that's supposed to cheer me up while I sit here in sunshine-filled hell, eating the best food and drinking tea by the gallon, reading parchment and watching tiny replays of arguments made through the ages.

And I do mean ages.

Magic has existed a long, long time. Longer than the United States. Longer than the Magna Carta. Longer than England or the Roman Empire or ancient Greece.

Our laws aren't based on Greek conventions or English common law. They're a modification—an improvement (believe me)—of magical law.

Which just makes it all the more confusing.

And, I'm told, defense attorneys aren't required here. So no one goes into that side of the magical legal system.

After reviewing one-one-thousandth of the documentation before me, I can see why. It's hard to defend these people against anything. And not just because of the convoluted law, but because of all the things they've done.

Fortunately for Palmer, I'm not one of those liberal-hippie types who gets appalled when his client is actually guilty. I'm not in this to provide a fair trial. I'm in this to provide the best defense I possibly can.

Because I like to argue, and I like to win against impossible odds.

And that's exactly what I'm going to do.

Call of the Second Wolf

Steven Mohan, Jr.

Last night about two in morning, after I left Charlene the blonde hooker and was home sleeping,
someone crept into burned-out south side warehouse
and iced five members of Chinese mob in middle of
business transaction.

I do not mean *killed,* I mean *iced,* changed into
crystalline statues of frozen water.

Good news is that it was cold last night, clear and
twenty-two at Midway, so Chinese thugs did not have
chance to melt before Chicago PD showed up in
morning and changed them back. Otherwise the
bloodbath would've already begun.

Bad news is anonymous someone stole 47 kilos of
Afghani H from the Chinese and, of course, they are
blaming us.

Worse news is Georgi Dorbayeva wants *me* to fix it.

I stopped at run-down storefront, dark green paint
peeling off the weathered wood in long curls like shav-
ings coming off pencil sharpener. There were dead
chickens in window, hanging upside down. Dead
chickens and dead rats and dead snakes and God
knows what else, but all of it skinned and ready for
pot.

"Traditional Chinese Remedies," said sign over

window, and that made me laugh. Sure, nothing's more traditional than heroin.

I shouldered my way through door. Store inside was tiny, six feet front to back and same side to side.

A wizened old man sat behind a polished mahogany counter watching me kick snow off fine leather boots I'd conjured up night before.

Behind him were shelves of everything practitioner of Chinese magic might need. I saw scorpions crawling over each other in glass jar, individually wrapped tiger penises, stoppered vials of snake venom, ground sea-horse, duck tongues, million other things. Shelves went up forever, so high I couldn't see ceiling.

"Valeri Kozlov?" said the man behind the counter. He was short, not much over five feet, and he really *did* look wise. I might've mistaken him for Confucius if he hadn't been dressed in jeans and a black Rush tee-shirt.

"Da," I said.

"I have your item, just as you asked." He showed me a square box, ten inches on a side, and pulled off the top.

Inside was a blackened monkey's hand, desiccated and curled into a claw.

I blinked. I'd never spoken with this man before, so why the "gift"? Was this some obscure message from Zhang Shaoming?

I smiled graciously. "Thank you. May we discuss after meeting?"

He bowed his head and raised a hinged section of the countertop. I stepped through and into sudden darkness. Just like that, I was somewhere else.

I pulled out my cell and glanced at backlit screen: "NO SERVICE." My network promises coverage in all of United States and three parallel dimensions, so wherever I was, it wasn't store.

I turned in a slow circle, seeing nothing but darkness. I turned again and this time saw a white light shining down on circular table fashioned from polished teak.

Two men sat at table. One I recognized as Zhang Shaoming, Chicago overlord of the Black Dragons.

Zhang was dressed like he just stepped out of *GQ*: periwinkle polo shirt and charcoal slacks. I'm not sure how old he was (it was rumored he'd been friends with one of the Ming emperors), but he *looked* late thirties, dark hair smoothed back, eyes black, handsome face relaxed and calm.

Next to him was a wisp of a man, frail and cadaverous. His clothes hung off him, his bony arms swimming in the sleeves of his white Oxford shirt. He wore dark glasses.

He looked like some species of undead. If Zhang thought he could unnerve me with zombie, he was badly mistaken. We Russians know zombies. During Soviet era Russia was even ruled by zombies. Twice.

Missing was any sign of muscle. That scared the living hell out of me. No one had bothered to take the Glock snuggled up against the small of my back, and there was no muscle. That meant Zhang wasn't worried about me at all.

I felt a little flutter of fear deep in my gut.

We were meeting under an assumption of neutrality, and my safety was guaranteed during meeting. That guarantee was built upon Black Dragon and Krasny Mafiya desire to avoid war.

But if Zhang had already decided that we had hit him, my life was forfeit.

I bowed politely. "It is always an honor, Zhang Shaoming."

"Valeri Kozlov of the Red Mafia," said Zhang in a pleasant, conversational tone. "Or should I say Krasny Mafiya?"

I shrugged.

"Someone has stolen my property, Valeri Kozlov."

I swallowed in a dry mouth. Right to business? No

intricate courtesy accompanied by a cup of jade oolong? This was not the Zhang Shaoming I knew.

He had to be angry.

"We also learned this," I said, "through our police sources."

"And you are here to tell me it wasn't you." I actually heard the tightness in Zhang's voice. *Very* angry.

I started to sweat. "I am here to tell you *truth*," I said. "Krasny Mafiya had no part in this."

"Then who do you think it was?"

I shrugged. "Maybe Yakuza. Or Vietnamese. Or Italians."

He snorted. "The *Italians?*"

"I do not know who it was. I *do* know it was *not* us."

And *that* was the truth. Georgi hadn't brought in any out-of-town talent, and the only Krasny Mafiya muscle in Chicago who could take down five Chinese magicians without being caught was him and me. Georgi wouldn't take risk if there was someone else he could use, and my evening had been spent with Charlene the blonde hooker.

Zhang studied my face for a long moment. "Please sit with us, Valeri."

I pulled out chair and sat down. The zombie still hadn't moved.

Zhang leaned across the table. "Why do you think Georgi Dorbayeva sent you to this meeting?"

"After what happened, you must be, ah, angry. And so a meeting like this carries with it certain . . . risks."

Zhang nodded. "So Dorbayeva would not come himself. Instead he sent someone who could be trusted to speak for him but who could also be sacrificed."

I said nothing.

"Dorbayeva has been head of the Russian mob in Chicago for eleven years," said Zhang. "How do you think he has lasted so long?"

"He is a great and terrible magician," I said. "And

he is surrounded by army of loyal supporters who would avenge his death."

"Like you," said Zhang.

"Like me," I said.

"I can't help but wonder if your loyalty has been repaid."

"What do you mean?"

"There are few in the Red Mafia who could steal our product despite our careful attention. If Dorbayeva took the heroin and sent you to this meeting . . ." His voice trailed off suggestively.

A twinge of doubt twisted my stomach. Still, I leaned forward and flashed him a wintry smile. "You will not turn me against my brother."

Zhang sat back and smiled innocently. "Of course not. We are just having a friendly talk."

I grunted.

"I have always admired you, Valeri. Powerful like Dorbayeva, but subtle, too. Smart." His eyebrows went up. "And courteous. So few Russians appreciate the value of courtesy. I have found our discussions to be most productive."

The zombie took off his dark glasses, revealing blank eyes like hardboiled eggs.

"I would like to keep it that way," murmured Zhang.

That's when I felt first feathery touch in my mind.

The zombie wasn't a zombie, he was *sifter.*

Right then I went for the Glock, but nothing happened. I couldn't move. Not even a twitch of my finger.

Zhang smiled. "The first thing Mr. Xi took from you was muscle control."

I tried to shout. *Nothing.*

"Don't worry," said Zhang in an easy voice. "You won't need to talk for this next part. Mr. Xi will search your mind for the appropriate information and bring it to the surface where I can read it. Now." He leaned forward. "Where were you last night, Valeri?"

I felt other seeping through my mind, trickling in like cold mountain stream working its way under and around and through stones. I tried to fight it, but it was *in* me and I just couldn't—

And then I was with Charlene, my hand combing through her thick blonde mane, my mouth on hers, tasting salt and vodka and bitter European tobacco, urgently pulling off her blouse, my hands on her breasts, astringent smell of sex, her body slick with sweat, moving together, together, together until—

Suddenly a flash of somewhere else: silver bright moonlight on snow, a crooked path leading down to darkness, darkness beneath a stone bridge. Something there—a, a *crucifix*—bone white in the moon's pale light, and then—

And then Charlene's body is moving under me, rocking with an ancient rhythm that is its own kind of magic, and my mind is lost to my need and—

I came out of the trance, trembling, soaked with sweat, my breath harsh and ragged in my ears.

"Well," said Zhang. "It seems you had a better evening than I did last night."

"Is dangerous," I rasped. "To use mind sifter. Sometimes." I paused to breathe. "There is damage."

"It is more dangerous to cross me, Valeri. A fact I trust you will share with Georgi Dorbayeva at your earliest possible opportunity."

And then I was standing in the store again, so stunned that I barely registered it when wise, old man in the Rush tee-shirt slipped the square box into pocket of my overcoat.

I fled into the winter cold. Head down, hands thrust into the pockets of my overcoat, scurrying up Federal Street. The sky was overcast, lending the berms of snow between sidewalk and street its gray color. The wind came up, picking up the chill off the lake. I huddled into my overcoat, but it didn't do any good. The cold knifed right through thin shell of warmth.

At least my feet were warm, thanks to my new boots—brown leather lined with lamb's wool.

We Russians know how to deal with the cold.

Not to mention Chinese.

Despite the cold, the street was filled with people going about their business. I passed multitiered temple, with three green tile roofs, the last topped with a scarlet and gold spire. I passed a bakery just as woman stepped out and was tempted by smell of ginger and warm bread. A dragon fashioned from golden light danced and capered over fireworks store. Well, the new year was coming up.

As I walked, an uncomfortable picture started to form.

First, mind sifter. Zhang had taken big risk using one on me. If the sifter had broken the mind of an apparatchik of Russian chieftain during a neutral meeting, he would've set off war. And war between Krasny Mafiya and Black Dragons would be brutal and dangerous.

So. Zhang had to be after something worth the risk. He wanted to know who hit him, yes, but there was something more important.

He wanted his heroin.

Only thing it could be. Forty-seven kilos of heroin was street value of 32 million dollars, American.

But we didn't take it, yes? After all, Zhang let me go.

Something kept returning to me: the image that interrupted my memory of Charlene's fierce lovemaking. Secluded bridge at night. Christian cross.

Surely Zhang had seen it, too.

Which meant he only let me go so his men could follow me right to the stolen drugs.

I had claimed we didn't steal Chinese heroin. Zhang believed we did and thought Georgi was using it as opportunity to rid himself of a dangerous rival.

Me.

But there was third possibility.

What if Georgi had ordered me to steal Chinese heroin and then covered up my true memory with false one? Such a thing was possible, but dangerous. Overuse of memory sculpting could leave victim lost in a maze of fantasy, unsure of what was real and what was not, lost to everyday world.

In bad sculpting jobs sometimes the actual memory *(bridge)* leaked through even though prompt *(cross)* was needed to bring true memories back. But Georgi would've gotten me the best sculptor in city.

Unless he wanted me dead.

Americans have always compared Russia to bear, but the truth is she is more like a pack of wolves. We follow lead wolf.

Until he shows even slightest sign of weakness.

Then the pack is on him, snarling and snapping, until the snow is stained bright red.

Maybe Georgi was looking to take out the second wolf as a warning to all challengers: no weakness *here.*

I turned the idea over in my head. After my father was killed by the KGB in the eighties, Dorbayevas took me in. Georgi and I had grown up together, we were brothers.

Still, I couldn't rule it out.

Tightness in my gut returned. I am not religious man, but I said little prayer to St. Peter. *Please don't let it be Georgi.*

The key to it all was the H. If I could just find heroin, I'd also find truth.

I stopped and looked up. Some time in my wandering I'd walked to a small park: dormant see-saws and swings blanketed with snow, naked elms mixing with lightly frosted pines, an unused path curling through the trees.

And beyond it the arc of a stone bridge, a pool of darkness at its heart.

While I stood there, it started to snow, big heavy flakes sticking to the cold, cold earth. The snow seemed to soak up all the sounds of the city, covering the park in a blanket of white silence.

There is a magic that requires no spells or charms, a magic older and more powerful than mankind itself.

The ancient forces of the earth had claimed this little park as their own. As long as silence of snow reigned here, no human being could follow me into this place. I would not be observed.

So much for Chinese tailing me to drugs.

I stepped onto the crooked path I remembered from vision, marking virgin snow with my boots, the crunch of snow the only sound in that winter refuge.

I passed under a cathedral of branches and emerged in clearing on other side. The land dipped down, curling into little depression that gave way to a twisted path of ice that would melt into a little stream in the spring.

It was here that someone had built bridge, a gray arch of stone and mortar fording stream. The bridge was small, just wide enough for man and woman to walk side by side.

It might've been charming, except here man had left his calling cards: an old McDonald's bag, a spill of white napkins, a crumpled section of *Tribune,* two crows fighting over the remnants of a half-eaten cheese-burger.

I heard the distant honk of a horn.

It was a warning. Focus on the signposts of man's presence, and magic of this holy place would be broken. And then one of Zhang's people could find me.

I turned my gaze from top of bridge. There was nothing for me there. What I was looking for was underneath.

In the dark.

I stalked down the hill, half-walking, half-sliding. Walked slowly toward shadow of bridge's arch. It was small space. Maybe three feet at top of the arch, the ground covered by perfect, white snow.

Undisturbed.

I crouched down, staring at scene for long moment.

The bridge should've sheltered ground from above, if snowfall had been light and gentle as it was now. No, *this* snow had to have blown in. And that couldn't have happened last night. Because last night was clear and twenty-two.

At Midway.

Meaning heroin wasn't hidden here, by me or anyone else.

Then what had drawn me here?

I looked again. If there is one thing we Russians know, it is cold. So much of our magic came from the need to endure the frigid winds that sweep down from the arctic north, freezing the land and everything on it.

To my trained eye, this pool of shadow beneath bridge looked like warmth. Small, yes, but large enough to lie down, keep out the wind with a flattened cardboard box anchored by a couple rocks. Hang blanket up on other side and you would have a kind of cocoon, far from prying eyes of Chicago PD.

So why was no one here?

There were no broken bottles, no used needles, no cast-off clothes, no used rubbers, no moldering paper bags. Up above there was discarded newspaper and crows fighting over fast food. Down here there was nothing? *Why?*

I got down in snow, crawled forward.

Looked up.

On the underside of the bridge, at the highest point of the arch, someone had drawn a cross

(bone white in moon's pale light)

using white chalk.

I reached for it with trembling hand. If this was the prompt, touching it would restore my memory instantly, feelings and facts and *knowing* coming back like an El slamming into me.

Had Georgi set me up?

I wasn't sure I wanted to know.

But the part of me that was kind of man that could

rise to be a lieutenant in Krasny Mafiya said, *Now, quickly, before winter's spell is broken and human eyes are upon you.*

I thrust my hand up and smacked my palm against the cold stone.

Nothing happened.

No drugs here and no memory, which meant what? A trick to throw Chinese off? Or to get me killed? Either way, someone had set me up.

And then I heard a familiar voice say: "Well, looky here, dammit it if it isn't my boy, Val. How ya doin', Val?"

I closed my eyes.

Dexter Johnson.

I inched out on my back.

"Slowly now," said Johnson and now his voice was deadly serious. If I moved wrong he would shoot me.

Or something worse.

I stopped when my head was clear and lay there in the snow, arms sticking up in standard "I Give Up" position.

Dexter Johnson was a tall black man. He was in his late forties, craggy, distinguished face, salt and pepper hair, trim goatee, soulful eyes.

And he was holding a Beretta nine millimeter on me.

"How did you defeat the spell, Dexter? Nothing human could've been watching me."

He spat out a piece of rancid hamburger. "You know the worst thing about stakeouts, Val? You eat like shit."

I let out slow, angry breath. Angry at myself for being so stupid. "You were crow."

He shrugged.

"What about second crow? Is that your partner?"

Johnson smiled, bright ivory against his dark skin. "C'mon, Valeri. Sometimes a crow is just a crow. Now why don't you tell me what you're up to?"

"I am doing nothing wrong, officer," I said innocently.

He looked at me a long moment, and then he said, "Carrying, Valeri?"

"Glock," I said at once, "small of my back." When it came to guns, Chicago PD didn't fuck around. "I have permit," I added as an afterthought.

"Roll over on your tummy, would you, Val?"

I did as he said and he took the Glock, patted me down, and cuffed me. "Where is the permit?"

"Wallet. Back pocket of slacks." I turned my head so I could see him.

He reached into pocket and grabbed wallet, flicked it open, and searched through contents until he found permit on official yellow paper. He pulled it out and, without looking at it, dropped it to ground. A stray breeze sent it flitting across snow.

Johnson smiled pleasantly. "Sorry, man, can't find it."

I knew better than to say anything.

He jerked me to my feet. "Valeri, my brother, I think it's time you and I had a confab."

Every interrogation room I'd ever been in is same, walls painted off-white or slate gray or pale green, a rectangular table, sometimes steel sometimes battered oak, window of one-way glass facing suspect, dim lighting, and one more thing.

The smell of fear.

Sweat, piss, grease, and BO, it comes off suspects in waves and somehow soaks into everything: walls, table, chairs, everything.

This time Chicago PD handcuffed me to the chair: steel frame painted gray, black cushion, better than anything I'd ever gotten in Novosibirsk. Johnson sat opposite me. I didn't know who was behind glass.

Johnson leaned back in his own government-issue chair and steepled his hands behind the back of his head, like this was his favorite place in the world. Hell, maybe it was. "We've got you on a nice weapons charge, my man."

"Lawyer," I said.

U.S. Constitution is only couple hundred years old, so is not very powerful magic, but sometimes is all you need.

Johnson sighed. "OK, OK, don't talk to me, then." He shrugged. "It's cool. Just listen.

"Last night we got a late tip that a drug deal was going down. We watched the place until morning."

"Hoping to catch someone in act," I said.

Johnson shrugged again, as if to say, "Can you blame us?" "Anyway, when we did go in, we found popsicles that had once been Black Dragons, but, and this is the funny part, no drugs."

"Only Black Dragons are stupid enough to do drug deal without actual drugs," I said.

Johnson laughed, a rich, musical sound. "Oh, that's funny, man, real funny."

"As funny as your weapons charge?" I asked.

"You know how I found you today, Val?"

Now it was my turn to shrug.

"Really? Not even a guess? I tailed you coming out of a Chinese medicine shop."

"Is a free country. I can get medicine anywhere I like."

"Yeah, I just think it's real suggestive when the Russian mob is talking with the Chinese mob the day after this deal went down at the warehouse."

"Detective Johnson," I said gravely, "I am not associated with organized crime in any way."

"Sure, sure," he said easily.

He knew I didn't have drugs. He arrested me for gun, hoping I'd be carrying heroin around. A magician powerful enough to take down five Dragons might've had juice to transmogrify drugs. Problem is, as with all magic, there are limits. The catch with transmogrification is that changed item retains its principal trait, even in changed form. And what is principal trait of 47 kilos of heroin?

That it is very, very valuable, of course.

No doubt Johnson had his lab rats work quick reveal spells on all my valuables: the Rolex, the $753.47 in my wallet, my gold rings, my diamond stud earring, and my platinum lighter. Apparently none had changed into mountain of drugs, and he was now grasping at straws.

He reached into the pocket of his suit coat and pulled out small, square box and slapped it down on the table. He pulled the top off, revealing the black, shriveled claw inside. "Care to tell me what this is?"

I looked down at it and then looked at him. "Is good luck."

"*Good luck?*" His eyebrows shot up. "A Chinese monkey paw? Man, haven't you heard the *stories?*"

I shrugged. Truth was, I didn't know what the hell it was. But I'd be damned if I'd admit that to Johnson. I'm sure his techs worked the reverse spell on the claw, too.

"Look, Valeri—"

"No, you look, Detective Johnson. You ignored my permit so you would have a pretext to bust me. By now you have cataloged my belongings and searched the small park. There is no trace of missing drugs in either place. Otherwise you would use evidence as leverage. So. I want lawyer and I want you to be releasing me."

Johnson flashed me a sour look, but he leaned forward, hands palm down on the table. "All right, Val. I'm gonna let you go. But I have one thing for you to think about. The Chinese think you have their heroin. You might just be safer talking to me than walking the streets."

He gave me meaningful look. I met his eyes and let my face settle into blank mask.

After a second he gave a little exasperated snort and walked out of room.

First rule of dealing with *militsia* is never let them know when they are right.

The lawyer that came for me was Stepan Balyuk. Most important thing to know about Balyuk was that he was Ukrainian, not Russian. He spoke Russian with accent, was Catholic instead of Orthodox, said "Kyiv" instead of "Kiev." Brilliant lawyer, but still Ukrainian.

None of the Russians liked him, which meant Georgi could trust him with sensitive information because he had no allies.

Balyuk said nothing until his silver BMW was cruising north. Even then he turned on radio and muttered a quick privacy spell.

Then he turned to me. "What happened?"

I shrugged. "Not sure. Both Chinese and *militsia* think we did warehouse job."

"What did you tell them?"

I snorted and rolled my eyes.

It was bad if Balyuk thought he had to ask that question. He had earned his position out of fanatical personal loyalty to Georgi. If Balyuk didn't trust me, neither did my brother.

My stomach tied itself into a tight knot.

For a long time there was silence as Balyuk fought his way through early afternoon traffic. After awhile I noticed that a dark blue sedan was following us a few cars back.

I was pretty sure it was Krasny Mafiya muscle in case I tried something. Was Georgi offering up Balyuk as a test?

"Where are we going?" I asked.

"Meeting," said Balyuk, tersely.

He slowed beamer down, stopping behind stalled moving truck.

I glanced at him out of corner of my eye: big beefy man in expensive suit, red hair, blue eyes, pale skin, the faint outline of a Roman cross under his pale green Arrow shirt. No way for me to read him. If only—

Something smashed through front windshield. It was the size of an anaconda, but ebony with scarlet eyes, as big around as man's thigh and impossibly long.

It wrapped itself around Balyuk and *squeezed*. I

heard *crunch* of ribs snapping. Then it reared back
and sank three-inch fangs in lawyer's neck.

"*Liod,*" I shouted, and suddenly the dragon was a
statue of crystalline ice.

Giving me time to pull my Glock and shoot the
Chinese thug coming up over the hood *pop-pop-pop*
three times in chest. Then I dropped guy coming
around passenger side with a head shot.

I put next bullet into the dragon. It shattered into
a million pieces, filling car with tinkle of breaking ice.

It was already too late to save Balyuk. His throat
was a bloody, broken mess, his stylish shirt stained
black with blood, his breathing labored and ragged.

But he was still alive.

I reached over and touched his chest, feeling the
cross beneath his slick shirt.

My eyes darted to the rearview mirror. The men in
the dark sedan were running up, weapons drawn.
About damn time.

I turned back to Balyuk and for a second our
eyes met.

Then I popped buttons of his ruined shirt and my
fingers found bloody cr—

Knowing shot through me like electric current.

*I stalked silently through cold warehouse, a wolf at
home in the frigid wastes of the world, winter's master.
From the shadows I saw Chinese and their heroin. The
Black Dragons were powerful and brave, but it would
not save them.*

They were in my *world.*

I must've passed out after that, because I came to
in hotel suite. It didn't matter, though.

Because I knew everything.

When I awoke, Georgi was leaning over me, and for
just a second I saw the boy I grew up with, not the
man I knew now. His eyebrows were hunched with
concern, his full, red lips slightly parted.

And when our eyes met a bright smile exploded across his face.

He glanced back at the others in the room. "You see? It will take more than Chinese tricks to kill my little *brat.*"

Brat.

Brother.

My throat closed painfully.

"You are well, Valeri Mikhailovich, yes?"

"Yes," I said weakly.

Georgi quirked an eyebrow. "Apparently your sit-down with Zhang did not go so well. Why do they believe we stole drugs?"

My eyes flickered to the guards and then back to Georgi. "When Zhang and I were talking . . . our minds touched. I saw . . .

Georgi shook his head, the question plain on his face.

"Georgi," I murmured.

He leaned in to hear me.

"There are traitors," I whispered.

His eyes widened. *"Nyet,"* he snarled.

I looked at the guards again.

It was impossible for someone to take advantage of Georgi's trust, for he trusted no one. No, the answer was *suspicion.* With Georgi, suspicion was the lever.

He turned to the guards. "Out."

One of them hesitated.

"Out," he roared.

The door snicked shut and just like that Georgi and I were alone.

There was a second of silence, and then he asked the question I knew he would. "You have proof?"

I nodded. "Square box in coat."

He pulled the box out of my pocket, opened it. Looked at the curled, black monkey hand. Picked it up and studied it, frowning.

Because, of course, there was nothing there. Just stupid good luck charm.

And for the second he was distracted, I pointed my right hand at him and shouted *"Siwang."* The Chinese death curse worked instantly, turning his blood to dust, squeezing the air from his lungs. He looked at me, eyes wide, mouth distended in a silent scream.

Then he fell, still clutching the monkey's paw in his hand.

And there he lay, chieftain of a mob at war with Chinese, a Chinese charm clutched in his hand, the taste of Chinese magic still charging the air.

What would you think?

Zhang would take blame, and I would lead war of vengeance. And anyone who did not show me proper loyalty would find himself on front lines.

And so I found my prayer had been answered. I knew who set me up, had arranged for poor sculpting job, who had bought monkey paw, who had been holding heroin all along, and it was not Georgi.

Was me.

I stumbled out of bed and found my boots. Johnson had been looking for an object of extreme value, and his glance had passed right over my boots. As a Chicagoan he thought he knew cold. Bah! He did not know cold. Anyone who has survived Siberian winter knows *true* value of good pair of boots.

I carefully tucked them away for time when I could use $32 million worth of heroin.

Then I went to the dried, blackened husk that was all that was left of Georgi Dorbayeva, and knelt down. A single tear slid down my cheek.

My *brat.*

But this is way of world. There can only be one lead wolf.

The thing Georgi forgot is that lead wolf owes his position to strength, but the second wolf owes *his* to guile.

I gently touched my brother's desiccated face.

Is not a lesson I will forget.

The Old Girlfriend of Doom

Dean Wesley Smith

Sometimes even superheroes can't save the day, or the girl, or the dog, and that fact is even sadder when the girl is one of the superhero's old girlfriends.

Honest, Poker Boy, and just about every superhero, once had a childhood, a life as a young adult, without powers. I only discovered my Poker Boy super abilities later in life, after I had lived a fairly regular life until the age of twenty-nine. Little did I know that someday I would put on the black leather jacket and the fedora-like hat and become Poker Boy, savior of blind women, lost husbands, and dogs.

It was Christmas Eve, a holiday for me just about like every other one. I was home, alone, in my double-wide mobile home that I had bought twenty years ago with the money from my winnings in a poker tournament. The green couch and chairs had come with it, and so far I had seen no reason to replace the perfectly good, but dog-ugly furniture. As a national-level poker player, I had more than enough money in a dozen accounts to buy a nice home and nice furniture, but since I was in poker rooms and hotels more than I was here, what was the point?

I was watching some lame Christmas program on television and eating a television dinner with fried chicken and the really good cherry desert. I had about two hours to get to the casino to sign up for the poker tournament, and I was enjoying the quiet, to be honest.

Then there was knock on my door.

As Poker Boy, I very seldom have the people who need help come to me, but there have been exceptions. And since I wasn't expecting any company, I figured right off this was one of those exceptions.

I opened the front door of my double-wide mobile home and saw my old girlfriend, Julie Down, standing there on the other side of the screen door. Of course, right at that moment I didn't know it was Julie. All I could see was that it was some woman about my age with a nice smile and an overbuilt chest.

"Hi," Julie said, smiling at me as I stood there, hand on the wooden door, staring at her though the screen.

Now I have a great memory for faces across poker tables. I can tell you the moment a person sits down if I have played with them before, the style of their play, and their poker tells. I won't remember their names, but I know the important stuff and how to take their money.

With old girlfriends, from the life before I became the superhero Poker Boy, I am lucky even to remember going out with them, let alone things like their names or if we slept together. I assume that any old girlfriend coming to find me years later is someone I must have slept with.

On top of my bad memory, Julie didn't look like the Julie of old. Granted, I'm forty-nine, and Julie and I were an item back twenty-five years before, when she was only twenty. But that said, she just didn't look the same. Not even close.

Julie of old had long blonde hair that had touched the top of her butt. I remember I used to love lying in bed and watching that hair flow over her back as she walked naked around the bedroom. This Julie standing in front of me had tight, short graying hair, curled in a style that made her look older and very businesslike.

Julie of old was rail thin, with no real breasts to speak of, and no body fat at all.

This Julie had filled out, as all of us have. She wasn't fat, but she wasn't that light and rail thin either. And she had had a boob job at some point. Or one hell of a growth spurt focused only on her chest. The white blouse she now wore under her open suede jacket made sure that everyone could see the growth spurts and the lace bra trying to hold back the progress.

"Hi," I said in return, at that point not yet knowing who the hell I was talking to. I wished at that moment that I had my black leather jacket and hat on and was closer to a casino. Then I could use my superpowers to help me figure out exactly what this woman wanted to sell me.

Or wanted me to do.

"You don't remember me, do you?" she said.

Okay, I have to admit that those words are the worst words any guy can ever hear from some strange woman standing at his door. I didn't have a clue who she was, yet she remembered me well enough to track me down.

A guy is never allowed to forget a woman.

Ever.

I glanced at her boobs, and since they were new since the last time I saw this woman, they didn't help. And her face rang a sort of bell when I looked right at her, and into her eyes, but not much of a bell. Actually, sort of a faint ding, like an oven timer going off in another room.

If I hadn't been a superhero, who didn't lie unless it was to save a life, or rescue a dog, I would have just laughed and said, "Sure I do, come on in." And then tried to figure out who she was through the conversation.

But she had asked me a direct question, and being

a superhero, I couldn't lie. So instead I said, "I can't really see you very well in this light. Come on in."

I honestly couldn't really see her that well in the porch light and through the screen door, so I didn't lie. I just bought a little needed time.

As I swung open the screen door to let her come inside, she let me off the hook.

"It's me, Julie."

For a moment, as she stepped past me, leading into the room with those new growth spurts on her chest, I couldn't remember any Julie's in my life either. Especially Julie with a chest the size of the Rockies.

"Julie Down," she said, ending all torture.

"Oh, my god, Julie," I said, "what a great surprise."

Actually I sounded happy mostly because she had let me out of the trap, and not because I was actually glad to see her. The last time we had spoken, she had called me a lazy bum, said I would amount to nothing, and that I should get a life. Or at least a reason for living and breathing.

Actually, at the point she left me, I was a lazy bum, and I really did need a life, but I wouldn't find that life until a number of years later, when I became Poker Boy.

In all, I think we dated seven months, or, more accurately, had sex for seven months. I don't remember much else in the relationship with her.

After I gave her the required hug, with her growth spurts holding us apart, she stepped back and studied me, then my abode, like a meat inspector looking over a side of beef.

"You look like you're doing well for yourself," she said.

Even without my superpowers I knew that was a lie. I was living in an old mobile home, with old, ugly furniture and a half-eaten t.v. dinner on the coffee table. I looked like, on the surface, the same guy she had gotten mad at twenty-five years before. If I had not had my Poker Boy identity, and a lot of money in different banks from all my poker winnings, I would have been ashamed that an old girlfriend saw me living like this. But superhero status and large bank accounts tend to make a guy not care, and I didn't really care what she thought.

"Actually," I said, "I'm doing very well. Can I get you something to drink? Diet Coke and water are the options."

She laughed, a high, soft sound I remembered from our past. Her laugh had been one of the things that had attracted me to her back then. That and sex.

Now I just wanted to know what she wanted. And the only way I was going to be able to do that with my superpowers was get my coat and hat on and get back into a casino.

My superpowers don't work a great distance from a casino. They are powered by the energy of a casino, as a flashlight is powered by a battery. My black leather coat and hat seemed to focus the energy from the casino and make me into Poker Boy.

"Wait," I said, "I have another idea. Let me buy you dinner and a drink at the casino." I pointed to my partially eaten t.v. dinner. "That just isn't doing it for me."

"That sounds great," she said.

No doubt she was relieved to get out of the old mobile home.

Fifteen minutes of very, very small talk later, we were seated in the fine dining restaurant at the casino. I had my leather coat and hat on and was in full Poker Boy power mode.

I knew with a quick scan with my Ultra-Intuition Power that she needed help. Poker Boy's help, actually, which was interesting that she had found me.

My Ultra-Intuition Power is my most used power. With a focused glance, I can tell what a person needs, what they might say next, or even their next action. The information comes to me by "little voice messenger," and I have learned to listen.

I could list all my superpowers right now, but that would be a dull monolog, not worth the time, since there are so many. Some of the powers I haven't even named.

"Thank you," she said to me after we were settled at a table and the waiter was off getting our drink orders.

"For what?" I asked.

"For being so welcoming, especially on Christmas Eve."

"Poker players are never much for Christmas," I said, shrugging. "The ones with the families miss days and sometimes weeks of play. The rest of us just continue on and mostly don't notice."

"You have no family?" she asked. "And you play poker for a living?" She sounded actually impressed about the second part.

"Right on both counts," I said. "How about you?"

She sighed, and then for the next twenty minutes, through drinks, appetizers, and into the main course, she told me about her family, her parents being sick, her brother being stupid, her last two husbands being abusive.

I wanted to ask her when the growth spurt on her chest had happened, but refrained. Some things you just don't ask a woman, I have learned, and that's one of them.

Suddenly, she stopped talking, afraid to tell me about something. She had been fairly graphic about her past husbands, what they had done to her. Some of it I couldn't believe she would just tell a stranger like me. Granted, we had a past, but after not seeing this woman for over twenty-five years, I was still a stranger.

She studied her salmon, forked it a few times, studied it some more, forked it again, all the time trying to say something. Whatever was now stopping her must be really something. It was, more than likely, the reason she had looked me up.

I used my Ultra-Intuition Power on her again, but I could see only blackness.

Deep, deep blackness.

Not good, not good at all.

I needed another superpower to help her out, get her to tell me her problem. I focused across the table at her, leaning forward, clicking my mind into a friendly, giving mode. A moment later I felt the superpower click on.

Empathy Super Power to the rescue.

I could make her feel better, I could make her trust me. My Empathy Superpower sort of radiated good feelings to another person, so it really wasn't empathy, by the standard dictionary definition, but Empathy Superpower was the only thing I could think to call it. I had tried Feel Better Superpower, but that had seemed silly. And so did Trust Me Superpower. So until I could come up with a better name, it was called my Empathy Superpower.

She looked up at me, her gaze holding mine. "I just feel like I can talk to you, and that you'll understand."

Empathy Superpower working just fine.

"I will," I said, easing my hand across the table between the water glasses and salt shaker to touch her hand.

Touch always made my Empathy Superpower even stronger.

"What's bothering you?" I asked.

She looked embarrassed for a moment, then took a deep breath and blurted out her problem.

"Aliens are trying to steal my breasts."

I knew there were no such things as aliens, at least at the moment on the planet. There had been in the past, and I am sure there would be again. They visited all the time. But right now they weren't around and hadn't been for at least five years.

But there were many, many other things that normal people confused with aliens. And there was an entire dark world that existed along with the light

world we all lived in. It was against creatures from
that dark world that I, and other superheroes, fought
so often.

"Aliens?" I asked, keeping my touch on her arm
and my super Empathy power turned on. "What do
these aliens look like? Have you seen them?"

She nodded. "Gray, short, with long fingers and little round mouths."

"Big heads?" I asked.

"Yeah," she said, staring into my eyes. "Big for
their bodies."

I could feel my stomach twist. She was even more
trouble than I had thought.

"And they want your breasts?"

She nodded.

I sat back, pulling my hand away and shutting off
the superpower. "You're not dealing with aliens.
Those are Silicon Suckers, a very dark creature of
the underworld."

"Silicon Suckers?" she asked. "How do you know
that?"

"I've had to deal with them a couple of times over
the years," I said. "They're not a nice bunch, and you
clearly have something they want, or they wouldn't be
showing themselves to you."

I knew exactly what they wanted, but I was going
to have to work into telling her what it was.

Silicon Suckers are a race of intelligent creatures
that have existed on Earth far, far longer than human
beings. They live in the deserts, burrow in the sand,
and have the ability to change their appearance and
blend with about anything. In this country, the Phoenix, New Mexico, and Las Vegas areas have the most
trouble with them.

"Silicon Suckers?" she said. "My breasts are silicon
implants." She was clearly starting to understand what
the little guys were after.

I almost said, "Really, I hadn't noticed." But I

stopped myself before that gaffe and instead just nodded. Then I moved to the next question.

"Where have you been living?"

"Vegas," she said. "I've been working as a blackjack dealer at Circus Circus for the last six years, since I left Bastard Husband Number Two."

"Good for you," I said, actually impressed. I knew how hard and how special it was to become a dealer on the strip. "When did you have the implants put in?"

"Twenty years ago," she said. "I did it between Bastard Husband Number One and Bastard Husband Number Two. But I upgraded them six months ago, and that's when the gray aliens started showing up."

"Oh, oh," I said.

"Oh, oh?" she asked, looking very worried.

And she should be worried. I didn't know how to tell her what had happened. The fight between good and evil, between the superheroes and the dark forces is always tough to explain to a mere mortal, especially when it concerns a body part.

Finally, looking into her worried eyes, I decided to approach the problem by showing her I knew what had happed.

"Dr. Doubleday did the upgrade. Right?"

She looked at me as if I had lost my mind, then nodded. "How did you know that?"

Actually, I wasn't reading her mind or using any other superpower. I had dealt with Silicon Suckers for a friend of a friend in Vegas five months before, on an adventure that also rescued three dogs. On that trip, I had discovered that Dr. Doubleday had been using a very special silicon mix taken from pure natural sand and then refined down into a very special silicon gel.

The problem was the sand he had been using was from a sacred Silicon Suckers burial site. Julie, my old girlfriend sitting across the table from me, had a real problem. She had dead Silicon Suckers for breasts.

"I know because one of the things I do is help people as I travel around the country playing poker," I said.

"I know," she said. "I've heard about you. Some people call you Poker Boy."

Since she clearly looked as if she didn't believe what she had just said, I let it pass and went on. "I helped a previous client of Dr. Doubleday. I assume you tried to go back to him after the Silicon Suckers started showing up and playing with your breasts. And I bet you found him missing."

Now Julie was looking at me as if I were the alien.

I knew for a fact that Dr. Doubleday had given his life for trying to improve his craft and find the most perfect silicon implants. After what he had done to the Silicon Suckers' sacred resting place, many of us in the superhero world thought he got off light by only being killed. His body will never be found. More than likely parts of Dr. Doubleday are tinting car windows everywhere.

"How did you know he wasn't there?" she asked.

"Doubleday is dead," I said. "Killed by the Silicon Suckers."

She sat there in silence, first staring at me, then down at her salmon. Finally she said, "Let's assume that I believe what you're saying."

"No weirder than thinking aliens are trying to steal your breasts."

She shrugged. "True. So what do I do?"

I put another bite of steak in my mouth, savored the flavor for a moment. There was only one answer to her question.

"If you're going to want to live, you have to give them your implants back."

"I'm not going to do that!" she said, her hands going to the monsters on her chest as if to protect the big girls.

I kept eating, staying calm. "You have no choice. If you don't have the money, I can pay for an exchange operation for the silicon implants you have now. All they want is those implants. They don't want you to be flat chested."

There was no chance at that point that the rest of her salmon was going to be eaten. She scooted the plate away and stared at me.

"I *wasn't* flat chested before I had the implants," she said. "You know, you're totally nuts."

I wanted to remind her that she had come to me for help, that she thought aliens were trying to take her boobs, but I didn't. Instead I just gave her the rest of the information, calmly and slowly, keeping my voice level.

"The creatures you are having trouble with are not aliens, but they are after the special silicon Dr. Doubleday used in those implants. If you have the implants removed, I'll be glad to help you give them to the Silicon Suckers in a special exchange ceremony. You give them back what they want, and you'll always be an honored guest in their sand castles."

She stared at me as if she were seeing me for the first time.

"Sand castles?"

"That's what they call their homes. I've been in a few of them outside of Tucson. Big, but kind of dusty and dry."

She stared at me again, then shook her head slowly from side to side.

"I knew better than to come to you," she said. "Even with Suzy's recommendation, I knew better."

She stood and thrust her chest out so far I was afraid she was going to go head first into my steak. Somehow, she managed to remain standing, although she cast a very dark shadow over the table as her breasts pulled an eclipse on the overhead light.

"These are mine, and I paid good money for them," she said, loudly, indicating what did not need to be indicated. "And I'm not letting any little gray alien suckers take them."

The guy at a table against the wall choked, then coughed, clearly trying not to laugh.

"Your choice," I said. "But I'm doing all right with money, and I would be glad to pay for replacements. Remember that. No strings attached. You can even make them bigger if you want."

"I'll give it some thought," she said.

"Don't take too long to decide," I said, staring up at her over the monster mountain range between us. "Silicon Suckers are not creatures to be played with. The only way they know how to get into a human body is through the anus, and trust me, taking those silicon implants out that way will not be fun. And more than likely fatal."

She sputtered, started to say something more, sputtered again.

I didn't blame her.

Finally she managed to get those sacred and very dead Silicon Suckers on her chest turned toward the door. Then, with one last withering glance at me, she stormed out.

The guy against the wall was laughing so hard I thought he would go face down in his soup.

For me, it really wasn't a laughing matter. She was in mortal danger.

I wanted to run after her and stop her, but I knew, for a fact, there was nothing I could do at this point. I certainly wasn't going to force her to have an operation. A woman's choice of what to do, or not do, with her body was not something a man, or a superhero, should get involved with. She was going to have to make that choice for herself.

For some reason that I didn't completely understand, Julie's entire self image must have been tied up in what the Silicon Suckers wanted back. And replacements might not be enough to matter to her.

I wished I understood Julie's side. I did understand the Suckers' side.

The guy against the wall finally coughed a few times,

shook his head, and went back to eating. I stared at
my steak for a moment, thinking over anything I might
still do to help her. Without butting in on her rights
to do with her own body as she saw fit, there wasn't
much.

She had come to me for help, then refused it. As
those of us in the superhero business know, there are
times you just can't help.

I finished my steak and just barely made it into the
poker room in time for the seven o'clock tournament.

I won the thing and put the money in a jar on my
kitchen counter, saved for Julie's operation. But I had
a hunch she would never call me, because after the
tournament, on the way home from the casino, I found
a German Shepherd laying in the ditch beside the
road. It had been hit by a car, but it was still alive.

I rushed it to the local vet, but the dog died on
Christmas morning.

On good adventures I save people and dogs. I
couldn't save the dog, so I had a hunch I hadn't saved
the person either in this one.

But that didn't stop me from trying some more.

I tracked down Julie and called her the day after
Christmas with the hope of trying to convince her to
change out the breast implants. She heard my voice
and hung up.

I called a few friends I knew in Vegas who could
be trusted to go talk to her. Both of them said she
got rude and angry at them the moment they brought
up the subject or my name.

Julie had made her decision, and by all the gambling
gods, she was sticking with it.

Somehow, I had to convince her to change that
decision.

I had to keep trying.

That's what superheroes did, usually against all odds
and at some cost and danger to their own lives. And
trying to convince any woman to change her mind
always had danger involved.

So throwing all caution to the wind, I jumped on a plane and headed for Vegas.

She wouldn't see me and had me removed from the Circus Circus when I went up to her blackjack table and sat down. Even my Empathy Superpower couldn't cut through the anger, although it made the guard very nice and apologetic for escorting me to the door.

Since the direct approach hadn't worked, I headed out into the desert, to where I knew the Silicon Suckers had a pretty good-sized village. It was impossible to see unless you knew exactly what you were looking for, and I did. The entrance to this one was hidden right under a billboard beside the highway.

The entrance led to a huge underground cavern cut out of the sand and rock and filled with castlelike buildings. I was welcomed into their castles, as I knew I would be, since I had helped them recover one of Dr. Doubleday's mistakes.

The main leader of this band clicked at me in Silicon Sucker language, and I used what I called my Understand Most Anything Superpower to talk with him, asking him for more time to convince Julie to get their sacred dead off her chest.

He clicked that he would give me two full moons, or something that meant two months.

I thanked him, backed from his castle in a show of respect, and went back to Vegas.

I left the message on her answering machine that I had the money for the exchange, had contacted the best doctor in Vegas to do the job, and had prepaid for it. All she had to do was show up. I left the time and date and address of the doctor, the most famous and expensive in Vegas, hoping that might convince her to change her mind.

Nothing. She missed the appointment.

So I pulled some strings in the Casino Gods area of the superhero world, and got the Blackjack God named Danny to talk to her pit boss at work.

That didn't work.

I talked to her friends, even called her mother, then I set up another appointment for her with the great doctor.

Again she missed it.

So one last time, with Danny, the god of Blackjack keeping the pit boss busy at another table, I went in to talk to her.

She was shuffling and didn't see me coming.

When I slid the doctor's business card with a third appointment written on it across the table toward her, she glanced up, the anger in her eyes almost knocking me back a step.

"Why are you insisting in meddling in my life?" she demanded, ignoring the stares from the older couple sitting at the table.

"Because you are in real danger," I said, using every convincing power I had in my superpower collection. With this much energy turned on at a poker table, I could have convinced a world class player I had a pair of deuces instead of aces.

Julie, on the other hand, was a little tougher. She just glared at me, so I went on.

"I have enough money to help. You won't ever see me again, but please, just do this. It's paid for."

She stared at me as I radiated super levels of good will and empathy and convincing. My superhero powers were on full tilt right at that moment, and for a second I thought she was faltering a little.

"I'm being honest with you," I said. "Your life is in danger. Please just do it, either with this appointment or on your own. It's your life, I know, and your body, but I care about your life."

Then I turned and walked away.

There was nothing else I could do.

I got back on the plane and went home.

I finally heard three months later that they had found her body face down in the desert, as flat-chested as the day she had come into the world.

I think back and wonder at times what more I might

have done to convince her I knew what I was talking about. More than likely nothing. She needed to believe I was still the loser she left for abusive husband hell all those years before.

She needed to believe that those special breasts made her a better person. For her, a certain self-image was more important than life itself.

For me, Poker Boy, I have my hat, my leather coat, and my superpowers. What more could I want out of life?

Nothing, except maybe winning every time. But even the best superheroes have to lose once in a while. I learned that lesson on the poker tables and with Julie.

Still, you have to feel bad for a person like Julie, caught in a self-image nightmare. And besides, pulling those sacred suckers out of her ass just had to have hurt.

Second Sight

Ilsa J. Bick

I

I'm not, she thinks, I'm not Lily.

Her brain folds like an accordion, because there's not-Lily, squeezing her consciousness against the bony vault of her skull.

I'm not Lily; I was, but now I'm not.

She's naked, legs scissoring spaghetti twists of off-white sheet. Her expensive dress Mother picked for her that evening, the scarlet one slit from her ankles to her thighs and a vee plunging to her navel, pools on the floor like hot, fresh blood.

(Mother? *Her* mother is dead. Cancer. When her father started up with someone else—twenty-two and Lily's only fifteen, and she might have to call that bitch *Mom?*)

Her mind is very cold. The weatherman is forecasting snow by morning, and the mayor promised salt trucks and snow removal crews at the first flake. *Yeah, and every guy in prison didn't do it. This is Washington, for Christ's sake.* This is what Call-Me-Bob, the bald man with the big nose who's chosen her for this evening, says as the news winks on. Call-Me-Bob's breath is sharp as burned wood from Scotch, but he wants to watch the late news at the same time. He makes jokes. *I like to watch, Eve.* Even though Eve is not her name either.

And there is no Call-Me-Bob, not in this room, *this* bed where Lily lies.

Her skin prickles with the memory of jungle heat, though the only jungles Lily has seen are concrete and tarry asphalt and rusted steel. The village Not-Lily remembers is like something out of a movie, populated with people who have almond eyes and wear straw hats.

But she—Lily—is hot just the same. A burning flush oozes across her skin like lava. With a small impatient movement, she kicks her feet free.

Just as Not-Lily did when she was very small: wanting to be free of the coarse blanket yet scared to death of the monster beneath the bed; how Auntie, a black stinking ghost smelling of rancid flesh and fruity Special Muscle wine, chanted her *muon* to bring out the *Rakshasas*. The demons erupted from Auntie's skin to sit on her chest, and they held her legs and arms so a son of Yama—naked, flat-faced and very hairy— could nibble her toes with his yellow fangs and bite her neck and hurt her in places that still cause her shame. Yet, always, her toes somehow grew back, and Auntie invariably melted into the Daylight Woman everyone else knew at the first hint of dawn. No one believed *her* about the nights. Every morning at the well the other girls tittered behind their hands even as they stoppered their mouths because it paid to be careful. You never could tell if a stray *Rakshasa* still lingered and might ride in on your breath so that not even a *kru khmae*

What? <u>Who?</u>

could help you.

A table lamp splashes a fan of yellow light, and a thin silver-blue wash pulses from the television, its screen of silver fuzz scritch-scratching silent hieroglyphs like the *yantra*

What?

which only the monks on Ko Len know. The DVD player's red light winks like a lost firefly because Call-Me-Bob

Mackie

likes to watch.

No, it's <u>Mackie</u> who can't get enough of the damn awful thing. It's Mackie.

There is enough light to see, or maybe she possesses some preternatural second sight, like a jungle cat for whom darkness does not matter and is, in fact, all to the better. Her eyes jerk over the ceiling of the hotel room. Tiny cracks fan the plaster, like the crackling glaze of a pottery vase, because the roof leaks and the way the manager figures it, the only people on their backs long enough to care are the girls. The johns aren't shelling out twenty-five bucks for the view, for Christ's sake.

Lying next to Lily/Not-Lily, Mackie sleeps, hugging the only pillow. Not Call-Me-Bob . . . and who is *that*.

Get up.

Gasping, she lurches upright, arms flailing, like a marionette whose puppeteer's been caught napping. Mackie mumbles, shifts, doesn't wake. The sheet pools at her waist. A scream balls in her Not-Lily mouth. But Lily doesn't scream. Can't.

Up, get up.

In the half-light, she staggers to her feet, clawing at air. The room's so cold her nipples stand, and the floor's icy against her soles, and she—Lily—wants her fluffy pink rabbit slippers, the ones her mama bought along with a thick pink terry-cloth robe for her thirteenth birthday. Lily wants to go home, where she was someone's little girl once upon a time.

Not-Lily doesn't care. Not-Lily can't go home either. *That* they have in common. And there are other things.

She—Not-Lily—takes two minutes to make it to the bathroom. By then, however, her movements are more fluid, as if all Not-Lily needed was a little practice.

Lily's mind screams, but her consciousness is like a spectator in the second balcony of a badly lit theatre, the stage faraway, the characters Lilliputian.

Pawing open the medicine chest, her fingers walk over bottles. Pills, lots of pills: Darvocet, Vicodin, OxyContin. And Mackie's works: two syringes, two halves of a Coca-Cola can, cotton balls for straining heroin, a lighter because discards are way too easy for the cops to match up to a pack. Mackie's knife, the one he uses on the cans. For an old guy—has to be sixty, if he's a day—he really goes through this stuff. He explained it once: Spoons are probable cause, but Coke, anyone can have a Coke can, for Christ's sake, this is America.

Pills. Jesus, but Lily wants pills. Pills make things hazy, so she doesn't care so much.

Mother

Who?

likes uppers. Feed a girl enough, she works for hours. And men will pay a lot of money for the young ones, especially the virgins. Virgins are good luck. They will cure a man of AIDS. Mother once knew a doctor in Poipet who could make virgins, over and over again. Doctors will do anything for enough money.

Not-Lily's fingers twitch, flex, grab the knife. The blade locks into place with that sweet, metallic *snick*.

She says his name three, four times before he rolls over. Mackie's fat, he's a pig. Too much beer and Thai takeout, and the grease they use in those spring rolls'll kill ya if the MSG don't. His belly jiggles like quicksilver in the light of the dead channel.

"What the fuh?" He scrubs eye grit with the balls of his fists, an oddly childlike gesture. "What you want, bitch?"

"I'm not a bitch," she whispers, the Lily piece of her mind finally realizing what is coming next, and, God forgive her, she wants it. She's even happy because this is revenge, a sort of *stand*.

"But I'm not Lily." And she brings the knife down. "I'm not."

She doesn't know if, through his screams, he hears. Certainly, in a little while, he's past caring.

II

I was dead asleep when my pager *brrred* at one A.M. Technically, I was supposed to be at the station for third shift, but plenty of guys took calls from home. Not that I was home, mind you.

On these odd Fridays, I was sure my colleagues in homicide didn't know what to make of me. I can guarantee you that the Black Hats at the synagogue—in Fairfax, off Route 236—thought my presence among them pretty weird. Me, too. Most days, I didn't understand why I chose to study with the rabbi or occasionally come for a Sabbath meal and good conversation.

We'd met years ago on a murder I and Adam—my best friend, my partner—caught. Later, he'd tried to help Adam. Couldn't, and Adam died. I don't know if he thought he was helping me now.

Mostly, I was the student. I listened. I asked questions, very pointed ones, mostly about Kabbalist mysticism. The rabbi had interpreted a spell left at the scene of that case, so he knew his stuff. Not like Madonna-kitsch. Oh, sure, Kabbalah was magic, just as the *mezuzah* tacked to virtually every doorway in the rabbi's house was an amulet. But Judaism was pretty specific: *Suffer not a witch to live.* Exodus 22, verse 18.

But. That's different from saying magic doesn't exist.

And Judaism has its protective spells and amulets. Every letter of the Hebrew alphabet has magical connotations. Name-magic, some of it. Heck, even Solomon bound demons to build the First Temple.

So we talked. Sometimes, we drank bad coffee, but only if his secretary was in that day.

I crept downstairs, guided by nightlights. The lights were on timers, as was the oven, the compressor on the refrigerator. The refrigerator light bulb was unscrewed. How Orthodox Jews made do before the invention of the automatic coffeemaker, I'll never know.

Halfway down the stairs, though, I caught the unmistakable aroma of fresh coffee. *Hunh.* Turned the corner. "Rabbi, what are you doing?"

Dietterich shrugged. He was a bearish man, with a thick tangle of brown beard that was showing more threads of silver these days. In his black robe and slippers, he looked like someone's scruffy, huggable uncle.

"I had . . . a dream. Don't ask me what. Anyway, I couldn't sleep, and I heard you moving around, so . . ." Another shrug. "You'll need coffee."

"You turned on the coffeemaker. Isn't that forbidden?"

"*Pikuach nefesh.*" Dietterich was a native New Yorker. Every time he opened his mouth, I thought *Shea Stadium.* " 'Neither shall you stand by the blood of your neighbor.' From Leviticus. To save a human life supersedes all other commands."

"Well, they usually call me when it's too late."

He handed me a travel mug. He *did* think ahead. "But when you catch a killer, he can't kill again, right? It evens out."

The coffee was hot and smooth going down. Clearly he hadn't taken lessons from his secretary. This was a bigger relief than you can imagine. "I suppose that's true."

"Think of this as an advance, a down payment. Save one life, it's as if you saved the world. Making coffee so you don't end up wrapped around a tree seems a no-brainer."

"What about the Guy Upstairs?" For the record, I wasn't sure where I stood on the God thing, but I can tell you this: I've seen what evil does, and I have no trouble bringing evil down. I'm not wrath of God about it. It's what I do.

"Hashem can take a joke." Dietterich hesitated, then said, "Jason, why do you come here? Don't misunderstand me. We're friends. But, in you, there is something missing. Here." His bunched fist touched his chest. "You're a detective, a seeker. You strive toward light where others see only darkness. But I still think you are a little bit like my hand here. You need to open, just a little." His fist relaxed. "Like opening a door to a second sight. You can't hold anything in your mind unless you open your heart."

I don't know how I felt. Not embarrassed. More like I'd been filleted and gutted.

He read my face. "I'm sorry. I'm intruding."

"No. Don't apologize. A lot of the time I'm stumbling around in the shadows."

"Then do something about it." He moved a little closer and pulled something out of a pocket of his robe. A glint of metal, a sparkle. "I don't know why I haven't given this to you before now. But now . . . *feels* right."

The metal was like nothing I'd seen. In fact, my mind must've been playing tricks because the light was very poor. The metal wasn't smooth but woven: gold filaments, I thought, and maybe silver? A hint of blue in the weave. I made out a five-by-five grid. A different gem sparkled in every square, both illuminating and magnifying a strange character—were they letters?—incised in the metal beneath. I counted five different symbols. Two were like runes, but the other three looked more like crude Egyptian hieroglyphs.

The center square was unique, with a character repeated nowhere else in the grid: a squashed teardrop canted right, tip down, broader bottom adorned with inwardly curved hooks or prongs. I thought: *Georgia O'Keeffe*. I rubbed my thumb over the gem there. A glitter of purple. Amethyst? "What is this?"

He opened his mouth, but my pager *brrred* again, and too late, I remembered I hadn't called in yet. "Sorry, I have to take this. I didn't want to use the phone in the house. But thank you." I slipped the charm into my trouser pocket. "And don't be sorry."

"It's fine, fine. We'll talk later." He made a shooing motion. "Go. Save the world."

The crime scene guys had finished with pictures and were working the room. Kay Howard, the deputy M.E., was hunkered over the body. My partner, Rollins, was downstairs talking to the night clerk, a diminutive Indian with coke-bottle glasses and an accent that got thicker the more questions we asked.

I waited, resisting the urge to crowd Kay, something that comes easy when you're as big as I am. People say I look like Patrick Ewing, except Ewing has the beard, and I'm two inches shorter and about eighty billion bucks poorer. I saw an opening when Kay bagged the hands. "Anything?"

"Well, she went right for the eyes." Her gloved finger traced a bloody orbit. "Very clean, no ragged edges, no evidence that she hesitated at all. She got him a good shot on the right." Kay gestured toward the evidence bag with a black-handled, blood-soaked pocketknife. The blade was serrated along two thirds of its length, then tapered to a sharp, slightly upturned point. A quarter inch was missing from the tip.

"We'll probably find the tip somewhere in the brain, or maybe wedged in the sphenoid at the back of the orbit, but that's not what killed him." Kay indicated a deep, ragged, fleshy necklace extending from MacAndrews's right to his left ear. Congealing purple blood sheeted the dead man's chest and there were drippy arcs painted on the wall immediately above the headboard. A slowly coagulating river of purple-black sludge stained his forearms, though I could just make out what looked like a tattoo on his left bicep. (Or it could've been a cockroach. If his toenail fungus was any indication, personal hygiene wasn't among MacAndrews's finer qualities.)

"She got both the arteries and didn't stop. Sawed right through the trachea." She looked up, and I saw a glint of steel in her eyes, a little defiance. "If it wasn't so politically incorrect, I'd say good riddance."

"The guy was an asswipe pimp. Won't hear me disagree."

"I did not hear that," said the tech. He was fiddling with the DVD player. "I'm not even in the room, and if I *am* in the room, I've turned off my hearing aid." His tone changed. "Whoa, we got a DVD here."

"So let's see what our bad boy here was watching," I said.

The film was clearly homemade but grainy, as if it might be a transfer from a VCR tape. It felt . . . *old*.

The room could've been anywhere, and the camera stayed tight on a single bed with a dirty brown blanket and a single pillow. No pillowcase. Nothing on the walls I could see right off the bat, though there might have been something on the corner of a night table protruding into the frame. Cigarette pack? And something green and white on the bed, near the pillow. Something else propped alongside. No sound.

A girl lay over the blanket, her head propped on the pillow. Ten, maybe twelve years old. She was Asian, with long black hair scraped back in a ponytail. She was naked and when she moved, she did so sluggishly as if moving through water. Drugged.

The man was also naked except for the black ski mask. There might have been something on his right ass cheek—a large mole, maybe—but I couldn't be sure. He loomed over the bed, then turned and flashed a V. Then he reached to his right, somewhere off-camera.

When his hand came back, I saw the tongue of a clear plastic bag in his fist.

"Oh, Jesus Christ," said the tech.

Kay let go of a small, sick gasp. "God."

I didn't say anything, but I knew: God had as much to do with it as the Tooth Fairy.

It took perhaps eight or ten horrible minutes, and that was only because he didn't flip her onto her stomach and tighten the plastic bag until the very end. Even then, he prolonged the moment, teasing her, rolling the plastic away from her gaping mouth so she might gulp a precious breath or two before cinching the bag tight once more.

Kay was crying. The color was gone from the tech's face. I was dry-eyed and shaking, my guts in knots, a black rage blooming in my chest.

Made me want to make an arrest somewhere dark and faraway. Maybe have a little accident, or something.

Something.

III

Jane Doe, mute and catatonic, had been taken to George Washington University Hospital.

The ER was hopping, so the bars must've closed. In the waiting room, the air smelled like dirty socks, musty and close; there was a motley assortment of frightened relatives, squalling kids with dead-tired moms in do-rags, the odd broken arm or leg.

In back, I waited behind the nurses' station. Nothing really going tonight. An MVA in one trauma bay: a weeping young blonde girl in a neck brace and torn blue jeans. A couple of heart attacks—that high mosquito whine of defibrillators charging, someone bawling, *"Clear!"*

One big moose with steely Old Testament prophet hair and a scruff of white beard. A Sixties throwback: black leather jacket with matching leather chaps, boots, aviator sunglasses in a breast pocket. He was Bay 4, very drunk, very busy bleeding all over his

Grateful Dead t-shirt and loudly harassing an earnest-looking female medical student, yelling that he'd taken worse in 'Nam and just needed a *"goddamned needle . . ."*

Across from Jerry Garcia's stunt double, I spotted an Asian family. Two women in their, oh, forties, fifties and one middle-aged guy clustered around a gurney. A shriveled, skeletal-looking guy with sickly yellow skin lay motionless as a mummy, tucked beneath a sheet. His bald head was cadaverous, the skin stretched tight across his skull. His black eyes were dull, fixed. Not just old. Ancient. There were blue-black sooty smudges on his forearms and several more on his neck.

Hmmm. In a fire, maybe?

Maybe it was because they were Asian, and I'd just seen that damn film. To this day, I don't know why they drew my attention. Now very curious, I tossed a glance at the whiteboard. which listed, in blue felt marker, each bay by problem.

Jerry Garcia was in 4: *ETOH, lac.* Doctorese for a drunk done busted his head.

My Jane Doe was in Bay 8: *?Sz. ? Head trauma Neuro.* Little red dot signifying she was a police case. As if the shiny black shoes visible beneath the drawn curtain weren't the uniform assigned to keep tabs on my suspect, and her being cuffed to the gurney wasn't like, you know, a giveaway.

The Asian family occupied Bay 7: Ψ.

Psychiatry. *Hmmm.*

"Detective Saunders?" A squat, utterly humorless doctor with gimlet, pewter-gray eyes and pale, nearly translucent lips stuck out his hand. The words **Phillip Gerber, M.D.** and **Neurology** were stitched in blue above the left breast pocket of his white doctor's coat. Ten to one, no one called him Phil. "Dr. Gerber. I'm the neurologist on the case." Just in case I couldn't read.

Gerber's palm was soft. Like shaking hands with a grub. "So what can you tell me about our Jane Doe?" I asked, taking back my hand.

"Well, she's no longer mute, for starters. Her name's Lily Hopkins. Don't have an age or place of residence, but we're running her through the NCMEC, but that's only good if she's been reported missing."

"She's responsive? Can I speak with her?"

"Yes, in a moment." He'd fingered up a chart and was now flipping pages. "Her neurological examination is unremarkable. Blood work was negative except for some alcohol in her system . . ."

I waited while he droned through the negatives. In Bay 4, I saw the medical student twitch a curtain around Jerry Garcia's gurney. She was pissed but trying to look as though getting cussed out by a drunken, bloody Sixties throwback was something you just took in stride. Her eyes briefly flicked my way. Lingered a sec, a sparrow of some emotion flitting across her face. I raised my eyebrows in my best *yeah, you really got an asshole there* expression. She got *that*. The corner of her mouth twitched in a tiny smirk as she slid behind the nurses' station, wrote *Surg* and Ψ on the whiteboard, then sat with the chart about two chairs down from where I stood with Gerber.

When Gerber came up for air, I said, "So you're thinking . . . ?"

He didn't look pleased at being derailed. Good. "I'll be honest, Detective. For the record, I'm not a fan of psychiatric diagnoses, though I'm no expert. They're only descriptive, not etiological. Having said that . . . You're familiar with multiple personality?"

"A little."

He stared at me a moment. "Well, you took that in stride. Mention DID to a detective or lawyer, and they roll their eyes."

I chose my words carefully. "I've seen a few things. Is she a multiple?"

Gerber's lips thinned to a paper cut above his chin.

"Personally, I think Dissociative Identity Disorder is ludicrous. But, no . . . Ms. Hopkins is not a multiple. She doesn't claim to have alters. I don't know about her past, but trauma in and of itself does not induce dissociative phenomenon."

Over Gerber's head Jerry Garcia hove into view, swaying. He'd changed into one of those flimsy hospital gowns. A wide gauze wrap stained with rust was wrapped around his scalp like a bandana. He listed, pulling hard to port, tacking for the wall to hold himself up.

I said to Gerber, "So what are you saying?"

To my right, a slender doctor rounded the corner behind the nurses' station and touched the medical student's shoulder. I laid odds she was the shrink. Just . . . something about her, the way she carried herself like an eye of calm in the center of a hurricane. Self-possessed. Confident.

She was also stunning: a long graceful neck, auburn hair she wore in a French knot, green eyes. Heart-shaped face exaggerated by a widow's peak.

Her name was embroidered in blue thread above the left breast pocket: **Sarah Wylde, M.D.** Below that: **Psychiatry**.

Wylde. A little *ding* in the back of my brain. That name . . .

As soon as I saw the two women together, I knew: sisters. And maybe she felt my gaze because she did the same thing her sister had. Her eyes touched on my face—and lingered there.

A tiny jolt of . . . recognition.

In my pocket, a strange heat. Puzzled over that a second and then remembered: that charm. What . . . ? I trailed my hand over the metal. It was warm, the gems almost pulsing, as if keeping time with a hidden heart.

What?

Gerber was saying, "The EEG findings are clear."

I wrenched my attention back to Gerber. "Clear?"

"Yes, you can't fake an EE—"

"Hey." Garcia bawled. Then louder: "Hey! You!"

Gerber looked over his shoulder. The usual bustle quieted as people paused.

The student pushed to her feet. "Mr. Dickert, if you wouldn't mind . . ."

"Fuck you say." Dickert was out of the bay now, maybe twenty feet into the ER. The student started forward, but her sister smoothly interposed herself between the two.

"Mr. Dickert," she said. "I'm Dr. Wylde. Can we speak for a few moments?"

Dickert's eyes jerked to her face, and then they got buggy. An expression that was equal parts horror and rage contorted his features. "No." He took a step back, swaying, and pointed with a finger that shook badly enough to be visible from where I was. "You, you stay away from me."

Wylde advanced slowly. "I'm sure we . . ."

"Gook." Saliva foamed on Dickert's lips. "You're a fucking *gook*." Then he seemed to see the Asian family for the first time. "Fuck *you* staring at?"

"Hey." I stepped around Gerber. I saw the curtain to Bay 8, Hopkins' bay, move as the uniform poked her head out to see what was going on.

"Please, Detective." (How did she know?) Dr. Wylde held up a hand but didn't turn around. "I can handle . . ."

That's as far as she got, but I saw it coming. "Doc!"

A fraction of a second too late.

With a ferocious bellow, Dickert launched himself at Wylde. He was on her in a second, his fist crashing into her jaw.

Her sister screamed. "Sarah!"

Wylde tottered, but he'd wrapped her up, an arm clamped round her throat in a stranglehold. "This is a fucking trap! You're *all* gooks! You think you can fool me? You're not smart enough, Charlie. You can't fool me!"

"Sarah!" The student started for her sister. "*Sarah!*"

Pandemonium now: a nurse jabbering into a phone, two security guards muscling their way through, the uniform drawing her service weapon.

"Holster your weapon!" I shouted. The last thing we needed was gunfire. "Now!"

"Gook *cunt!*" Dickert had a hand clamped around both Wylde's wrists. Whirling her around, screaming, spit flying—and then his voice changed, went guttural: "Be gone until I com . . ."

Without warning, his head jerked, a whiplash snap, and then he was staggering back one step, two. Blood spurted from his nose, and he dropped.

In my pocket, the charm heated. And that's when I saw it, or maybe it was a trick of the light. But in the space between the two—between Dickert and Wylde—the air danced. It quivered, rippling like the surface of an ocean breaking apart.

What sprouted from Wylde's body was white then black. Cohering in a roiling ball of vapor, it verged on the brink of solidity. Of reality.

And then in my head: *Not yet time.*

I didn't stop, didn't think what that meant.

"Dr. Wylde!" Closing the distance, I grabbed her by the arm and yanked, hard. A queer electric thrill, like a charge jumping from a Van de Graaff, cracked, but I hung on. *"Wylde!"*

Either I'd broken her concentration, or she—it— was done.

Or I was nuts because nobody said anything like *Hey, you see that?* Or *Jesus, she's a witch*!

And ten to one, they weren't hearing voices, either.

The air pruned. Whatever that thing had been— it vanished.

On the floor, Dickert drew in a wheezy, rattling breath. His nose was streaming blood.

Wylde turned. And then, for the briefest of moments, Sarah Wylde was not . . . all there.

Superimposed upon her body, like the ephemeral penumbra of a darkened sun, was the smeary translucent avatar of the girl from the DVD. The girl's imago drew in upon itself, folding into Wylde's body until she was gone.

And then it was just Sarah Wylde, her brilliant green eyes firing to emeralds.

"I'm not a gook," she said, reasonably. I saw where Dickert had split her lip. Blood dyed her teeth orange. Her eyes rolled. "*Devaputra-mara.*"

I caught her before she hit the floor.

Later, when I remembered, I drew the charm from my pocket. But it was just a pretty piece with weird symbols and gemstones, and cold.

IV

". . . What you'd expect after extensive blood loss," Kay was saying. "Official cause of death is cerebral anoxia secondary to exsanguination."

"No surprises there." I stood beneath the ER's breezeway off Washington Circle. Freezing my ass off, but you can't use a cell in a hospital. Messes up the machinery. The sun had staggered up to lighten the clouds to pewter, and the traffic was picking up. "Anything else?"

"Just interesting: MacAndrews served in Vietnam. Army, Third Brigade. He even had this funky tattoo on his bicep. Rollins could run down his service record if you want."

"And that's interesting . . . how?" But then I answered my own question. "The DVD."

"That's what I was thinking."

Hunh. The disk was being looked at by the computer guy to see if he could clean things up. "Kay, you at your computer? Can you Google . . ." I spelled the name. "Check for family."

She was silent a moment. Then: "Don't tell me Preston Wylde's involved."

"I don't know yet. What'd you get?"

"Hang on." Sound of typing. "Lot of hits, but . . . here we go. Just says that he's got two daughters. No wife mentioned. No names."

That tallied. Guys like Preston Wylde might not want too much personal information out there. "Try Sarah. Same last name."

More typing. "*Hunh*. Well, this is interesting. She comes up as faculty at the medical school. Her specialty is transcultural psychiatry. She's been all over, most recently a couple of years in Thailand and Cambodia researching cacodemonomania . . ."

I thought of that Asian family. That Ψ. "What's that?"

"I don't know. I'm a pathologist. Hang on . . . *hunh*."

"You keep doing that."

"Well, that's because it's *hunh*. Cacodemonomania is the delusion of being possessed by a demon."

This time *I* was quiet. My mind jumped to something that most cops would find well-nigh certifiable. Maybe if I'd been more open to *possibilities*, though, Adam might still be alive.

See, I'd investigated an angel.

It was complicated.

And I know what I heard out of Dickert's mouth. And what Sarah Wylde said . . . "Anything else?"

"Well, there's a pretty funky paper entitled 'Green is for Goblin: Exorcism in Buddhist Magic.' "

I closed my eyes—and saw Wylde's own glittering, emerald eyes.

Kay: "Is there something you're looking for in particular?"

Yeah. Try Googling Wylde *and* witch *and* Satan. "I don't know. That's okay. Thanks, Kay." I disconnected, then dialed Rollins. He answered and I heard background noise: men's voices. A phone ringing. "Where are you?"

"In the office, finishing paper. I hate paper. What's up?"

I filled him in, then said, "Run Dickert through the system, see if you get anything."

"And he's connected . . . ? You'll notice the ellipsis."

"Well, he's an asshole."

"The world's full of them."

"So I'm betting there's something."

"And it connects . . . ?"

"You're repeating yourself."

"So observant. You must be a detective."

"So will you run him?"

"Okay, okay. What about *our* case?"

"I still haven't had a chance to talk to the girl. I was going to interview her now."

"Wait for me. Give me twenty minutes."

"This is Washington."

"Forty."

"That'll do." I closed the phone and ducked back into the ER.

Things had more or less gotten back to normal except Gerber was nowhere in sight and Dickert was in leather restraints, snoring from whatever he'd been given. Someone had also taken soap and water to him. Didn't really improve his looks. A walrus in a flimsy hospital gown that had hiked up in unfortunate places. Obligatory biker tattoos: a ring of barbed wire around his left bicep that, with gravity and a couple years, would end up a bracelet; an American flag on the right. He had a thing about skulls: skull on fire, Jolly Roger centered in an ace of spades peeping from an ass cheek (too much information!), Grateful Dead skull haloed with red roses.

I hoped Wylde pressed charges. There was just something about Dickert I didn't like, and it wasn't about the t-shirt or that he was a drunk and a bully. His tattoos were unoriginal, but you couldn't throw a guy in jail for his taste in tattoos.

Just . . . something. That voice, for starters.

And the one in my head . . .

Oh, don't go there. I'd just about convinced myself the whole thing was stress.

The medical student sat on a stool next to a surgical resident who was stitching Dickert's scalp back together. "Your sister around?" I asked the student.

If she was surprised that I'd put it together, she didn't show it. "Zoe," she said, and stuck out her hand. We shook; her grip was firm. "Sarah's with the Chouns." Zoe tilted her head toward the bay where the Asian family was hidden behind a drawn curtain. "She might be a while. They're family friends."

"She okay?"

"Sure. I don't think she's going to press charges, though."

"That's a shame. And here I was hoping."

"The guy had an idiosyncratic reaction to alcohol. It happens. Once their BAL goes down, they're pretty reasonable people. Well . . . maybe not *him*."

"Your sister always take risks?"

"Yes," the surgical resident said, without turning around. "Rushing in where angels fear to tread. Can't tell Sarah anything and never could, if you listen to the attendings. On the other hand, can't tell Zoe anything either. I pity the chief resident of whatever specialty she ends up in."

"A fan club," I said to Zoe.

"Part of the family charm. We go all sorts of places." She mock-punched the resident. "Harry's just worried that I'll end up his intern for his first big case."

"Are you kidding?" Harry tied off, snipped. "When that day comes, and if you're very, very good, I'll let you staple the skin."

"So generous."

I debated a half second about waiting for Wylde—to ask her . . . what? Hey, whoa, nifty parlor trick. Do all the witches in your coven do that? But then I spotted Rollins trundling in, and I really did have work.

"Hey," Rollins said. He was open faced and big in a solid, apple pie, Midwest kind of way. Last person in the world you'd peg as a computer geek. "Computer guy thinks he might have something. I'd have given it a shot, but I was doing *paper.*"

"My, my, everyone is working hard and on a Saturday morning. What's the story on Dickert?"

Rollins fished out some flavor of PDA and started tapping. "Mostly small stuff. Couple DUIs. A breaking and entering kicked down to illegal trespass, along with two assault charges. All three were in connection with a girlfriend. Charges were dropped after the girlfriend didn't show to testify. Got an address out in Springfield, and a couple rental properties in Arlington. Looks like that's how he makes a living, renting out the houses and general all-around handyman."

Odd he lived out there, given his reaction to the Chouns. Route 50 near I-495 was wall-to-wall Korean, Vietnamese, Thai. "What about military? He said he's a vet. Well, *implied.*"

"Drafted in '65, did two tours. Army. Third Brigade, Twenty-fifth Infantry Division."

Hmmm. "Two tours? He volunteered?"

"Dunno. Honorable discharge in '69 and then nothing until the DUIs start up. You're looking for . . . ?"

"Nothing." I let it go. Dickert was trouble, but a brigade was a big place, and I had plenty to deal with.

Lily Hopkins looked very young and very scared. A trace of baby fat under her chin. Maybe thirteen. But there also were purple smudges in the hollows of her cheeks and beneath her eyes, and she had that kind of haunted, hunted look you saw in runaways.

"I don't know what happened. I just . . . it was like

I was dreaming. Only I couldn't move at first. I almost couldn't breathe. Like someone sitting on my chest. Then it was kind of like . . . You know how you get in a crowded room and people are shoving you and shoving you? That's what it was like. I got shoved aside." A quick flick of her eyes to my face and then away. "There was somebody else."

"Somebody. Not something?"

Shake of the head. "A girl. She talked about her mother and an aunt."

"You heard a voice?"

Really hesitant now. "N-nooo. Know how you hear your own voice in your head sometimes? When you're reading? Like that. Her voice but not really talking to *me*. I don't think she was American."

Rollins and I looked at each other. "How do you mean?" I asked.

"I mean, she didn't sound American. Like she thought about this guy. I think he was . . . you know, she . . . was doing what Mackie made *me* do. Only either his name was like a joke in her head or she really didn't get it."

"Get what?"

"In my head, she said he was *Call-Me-Bob*. You know, the old joke. Guy shakes your hand and you say, 'Lily' and he says, 'Call me Bob.' Like that. And she mentioned a place named Poy . . . Polypett or something, and said a bunch of words . . . *yama* and *mutra* . . . stuff I didn't get."

I snagged on *mutra*. Like Wylde . . . "Tell me the rest."

She did. It gave me a little chill, the way she described a presence residing in her mind, watching, waiting. Of being yanked around like a doll and commanded to do a horrible thing.

I couldn't help but think of Wylde.

I expected to see Gerber waiting when Rollins and I pushed through the curtain. But he wasn't.

"Detective Saunders?" Dr. Wylde offered her hand. "I haven't had a chance to thank you properly."

I liked her grip: firm but not overly so. I introduced Rollins, then asked, "How's the lip?" Actually I could see how the lip was: swollen.

She touched the knot with slender fingers. "I think the plastic surgeons were disappointed. My dignity's hurt more than anything else. We usually don't have situations like that get so out of hand here. Anyway." She held up a chart. "Ms. Hopkins has been transferred to the psychiatry service for evaluation. Dr. Gerber will consult, if needed. He said that he hadn't had a chance to go over the EEG results with you. So."

We followed her to the nurses' station. A quick glance at Dickert's bay—empty now, I saw. Ten to one, his ample butt was parked on his Harley. Ten to one, he didn't use a helmet.

Good. The world needs more organ donors.

Wylde flipped pages. "Okay, here are the EEG findings."

A lot of scratchy scribbles. "What am I looking at?"

"We do a routine run to get a baseline, and then we introduce various types of stimulation to evoke a response. For example, here, you see normal brain activity and then, with photic stimulation—light— there's activity in the occipital lobe, where visual information is processed."

"Okay. So?"

"So, everything's going fine, with no abnormalities until . . . right . . . *here*." She stretched past to point with a pen, and I saw the vivid scroll of a tattoo at her right wrist, a weird line of script.

Angelina Jolie.

What?

Before I could figure out what my brain was trying to tell me, she rolled on: "Time index is plus thirty minutes. Where the waves are faster, closer together? That's called beta rhythm. You see beta in REM sleep, when we dream. But she wasn't asleep at the time. This rhythm just appeared."

"Was she having a seizure?"

"No. If she'd been asleep and then awakened, I would've said sleep paralysis. In REM sleep, we're all partially paralyzed. It's called REM atonia. Perfectly normal. In sleep paralysis, the subject awakens, but the paralysis persists. Many subjects experience quite vivid hallucinations. In some cases, sleep paralysis will transition to what we call lucid dreaming. For all intents and purposes, the person is conscious, but the brain is still in REM sleep. If you listen to Lily, she was in deep sleep, and then she awakened, convinced there was someone else in her mind. *This* EEG records REM breakthrough into the conscious state, which you might interpret as a lucid dream. But I don't think so. Here, it's as if there are two brains. Two people. One's Ms. Hopkins," she indicated a set of tracings, "and the other's not. Like a split brain: two completely independent patterns, but her CT is stone-cold normal."

"Was she aware of it when *this* happened?"

"Yes. She said someone else came *in*." Wylde paused. "Not-Lily was how she put it."

"Is she . . . ?"

"Crazy? No."

I said nothing. My eyes dropped to the EEG again, those two independent brains occupying the same space at the same time. Then my eyes snagged on the initials on the front sheet. One set was P.G.: Phillip Gerber.

The other: S.W.

She said someone else came in.

I said, "When did *you* come into the EEG suite, Doctor?"

Rollins said, "What?"

Her expression was unreadable, though I saw her pulse bounding in her neck. She opened her mouth to reply, but Rollins's pager chirped. "Computer guy," he said, heading for the exit. "I'll let him know we're on our way."

I waited until Rollins had gone and then looked back at Wylde. Just came out with it. "You're Preston Wylde's daughter."

"It *is* an uncommon last name. My father's always tried to maintain a distance between his professional life and home, but . . ." She shook her head. "Things have a way of coming to roost."

An odd statement. I let it hang.

She said, "Is the fact that my father works for the FBI a problem?"

"No. But I can't imagine it's easy being the daughter of a famous profiler, especially given the men your father tracks down."

"Demon hunter is what the press prefers."

"I don't get anything near that sexy when the press talks about me."

"Maybe you need to get sexier then." She checked her watch. "I have to go. Was there anything else?"

"Yes. What was that, Doctor? With Dickert? And don't tell me nothing. I know what I saw, damn it."

Her face was still as smooth glass. "What do you believe happened, Detective? What do you think you saw?"

Not what, who. And I believe you stopped him somehow. I believe you command things the rest of us only have nightmares about.

And does it have anything to do with what's happening to me?

When I still said nothing, only then did her expression shift: a tiny blur, as if she were a projection going briefly out of focus, the pixels scattering, then coalescing around the edges until she was sharp edged, like something scissored out of black paper and superimposed upon a perfectly white background. She was almost too real.

"I've got work." She turned to leave.

For no reason I could think of, I said, "Dr. Wylde, how is the old man? Mr. Choun?"

Her back stiffened just the tiniest bit, and when she turned her face was midway to rearranging itself into something close to neutrality. But I saw the emotions chase through—and there was grief, most of all.

"He's about to give up the ghost," she said.

"That's an odd way of putting it, Doctor."

"I guess it depends on your point of view. One thing, Detective, about my father? What they call him?"

This was not what I expected. "Yes?"

"Sometimes, a name isn't all about sex. Sometimes, Detective, the truth is right under your nose."

V

"I've been able to clean up the image pretty good," said the computer guy. "Best I can tell, this is old stock film transferred to three-quarter inch and then to disk. A lot of degradation in the transfer. Black and white, silent. Almost looks like newsreel footage, you know what I'm saying?"

Black and white? I could've sworn *I* saw colors: the dirty brown of that bedspread, that girl's black hair. The blood where she'd bitten her tongue. That green and white thing on the bed. "Let's see it."

The thing was no easier to watch the second time around. But the computer guy had been right: black and white.

Hunh. "Can you tell us anything about where and when?"

"Yup." The computer guy tapped keys. "I've isolated a couple items in the room, did freeze-frame, blew 'em up."

What he brought up were two stills of objects on the bed: one, a triangle protruding into the frame from the right, and the packet alongside the pillow, only black and white now instead of green and white. He zoomed in on the latter with a couple of mouse clicks.

I stared for a few seconds. "Chiclets?"

"Chewing gum?" said Rollins.

"But a very special pack of chewing gum. It's only two pieces, and what store sells that? Then this other thing." He did the zoom thing again, and I now could see that the triangle was the bottom third of a box.

I said, "Does that say what I think it does?"

"It does indeed."

First line: **Marl**

Second line: 4 CLASS A CIGARE

"Who sells cigarettes with only four smokes a pack?" Rollins asked.

I thought I knew.

The computer guy looked smug. "Before I get to that, there's one more thing. This is from the guy. That splotch there?"

"Yeah, I thought that was a mole," I said.

"Not a mole. Let me just enlarge it here . . . clean it up . . . there."

My whole insides went still.

Not a mole. A tattoo. One I recognized.

An ace of spades with a Jolly Roger in the center.

The computer guy said, "The gum and the cigarettes were standard C rations for American soldiers. That tattoo is a copy of a death card, what PsyOps developed during Vietnam and which some soldiers used to leave on the bodies of dead Viet Cong. Here." More mouse clicks, and this time a webpage came up with a screen, the kind on YouTube. "This is actual footage of something called Operation Baker. Happened in 1967."

About ten minutes long, the film was silent and consisted mainly of soldiers on patrol, burning a village. Then, at the end, footage of American soldiers putting cards in the mouths of dead Vietnamese.

"Ace of spades," Rollins said. "Looks like a regular card from a Bicycle pack."

The computer guy nodded. "Some lieutenant got wind that the ace of spades was some kind of bad luck symbol to the Vietnamese or something. He was wrong, but he contacted Bicycle, and they sent over thousands of packs. Said *Secret Weapon* right on the pack. Not all units used the same cards, though, and some designs were more popular than others."

"You know what company that was?" I asked. "In the film?"

"Yeah. Third Brigade. Twenty-fifth Infantry Division."

"Dickert," said Rollins.

"And MacAndrews." Opening my phone, pressing speed dial.

When I got Kay on the line, I said, "MacAndrews . . . did he have any identifying marks?"

He did.

Thirty minutes later, Rollins was still tapping keys and frowning. "Can't you go any faster?" I asked.

"Learn to use the damn computer," Rollins said, though he didn't sound mad. It was a partner schtick. Just as Adam and I'd had ours. "Okay, it says here that Jolie has several tattoos."

"Go to Google Images. I want to see them."

"You want to drive?"

"I like watching you earn your pay." Pictures winked onto the screen. Obscure tribal signs, a huge tiger on her back, several dragons, a *large* cross. "The woman's a walking billboard . . . There, on her left shoulder blade. What is that?"

"Supposedly, a magical tattoo," Rollins said, and read. "Says here it's written in Khmer and is supposed to protect her and her loved ones from bad luck, evil, stuff like that. It's a . . . yantra tattoo."

Bingo. "That's it, *that's* what she's got."

"Who?"

"Tell me about yantra tattoos."

"Jesus, you're demanding. Hold on, hold on . . ."

A lot of hits on Google. Silence as we read.

Then Rollins said, "This is some funky shit."

Here was how it worked.

A yantra tattoo had to both adhere to a certain Sanskrit pattern—the *yantra*—and be coupled with precise *muons*, chants dating back to the Vedic religion, the historical predecessor of Hinduism, which the monk who applied the tattoo was to recite.

A monk. That old man, Chuon. And those smudges on his forearms and neck: They'd been tattoos.

The actual verses tattooed in special ink were in Pali, the religious language of the earliest Buddhist school, Thervada, or "The Way of the Elders."

If you believed these things actually worked, there were patterns that might make a warrior stronger, give someone good luck, allow someone to become invisible. Give you superstrength. If you believed in magic.

I thought Sarah Wylde might.

And me? Well.

I *had* met an angel a year ago. Maybe I was due a visit from the other side.

And I found out one more thing, courtesy of one of Wylde's papers.

In Cambodia, sleep paralysis has a very specific name: *khmaoch sângkât.*

Translation: The ghost knocks you down.

Because the people who suffer from this also report seeing demons that hold them down. Another paper suggested that the symptoms were really PTSD; one woman suffered an episode whenever she remembered how soldiers razed her village and killed everyone.

I don't think it was either-or. Could be both. Could

be, maybe, that the old monk had been carrying the girl on the DVD. And maybe now, Sarah Wylde was picking up the slack.

Like she said: Right under my nose.

VI

Wylde wasn't at GW.

"This is nuts." Rollins was driving fast, no flasher, the light fading and the day slipping away. Flakes beginning to fly. "We're driving a million miles an hour to intercept someone you're not even sure will be there so we can deal with a murder that's over forty years old in a country we're *not* by two guys—"

"Maybe just one. Maybe two of them, or even more. And this isn't about just the past. Remember what Lily said: The girl in her head had a red dress. There was the TV news saying snow in Washington."

"So you're saying—"

"We know Mackie was a pimp, and we *know* that Dickert's got rental properties in Arlington, right? So maybe he's renting to himself. Maybe what he's got are a whole bunch of little girls just like Lily, only they're Asian."

"Because that's where they'd have started, when they were in Vietnam. I can't believe I'm even thinking this. Jason, you're taking the word of a *kid* who killed a guy and said the devil made her do it. Man, are you *hearing* yourself? How are we going to explain this? And it *still* won't help Lily. She killed a guy. It's out of our hands."

But this was the right thing to do, I knew it. As soon as the idea set in my mind, the charm Dietterich had given me had begun to warm, heating the skin of my chest as soon as I slipped the cord around my neck.

Why was I wearing it? Beats me. Same reason I didn't tell Rollins what I thought about Wylde.

We were racing down Route 50 now, the strip malls

blurring, and then the traffic starting to pick up. Cars started creeping. At the first flake, everyone in Washington panics and crashes into each other out of sympathy.

Screw this. I stretched, reached into the glove compartment, reeled out the flasher and slapped it onto the hood. "No choice, just don't use the siren. Go, go!"

It was like the Red Sea parting, cars scuttling right then left like headless chickens. Rollins swore, jinked the car. I hung onto the safety strap on my side as Rollins took a hard right, accelerating through the turn. "You know, it'd be real nice if you get us there in one piece."

Rollins was grim. "I'll get us there. Just hope it's the right *there*."

Dickert's rentals were in Arlington, but his house was in Springfield, an older section of identical 1950s ranch houses near I-495. It was dark by the time we made it. Snow silting down. A meager puddle of silver light from a street lamp illuminated the front drive, but I knew it was Dickert's place as soon as I laid eyes on a Harley in the driveway.

There were no lights. The house felt empty. I didn't see a car—I had no idea what Wylde drove—but I did notice that the house backed on dense woods. Lake Accotink Park. "They're not in there. But I think." I pointed at the woods.

"How do you *know* that?"

"Just do." I popped the car door.

"Damn it, Jason, wait up!" Rollins pushed out of the car as I started around the back of the house. He grabbed my arm. "You have no idea where you're going. Let me call for some backup. Man, we're not even on our own turf. We're going to end up getting our asses fried."

"You're right. So you should stay here." I pulled free before he could protest and started for the woods.

"Call for backup, Justin. Cover your ass. Better yet, go to those rental houses and see what you turn up."

"I don't have probable cause."

"Find a busted window."

He stood there a second, then hissed after me: "Jason, you don't even have a fucking flashlight!"

"I know," I said, and then I plunged into the woods.

I didn't have a flashlight because I didn't need one.

Reeling out the charm on its black cord, I let it hang outside my clothing. It was white-hot now, though it didn't burn. The gems glittered in brilliant colors and shone beams that lanced the night. Showing me the way.

And my path was clear. Monstrous gleaming prints, partly human but clawed, tearing up and trammeling the earth. Think of the way white glows under UV and that's how they looked.

Just as I also knew that anyone looking at me would've seen only a dark silhouette and no light at all. The ability to see—my second sight—was coming from within.

That there was only one set of prints worried me. I was pretty sure the prints belonged to Dickert—or whatever lived inside. But where was Wylde?

I couldn't believe my intuition about this was wrong. Although I hadn't seen her car on the street. Maybe she wasn't here at all.

So I'm finally cracking up. Well, that's just great.

But, no, I felt something striding alongside in my mind, a presence. Adam?

In my mind: *Hurry, Jason.*

The voice was sexless. I couldn't place it.

I moved swiftly, silently. Almost too quietly; I should be making all kinds of noise. But there was none, as if I skimmed the earth. Snow getting thicker. Ahead, I sensed a space opening up, and in the next moment I smelled water. Getting close to the lake.

Ahead, I heard a low basso rumble, the sound of a

man's voice—and then the higher tones of a girl. And
I knew: I'd found Dickert. Heart hammering, I ducked
into inkier shadows at the edge of a clearing.

In the center stood Dickert, naked in the glare of
my second sight. He seemed, if anything, larger than
I remembered, and his skin was shifting as his body
rippled, changing colors before my eyes, going from
pallid white to a deep cobalt that was almost black.
His eyes reddened to fiery pits; slashing white fangs
sprouted from fleshy, crimson lips; the skulls on his
body grinned down—

At a slip of a girl cringing on the ground in a pool
of blood-red gown. Not the girl I'd glimpsed in Wylde;
this was the one who'd inhabited Lily's mind.

But where was Wylde?

The air was getting thick, gathering and bunching
on itself, and now I heard the whisk of many voices
swirling on eddies and currents that were not breezes
but liquid and sullen, with the feel of fingers dragged
through tar.

The realization flashed into my mind with all the
immediacy of insight.

The clearing was a perfect circle. The perimeter
thrilled in the air with a slight tang of ozone, and the
hackles of my neck prickled.

An absurd thought, entirely my own: *Like a force
field.*

Stupid. But I reached a hand, felt the jump and
shock of electricity as the field reacted, puckering into
knives of energy that burned seams into my palm.
With a hiss of pain, I pulled back.

At the sound, Dickert—or whatever he was
Devaputra-mara
pivoted. He didn't even seem surprised. His eyes
danced flames, and when he laughed, the sound burst
inside my head like napalm. Pain hazed my vision,
and I staggered, went down on one knee, then grunted
when another white salvo exploded in my brain.
Maybe Dickert said something, but I couldn't hear it

over the roaring in my head. Gasping, I pressed my palms against my skull to keep it from blowing apart.

The little girl shrieked, something pointed and piercing that was a stake through my heart.

Had to do something. My slack fingers slapped against the butt of my Glock, and I concentrated on wrapping my hand around the grip, heaving it from my holster. There was a shell in the chamber. The gun was very heavy; my hands were shaking, and I thought: Can't hit the girl, just don't hit the girl . . .

Now, in my head: *Jason, no!*

I pulled the trigger.

Rocketing from the Glock's barrel, the bullet whammed against the invisible force emanating from the circle. The circle sheeted purple; the air sung electric. In the next instant, a fist of energy hurtled with all the force and fury of a blow. Pain erupted in my face, and I was lifted off my feet and dashed broadside against a very solid, very real oak with a jolt that shuddered through my bones.

Wind knocked clean out. Unable to breathe, I clutched at my chest, writhing in the dirt, struggling to pull in a precious mouthful of air—and I thought of that poor girl from so long ago.

A mistake. Suddenly, it was as if a giant hand had descended from the sky, clamped around my throat, my mouth, my nose. I couldn't breathe. Mouth dropping open in a silent scream, gawping, trying to make my lungs work, drink in air. My chest burned; something was squeezing, cinching down around my ribs. My world shrank, my vision nibbled away at the margins, and if that amulet still burned, I no longer felt it.

Darkness before my bulging eyes. I was on my back, staring into a canopy of a blackness darker than night. Couldn't feel the snow. Pulse thudding in my temples, my mind slowing down, the thoughts like single words sketched in black marker.

Need.

Air.

From the space above my body, the darkness . . . shifted.

The night peeled away like a wrapping tugged to one side, a curtain lifted, a door opened—

And then Sarah Wylde was there.

She said something and moved her hands over my body. I don't know what she said, couldn't tell above the roar in my ears, but then the ache in my chest eased. My throat opened, and I pulled in a shrieking, burning breath of cold air—and then another.

A hand taking mine. Sarah's grip steady and sure, and now it was her voice in my head: *Get up. We have to go together. You have the Sight, now use it!*

Somehow I was on my feet, and it was as if things began to tumble into place like cogs meshing with new energy. Perhaps no more than a minute had passed since I'd fired my weapon, but I saw that Dickert, blue and terrible, was bestride the girl, and Sarah's face was a shimmering oval of pure white light in my new eyes.

What Rollins had said about yantra tattoos: *Some make the wearer invisible.*

She'd been the presence at my side. Needing *me*?

Yes. I was the Sight. I could lead. I was the light she needed to see.

"Open the door, Jason." Speaking now, her voice humming with urgency. "We have to cross into the circle, but we can't do it unless you open the door."

"I don't know how," I said.

I shouldn't have been able to see the green fire in her eyes, but I did, just as I knew Dickert's were red coals. "Open your hands, Jason. Open your *hands*."

What? An image shot into my brain—the rabbi, in the kitchen, his fist bunched against his chest: *Open your heart.*

My palms itched. They began to heat. I stared, and they were glowing, beginning to crackle, and now the air they held whirled, the strands of two glowing orbs of energy coalescing, one in each palm, pulling together like the arms of a Milky Way galaxy spinning backward.

Without knowing why I did it, yet understanding that this was the only way, I thrust my hands toward the field. The moment of contact was brutal and solid, like twin jackhammers punching through concrete that rattled to my shoulders and down my spine. A tremendous BOOM, and then the field shattered, turning into opaque shards that sprayed indigo rooster tails of eerie light.

And then we were through, Sarah's hand clamped firmly around my wrist, moving with the speed of avenging angels.

Dickert—whatever he was—roared. Wheeling about, he started for us. His body bent, shifted, transmogrified, and now a fan of sinewy dragons sprouted from his torso. They bellowed.

"Get the girl!" Sarah shouted. She let go. "Then get out of here!"

"Not without you!"

"No time!" And then she was sprinting for Dickert, driving hard, running full tilt, hair billowing.

Rearing up, the dragons spouted fire.

"Sarah!" I shouted. Somehow I had reached the girl; she was quaking under my hands, shivering as if with a lethal fever. "It's okay," I said, thinking, *liar, liar!*

With a bugling ululation, the dragons let loose fireballs: huge, all orange-yellow flame.

Sarah saw them coming. Still running, she lifted both arms in a great fluttering motion as if snapping a sheet. An instant later, the fireballs connected, squashing flat against some invisible mantle, raining flames on either side of an invisible dome.

Her tattoos—how could I see them? Her tattoos were moving. A spray of arms, muscular and thick with scythe-like talons, unspooled from her body, like those from a many-armed goddess. They whip-snapped the distance between her and Dickert, powerful hands clamping around the dragons' necks even as the dragons twined round her arms. When they crashed together, the air split with a cannonade of thunder.

And then the most remarkable thing: Sarah's form blurred, got fuzzy—and then the girl, the one I'd seen die in silent agony over forty years ago, stepped away from Sarah's body. The girl was all colors and no colors; her eyes were white light, and when she opened her mouth, brilliant lambent pillars shot forth as if all the heavens had gathered in that one place, in that one time.

Dickert bellowed as the light splashed and broke over him, and he backpedaled, off balance. The dragons' heads smoked, then sprouted frills of fire. The air thrummed with a high-pitched squealing that shook the earth beneath my feet. The dragons dissolved, and then Dickert—just a man, now—went down.

Sarah reeled, then stumbled backward as the girl tore herself free, spreading upon the air, now white, now black as a mantle of the deepest starless night— and flung herself over Dickert's body.

And yet I could see everything, and I knew that what I saw now was tit for tat. Death dealt out in equal measure.

Dickert's back arched, yet no sound issued from his wide open mouth. He was slowly suffocating, and I knew just what that felt like. His legs flexed and pedaled to nowhere. His hands were at his throat, his fingers clawing his own flesh to bloody ribbons. His face was going plummy purple, eyes bulging now not in rage or triumph but terror.

Still holding the girl, I knelt beside Sarah. Touched her shoulder. She pulled her head around, and with my strange new sight, I saw that her eyes were still green, but for the moment, there was no one else there.

I looked at Dickert. His legs were shivering, his hands fluttering in death tremors.

"It's over," Sarah said. "Until next time."

VII

When Rollins and Arlington's finest showed up at Dickert's rentals, they found a clutch of seven girls in each. The youngest was ten, the eldest seventeen. Each had either been sold by their families or simply kidnapped. Of the twenty-one girls, thirteen were from South Vietnam, seven from Thailand, seven from Cambodia; all were smuggled in by way of the Canadian border into Minnesota. The houses were overseen by "mothers" hired to run the brothels.

They never found Call-Me-Bob. But the girl's name was Tevy.

Cambodian for "Angel."

In time, the DA saw the wisdom of not stringing up Lily Hopkins as an example. A smart DA, he got her remanded to a psychiatric facility and from there, probation and home.

I'm told Lily wasn't in an institution very long. Her father came to be with her. They probably have a long row to hoe before they're a family again.

But.

We live in hope.

Never did figure out who that poor Vietnamese girl had been. Sarah didn't get a name, sorry, but she thought the girl might have been a collective Presence. Many villages in Vietnam and Cambodia had spirits attached to them. So perhaps the girl was the village, and the monk was dead. So.

What was past was past.

We couldn't have taken it further, anyway. When I went back to look at the DVD, the disk was empty. Poof. Like magic.

As if I'd been allowed to see only what was required to act.

All accounts balanced.

*　　*　　*

And Sarah Wylde:

"A seer?" I asked. This was five days later. We were drinking good coffee—excellent coffee—at a little Ethiopian bakery-café off U in the Shaw District. "I'm no prophet."

"Not a seer. A *See*-er. You've got the gift of Sight, not Future Sight, not clairvoyance, but the ability to see manifestations no one else can—and probably more abilities you don't know. It's what makes you a good detective. Your hunches? Those sudden *aha* moments when everything clicks into place?" She gave a lopsided smile, but her lip was almost normal. "That's part of it. You've got something special."

Then she touched her fingertips first to my forehead and then my chest, over my heart.

The place where, a year ago, another woman— different and yet somehow the same—placed her hand and told me why she'd waited around until I'd figured things out. Her mission, you might say.

"There and there," Sarah said. "You've been . . . marked. You're different."

"But I'm just a cop."

Who's been touched by a woman who might have been an angel.

"If you were just or only a cop, you couldn't have seen my avatars. Dickert would have been just a man. You'd never have found him. I'd never have found him either. Oh, I was . . . *drawn* to a certain point in time just as you were, and Dickert and MacAndrews and Lily Hopkins. But I don't necessarily know a Malevolent when I see it. That's why I mantled myself, so I could remain invisible until you'd found him or . . . you needed me."

I touched the place where the amulet nestled against my skin. "Do you think the rabbi . . . that Dietterich . . . ?"

"He sounds pretty intuitive. He must've sensed something, then given you the amulet, not really knowing how it was going to help."

"And how did it? I still don't get that."

"Let me see it again." She took the charm I proffered. Stared at it. Then she made a little *aha* sound and started digging through her purse. Fished out a compact. "Not gibberish. I just wasn't looking right."

"A compact? I didn't know you were vain."

"Don't be mean. Look." Opening the compact, she held the amulet so I could see its reflection in the compact's mirror. "It's a mirror script, like da Vinci's handwriting. That's ancient paleo-Hebrew from before the First Temple Era. Say, five thousand years ago. That one in the center with hooks like a bull's skull?"

"Yeah. I thought of Georgia O'Keeffe."

"Close. It represents an ox head, but it's also an 'aleph,' the first letter of the Hebrew alphabet. In their modern equivalents, the letters spell *Elohim* no matter if you read them right-left, diagonally, or up-down." She paused expectantly, and when I didn't jump in, she said, "God, Jason. It's *God*, or whatever power you want to call on. And the gems, these are all from the high priest's breastplate, each letter associated with a specific jewel. The amethyst in the center: Purple is the color of spirituality. Amethyst is the stone of clarity and transformation. Coupled with aleph, it is the power of one, the power of that which is unique and like none other. It's *you*, Jason."

I chewed on that a minute. "What about those things I conjured up in my hands? What were those?" But what she'd said was already triggering associations I'd look up later.

"Dunno. Be interesting if you can conjure them again."

"How do you know so much?"

"I read a lot. And when you're in a family as odd as mine . . ."

"Uh-huh. Tell me something: Your dad being a demon hunter. Is that all hype? Or are we talking like father, like daughter?"

Her emerald eyes sparkled. "I have a very interesting family. Want to meet him?"

"What are you offering?"

"This." Then she cupped a hand to my cheek, and I felt something almost unbearably sweet, and yet also like pain, loosen in my chest. As if by losing one thing I had gained something much greater, even if I could put no name to it. Not yet anyway.

"A door, Jason," she said. "All you need is the courage to open it and step through."

It was going to be complicated.

Later, in my apartment, I Googled: *Ummin. Thummin.*
    Read and Googled some more.
    Thought: *Hmmmm.*

Two days later, on Saturday night:
    I watch as Rabbi Dietterich blesses a cup of wine to begin the ritual of *Havdalah*, marking the end of Shabbat. The word means *separation*, and he once explained the ceremony as not only signaling the start of a new week but as a literal separation of one state of being from another. The Orthodox believed that all Jews received a second soul for the duration of Shabbat, and so this ritual marked that separation as well.

What is this second soul? Who? Always the same one, or can any restless soul come calling? I don't know. I suspect it's complicated.

Someone passes the spice box, and I sniff the heady aroma of cinnamon and nutmeg, of cloves and allspice. The Kabbalists say that the scent might also entice that second soul to linger just a little while longer.

People don't like to let go, even when they know they have to.

Chanting the blessing, Dietterich lights the long braided candle with its two wicks. The flames leap heavenward. The light is full and rich and makes Sarah's hair shimmer with sudden startling flashes of ruby and gold. When she looks at me, I see the light reflected there.

"Just as light illuminates the dark, so we see that there is a clear distinction between darkness and light, between confusion and clarity," Dietterich says. "To linger in the light is to know wisdom. To know wisdom is to banish loneliness and doubt and fear. So we are sad as we take leave of this Shabbat and of this soul, which has blessed us by its touch, yet we take comfort in what we have shared and what lies ahead knowing that what is now will be again."

As the rabbi douses the flame in a small dish of leftover wine and for some reason I do not understand, I close my eyes. Maybe it is because, for the first time, I *do* feel something leaving. Something is letting go. It is not quite loss, but it's that same feeling when Sarah touched my face.

Is it—was it—*Adam*? Has he always been there and it's only that I've never rediscovered my old friend, there all along, because I haven't known how to look? How to see?

How many other souls are worth knowing?

"Jason." I open my eyes, and it's the man to my left. Saul, I think his name is. He extends the basin of wine. "Your turn."

"Thank you, Saul." I dip my finger in the wine, close my eyes once more, and dab a drop to each.

The command of the Lord is clear, enlightening to the eyes.

Psalm 19:9.

We live in hope.

And when I open my eyes and pass the basin, Sarah is there.

The True Secret of Magic, Only $1.98, Write Box 47, Portland, ORE.

Joe Edwards

It used to be more than a grift. She'd never meant this to be a con. Even now, she could sense her grandfather frowning from the spidered darkness of his grave. "My sweet patoot," he'd say in that gravelly voice that always brought in a few extra dollars from the middle-aged women in the audience. "You can't never lose track of which part is from the world of light and which part is from the world of shadow."

"Yes, sir, pappy," she whispered.

Bringing in money through the mails was a risky proposition even at the best of times. Postal inspectors took a dim view of mail fraud. The murmured cant by candlelight in a sideshow tent became a felony when she wrote it down and put a five-cent stamp on it.

It wasn't the money that was interesting.

She lived in a little walk-up on the third floor of a decaying Victorian apartment house on Portland's east side. Buses and trucks wheezed in the street by day, railroad cars rumbled down the pavemented sidings by night. It was never silent here, always too damp,

168

nothing like the bright fields of home. There was little to do here except listen to the ache of her bones. If it weren't for the mail, she'd have cracked like an old chamber pot long before.

The mail was interesting, not the money. It brought questions—the same kind of sad and quiet whispers people had come into her tent with during the years before and during the Depression.

Dear sir can you pleese find my dog Freeway?

How will I find love?

Where did Aunt Irma hide the silver?

She didn't even mind the sirs. A whole generation had grown up since the war not knowing that women had done anything besides wear sunglasses and capri pants while lounging outside their husbands' Levittown homes. The ones who were old enough to recall the Depression, and women working swing shift at the factories after that, they preferred to forget, to pretend. Now America had that nice Catholic boy as president, who'd fought the Japanese armed only with perfect teeth and a Cape Cod tan. He was every woman's dream and every man's envy. Not like the wrinkled old men who reminded everybody of the bad times.

She took the money in, a few dollars some weeks, more others, because without it she would have been living on dog food in someone's cellar. But the money was nothing more than the river on which the questions flowed.

This past week there had been a postcard from Dallas, Texas. A question, of course—money came in envelopes.

Why must he die? it said on the back. The handwriting was strong, with a thick marker pen, like a man labeling a box. There was no return address, only the postmark.

She turned it over as she had every day since receiving it. Texas Theatre, Oak Cliff, Dallas, the letters on the front proudly proclaimed. The movie house's

marquee advertised Cary Grant in *The Grass Is
Greener*, which made the photo several years old.
Somehow she doubted the postcard concerned itself
with the passing of an actor.

No clues at all. The question was nonsense, and
there was no way to answer it anyway. She tucked the
postcard into the frame of her mirror, where she kept
the saddest and most puzzling ones. It was past time
to fold a few more of the brochures to mail to the
people who'd sent actual cash money. The money orders she simply tore up and threw away, though those
people also received a brochure for their efforts.

*There is magic everywhere in this world. From
the voodoo priests and priestesses of New Orleans
to the smoldering altars beneath castles and pal-
aces of Nazi-occupied Europe, misguided persons
have always come together to call power. Professor Marvel LaCoeur's patented magical pathways
will show you the true secret of magic, safe and
effective. Win over friends! Get the girl! Have
more money than you'll ever need!!!*

Her favorite time to walk was twilight. That was the
hour when the distinction between light and darkness
melted to a quiet silvery glow, and anything was possible. Sometimes her grandfather whispered to her then,
or even walked a few paces beside her. It was hard
for him to reach back from where he had gone, but
she knew he loved her.

The city was that way everywhere—the day birds
were not quite all sleeping, and the night birds were
not quite all out. Mercurys and Buicks fled downtown,
heading for the nicer homes in Gresham and Milwau-
kie, even as the first cab loads of drinkers and louche
women were already passing west, into the bars that
were just awakening. Sun touched the West Hills, but
she could see stars over the mountain.

Her time, her day, when answers would come un-
bidden to questions she had not yet heard. The challenge in her life was matching them up once again.

Blue shall always be unlucky for you.

Trust her tears far more than you trust your smiles.

Take the job, even if it means moving to Mexico City.

It was like having one piece each out of a hundred
different jigsaw puzzles. Still, she kept a pencil stub
and a pocket memo pad in her purse. When the answers came, she wrote them down. They always mattered again later.

Papa leaned so close she could smell the cloves and
hemp on his breath. He whispered: *Because otherwise
the boatman would be king.*

She hadn't put her memo pad away yet, but she
thought long and hard before she wrote that answer
down.

The next day she shuffled off to the post office to mail
the three brochures she'd received payment for the
previous week, as well as the one money order she'd
thrown away. Portland at the end of summer was already crisp. The air was like the first bite of an apple
even though the sun was still brass-bright. Nothing
like the golden fields of her youth, but little else in
life was like her youth either.

There was no one outside the East Portland postal
station. She stopped to examine the rhododendrons
that struggled in their concrete-lined beds. The season's last spiders hung on in their optimism, webs
strung to catch the straggling flies.

She looked up through the windowpane by the door
to see a man in a cheap gray suit looking back at her.
Time to go home, she thought, but even as she turned
away he stepped out the door.

"Box 47." It wasn't a question. His voice,
though . . . this one could have worked beside pappy
back in the good days. A big man, shoulders that

pushed skinny kids around on the playing field not so long ago, with close-cropped black hair and narrow gray eyes.

She might have fancied him, decades past.

"*Es tut mir bang*?" She used the voice she always used for pushy strangers and people who asked questions—thick, European, confused. "I'm sorry?"

"Ella Sue Redheart." His smile didn't try very hard. "You're no more Yiddish than I am, lady."

So much for the accent. "That's *ma'am* to you, sonny."

"Ma'am." You could have sliced the sarcasm in his voice and sold it by the pound. He pulled a sheaf of papers out of his coat pocket. No, letters, she realized, two envelopes and a postcard. "You are the box holder at number 47?"

"Who knows?" She shrugged.

His smile quirked again, with a dose of sincerity this time. "I do."

"Big government man, shaking down little old ladies. Your mother know you do this?"

"Cut the crap, granny." He reached in again and pulled out a badge. "We both know I'm a postal inspector, and we both know you're Miss Redheart of Box 47." He snorted. "Magic? Really? You got supernatural powers?"

"Oh, I got supernatural powers, boy. They tell me you're going to buy me a cup of coffee down the street there, and we're going to talk real nice."

"How's that?"

"Because you haven't yet told me your name. A cop always starts out either with the truncheon, or the *I'm Officer Blueshirt of the pig farm* routine. You want something. Don't try to grift a grifter, boy."

"Coffee it is." This time he really did smile. He didn't give her the letters, though.

The source is within you. Every one of us is born with a shard of the Pearl of World deep inside our hearts. Most children have it taken out of them by spankings, by prayer, by the mindless lockstep of school. Free yourself and you can find that Pearl. Once you take it in your hand, you can make the world your oyster! You begin by looking back before your first memories, when even your mother was a stranger to you.

She blew across the coffee cup. It was beige with green striping and could be found in any diner in America. The coffee within was as dark as a Chinaman's eyes. No cream, no sugar, not her.

The postal inspector stirred his tea. She'd been surprised by that. She'd have thought him a coffee man. All the big ones were. Coffee, and scotch in the afternoons.

Pappy's first rule was never volunteer anything to the heat. She wasn't pappy, and besides that she was as small time as they came. Still she held her silence as tightly as she held her cup.

He finally put the letters on the table. "Two days, three letters. That's what, six simoleons in your pocket?"

"Less advertising, printing and mailing," she said quietly.

"I've seen your little booklet." He leaned close. "A moron wouldn't believe that stuff."

"You'd be amazed what people believe, copper." She sipped her coffee. "You'd be even more amazed how many of them are right."

He kicked back and drank some of his tea. "Maybe. I seen a lot. First Korea, then a flatfoot in Seattle, now minding the mails for Uncle Sam." He examined the letters. "That's six years right there, three instances of postal fraud. For you, I'm guessing it don't matter what the fine is, you can't pay it."

She hunched down. She wasn't often ashamed of herself, but this man opened doors in her memory. "I live on ten dollars a week, fourteen in a good week. What do you think?"

"I think, why the hell is someone committing federal offenses for ten dollars a week?"

"It's a living."

"Not much of one."

She put her cup down and took the letters from his hand. "Sonny, I'll be seventy in a couple years. I ain't never had no Social Security number, been cash and carry all my life. It's what I got."

He tugged the postcard out of his pocket. "No, *this* is what you got." He turned it over in his finger like a stage magician with the Queen of Hearts.

She looked, suddenly terrified it might be from Dallas, Texas. But no, this one said, "Greetings from Scenic Lake of the Woods!"

The card stopped flipping. He read aloud, "I can make fifty dollars a week and send my kid to college, but I have to go so far away. What should I do?"

"*Take the job*," she whispered. "*Even if it means moving to Mexico City.*"

"You don't charge for those," he said flatly.

She shook her head. Two bits a reading, a long time ago in a tent beside dusty red dirt roads. Not now. Not any more.

He pulled another card out of his coat. A photo, she realized. A head shot of a man of medium build, average looking with short dark hair. He seemed like an earnest fellow. This one could have been her son, if she'd ever had a son. "This tell you anything?"

Someone has a camera, she thought, but bit off the words. "N-no."

"Hmm." He stared. "I'll buy you coffee again next week. You think of anything, you write it down in that little book." He left thirty-five cents tip on the table and stood, taking his hat off the coat hook on the wall.

As the postal inspector left, she realized two things. She hadn't pulled out the memo book since meeting him, and he'd never told her his name. At least he'd left her the letters.

She palmed the tip as she picked up her mail and shuffled off for home.

That Friday there was another postcard from Dallas in her box. This one showed a city park, with a road running through it to disappear under a railway overpass. There were a few monuments scattered around. She looked at the back, at the almost familiar handwriting.

Why not tell him to stay in the white house?

Hands shaking, she set the postcard down. She laid her copy of Eugene Sue's *The Wandering Jew* atop it and set to folding more brochures.

She spent the entire weekend wondering if the postal inspector would reappear. She assumed he'd be at the East Portland postal station, but with him anything seemed possible. She sat on bus benches and waved the drivers past, then shuffled onward when she'd been in one place too long.

They'd run more than a few times, she and pappy back in those years. Somehow it had always been funny. Afterward, at least, if not in the moment. Sheriff's deputies, town constables, preachers, angry wives, angry husbands—her memory was a parade of red faces and southern accents and the squeal of tires on gravel. Even when they'd been cornered, as happened once outside New Orleans, and probably a few other places as well, pappy would launch into some oration in that voice of his and eventually find the keys to unlock the hearts of their pursuers.

She'd thought her grandfather was old then, but she would swear to being older now. His gift had been the gift of gab, the flim flam grift that flowed from his lips like sand from a child's fingers.

Her gift was real. They both knew it back then. They just never used it for anything. She could have played the ponies, picked stocks, found *some* way to make it into real money so they could retire to Havana or Miami or Nag's Head. But it was never time, and there was always an element of danger, of betrayal.

So she'd told fortunes across the south and west for so many years she'd forgotten to ever make her own. Besides which, people didn't want to know their real future. They wanted to know their imagined future, the one they cherished instead of fearing.

He was waiting for her Monday. He had her mail again, one grubby letter. Sometimes those didn't even have money, just a simple request. Rarely begging, but she knew how to read an envelope just like she knew how to read a mark.

"Tell me," the postal inspector asked as they walked to coffee-and-tea. "What is the true secret of magic?"

In spite of herself, she laughed. "You really want to know?"

"Sure. We got time."

She heard the lie in his voice and knew that something drove this man, something invisible to her but as real as cholera in a well. "A dollar ninety-eight."

"You want me to pay you?" He sounded disgusted now.

"No, no, you don't understand. The true secret of magic is in the numbers. You have the numbers, you have everything. Like elections, you see? It's not the votes, it's the counting."

"Hmm."

She went on. "Wall Street. Who makes money? The brokers, not the poor bastards who pay for the stock. Numbers are magic."

"That's not magic. That's . . . that's economics."

"An economist can tell the future."

"But he's not right," the postal inspector protested.

"How do you know? Anyone can call spirits from the vasty deep, but will they come?"

His eyes narrowed. "You're twisting the question."

"Oh, a big cop like you, he never did such a thing?"

He laughed. "You must have been quite something in your day, lady."

"Ma'am," she said quietly.

"Ma'am."

"I'm still something today, sonny. I'm just something different."

A few minutes later, over their steaming mugs, he leaned toward her. "So, what do you know about my boy there?"

"Texas," she said, surprising herself. She wasn't inclined to trust him, not a cop, especially one who wouldn't even give her his name.

"He the one sending you those postcards?"

"Who knows?" She sipped. "All I can say is Texas. I don't know why."

"I hope you get better at spirit calling."

> Step outside on a new moon night. Walk to a park or a railroad siding, or even a rooftop, somewhere away from the street lights and the late night buses. Now look up and try to count the stars.
>
> How many did you find? How many do you think there are?
>
> Magic tells you that you don't need to know, that there are as many stars as the sky can hold. Magic tells you how to find the one you want, like looking for a diamond in a mile of beach sand. Magic is the art of picking out the impossible from all the things which might be or have been. Magic is the star under which you were born.

They went on into the autumn, meeting every week or two. He badgered her, he twitted her, but he never pushed her. She came to respect him for not trying to pull the answer from her. Somehow this man with the gray suit and the badge understood at least that much about what she did.

He let her keep answering her letters. Eight dollars one week, twelve the next, once a twenty-dollar week. She put three dollars aside that week, in her coffee can, and that was after buying a pork chop at Fred Meyer's.

Still, something drove him. His attitude became slowly more urgent. She got more postcards from Dallas, all of them cryptic. Pappy whispered the answers to her, no less strange.

A textbook killing.

Hobos hidden atop the grassy hill.

Officer Tippit has three children.

She kept the answers to herself. There were some things he did not need to know. Coffee every week or two did not buy trust. Besides, he'd surely read all the Texas postcards.

In mid-November, she got another one of the postcards from Texas on a day when there were no other letters. This one had a mail order rifle ad from the Sears catalog pasted over the face. On the back it read, *Why only one bullet?*

She stood in the post office, looking at the card. His hand reached around and plucked it from her grasp. "You've received one hundred and two letters since I've had you under surveillance, Miss Redheart. That's one hundred and two separate counts of postal fraud. You've also received twelve of these postcards from Dallas, mixed in with thirty-eight others from around the United States. A secret admirer in Texas, perhaps?"

"I'm sure I don't know." She thought of the earnest young man in his photograph of the previous summer. "Maybe you should ask that fellow whose picture you showed me."

"I'd like to," he said. "I really would. I just don't know who he is."

"Why did you bring him to me?"

He glanced at his shoes a moment. "Because I saw your classified in the *Oregonian*. I . . . I received that photo in a very strange fashion. Nothing I could make sense of." He tugged it out of his pocket and turned the picture over. On the back was written *11/22/63* in the same bold, black handwriting as all her postcards. Below it was a drawing of a goblet with a line through it. He continued, "I've been waiting for an answer I could give someone. Something I could say."

"An answer about what?" she asked, her voice so soft she could barely hear herself.

"Why I'm so afraid of this picture."

"Big man like you, afraid of a photo?" She was sorry for the words as soon as she said them, but it was too late. His face hardened and he turned away.

Go to Dallas, said pappy plain as day just behind her ear.

The postal inspector turned back. "What?"

"My father says you should go to Dallas."

He drew a deep breath. "It's too late, I think. You should have told me that a long time ago."

"I told you Texas, the first time we met."

He nodded. "Yes . . . I suppose you did."

She went home and folded brochures. It all made sense now, except the why. Something in the numbers of the world had tried to warn her of the true secret that would arrive tomorrow. A man, a gun, a bullet. She wondered if the postal inspector would board a night airmail plane and fly to Texas, looking to stop whatever might have been.

The shadows deepened in her tiny apartment, day slipping westward as the night took up its watch on the horizon's battlements. As the first stars came out, she found her coffee can and took five of the eleven dollars out.

She hadn't eaten steak in years, and besides, the world was going to end tomorrow, or good as. Magic was little more than grift, pappy had been dead for years, and the postal inspector had never asked her the right questions that might have saved a man's life on November 22nd, 1963.

The boatman who would be king was going to die tomorrow. She ate well on the scant proceeds of her mail fraud and drank to his life, before stumbling home amid the memories and ghosts of night.

Maybe it was time to change her ad.

The Sweet Smell of Cherries

Devon Monk

Mama's restaurant is a greasy dive hunkered in the kind of neighborhood outsiders avoid during the day and insiders try to ignore at night. Magic isn't what's wrong with the neighborhood. It's a dead zone, far enough outside the glass and lead lines that carry magic throughout the rest of Portland that it takes someone with college learning, or a hell of a knack, to cast anything stronger than a light-off spell. Yet even without the help of magic, dark things move on these streets. Very dark and hungry things.

But I was there because Mama's food was so cheap even I could afford to eat out once a week. A girl needed a place to get away from her job, right? This was my place. Or at least that's what I'd been telling myself for the last month. What I didn't like to admit was that I wasn't sleeping so well any more, wasn't eating so well, and lately had been having a hard time deciding if I should spend my money on rent or booze. Rent still won out (what can I say? I'm a creature of comfort and like a roof over my head), but it didn't take a genius to see how dangerously close I was to burning out.

And burnout is a fatal sort of situation in my line of work.

Hounding magic is not for the weak of heart. Use

magic, and it uses you right back. And I'd been magic's favorite punching bag for months now. It wasn't any one thing—I knew how to set my disbursement spells, I knew how to choose what price magic would make me pay: headache, flu, bruises, bleeding, breaks—all the old standbys. But after a year of Hounding on my own, the little pains were starting to add up.

I needed a month—hell, I needed a week—off. I'd even settle for a full twenty-four hours blissfully free of any new ache or pain. After this job, just this last one, I'd take some time off.

Yeah, right. I'd been saying that for a year.

"You eat, Allie girl." Mama, five foot nothing and tough as shoe leather, dropped a plate heaped with potatoes, eggs, and onions on the table in front of me. I hadn't even ordered yet.

"Someone skip out on the bill?"

She pulled a coffee cup out of her apron, set it on the table, and filled it with coffee that had been sitting on the burner so long it had reduced down to a bitter acid syrup.

"I know you come tonight. You meet with Lulu for job."

Apparently this Lulu—my might-be client—had a big mouth. It irritated me that she had spoken to Mama. I'd been doing my best to keep a low profile since coming back to town, but really, who was I kidding? Everyone knew my father—or knew his company. He was responsible for the technology that allowed magic to go public: all those lead and glass glyph-worked lines that ran beneath the city and caged in the buildings, all those gold-tipped storm rods that sucked magic out of the wild storms that came in off the Pacific Ocean. A modern miracle worker, my dad. The Thomas Edison of magic. And an empty-hearted, power-hungry bastard I was doing my best to avoid.

I shoveled a fork full of potatoes into my mouth and almost moaned. I was hungry. Really hungry. I had no idea how long it had been since I last ate. Maybe yesterday? Night before?

"It's really good." And it was. The best I'd ever eaten here. Which might make me suspicious, if I were the suspicious type. And I was.

She scowled. "You surprised Mama cook you good food?"

I thought about telling her well, yes, since I'd never tasted anything here that wasn't too greasy, too spicy, or too cold before, it did seem strange that she'd be waiting for me on this particular evening with a plate of killer hash browns.

I took a drink of coffee to stall while I thought up a convincing lie. The coffee hit the back of my throat in a wave of bitter and burned, and I suddenly wished I had about a quart of water to wash it down with. Forget the lie. Mama was the kind of woman who would see right through it anyway.

"I'm not surprised, just suspicious. What's so unusual about this Lulu friend of yours that I'm getting the special treatment?"

Mama held very still, coffee pot in one hand, her other hand in her apron pocket and quite possibly on the gun she carried there.

I kept eating. I watched her out of the corner of my eye while trying to look like it didn't matter what she said. But my gut told me something was wrong around here—or maybe just more wrong than usual.

Finally, Mama spoke. "She is not my friend. You Hound for her, Allie girl. You Hound."

So much for keeping a low profile. I wanted to ask her why she thought I should take the job, but she stormed off toward the kitchen yelling at one of her many sons who helped her run the place.

If I were a smart girl, I'd eat the food, leave some cash, and get out of Dodge. If I paid my electricity bill short, I could probably make rent without this job. I could take my day or maybe a whole week off right now. There were too damn many crazy people in this town who had access to magic, and my gut was telling me this whole Lulu thing was a bad idea. I swigged down as much of the coffee as I could stand and ate one last bite of potatoes. I put a ten on the table, hoping it would cover the bill.

That was when the door swung open, and in strolled Lulu.

How did I know it was her? Let's say it was the way she stopped, like a child caught with one hand in her mother's purse, when she got a look at me. Let's also say that I didn't even have to Hound her to smell the stink of used magic, the sickening sweet cherry smell of Blood magic to be exact, that clung to her thrift store sun dress. From the glassy look in her eyes, she'd been mixing Blood magic with something that had her soaring high out of her head.

Blood magic was not something I wanted to deal with. Not today. Not any day. Time to cut out and call it good.

I walked toward her. Since I am a tall woman, six feet barefoot, and since I also had on three-inch heels, I towered over Lulu, who probably clocked in at about five-five and maybe a hundred pounds. I had the physical advantage, which meant I had the power of intimidation on my side.

Hooray for me.

"You're Lulu," I told her.

She did the one thing I didn't expect. She whispered a soft mantra—a jump-rope rhyme—and moved her left hand in an awkward zag. She might be an awkward caster, but she was fast. I didn't even have time to pull magic, much less a defense, before she and I were surrounded by some sort of sound-dampening spell. The clatter of dishes and Mama's constant yelling weren't gone, they just sounded very far away.

A sheen of sweat spread across Lulu's face and dripped down her chest. Along with the smell of sweet cherries, I caught a whiff of a vanilla perfume that wasn't doing any good to cover up the stink of her terror.

"He already told you, didn't he? Sent you to find me?"

Great. She was one of the crazy ones.

"No one's sent me anywhere. I'm not going to take the job," I said. "Get yourself another Hound—try the phone book and the net."

Her eyes, which were so brown they were almost black, narrowed. "You don't even know what the job is."

I didn't answer. I actually did know what the job was—or rather I knew what she had told me it was over the phone. Her dog had been lost, she thought kidnapped, maybe by an ex-roommate. I thought it would be easy money. I thought wrong.

"I'm out." I said. "Nice meeting you." I tried to move past her, which shouldn't be a problem because even though we were in a quiet zone, it wasn't a solid sort of thing and would unravel as soon as I got out of her range. But she was quick, that crazy Lulu.

She took my hand and pressed her palm to mine. Her hand was hot—fever hot. I felt the cool press of paper, maybe a photo, between us. Lulu smiled, shook my hand as though we were old friends, and let the spell drop away. She wavered, just slightly, and I wondered if I was going to have to catch her before she passed out.

"Sorry it didn't work out," she said. And there was more she didn't say, in her body language, in her eyes. There was "please help me."

Sweet hells. Nobody should love their dog that much.

I gave her a noncommittal nod and walked out the door, but not before sticking the photo in my pocket.

I hit the night air—humid and too hot for a Northwest summer—and headed into the city at a brisk walk. Evening was just coming on. Streetlights sput-

tered to life and cast an orange glow that only made
the night feel hotter. I wanted some distance, like
maybe half a city, between Lulu and me. I cut across
a few streets, mostly to make sure no one was following, and ducked into a bar to use the bathroom. Only
there, with the bathroom door closed, the overhead
fan humming, and the lock set, did I pull out the
photo.

It was not a dog in the photo, it was a woman.
Maybe twenty years old with short, dark curly hair
and a white, white smile against her maple-honey skin.
She wore a t-shirt, looked as if she should be in college and wasn't, and had Lulu's eyes.

A sister maybe. Too old to be a daughter. She might
be the roommate Lulu thought kidnapped the dog.
But Lulu had said something about a man, about "he"
already telling me something.

Let her be the roommate, let her be the roomate. I
turned the picture over. Written on the back, in very
small, very neat handwriting was a name: Rheesha
Miller, her age: fifteen, and the last place she'd been
seen: at a convenience store on Burnside.

A chill ran down my neck even though it was hotter
in the bathroom than it had been outside. I'd seen this
girl's picture on the news. Missing person, no leads.
Disappeared in broad daylight. One minute she was
on the street. The next, she went into the store and
never came out. The owners, an elderly Asian couple,
hadn't seen her come in, nor was there any trace of
her on the store's security camera. Strange, to be sure,
but the Hounds who freelance for the police hadn't
picked up any traces of magical wrongdoing. It was a
runaway or a kidnapping, straight up, no magic.

There was nothing I could do about this. Nothing.

I committed her face to memory, just in case, then
tore the edge of the picture, intending to flush it down
the toilet. A chemical and fertilizer smell rose up from
the photo. I held very still. There was a trip spell on the
photo. Maybe it was for tracking where the photo

went. Maybe it was supposed to make sure the photo couldn't be damaged. Or maybe it was set to trigger an explosion spell. Damn, damn, damn. I knew I shouldn't have taken the photo. I knew I shouldn't have gotten involved in this mess.

I took a deep breath and tried to think calm thoughts, because magic is a bitch and you can't cast it when you're angry. I whispered a mantra until I calmed down a little. Then, while carefully holding the photo in my left hand, I drew a quick Disbursement spell with my right. I'd have a migraine in a day or two, but at least I'd be alive. I drew upon the magic stored deep in the ground below the building and traced two spells, Sight and Smell.

Magic flowed into the forms I gave it, and my vision shifted. Like turning on a single light in a dark room, I could now see the traceries of spent magic and old spells hanging like graffiti in the air. And since I was a Hound, and good at it, I could smell even more than I could see: the too-sweet cherry stink of Blood magic mixed with drugs, the slightest hint of Lulu's vanilla perfume, and something else—a subtle spell that stank of hickory and smoke.

I leaned forward until my lips were almost touching the photo and inhaled. I got the taste of the spell on the back of my throat, the smell of it deep in my sinuses. Not an explosive. A tracker. Someone had gone through an awful lot of trouble to know exactly where this photo was going—or maybe where I was going. This was a complicated spell. One that took a hard toll on the caster. And I knew the signature of the man who put it there. A Hound named Marty Pike. He freelanced mostly for the cops. I was pretty sure he was ex-Marine.

I let go of Sight and Smell, and the room settled back to normal. Except for the fact that I was sitting in the bathroom stall of a bar being tailed by an Hound who worked for the police, I wasn't in any danger, hadn't done anything wrong, and could still back out of this job by flushing the photo down the commode.

But here's the thing. Lulu had said "he." And right this minute, I'd take bets that "he" meant Pike. There hadn't been any real reason for Lulu to put the quiet on our conversation back at Mama's, there hadn't been anyone but a few regulars at the tables. If Pike thought she was going behind his back and hiring a second opinion on her sister's disappearance, then I could see her wanting to keep it quiet. Cop Hounds don't much like it when freelancers take a piss in their sandbox. Hell, Cop Hounds don't much like freelancers, period.

So I could either believe that Pike didn't want Lulu going behind his back, or maybe that he was counting on her to do just that. To hand off the picture to some sorry sucker—say me, for example—and that I'd . . . what? Find something he hadn't or couldn't find? Come up empty-handed? That didn't make any sense.

Well, screw this. I was not going to be used for anyone's patsy. I kept the photo and headed out into the bar. Tracking spells don't work over great distances, so Pike should be close by. I scanned the crowd, a humorless bunch of hard drinkers who were watching the game and ignoring everything else. It was a small enough place there wasn't anywhere for Pike to hide.

Plus, I couldn't smell him.

Outside then. I made a point of leaving the door open nice and wide and stood there for a couple of extra seconds, just so he'd know I knew he was following me. Sure enough, the familiar short and shaved figure of Pike emerged from the shadows between a couple of parked trucks and started across the parking lot toward me. I'd heard from someone down at the city that the cops had nicknamed him Mouse. That was before his first case with the police. It was a high profile situation, and bloody. He saved a couple of guys on the force and did some other medal-worthy things that fell into the above-and-beyond-the-call category. Ever since then, the cops just called him Pike.

I still couldn't smell him—he'd been standing upwind, the clever boy.

I walked down two steps and out into the parking lot, my heels making a solid, staccato sound.

"Allie." His voice was low and carried the hint of a prior life spent in the south. His hair was gray, buzzed, and in better light his eyes might be brown instead of black. The lines on his face made him look angry without even trying. This close, I could smell his aftershave—something with a helluva lot of hickory overtones.

"Pike. You lose something?" I held the picture out for him.

He was wearing a long-sleeved button-down shirt, which seemed odd in the heat of the night. Both his hands were in the front pockets of his jeans, and he did not move to touch the photo.

"Lulu talk to you?" he asked.

"You know the answer to that."

"No, I don't. I haven't seen or heard from her in three days."

Wasn't that interesting? If he didn't know where Lulu was, then he couldn't have been the one who put the tracker on the photo. But that spell had his signature on it. You can't fake a magical signature. It's just like handwriting. Every caster has his or her own unique style.

And if he had put the spell on the photo, then he knew where Lulu was. He could have followed her around twenty-four seven and still had time for an ice cream cone. Not that Pike looked like the type who ate frozen desserts.

I found myself not so much caring what part Pike played in this but why the hell the girl, Rheesha, hadn't been found yet.

"What's going on with this girl?" I asked.

"Did Lulu hire you to find her?"

"No."

"She was just handing out pictures to strangers when you happened by?"

"Has anyone ever told you you suck at sarcasm?"

"No."

Yeah, that was probably true. "You know what?" I said, "I don't have to tell you anything, but here's the truth. I'm out. Good luck finding Lulu and Rheesha. I want nothing to do with it." I held the photo out for him again. He kept his hands firmly in his pockets.

"It's too late for that," he said.

"For what?"

"Backing out. You're a part of this, Beckstrom."

"Really? Since when?"

"Since you touched that photo. They're looking for you now. And they'll find you."

Then the bastard turned around and started walking away.

Oh, no. Hells no. He was not going to leave me with some cryptic statement and fade to black. I caught up with him. "You know I haven't ever gotten in your way—on a job or any other time."

"So?"

"So level with me. Tell me who's looking for me. Tell me why. I know how to lie low. This is your job, Pike. I don't want anything to do with it."

He stopped next to a beat up Ford truck and opened the passenger door. "Get in. We'll talk."

"What about . . ." I held up the photo.

Pike shrugged. "Keep it. At least we'll know where they'll be: right behind us." Then he gave me a sideways glance. "You might be useful after all, Beckstrom."

Comforting. I tucked the photo in my pocket and climbed into the cab. I wanted to know what Pike knew. Or at least enough of it to keep myself alive.

I half expected his truck to be loaded with secret

military gear, but I didn't see anything unusual, unless you counted the bobble-headed dog on his dash.

"Cute."

"Grandkid gave it to me."

He started the car and headed out of the parking lot, which was fine with me. I had no idea Pike had a family. For that matter, I had no idea he had a life except for Hounding. Hounds tend to be loners—the kind of people who work nights and dull the pain of using magic with pills, needles, and booze. Not exactly white picket fence compatible. Still, watching Pike in the sliding light from the street gave me a sort of morbid hope. He was not a young man, and he seemed to be holding up okay.

"How long you been Hounding Portland?" he asked.

"About a year."

"Before that?"

"College. Don't you read the headlines? Billionaire Daniel Beckstrom's Daughter Drops Out of Harvard."

He glanced at me. He was not amused.

"Why did you come back here?"

That was a question I'd asked myself almost every day for a year. Maybe because Portland and the Northwest were familiar to me. Home. Or maybe because I wanted to succeed on my own terms, right under my father's nose.

Yeah. Mostly the second thing.

"Family ties," I said. Then, before he could ask anything else: "Who's looking for me, what does it have to do with Lulu and Rheesha, and where the hell are we going?"

"Do you know Lon Trager?"

"No."

"High-end dealer. Blood magic mostly. Owns a place down Burnside. Likes to make the rich come begging him for it." He turned a corner and we were heading down Burnside. About every other streetlight worked, and there were an awful lot of people leaning against buildings for this late at night.

Pike turned down a side street and into the neighborhood a bit. He parked and turned off the truck engine.

"You any good at lying, Allie?"

"No," I lied.

That almost got a smile out of him.

"Good. Here's what you're going to say. You want to see Trager. Tell them your name—they'll know who you are, because they're the kind of people who do read headlines."

"Wait. I am not going into the office, drug den, or whatever the hell it is, of a known Blood magic dealer. I wanted out of this, remember? I wanted to lie low."

Pike just sat there and stared at me. Then, in a voice devoid of inflection:

"The cops think she's a runaway. There's no evidence of kidnapping. None. There're no lines of magic to sniff down. But I know she's in there. And you know why I'm not going in after her? Trager and I have history. Bad history. For all I know, she's already dead. It's been two weeks. Two weeks." He stopped as a car passed by. I had the strangest feeling he wasn't talking to me, that he was looking across the cab of his truck and staring down demons I could not imagine.

"I can't get in there short of blowing up the building," he finally said. "There's no proof. No evidence. The cops won't push for a search warrant on a teenage runaway. But you fit Trager's clientele." He nodded. "Rich, young, looking for a good time. You can walk right in there. And the best thing? Trager doesn't know you're a Hound. If the girl, if Rheesha's in there, you'll know. You can get her out."

Okay, this had just gone way out into holy-shit crazyville territory.

"Listen Pike. I'm not a cop, a private detective, or a secret agent. I have no military training. I'm just a

Hound. I can track magic better than anyone out there, but I have no idea how to rescue kidnapped girls. I don't even know how to shoot a gun."

That got through to him. He blinked, and his eyes cleared. I knew he was looking at me. Right at me.

"Rheesha's my granddaughter."

Oh, fuck.

My mind started working through all the things that one statement meant.

"Lulu?" I asked.

"Her half-sister. She's—" He took a deep breath and let it out loudly. "She's not the girl she was before the drugs and Blood magic. I think she sold Rheesha for her debt, for her fix. She doesn't know I suspect her. I haven't told the cops. Yet. I can't—I just can't. Her mother is all I have." He laughed, a raw bark that sounded more like a sob. "You still want to be a Hound, Allie? Want to become a sorry son of a bitch who's too afraid to save his own grand-daughter?"

"What does Rheesha smell like?"

"What?"

"Does she smell anything like you? Like Lulu? Do you know what the last spell was that she cast? What are her favorite spells? Does she have any pets? Has she ever touched this picture?"

Pike's eyebrows arched up, and he gave me one respectful nod. He was going to owe me a lot more than that for Hounding his granddaughter. Still, the questions and my all-business, no-bullshit attitude seemed to pull him out of what I feared was a sui-cidal spin.

That was another way Hounds died young. One of the easiest ways.

He took five minutes telling me what I needed to know, the perfume, her pets (snakes), and the spells she most used.

"I'm not going to get her out," I said, "but I'll try to find her and get out as soon as I can. If she's in there, we'll call the police. I'll tell them what I know, and I'll try to keep Lulu out of it. We'll let the law take over from there."

Pike nodded. "She was right about you," he said.

"Who?"

"Mama."

Sweet hells, who wasn't trying to make me Hound this girl? I decided to get angry at Mama for selling me out later.

"Tell me about it when I come back."

I left the photo on the seat of the car and headed down the street toward Trager's address. After about fifteen minutes, I was right in Trager's backyard. If any of his people had brains, they'd come out and escort me to their boss.

"What's a lovely lady like yourself doing out alone tonight?" A man appeared out of the building's corner shadow and took a few steps toward me. He was dressed in a suit and had one of those cell phone things sticking off of his ear.

"I'm looking for Trager. Is his place down this way?" Here's one of the things I didn't think Pike, or really anyone, knew about my family line. We are very, very good at Influence. With just the slightest nudge of magic, we can pretty much make people want to do what we tell them to do. And this guy was not immune. I hated using it, because it wrecked hell with a person's free will, but, hey, there could be an almost-dead girl in there who needed my help.

Suit smiled, and the streetlight caught a glint of gold off his incisor. "Yes, it is. Who may I say is calling?"

"Allison Beckstrom. I'd like to see him now. Take me inside."

"Of course. Right this way."

Bingo.

I gave him what I hoped was a bright smile. Inside I was pretty terrified. I wasn't kidding when I told Pike I didn't own a gun, and it took more than Influence to dodge a bullet.

Note to self: If I survive this, take a martial arts class and go to the shooting range.

The walk wasn't far—just two more doors down. Okay, I don't know what I was expecting—a seedy room, people lying around in their own filth, maybe. Bad lighting at least. But the room looked like a fine restaurant. White linen tables all arranged behind silk privacy screens were tastefully up-lighted to give off pastel tones of gold and amber and plum. It looked trendy, expensive as hell, and stank of cherries, cherries, cherries.

"Very nice," I said. I was starting to sweat under the strain of Influencing Suit. He wasn't resisting, but I think deep down, he knew he was screwed. "I'd like to see the girl named Rheesha Miller. Take me to her." I dug magic out of the ground and threw it behind my words. Unlike other spells, I could use Influence without a mantra and without tracing the glyph for it with my fingers. But it still took effort, still took magic, still took calm and concentration.

Suit's smile slipped just a little, but he couldn't break the Influence. "Follow me."

He butlered me along a walkway that obscured the occupants behind the screens, then down a plush, red-carpeted hallway. At the end of the hallway was a modern glass and lead door that both contained and blocked magic. Behind that was probably Trager's suite.

My heart started beating too fast. I didn't want to go behind those doors, didn't want to see what kind of man Trager really was.

Suit walked up to the door, and my stomach tightened in fear. *Please, no. Don't open that door.* He walked past the door and down the darker hallway to the left. Plain wood doors were spaced out evenly on either side of us.

Now would be a good time to try Hounding. I wasn't kidding when I said I went to Harvard. I knew how to recite mantras silently. I knew how to draw magic into my sense of sight and smell by casting the spell with one hand and adjusting my bra strap with the other. It was similar to how stage magicians keep the audience's eyes where they want them to be, except, you know, this might be a lot more dangerous because there might be people with guns pointed at my head.

I pulled magic into my senses. The stink of Blood magic went from overwhelming, to so thick I gagged. Sweet cherry mixed with too many other odors: turpentine, animal sweat, rot, sex. I inhaled carefully as we strolled down the hall. It was damn near impossible to untangle the smells and signatures of the hundreds of spells that lingered in the air. I couldn't smell anything that might be even remotely close to Rheesha's scents.

Maybe Pike was wrong. Or crazy. That thought had crossed my mind. Maybe he was grieving for his granddaughter and grasping at straws. Or maybe he'd been part of a plan to get rid of me—take out the newest Hound on the block. Suit could be in on it. Maybe Suit wasn't really under my Influence. Maybe I was about to lose hold on my concentration, my spells, and really fuck this up.

Fingers of panic rose up my throat.

I thought calm thoughts, took a deep breath, and tried not to choke. If I panicked, this whole charade was going to crash around me.

Then I smelled it, the hint of Rheesha's perfume and the musty smell of snake. Not a sure thing, but something to hope for.

Suit stopped at a door and scanned a key card over the lock. He opened the door and stood aside.

"Thank you," I said. "Now, walk to the nearest empty room and go to sleep."

He stood there, and my heart beat harder. "Be a good boy. Go to sleep."

Suit walked woodenly down the hall to the right.

I stepped into the room and turned on the light.

Small, with just enough space for a king-sized bed and two chairs. There was also a table on top of which were tubes and rubber hoses, knives, and other things I didn't have time to get pissed off about.

Rheesha Miller sat with her back against the headboard. Her legs were drawn up close to her body and her wrists were tied to the headboard, just high enough that her hands were blue. Her bare arms looked as though someone had inked a red tattoo from wrist to shoulder, but the smell of her blood and sex was heavy in the room. That wasn't a tattoo—she'd been cut. Since she was naked, I knew they hadn't had time to carve up the rest of her yet. It took her a full minute to look over at me. Brown-black eyes like her sister's but wide, bloodshot, and doped up.

Note to self: After I learn to use a gun, come back here and kick some ass.

Screw the call-the-cops plan. I was getting this girl out of here now.

"It's okay," I said softly. "Stay quiet." I put Influence behind it, but I don't think I had to. By the time I found a knife from the table and had cut her free of the rubber shackles, she had passed out.

Which presented another problem. How was I going to nonchalantly stroll out of this place with a naked girl over my shoulder?

Sweet hells.

I looked around the room for clothing, found nothing.

Think, Allie. You went to Harvard. You're supposed to be smart. I couldn't Influence everyone in the building—I was already fatigued and headachy from pushing Suit around. I didn't have time or the equipment to set something on fire, couldn't afford a stupid cell phone.

What was it one of my roommates had once told me? It was easy to steal something big if you just looked as if you had already bought it.

And since I didn't know where the exits were, didn't even know the floor plan, that's exactly what I was going to do. Walk out of this place with a naked girl on my shoulder.

First, I repeated a mantra. My voice was shaking—hells, all of me was shaking. I pulled magic up into my hands and then into a glyph of Obscuring. That spell was most often used by people who wanted to cover up dry patches in their lawns or fruit sellers hiding bruises. It didn't work well on large-scale things like people, but it was the only thing I could think of at the moment.

I arranged Rheesha's arms and legs and lifted her across my shoulders in a fireman's carry. She probably weighed ninety pounds.

I took a deep, calming breath, opened the door, and strode down the hall.

I have never taken a longer, more nerve wracking walk in my life. *Calm, stay calm.*

The door to my left, one door away from the glass and lead monstrosity, opened.

Don't look, don't look. But I looked.

His eyes were soft brown with flecks of gold, and they widened in surprise when he saw me. He was dark skinned and had the bone structure that hinted at Native or Asian in his blood. It was just a moment, but I was sure he recognized me. Too bad I'd never seen him before.

He stepped closer, and I noticed he wore a clean white shirt and black slacks—a waiter's uniform—and he smelled of pine cologne. He touched my wrist gently.

"This way." He tugged me back through the door he'd just come through and down a windowless passage that was maybe a delivery entrance. I noted belatedly that he was muttering a mantra, throwing around hiding, warding, and other high-level spells that I wouldn't expect a waiter to know, spells that left the taste of mint in my mouth.

We exited on a side street. He let the door close behind him.

"Who is she?" He pulled off his shirt and handed it to me.

"Rheesha Miller." *Smooth, Beckstrom. Way to keep a secret.*

The man shook his head. "I didn't know. Do you have a way to get her to the hospital?"

Before I could ask him why he was helping or even who the hell he was, the sound of a Ford truck started up. Apparently Pike had no trouble Hounding me. "Do I know you?"

"No. But you're Beckstrom's daughter, right?"

I nodded.

"Welcome home." He glanced over as Pike's truck turned the corner. Then he ducked back inside, as if maybe he didn't want Pike to see him.

Crazyville. But damn, anything that got me out of that hell hole was okay with me.

Pike got out of the truck and left the engine running. "Allie?"

"She's alive."

Pike helped me get her inside the truck, and I draped the white shirt over her. Neither of us said anything on the way to the emergency room. Rheesha slept. Pike didn't look over at me, his gaze locked grimly on the street ahead. Only the bobble-headed dog nodded like everything was going to be okay. I, for one, hoped the dog was right.

I spent the next month dealing with the police, the courts, and a constant migraine. I got one look at Trager during a hearing, and he got one look at me. He was a frightening man, and he has since taken up residence in my nightmares. From what the police told me about him, I had just made myself a very dangerous enemy.

Pike didn't call, didn't thank me in any way. He really was a bastard. He owed me a hell of a favor, and I was not going to let him forget it.

But right now, there was someone else I wanted to talk to: Mama.

I strolled into the restaurant and took a table near the window. The smell of coffee, steak, and onions made my mouth water. I looked around for Mama and spotted her coming out of the kitchen. She strode straight over to my table, filled a cup with coffee, and set it in front of me.

"Why did you tell Pike he should send me in after that girl?"

She shrugged one shoulder. "You are strong, Allie girl. She needed you. Pike needed you."

I took a drink of coffee. It was fresh, rich, and hot. "This is really good," I said. And yes, I was surprised.

"You come here any day or night. Any time." Mama nodded. "Coffee always be fresh for you, Allie girl." I knew that was all the apology and thank you I was going to get out of her. That, and the best steak dinner I'd had in years, were enough for now.

Eye Opening

Jason Schmetzer

Eddie Timmser didn't know where Gong had gotten the pistol, but he did know he didn't like looking down the barrel of it. He leaned away from the safe and held up his hands. "Hey, come on, man," he said. "It's not my fault. I can't see this one." *Jesus, I should have stayed home tonight.*

"What's your deal, Eddie?" Gong asked. The light from Eddie's penlight reflected from the burnished steel of the safe door and cast shadows across Gong's narrow eyes. The pistol jerked an inch closer. "All the places we been together, buddy. Now you can't see this one safe?" A sneer twisted across Gong's lips, making the perspiration on his upper lip shimmer in the light. "I'm not buying."

Buddy? The last time they'd worked together, Eddie'd spent three months in lockup before his public defender got him out on a technicality. Gong had make it clear away, with the loot and the rep to go with it. And now he was back, forcing Eddie to work again, to use his sight to make a fast score. As if there weren't enough honest jobs where a guy who could see through walls could make a living.

"I can't see it," Eddie said. "It happens."

He resisted the urge to rub the bridge of his nose, between his eyes. It hurt to look through metal, hurt

right behind his nose when he concentrated and
squinted and looked with the eye he couldn't see. It
hurt more when he looked at something he couldn't
see through, like now. There was a mother-big headache brewing behind his eyes, and his pills were in
the truck.

This always happened to him. Every time he tried
to go straight, something happened. Someone would
call with a big score. A favor he'd forgotten all about
would get called in. He looked at Gong. Someone
would threaten him.

He looked away from the gun and played the light
across the surface of the safe again. Something flickered. Eddie leaned in close, ran his fingers across the
metal. There was a pattern etched in the tough steel,
just barely there. He held the light close and moved
his head alongside the safe.

"What is it?"

"There's something here," Eddie said. "Some kind
of pattern."

Gong lowered the gun. He bent down and held his
head close as well, close enough that Eddie smelled
the sweaty stink of fear and the beer on his fetid
breath. Eddie wrinkled his nose and slid back a bit.
"That's got to be it," he said.

"Got to be what?"

"That's what's blocking me," Eddie said. "I don't
know how this works, but maybe somebody does.
Maybe somebody knows that there are people that
can see through metal like freaking Superman. And
they know how to block it."

Gong frowned. "What, like magic?"

Eddie stared at him. "I can look through metal,
Gong. What the hell do you think that is?"

"It's called magic," a deep voice said from behind
them.

Gong spun, the pistol already coming back up.
Eddie just let himself fall backward off of his
haunches, against the safe, and twisted to see what

was going on. He didn't have a gun—hated guns—and wouldn't have used it if he did. Gong was shouting something, brandishing the gun, but Eddie barely heard or saw him.

Eddie was thinking about going back to jail. *Not today*, he thought.

A small man stood in the doorway to the study, an Asian man. His expression was calm, and he wore a simple white shirt with black trousers. His hairline was receding. He wore large wire-frame glasses. Eddie stared at him, blinked. Looked again, concentrating. He blinked again and then saw something else.

"Jesus Christ!" he muttered.

A black haze flowed around the man in the doorway. It filled the corridor behind him, peeking through over his shoulders and whirling like angry tendrils of dark-white cloud. When Eddie looked again at the man, a symbol burned in gold on his forehead. Eddie blinked again, lost his focus, and the cloud and symbol disappeared. The man appeared smaller.

"That is my safe."

"We was just looking, man," Gong said. His pistol was pointed straight. "And now we'll be leaving. Come on, Eddie," he said. He took a step forward, leading with the gun. The man in the doorway smiled, then shrugged his shoulders. Shivers raced up Eddie's spine.

Gong screamed. His arm—and the gun—vanished. Eddie stared at it in horror. Gong screamed and screamed and screamed, waving the steadily shrinking stump of his arm as if he could fling whatever was eating it away. Eddie concentrated and looked again.

The cloud was climbing up Gong's arm. Tendrils were already starting to encircle the small man's head, caressing the loose ends of Gong's hair and his ears. The screaming stopped. The Asian man at the door chuckled.

And then Gong was gone.

The Asian man smiled with satisfaction and turned

to Eddie. Eddie felt the blood drain from his face. The cloud—was Gong really gone, or had it eaten him, or what?—rolled backward through the air and whirled around the Asian man's head. "You can see it," he said.

Eddie grunted and shoved himself up off the floor. The desk was between them, with Gong's case still lying open. Rows of gleaming tools, a drill, and little odd-ended picks for locks flickered as the penlight played across them. Behind the case, off the edge of the blotter, were two ornate golden goblets.

"He called you Eddie," the man said, softly, as if it were an everyday occurrence for a shimmering monster cloud to eat someone in his presence. "Is that your name?" The cloud flickered, shimmered a deepening blood red, and slid forward.

"Nope," Eddie said, and took two steps forward—*Jesus, here it comes*!—and grabbed the goblets. The man's eyes widened behind his glasses. He reached out, taking a step forward. The goblets were heavier than they looked. Eddie looked around, desperate. The window was large, a few feet behind him.

"Put those down," the man in the glasses said. His voice held a tinge of steel, all the softness and humor gone.

"Where's Gong?"

"Nowhere you would like to be," the man said.

"Bring him back."

"That's not possible."

Eddie shivered. The cloud was hanging between them, a malevolent mist, the haze a harbinger of pain and death and somewhere he'd rather not be. He hefted the goblet. "I just want to leave."

"You never should have entered," the man said. His mouth moved, whispering words in a language Eddie had never heard, not Korean or Chinese or Japanese or anything else he expected. The haze pulsed, deep golden, and then undulated larger, redder. The golden symbol glowed brighter. Eddie looked down at the goblet, expecting to see the golden light playing across the decorations, but he saw nothing. There was nothing to see.

Light reflected . . . not whatever he saw, whatever let him see through metals and walls and safes and the dressing room doors at Macys. What he saw wasn't real. What he saw didn't affect the real world.

But Gong was still gone. *Damn it.*

Eddie spun and hurled the goblet in his left hand at the window. It was heavy enough, but if the man had spent as much money on his windows as he had on his safe it would be transparent plexi and not glass, and the goblet would just bounce off it. He dove after the goblet, toward the window.

The window broke.

Eddie fell through, tearing his arm and his sleeve on the jagged glass. He heard the man scream from behind him, and then the first crash of thunder as a storm rolled in. He hit the ground hard, grating his arm to the bone on the pavement, but he forced himself up and into a run. He still held the other goblet.

Peeve would know what to do. If he could get that far. Lightning crashed around him, casting great shadows against the alley walls.

He didn't look back.

There was a guy at Peeve's when Eddie got there, a big black man in a nice suit with a wet overcoat. His head was shaved bald—not just his hair, either . . . no eyebrows, no beard, no nothing—and he was standing near the end of the counter, ignoring Peeve.

Peeve was Peeve. He stood about five-ten, two hundred pounds. His hair was receding, but he kept spiking it up in the front like he had a shark fin on his head. Hawaiian shirt, shorts, flip-flops. He was four or five stereotypes rolled into one. He looked up when Eddie came in, frowning.

"You're dripping all over everything," he said.

"Sorry. Listen, Peeve . . . I need you to look at something."

"Did you get them?" the black man asked. Eddie looked at him.

"Get what?"

"The rings," the man said. "The things you were sent to retrieve." He looked past Eddie at the door. "Where is Gong?"

"Gong's dead."

"What?" Peeve hustled out from around the counter. He locked the door behind Eddie and then turned around. "How?"

"Did you get them?" the black man asked.

"Who the hell are you?" Eddie snapped.

"Edan Boukai," he said, bowing his head slightly. "I am the one who hired Gong to enter Mr. Kim's home." He looked at Peeve and then back at Eddie. "This was to be our meeting point." His voice was think with accent but understandable.

"We never got the safe open," Eddie said, and turned away from him. "Listen, Peeve—" he began.

"How did Gong die?" Boukai asked.

"That guy—what's his name, Kim?—he killed him, all right?" Eddie snarled and shook his head. "Listen, Peeve, I need you to tell me what this is." He reached into a pocket and brought out the goblet.

"It's a cup," Peeve said.

"God damn it, Peeve," Eddie started, but Boukai cut him off.

"Where did you get that?"

"It was on his desk," Eddie snapped. "Shut up a minute, will you?"

"Were there two?"

Eddie waved the goblet. "I've only got the one."

Boukai looked down at his hands. "Then they are separated . . ." He turned away, muttering under his breath. Eddie stared at him for a minute, then looked at Peeve.

"Tell me what happened," Peeve said.

"We were working on the safe, but it wasn't going well." He told him how Gong had pulled a gun on him. He explained the markings on the safe and how he couldn't see inside it. "It was like the markings blocked me."

Boukai spun around, eyes narrowed. "What do you mean, blocked you?"

Eddie steeled himself. He didn't advertise, but the guy had already heard most of the conversation. "I can see through things, okay? Walls, doors, metals, anything. Just like Superman. Except I couldn't see through the safe."

Boukai's eyes widened, white-rimmed against the black of his skin. "You are a seer?"

"A what?"

"You can see the inside of things?"

"I just said that, didn't I?"

"Prove it. What do I wear around my neck?"

Eddie stared at him. He opened his mouth to argue, then thought about it. His head already hurt. His friend was dead. There was a good chance this guy was nuts anyway, and if nothing else, the whatever-that-ate-Gong might catch up with him. He concentrated. "A horse."

Boukai stared. "Who trained you?"

"No one trained me."

"A natural . . ." He shook his head. "How did you come to learn this?" Then he saw the goblet and shook his head. "Never mind. Tell me of these markings."

"Why do you want to know?"

Boukai took two steps until he was face-to-face with Eddie. "Because I hired you and your friend to retrieve something from Kim's safe, a pair of rings. Because I recognize the chalice you bear and know that it has a mate that appears identical." He paused. "Because I know it hurts you here," he tapped between his eyes, "to use your Sight." He looked past Eddie, out the window to the rain-filled alley.

"Because I know what is coming, boy. Now tell me everything, beginning with how Gong died."

*   *   *

"You are very lucky to be alive," Boukai said when Eddie was finished talking.

"That's messed up," Peeve said.

"Yeah." Telling the entire story again made Eddie's stomach tighten. He rubbed his sore arm and looked at the cracked linoleum floor. It could have been much closer.

"The cloud you describe is a *fakir*. That is not its true name, but it serves. It is a servant from another realm, and Kim controls it. He has bound it to his command using black sorcery." Boukai faced them, Eddie and Peeve, as they sat on the counter. "He uses it to get what he wants." He spat the last sentence with a vehemence that even Peeve couldn't miss.

"You really hate this guy, don't you?" he asked.

Boukai ignored him. "The reason you could not see through his safe door to the tumblers beneath is indeed magic. There are charms that can be worked into metal that protect it from seers or other magical attacks." He reached into his coat and produced a silver flask. When he held it up, it flashed in the light. "Look inside this."

Eddie frowned and shook his head. "It's got booze in it."

"You haven't looked. I didn't ask what was in it. I asked you to look inside."

Eddie swallowed the angry reply that his headache wanted to shout and concentrated. He stared at the flask in Boukai's hand. He saw the metal. He set his mind, saw the metal again, and *pushed*. Then he gasped.

Golden letters flickered on the inside edges of the flask. They were written far too small for him to make out from that distance, and yet they showed clearly in his vision. The letters glowed brightly. He didn't recognize the alphabet.

"I can't read it," he said, after a moment.

"It's not a language of man," Boukai said. "I could teach you."

"Not in an hour," Eddie said, shaking the Sight from his head. "So I'm a seer. So what? That's not going to stop Kim from siccing his *fakir* or whatever its called on me." He hopped down from the counter and stumbled. His leg had gone to sleep. He bent over to rub the blood back into it, cursing under his breath at the pain of the pins-and-needles sensation.

"You are right. We must deal with Kim first." Boukai looked around. "He will surely be here soon."

"Whoa," Peeve said, standing. "What do you mean, he'll be here soon? Why would he come here? Why would he even know where here is?" He walked past the two of them and peered out through the store's front window into the steadily falling rain.

Boukai pointed to the goblet sitting on the counter. "Because of that. Its mate will lead him here as soon as he recovers it. They are linked, you see. In the other realm." He picked the goblet up and cradled it in his hand. "But perhaps . . ." He looked at Eddie. "Have you attempted to See this?"

"It's right there," Eddie said.

"You know what I mean."

"Do you have any idea how much my head hurts?" Eddie turned away from him and leaned over the counter. He wanted to rub his head, to reach beneath his skin and stamp out the pain between his eyes. But he couldn't. He knew if he tried it would only hurt more.

"Your pain is a manifestation of your Sight. Because you're not trained, you're forcing it. If you could learn to control it more easily, the pain would lessen." Boukai's voice trembled and dropped an octave. Eddie looked over his shoulder. The black man was holding his hand over the top of the goblet and chanting. The words were similar to those Kim had said but not the same. "It's possible," Boukai said, a moment later in his own voice, "that you could be shown."

"How?"

Boukai held up the goblet. "Look at this, and we'll see."

Eddie turned back to face him. "Why are you doing this?"

Boukai straightened. "Because Kim Lu stole something from me, something very dear. And because he took that, I will take everything from him." He held out the goblet. "And you're going to help me. Now concentrate."

Eddie held his gaze for a moment. Looking at Boukai's eyes was like looking at rocks. Finally he sighed and lowered his line of sight. The goblet beckoned at him. He concentrated on the goblet's rim. Lightning flashed outside. The light flickered against the golden cup but didn't fade. Eddie's eyebrows rose. The light kept growing. And growing.

Until finally it became so bright and white and the pain replaced everything else.

"Eddie?"

The pain was gone.

"Can you See?" Boukai asked.

Eddie opened his eyes. He was flat on his back on the floor. From the feel of things, lying in his own puddle of rainwater. He squinted as the fluorescents in the ceiling cut at his eyes. And suddenly he was looking at the stars. He snapped his eyes open. Ceiling. Squinted.

Stars.

"Wow."

"I will take that as yes," Boukai said. "Can you stand?"

Eddie shrugged and sat up. His head swam a little. He put a hand to the side and waited a moment. It passed. Taking Peeve's hand, he stood.

"What's it like?" Peeve asked. Eddie gave him a look. "Sorry."

"We need to find out what you've learned," Boukai said. "He will be here soon."

"Why aren't we running away?" Eddie asked, looking around for the goblet. "I mean, that's what you do, when someone is chasing you. You run away."

"We cannot escape the *fakir*." Boukai brought the goblet around from behind his back. "Tell me what you see." But Eddie had already stopped listening.

The goblet existed in four dimensions. That was the only way Eddie could express it to himself. He saw the goblet in Boukai's hand, radiant gold against the soft brown of his skin and the deeper black of his coat. But he also saw the ones next to it, on either side, that shifted out of his sight if he tried to look directly at it. "It's like it's shaking," he said.

"That is because this chalice exists in all realms," Boukai said, looking down at it himself. "You see this one and the two nearest it. When you bring it together with its mate," he brought his hand overtop the goblet, coverings its mouth, "you can open the way to another place."

"That's neat and all," Peeve said, looking out the window again, "but if we can't get away from the faker or whatever you called it, what are we going to do?" Eddie looked at Peeve and then at Boukai.

"That's a fair question."

Boukai smiled. "We shall take it from him."

Peeve stared. Eddie stared. Boukai laughed.

"First I need to see what Eddie has learned," he said. He held up his flask again. "See again."

Eddie looked at the flask and squinted. The letters appeared before his eyes again . . . but this time with more meaning. He read them. He *could* read them. He looked at Boukai. "How did you do that?"

The black man smiled and bowed. "I am not untrained myself," he said.

Peeves looked at them. "What's going on?"

"I can read the words," Eddie said. He looked again at the flask—through the fabric of Boukai's pocket this time—and read them again. "Who is Mariel?"

Boukai's face hardened. "She is dead." He took a deep breath, closed his eyes, and held his breath for a long moment. Eddie waited. Finally the black man exhaled and opened his eyes.

"When Kim arrives, he will have the other chalice." He held up the one in his hand. "It is important he not join them." He held the goblet out to Peeve. "You must hide this somewhere out of sight, but somewhere you can reach it when we need it."

"Where I can reach it?" Peeve asked.

"We?" Eddie asked.

"When Kim comes, he will have the fakir. We must be able to overpower him and get the chalice away from him. If we can, we must get the rings from him as well. They control the fakir. It is through them that he binds it to his will."

"The thing that ate Gong. The cloud." Eddie traded glances with Peeve. "You want me to fight that."

Boukai smiled, a predatory smile a wolf might have worn. "No. I want you to manage Kim. I will handle the fakir." And then he laughed, a great and terrible laugh, and shrugged out of his coat. He threw the overcoat on the countertop and stopped laughing as suddenly as he'd begun.

"Hide the chalice," he said. Then he spun to face the door. "He is here."

Peeve scooped up the goblet and ran behind the counter. Eddie moved halfway down the counter, out of direct line of the door. "What do I do?"

"You must See," Boukai said, unbuttoning his shirt halfway. His sleeves were already rolled up, revealing blue-ink tattoos covering both his forearms. When Eddie squinted, the tattoos shimmered as the goblet had. "I will fight his magic. You must fight the man."

The plateglass window exploded.

Eddie looked out into the storm and screamed.

In Kim's study the fakir had been a cloud, a hazy harbinger of death and dread. To his new Sight it was much more. It was a wraith. A demon. A creature of mist and malice with wings and talons and great gaping teeth. It wove its way through the window even as the door opened and Kim stepped through, the other goblet clutched in his hand.

"You!" he shouted, when he saw Boukai.

Boukai smiled and gestured. The tattoos on his arms flowed forward, dark and shiny tendrils to duel the fakir. Where they touched, arc-white sparks danced. Sounds crackled inside Eddie's head, and he realized he was standing still. *What the hell do I do know?*

"Get out of here!" Peeve shouted. He popped up from behind the counter with a pump-action shotgun leveled. Eddie swore and dove to the side. The gun's explosion was just as loud as the sound of the demons fighting, but this sound shook his chest and echoed through the small shop. Eddie twisted his head to see the shot, expecting to see Kim's bloody body slumped to the floor.

He was still standing, arms outstretched, watching the fakir duel whatever Boukai had summoned.

Peeve ratcheted the slide and fired again. This time Eddie was looking that way, and he Saw what happened. The buckshot blazed into the fakir's center and sparkled like fireworks for a brief instant before it disappeared to wherever Gong had gone.

"Son of a bitch," Eddie whispered.

"You cannot fight it," Kim screamed.

The fakir circled the black man like a hound on the hunt. Boukai kept his eyes on it, his arms raised. Eddie tried to focus on whatever was growing out of his arms but they moved too fast. Like the goblet, they were there and they weren't. What if the fakir was like that? He looked at it, but it still appeared hazy.

Kim lunged two steps forward. The fakir advanced,

crackling with energy, struck the tendrils along their length. Eddie was forced to look away. The light was so bright it hurt his eyes, but when he looked down he saw it cast no shadow. Just as at Kim's place.

"Eddie!" Boukai cried.

Eddie looked. The fakir was high off the ground, with just enough of itself lowered to guard Kim from Peeve's gunfire. As he watched, Peeve ratcheted and fired again, but this shot went the same way as the rest. He squinted, and looked. The goblet was inside Kim's coat, tucked there as he used both hands with the fakir.

There was a crack, and Boukai fell. The fakir flickered at him, caressing his head and shoulders, but the tattoo tendrils were still there and held it at bay. Eddie's brow furrowed in amazement as Boukai himself seemed to shimmer and bounce between realities, but he steadied back to one person. Eddie ground his teeth and looked around for something, anything. It was obvious Boukai was losing. He had to do something. He looked around him, around the store, trying.

But there was nothing to See.

"Do something," he whispered to himself. And then he Saw it.

Kim was holding his elbows tight against himself, holding the goblet secure around its side. Eddie concentrated, squinting with his mind even as his eyes narrowed. A slender chain appeared, trailing off the goblet toward the counter, toward Peeve. Eddie twisted that way, thinking to warn Peeve, when it hit him.

The other goblet. And then he looked again and saw the chain pulse and undulate, toward Kim and his rings. When the pulse reached him, the gold symbol on Kim's forehead glowed a little brighter. And then the fakir advanced, a bit stronger. It was feeding off the goblets somehow. It was magic.

"I will fight the magic," Boukai had said. "You will fight the man." Eddie frowned.

The magic is kicking his ass, Eddie thought. *But Kim's still a man*. And that was it.

"I know how to fight a man," he said, and clambered to his feet.

He charged.

He was within two steps before Kim dragged his attention from the battle with Boukai to see the threat. All he had time to do was shout "No!" before Eddie slammed into him. He hit Kim in the midsection, crushing the goblet between them. The rim of it cut painfully into his shoulder even through the fabric of Kim's coat. They fell in a pile on the floor.

Boukai screamed. "The chalice!"

Eddie fumbled for the goblet. Kim brought one hand down on it and wrapped his other around the back of Eddie's neck. His touch burned like fire. Eddie screamed and lashed out. His fist connected with Kim's chin. The fiery touch disappeared. He looked down. Kim was conscious, but his eyes were wandering. Eddie dug through the man's coat, found the goblet, and flung it behind the counter toward Peeve. He heard it clank against the floor. He glanced back long enough to make sure the ethereal chain had gone with it and then looked back at Kim.

"Got it!" he called. There was no answer. He looked.

Boukai was on his knees, his arms held above his head. The tendrils that had so adroitly fought the fakir were slender shadows of themselves, and white had leached its way up the tattoos on his arms. Eddie looked at the fakir, writhing above him, probing with taloned wings. He turned back around, cupped Kim's head in his hands, and slammed it against the floor. The man whimpered. Eddie did it again. And again.

He stopped.

The rings. He reached down and grabbed Kim's

limp hand. He clutched at the ring there. It burned his fingers. He yelped and let go. Checked over his shoulder. Boukai was on his back, but the fakir was motionless, waiting.

"Peeve!" Eddie called.

"Is he dead?" Peeve asked, peeking over the countertop.

"Get over here. I need you to take his rings off."

Peeve crept out from behind the counter, leaving the shotgun where it was. "Why can't you do it?"

"Because they burn my fingers."

"Why are your fingers more important than mine?"

"Peeve, damn it. Just do it."

Peeve reached out with one finger and tapped the ring. Nothing happened. He tapped again. Then he grabbed it. "It's barely even warm," he said.

"Take it off," Eddie said, watching the fakir. He felt something nibbling at the edges of his awareness. He hoped it wasn't the cloud starting to gnaw on him the way it had taken Gong's arm off. "Then the other one. Be careful."

"Careful of what?"

"I don't know, do I?" Eddie waited. Peeve got both rings off, and nothing happened. The fakir didn't move. Neither did Boukai.

"Now what?" Peeve asked.

"The chalice," Boukai whispered. "Get the goblets."

Eddie scooted over to where the man lay motionless. His arms were at his sides, all the color gone from the tattoos. The skin beneath them was as white as porcelain. Eddie looked closer, saw the lines etched in Boukai's face. His breathing was shallow. Peeve came back with a goblet in each hand.

"The rings," Boukai breathed. "Put one in each cup." Peeve dropped them in. "Now hold the tops together." Peeve tipped them against each other. Boukai's hand came up and grasped Eddie's wrist weakly. "Now, seer. See the words inside."

Eddie looked at the goblets, squinted. He saw many goblets, one after the other. Where there had been three before there were ten, twenty, a hundred. He concentrated on the center. He saw inside, saw the rings swirling in a vortex of light. He saw the words flare to life on the inside of the cup. He spoke the words.

There was a great tearing sound, a flash of light and pain, and then cold.

"Ow!" Peeve cried, dropping the goblets. "They're frozen."

"It is done," Boukai breathed, letting his head roll to the side. Tears leaked down the side of his face. "Mariel, it is done." He looked back at Eddie, smiling. It seemed some of his strength was returning. "Look," he said.

The fakir was gone. Eddie picked up the goblets, looked inside. The rings were gone. Behind them, Kim moaned. Peeve looked over at him and then stood. "I'm calling the cops," he said.

"Go ahead," Eddie said. "They'll never believe it."

Boukai shuddered and laughed. "You are right," he said. "But it does not matter. Without his fakir Kim is nothing." He rolled onto his side and reached toward his coat. "We must be going, Eddie," he said.

"Where?"

Boukai sat up. "You've learned much tonight," he said. "Think of what I can teach you tomorrow." He chuckled and jerked the coat down from where it had lain across the counter. He dug in the folds until he produced the flask. A swig seemed to give him the strength to sit up and start rolling his sleeves down.

"What else can I learn?" Eddie asked, standing. He looked down at the exhausted man sitting beside him.

"You can See," Boukai said, extended a hand. "Now you must Do."

After a moment, Eddie took the proffered hand.

Faith's Curse

Randall N. Bills

They say a body isn't dead until it's at your feet. And warm.

Adrian Khol's eyes traced the outline of the victim, trying to find recognizably human features. No clothing was apparent; the ash that coated everything within arm's reach? Stranger still, no marks marred the concrete of the connecting tunnel between the Red and Blue lines at the Jackson stop. No signs of a struggle—unusual scuff marks, high velocity blood spatter or scorching, in this case. Even odder, despite the apparent ash, the body didn't appear burned so much as . . . melted. As though someone took one of those exquisite wax figures from Madame Tussaud's and put it to a blow torch. The arms fused to the chest and legs in a single, long stump, body devoid of hair. And the face? The noseless, eyeless mask runneled and pulled, like taffy, a true horror in the dim, florescent lighting.

"Yeah, that's warm enough, alright."

"Uh?" Martinez' response barely came through the donut filling his mouth to bursting. His smacking lips echoed in the starkly lit tunnel, the grimy tiles amplifying the sound as though taunting the man's slovenly habits.

Adrian managed to keep his lips sealed around his

reaction to his assistant's inability to take four steps before tearing off a wrapper from some chemical-packed sugary bar and slamming it past bleeding gums. A look at his aura almost a year ago during the first interview had been painful, his body tainted with such vileness. How could he ingest such filth? After a year, he knew it wouldn't do any good to voice such questions.

This is the best I can get? Adrian sighed heavily as he pushed fists deeper into his long overcoat's pockets against the cold—with only his assistant around, it wasn't worth the expenditure of energy to alleviate the discomfort—and moved around the body to get different perspectives. He carefully stepped to avoid placing his imported leather shoes in the strange ash.

"You say something, boss man?" Martinez managed to speak again, this time without an accompanying crumb shower, though the yawn at the early morning hour ruined the effort.

"Nothing that need worry you," he replied. Through dozens of assistants across the years he'd learned that nice or curt, it never mattered. What mattered was what their brains could handle. After that prerequisite, his manners were irrelevant. And abrasiveness was so much easier. So much more the natural human state. With everything else he fought with in his life, being nice to people when he didn't need to be . . .

The other man shrugged the snappish response away easily.

. . . point.

Martinez shoveled in the last of the donut and pulled out a liter of Mountain Dew he'd somehow managed to fit into a pocket of his oversized, thread-bare coat. He started to untwist the cap before he spoke again. "Man, what the hell. Dude's like a human stick of butter."

Early, even for you, Martinez . . . been asleep yet?

"So, what we got here, boss man? Spectral phantasm? Werecreature?"

Adrian glanced toward one end of the tunnel and then the other, noting the uniformed officers keeping anyone from entering. Lips sardonically stretched. *Facing away, as ever, well out of earshot. They can head into the squalor of Cabrini-Green and face the worst horrors that humans can inflict on each other, yet they flinch like schoolgirls watching their first horror film whenever I walk by. They use me to get what they need when it comes to the darkness and the places they won't tread, but they won't even look me in the eye. Won't even shake my hand. But who am I to complain? I use them equally as well. Mutual parasitic whores.* The image swelled the bitter smile further.

"Maybe it's an undead," Martinez continued yammering. Always yammering. "I keep asking, and you're never telling. But yeah, could be undead. That'd be cool. Wait, wait," Martinez said, his mangy beard quivering with excitement, glasses above his blotchy cheeks almost fogging with exhalations. "An unbound spirit?" he softly breathed, as if it were a holy prayer over rosaries at a pew on Sunday.

Adrian shook his head slowly. *Where in the world did Martinez obtain such information?* He knew to the word exactly what he said around his assistants, especially once they'd been around long enough for him to start mentally referring to them by their names (though he never deigned to voice them). And something as dangerous as an unbound spirit? Never. "Too many movies," he finally said.

"Huh," Martinez responded, eyes blinking as he mentally stumbled to a halt, his childish glee fading under confusion.

"Too many movies. Such creatures do not exist."

A knowing look replaced confusion, a child convinced he'd caught an adult in a lie. "Right. Sure. What ever you say, boss man." He took another giant swig of his teeth-killing sugar water and then waved the bottle like a laser pointer, his voice a cable infomercial salesman at three in the morning, deep into the hundreds. "But I'm looking at a corpse that died in no human way. Explain it."

Adrian stood perfectly still, his smooth, angular face a pale slate statue to house his dual-colored eyes. Martinez' arrogant smile slowly faded, and he gulped several times under Adrian's piercing blue/brown gaze before his eyes fell to the floor.

"I explain to no one," Adrian spoke, voice never wavering off its even keel—all the more powerful.

"Didn't mean anything by it, boss man. Just, well, *something* killed this guy. And it ain't normal." The last almost a mumble.

Yes, you did. But he didn't respond, knowing that despite his distaste, he needed the repugnant man. He reached inside his posh coat. Pulling out a silver-threaded pouch, he unwound the drawstrings and dipped fingers into the hideously expensive rare metallic dust mixture. With practiced ease he rewound the cords one handed and slipped the pouch away. He then stretched out his hand and waggled his fingers over the body with ludicrously over-the-top showmanship that almost brought pink to his ears despite the years (why, for the love of all that is holy, why?!) until he caught Martinez' eye. Then he flicked the sparkling dust into the air; he ignored the gleeful, anticipatory look that swept the other man's face.

Adrian cleared his voice to cement his hold on his audience of one; he struggled to concentrate. Such moments always invoked childhood memories like incantations to raise the unwanted corpses of the long dead. Of make-believe games with his little sister when they wished to keep their parents ignorant of their talks even when in their presence and the made-up language that became so much more; of hide-and-seek in the back woods when he lost his mind for some time, his spark of talent found and the spirit world revealed; endless time spent honing his craft by trial and error, and all the lonely, desperate years to find someone, anyone, like him. He fought to keep a darkly sarcastic laugh from tearing free at the ludicrousness of it all. He pulled his thoughts back to the moment, all too aware of the dangers of letting his concentration slip. He spoke forcefully, the alien tongue rolling easily off his, a guttural snarl that clawed at the walls and dimmed the harsh electronic lighting. The glittering dust pulsed as though in sympathetic vibration to a monstrous, unheard heartbeat that filled the universe. Susurrations of unfelt wind wafting down the long subway corridor, twisting the dust into a vortex of microstars squeezed into a miniature black hole. He clenched his fist and barked out the final words, the vocal sounds like claws tearing up out of his throat into existence. Abruptly the dust strobed in a pyrotechnic flash of unearthly fury that threatened to etch their shadows into the tiled walls like Nagasaki victims from that long ago nuclear blast: hell's own flashbulb.

In that instant time ground to a stop as the footprint from the astral plane lay revealed to his trained senses. The last several days lay juxtaposed in a mind-numbing snarl, like thousands of photos developed onto the same film stock. As each living entity moved through the mundane world, they left a trail, a smear of their own life essence. An indelible mark on the underpinnings of existence and the realm of spirits and so much more: the astral plane. While it faded with time, he'd taught himself to read such signatures, more pure and sure than any biometrics of fingerprints, eye-scans and DNA samples. He concentrated, quickly stripping away layer after layer of the mundane masses moving about their inconsequential lives, completely unaware of the world beyond their own. The sheer volume took some time, but he knew it was all subjective; hours might pass in the astral plane, and yet it was all just an eyeblink.

He abruptly found the layers for when the man appeared. Late last night, not a soul in the tunnel—

strange, for a Saturday—hands deep in coat pockets against the cold as he climbed down from the Red line stop and began to make his way toward the Blue line. Features tired but resolute, marching toward a destination only he could know. If the man still lived, Adrian might expend more energy—even if only Martinez were present, the energy drain was not significant—and follow the trail to his living essence, perhaps tweezing out additional details of feelings and thoughts. But the trail ended messily in a hazy, indistinct glob, like a badly fuzzed image on those late-night cop shows Martinez loved to watch, where the producers only haphazardly paid lip service to a citizen's right to privacy.

A frown pulled at his features. Deaths—even non-mundane deaths—always left a clean break as the life energy evaporated back into the astral plane, like a rope smoothly cut. And in such deaths a multitude of details could be found. Almost too easy for Adrian and his skills. But this? This was altogether different. No details at all, just an . . . opacity . . . almost as though . . . no, that could not be possible.

His mind traveled down multiple paths simultaneously as he struggled with the problem. All the while something bothered him, as though he should recognize the strange astral print, but nothing came to mind. Though he eventually came up with nothing, he knew one thing for certain. This was new. And Adrian hated new.

He sucked on his teeth momentarily, then braced for the pain and relaxed his fist; he unleashed his iron-clenched will and slid from astral space, the frozen flash gone in an instant. The pain enveloped him as the clockwork mechanism of the mundane world hammered back into motion and the astral inertia it imparted slammed into the one responsible for its arrest. Despite the years of practice, he staggered under the molten spike stabbing downward through his chakra points across head, spine and finally into the belly, where his intestine stretched under the final throes of the energy until only clenched teeth kept the scream at bay.

"What did you see, boss man?"

Adrian breathed in deeply, nostrils flaring as he sought to extricate his mind from the pain's tentacles. For once Martinez' unwashed pungency remained mostly buried under the harsh chemicals used to keep the subways clean, with a hint of sulfur quality behind it all; the victim and whatever had happened.

"Nothing," he finally rasped out. "I saw nothing."

"Right," Martinez responded, voice childlike in its sullenness. "What ever you say, boss man."

Adrian took another deep breath to finally start the pain onto the path of distant memory, nerves more jangled than ever. But I did *not* see anything. Anything at all.

God, Adrian hated riding the subway.

Despite such a short distance as two stops, he hated stepping foot on the crowded meat carriers. Hated the occupants and their vacant stares as they tried to pretend they were anywhere but wedged into cars like cattle to the slaughter. Hated their hostile and fearful, surreptitious glances. Most of all, hated that he needed them. Needed every one of them.

They pulled into the Harrison stop, and a new gaggle of warm bodies squeezed in. The bitter December cold—much more acute above ground, the lake-effect snow and wind swirling with gusto across the concrete platform—pushed in as well. Others shivered uncontrollably at the gusts, but with so many about, he remained blank-faced, coat undone, unfeeling of the cold.

The greatest show on Earth . . . his sardonic inner voice never strayed far.

Despite the press of bodies, Adrian's cool gaze and body stance—the absolute knowledge in those bicolor eyes that the cold *really didn't affect him*—kept an invisible shield all around him. A modicum of breathing room, more effective than a real force screen. Despite his obvious wealth—the subtle hint of silver threads woven with intricate runes along the coat sleeves and down the front and back almost gluttonous in this impoverished part of the city—no pickpocket dared approach. No ganger moved to bully with a raised gun. It'd happened in the past. Still did happen now and then when someone new came along. But these? They were regular commuters. Knew him. He'd made sure of that. Had to make sure of that all the time. Why he chose the stinking cattle car when he traveled throughout Chicago.

God, he hated them.

Despite his best efforts to avoid focusing on any of them, he abruptly noticed a face in the crowd. A female face. One he recognized with a jolt of echoing pain. Regardless of resolve, he swept into motion, the crowd parting like the Red Sea before a mad Moses. He stopped mere feet from the terrified woman, mind finally registering the only passing resemblance to *her*.

Of a sudden he shivered. Must be the cold. Must be.

The train dragged to a halt at the Cermak-Chinatown stop, and Adrian was out the door with a flourish of the floor-length coat (never forget the charade!), the hard air almost burning his lungs as he pulled in huge amounts to banish the stink of the L-car. To forget what just happened. To forget. . . .

"So what do you think's up, boss man?" Martinez asked, apparently unconcerned with Adrian's strange behavior, already over his petulance from the scene of the murder. "I spoke with the cops, and they got nothing."

As if they'd tell you anything of worth. "Of course they have nothing. If there were even one scrap of evidence that pointed to a mundane murder, they'd hound that trail wherever it led, even if it was a dog chasing its tail round and round. Anything but call in my services." Now away from so many people, he was forced to cinch his coat up as the cold worked past his shield. Stepping carefully down the stairs, he came out under the El—no pigeons overhead to drop their surprises during winter—Cermak Street running left to right directly ahead. The sand/salt station to the left, across the street, looked like a kicked anthill as trucks and personnel prepared for the coming blizzard. It was nearing January after all, and Chicago almost never failed to deliver its annual dump of two feet of solid cold.

"So, what we doing, then?"

"Back to the warehouse."

"Not the estate?"

"Are we not here in Chinatown?" he responded, arm sweeping to the right to take in Chicago's Chinatown. "Would we not need to be someplace markedly different if we were heading to the estate?"

"Right . . ." Martinez responded, voice trailing off as though in amazing discovery. "Will I finally get into the sanctum, boss man? Or do I have to stay in the mundane again? It's been a year."

Adrian's silence was answer enough.

"Right." The man could teach a course on sullenness. "So why the warehouse?"

A sigh. He glanced to the left to see how long the Cermak bus would take, and a reminder that he needed the man. Would never be caught without a follower again. "Because there's something about that death, some astral signature that reminds me of . . . something."

"Yeah, boss man? You remember everything. I bet you remember exactly what I said to you the first time we met, after your other assistant ran away."

In excruciating detail.

"So how you couldn't recognize an astral print . . . wacky."

From Adrian's peripheral vision he watched Martinez put down the last of the teeth-killing drink. He then flicked the bottle toward the trash can with its

side opening and it sailed right in. Adrian slowly
blinked at the surprising dexterity from the usually
ungainly, overweight man.

"Yes," Adrian spoke slowly. "As you say. Wacky."
The few other individuals at the bus stop abruptly
began shuffling toward his position at the edge of the
street, a sure sign of the approaching bus that they
dared come so close.

The tick in the back of his mind became an itch,
one that he finally acknowledged after leaving astral
space and the murder scene with only a negative shake
of his head to the on-scene officer; they knew he'd get
back to them. *There's only one way that I couldn't
recognize the astral print. That's if it was obscured.
No undead, werecreature, or spirit—unbound or not—
would think of obscuring its astral signature. Most
wouldn't even know how, and the few spirits that have
pilfered enough essence from the mages that have
summoned them to know such a thing was possible
wouldn't consider it. No, this was different.* Trepida-
tion and yearning filled him in equal measure. There
was only one answer. An answer to a question he'd
spent his life trying to find.

Another magus.

A lifetime of learning through ancient, crumbling
tomes taught him that magus existed in the past, oftimes learning and teaching together. Yet he'd almost
given up, convinced that he alone wielded magic in
this modern world. The abrupt irony was almost more
than he could take. For though the answer must be
another magus, it was someone that knew Adrian . . .
and Adrian didn't know this man! He knew enough
about Adrian to know exactly how to obscure his astral print, to bar him from any ability to tweak out
the littlest detail. That type of intimate knowledge
wasn't just unnerving—it was down right terrifying.
He'd read of what could happen under these circumstances. Such intimate knowledge conveyed immense
power over Adrian.

He gingerly stepped onto the bus, ignoring the gasp of foul, black smoke from its diesel engine and the fearful look on the bus driver's face as he passed by without paying the fare. He sat down at the rear of the bus—sending one occupant scurrying toward the front—but the sudden in-rush of people allowed him to uncinch the coat once more.

He needed to find who was responsible for the murder. Needed to find him right now, before the man moved against him. That he might have to kill the magus after all the years of searching was a bitter bill to swallow.

Adrian stepped off the bus at 1100 West Cermak, across from the Fisk coal-burning power plant, Martinez at his heels like an obedient pup. Though he could easily walk through the front door, as ever—especially with the conjuring he planned—he walked briskly toward the road entrance to the inner dock. Once he hit the shadows of the tunnel, he stepped carefully, for patches of black ice might have formed overnight, then moved into the inner parking lot proper.

A twenty-four-foot truck already sat at the dock, driver talking animatedly to the building supervisor. Several handlers—puffs of breath in the cold actually larger than the smoke rings they'd be blowing on break—easily maneuvered pallet jacks with their paper cargo to be warehoused on the fifth floor.

Taking the steps two at a time up to the loading dock, he almost reached the group of men before they noticed him. The building supervisor blanched, cutting off mid-discussion, while the driver looked around confused at the other man's shocking change of demeanor.

"Good morning, Mr. Kohl," the building supervisor spoke, voice brittle as the icicles clustered along the corrugated awning all along the dock.

Adrian stared right through the man.

"If you'd like to go right up, the freight elevator can take you immediately."

Adrian swept past the super without a nod, ignoring the confused driver as well; no time to educate the man on why he should fear Adrian. A single man—especially if he proved somewhat intractable to the mind-bending realities that Adrian would unveil for him—would not make that large a difference.

The lift took them quickly up to the third floor, where the building supervisor managed to open and close the heavy doors, and slide in a hasty "good day," all without once glancing into the interior.

As the rumbling lift took the repellent man away, gloom descended onto the room, the single bulb at the entryway barely making a dent against the thickness; a perfect mood setter for the type of work accomplished in the setting. A long-used wooden blank floor covered every square inch of the four-thousand-square-foot warehouse. Boxes and bundles and packages seemed to rise out of the ground like grotesque trees, festooned with a myriad of rotting, ancient vegetation: cloth and dust and mildew. Adrian reviled such filth and clutter. Yet years ago he'd tried cleaning the entire area, installing full lighting and generally making the place habitable for humans, only to lose control of those who worked this sanctum; sickening how much humans relied upon trappings and regalia for their faith to flourish. Lost to the point where, in disgust, he was forced to dispose of them all and start again new. He hated new. It took so long to work with what he had. Starting new was anathema to the very core of who and what he was, to the arts he practiced.

A woman moved out of the gloom, coarse shift barely covering a thin frame, a holy sheen in her eyes and an obsequious bow practically taking her forehead to the ground. Years before he thought he'd get over it. Thought he'd eventually take it for granted, or perhaps come to enjoy it. Finally prayed that he would at least forget about it. But it never seemed to happen. The guilt over what he'd slowly done to this, his inner cadre, always twisted like a rusty shiv. That it happened to this very woman . . . bile threatened; a quick snag at a white cloth, from an interior pocket, pressed to lips the only salve to kept his rebellious stomach under control.

"We serve, my lord." Her voice, soulless as an automaton, raised the bile again until he coughed several times, dry heaving before he remembered the urgency propelling him here: the thought of another man with such intimate knowledge concerning Adrian; another magus with the ability to strike him with deadly force from afar. He glanced toward the walls, floor, and ceiling and noted the carefully tended ruins that marched like horrific hieroglyphs, twisting, fading and throbbing even as he watched. A faraday cage for magic, one might say. But much, much more. That power, that safety brought a small measure of respite.

"We've work to do," he clipped after several more moments to assure his voice was back under his control. Without a further thought for Martinez—the man would stay behind, as he always did—he began to follow the winding path through the stacked goods. He immediately felt a shift in perception, as though a breeze he could not feel were ruffling his close-cropped hair, a fairy's blown kiss caressing a cheek. After long years, the trail seemed natural, his feet automatically finding the proper runes. Here, in his inner sanctum, where the faith of his workers lay embedded in the walls so thick they actually appeared solid in astral space, flowing with that power like pulsating veins, he might manage the transfiguration by himself. Yet it would require a needless expenditure; instead, one of his workers always met him at the portal to allow an easier passage.

That soft, unfelt breeze became a tangible force as they continued the seemingly random twist and turn down strange corridors of crookedly stacked, mysterious boxes and crates, always following the unique path marked on the floor, a path only a select few even knew existed, much less could manipulate. An uninitiated mundane, if he managed to cross the initial threshold and live—highly unlikely—and then managed to trail him—almost beyond comprehension— would see him slowly fade from existence until they were left in a warehouse devoid of human life, simply piled with incomprehensible bits and bobs from around the world.

As Adrian neared the final gate and the end of the piercing of the veil by the path, the power built up along his chakra until his skin vibrated with pent-up energy. With a last step onto the final glyph, he opened both hands wide and released the energy, like the greatest static charge release imaginable. Unlike the viewing of astral space while still in the mundane—as accomplished in the subway tunnel— this didn't bring pain. This brought ecstasy as he and his follower finished the transfiguration of flesh into pure energy that allowed them to occupy the astral plain.

Still shuddering from the echoes of that energy, which far outstripped any sexual experience of his life (even that he'd experienced with *her*), he stepped into the warehouse. Yet one unrecognizable from anything viewed by human eyes. Ghostly and ethereal, yet as solid as anything touched in the real world, every part of the warehouse shone with an inner light covering a rainbow of colors beyond imagining, luminosity varying depending upon the object. Bought, scavenged, and oftimes outright stolen by a network he'd spent years building, to the mundane each object was simply a rare artifact or beautiful, precious stone. But each was in reality an item imbued with astral force that he could manipulate, some naturally occurring, others created by ancient magus, some dropping back as far as the dawn of mankind when man first discovered the meta planes of astral space, the spirits and monsters that resided there and that, like gods, men could learn—albeit very painfully—to manipulate to their bidding.

"Master, we serve," a half dozen men and woman intoned, their naked bodies translucent like crystals, energy pulsing in one rhythmic swell. While each beat to its own rhythm, all immediately fell into a single chorus shimmering with latent potentiality; he closed his eyes, felt the power mirrored in the thrum of his own heartbeat.

"Someone has cracked my inner sanctum," he spoke, eyes opening. He took a step and crossed the entire distance of the warehouse to his worktable— after all this time he did not know if he instantaneously crossed that distance or whether that distance crossed to him.

"That is not possible," the woman who met him at the portal said, appearing next to him, her shift gone, her luminous energy brightest of all.

His urgency wavered once more, knowing that he couldn't even bring himself to use their names anymore. For one mind-numbing moment he thought he detected movement out of the corner of his eye, as though she were on the verge of touching his arm. *No one* touched him here, *especially* her. But he only imagined it. He knew she would never violate such a dictum. Yet he still jerked upright—now on the other side of the table—and forced his iron will to control his mind and force it back to the task at hand.

"It is possible," he spoke, relieved at the same even tone as ever. "There is no other explanation for what's occurred. There's another magus." Saying it aloud was still astonishing. "And that magus cannot possibly have obscured so much of an astral event from me, so much of his own print, without intimate knowledge of me. He's good. He's very good, or I would've noticed something wrong with the sanctum. Therefore, we will summon an unbound spirit to find that crack in the astral façade of the sanctum. And from that crack we will find the thread that binds the magus to the breach and follow it until we find him."

While his followers rarely spoke without a direct query, their silence almost deafened. They would never gainsay his word, but an unbound spirit could be a thing of horror if even the smallest mistake in the summoning occurred.

He began thinking of the needed ritual objects and tapped the worktable, each appearing from their stored locations throughout the warehouse with each finger strike. Yet despite trying to focus on the work of constructing a perfect summoning, the itch that rode the back of his mind became a furious burn. Something wasn't right? What wasn't right?

An Olmec statue appeared on the table. Two thousand years old, its ornately carved jade a pulsing green of the living energy fused with the stone by the magus that crafted it millennia ago. Grasping the statue, he opened his mind and fed it energy, and his senses catapulted to new heights. The wrongness he knew to be in his inner sanctum abruptly spiked until he could sense it. His astral perception roved the walls and ceiling and floor as he flashed around the warehouse from one thought to the next, trying to find the breach.

In mid-thought-leap, he froze as he caught a hint of the wrong essence, as though a wolf passing through the scent trail left by prey. He unleashed more energy to focus his senses as much as possible, the force becoming painful as it hammered through the statue, on the verge of incinerating the irreplaceable item.

Zeroing in on the trail, it finally led back to Martinez. Confusion sundered his concentration, and the energy drained away, the dust of the vaporized statue drifting unnoticed. What was Martinez doing here?! The man followed him into his sanctum? How? He'd not allowed it. Not yet. That man needed another year, five years, before he could be trusted so much. Yet how . . . the slow, awful truth wormed past the confusion, setting the hair on his arms and legs to standing.

"No," he finally managed.

"Oh, yes," the man spoke, voice a complete octave lower then his normal range, the teenage-boy-in-a-man's-skin mannerisms gone, sloughed off like so much dead skin.

"How? You were never initiated."

A bellowing, mocking laugh ripped from the man's large chest. Adrian started, another shock stabbing further into his ability to handle the situation as the astral plane nearest Martinez responded violently to the emotion. *He can't be a magus!*

"Ah, you've finally figured it out. Watching you flit about like a mad fairy was most amusing. Almost made up for the shit I've had to eat at your hands for the last year."

"But it's not possible," Adrian continued stoically, unable to get beyond the obviousness of the man's presence in astral space, in Adrian's own sanctum. His mind worked furiously, and an idea emerged from a text read long ago. "You have to be bound by another magus. You've never revealed the slightest hint of potential. Nothing to convince those around you so you can draw power from their belief. These followers are mine, bound across most of a decade. You cannot draw anything from them. I would know it."

Martinez shook his head, smile as condescending as any Adrian handed out. In another time, another place, Adrian would've bristled. But here it terrified. Where was the man drawing his power? Another, even more horrific, thought surfaced. Had the man managed to bind an unbound spirit? He'd read of such acts in only remnant pieces from ancient books filled with the art as black as the deepest cave. But to fail, to be dragged off to suffer torment for eternity? Not even a madman would risk such, despite the continuous flow of power that would render all the hated charades meaningless.

"You still don't get it, Adrian. Your grasp of the arts is intuitive and even masterful. But the foundation of your art is mind-bogglingly limited. When I first met you, I did not believe it possible to construct such limitations and reach the height of your art. I certainly didn't believe that you'd managed to craft an inner sanctum carved into a bubble of astral space. I thought I'd be able to convince you earlier, but your paranoia was simply too much to breach. So I had to do something that might send you scurrying to your sanctuary with such haste that I might finally follow."

The pieces, despite the lunacy of the image they created, began falling into place. The strange astral print he couldn't identify . . . the filth the man poured into his system. His mind simply refused to accept the possibility, despite it staring him in the face. "You murdered that man," Adrian continued, unable to voice the painful truth of his own arrogant blindness. "After this much time you know me well enough to have crafted such a snarl that I couldn't see anything." As he spoke, he carefully began to channel energy, knowing that despite their silent words, his followers knew their lord and master would be triumphant. Knew that here, in his inner sanctum, nothing could touch him. That absolute knowledge, wedded to the years of unceasing faith directly crafted within astral space, gave him a reservoir to tap that he'd never come close to plumbing. "Why?"

"I already told you. I couldn't believe you'd managed to gain such knowledge and power with the shackles you've given yourself. We'd heard of you and finally managed to track you down. But we had to be careful. Had to approach you in a way that wouldn't endanger us."

Despite the situation, Adrian couldn't help the words as they slowly dragged out of him. "What . . . are . . . you . . . talking . . . about?"

Another giant belly laugh. "You think others must believe you are a magician for your power to work. The more powerful that belief, the greater magic you have; hence all your silly public rituals. It's rubbish.

All rubbish. Power is power, and you've shackled yourself with meaninglessness. If one of my pupils taught you in this fashion, I would have him killed for such stupidity. Who taught you, Adrian? That's what I've wanted to know all along. What we must know. Why I've put up with your insufferable arrogance. Your teacher is twisting magic learning and twisting minds in the process. Who knows what effect that might have on the meta planes? I can already see what you've rendered here through actually using other human beings as part of your rituals. Do you have any idea of what you've done to them? Who knows what other damage you might be wreaking on the natural order of things?"

Adrian's mind worked feverishly, trying to figure the other man's angle. Was he trying to distract me with such lies? Trying to delay my assault? Make me doubt my art? None of it made any sense. And of *course* he knew what he'd wrought on these people. Despite their devout belief that had become faith and then so much more; despite that natural progression that involved no coercion at all on his part, making it all the more difficult to bear; what he'd wrought twisted with pain continually.

"No one taught me."

For the first time since dropping his disguise, Martinez seemed thunderstruck, out of his element. "What?"

"No one taught me. All I've learned I taught myself. I've spent my life hunting for other magus. And now, when I finally find one, he's mad. Mad and possessed." His skin began to tingle with the energy build-up as it neared the flash point, and Adrian prepared to unleash all its fury.

Martinez opened and closed his mouth several times before finding his voice again. "That's just not possible. You can't learn alone. You cannot stumble upon the art. It must be nurtured and drawn from you like a tree from fertile loam. It's not possible. Someone self-taught doesn't have the right control. Is a danger to everyone around him. Is—"

In mid-word Martinez struck, the hammer blow of argent energy flung off the man's abruptly outstretched arms, double fists of energy to crush Adrian.

But this was *his* inner sanctum, crafted across long, long years. And he'd been slowly building energy for longer than Martinez. In a fiery cascade of force Martinez' attack fell against his own force screen, the blow easily diverted in a shower of sparkling energy. With the last of his confusion falling away, Adrian knew he did indeed look at a bound spirit in the shell of a man: a possessed magus. The only explanation for how the man wielded his art without a single soul that believed him to be a magus at hand.

The single greatest yoke that bore down a magus. The yoke that forced medicine men from time immemorial to be showmen; the same heritage that found its way down into snake oil salesmen and finally sleight-of-hand magicians of the modern age, with all the trappings of a true magus but with none of the spirit that such rituals allowed a user to invoke. A hollow shell, missing the true forms of power beneath.

With his true believers and their towering batteries of faith hyperactivating his power within his own inner sanctum and fortress, he drew in energy from the astral plane until he screamed out loud from the pain of it; he unleashed the gates of hell in a raging inferno that struck from all sides simultaneously. Martinez' life was cut from existence with such force that astral space itself trembled. The energy, with far too much power and inertia to be expended after the ease with which it killed the other man, cascaded back along time itself, withering the mundane world's memory until Martinez ceased to ever exist.

Adrian collapsed into unconsciousness.

Adrian slowly woke, his twelve-hundred-thread Egyptian cotton sheets a balm to sweaty flesh. A cloth slowly sponged cool water across his forehead before a hand gently lifted his head to pour liquid ambrosia in the form of water onto parched lips and a throat scarred by what must surely be the fires of hell.

He cracked his eyes to pain, despite almost no light in the room. Long, almost silent minutes of such ministrations passed, the pain receding further and further. Finally, the dim outline resolved into an intimately familiar shape, though one he never thought to see here, in his own home, again.

"You."

"Master, I live to serve. After your collapse you became sick, feverish. We knew not what to do. So some of us . . . we touched you," her words continued, timid and terrified and filled with that worshiping tone that twisted the knife deeper. "Laid ointments as best we could. Brought you here to heal."

Through the haze of lethargy, pain, and the blackness surrounding any events after Martinez, his inner voice began its sardonic subtext. He had begun to take them for granted. Had gotten used to what he'd done. Used his sense of guilt for a shield that allowed him to continue to use them in such fashion, ignoring his own humanity being lost.

The memories of the whole, fantastic ordeal unfolded like an unlocked treasure chest. The betrayal by his assistant, a possessed magus, with his ludicrous attempts to distract Adrian with outrageous lies. Despite it all, despite the lunacy of the man and his failed attempt to destroy Adrian, he knew the man did speak one word of truth. He *had* taken too much for granted. *Had* turned humans—once friends, once . . . lovers (even now it hurt to think about it)— into something less. Less than human. Knew he must start down a different path if he was to avoid becoming mad. Avoid becoming Martinez and embracing magic to the point of allowing a spirit to possess him in his feverish desire to find other magus. Knew now that other magus did exist, that other magus could be found, but the current price for finding them was unacceptable.

That different path must start now. His tongue scraped at lizard-dry lips, working moisture into his mouth before he spoke her name with as much reverence as she intoned his.

"Kim."

The Wish of a Wish

Robert T. Jeschonek

You'd think genies might get a wish to themselves now and then . . . but from the pain in Magda's eyes when she opens the mansion's door, I can see she's getting zero wish fulfillment out of life.

"Yes?" Her eyes are beautiful, an unearthly bright greenish gold, but the look in them is one of pure misery.

"Good morning, ma'am." I flash her my badge, and she winces. "Oliver Singel, State Department of Mystic Revenue. I'm here to see Mr. Rudolph Gunza."

She ushers me in without hesitation. She doesn't fear me at all; as a genie, she need fear only one man in all the world.

That man is her master, Rudy Gunza.

As she closes the heavy door behind me, I gaze around at the opulent entryway. Everything is glittering gold and crimson velvet and gleaming marble, from the winding staircase to the fountain in the middle of the giant room.

Ill-gotten gains, all of it. Whipped up on a whim and a wish by the magical beauty standing in front of me.

She tosses her head, and the lush, black curls flop about her shoulders. She straightens the dark blue satin bodice of her outfit, smooths the silk harem pants below her taut bare midriff.

Even with the beaten look in her eyes, even with her mouth and chin covered by a pale blue veil, she looks breathtaking. She looks more perfect and radiant than any woman alive, as beautiful as any fantasy sculpted by a man's imagination.

Then again, she *has* to, doesn't she?

"What business do you have with Master Gunza?" There's a hint of a glint in her eye as she says it—a flicker of power. She might not be able to exercise it against her master, but that doesn't mean she can't use it against someone else, like me.

"Serious business," I tell her. "*Tax* business."

"Oh-ho!" Gunza's jolly voice booms from the top of the staircase. "And here I thought this was purely a *friendly* visit!"

A weak smile doesn't quite make it onto my face. "Hello, Rudy."

Gunza wobbles down the stairs, looking like a tubby sheikh. His glittering red robes can't hide the stupendous gut wagging in front of him.

When he and I were partners, he never had a gut at all.

"Long time no miss!" says Gunza as he drops from the last marble stair to the floor. "How's the old gang of idiots?"

"Better than ever, now that you're gone," I tell him.

Gunza throws an arm around Magda's shoulders and squeezes her tight. "Oleo and I used to work together! Isn't that something, Magda? We was *revenooers* together."

Magda's head bobbles as he jerks her around. Her flat stare drifts past me like litter on a breeze.

"Went after *tax evaders*, didn't we?" says Gunza. "Folks who didn't pay the state a piece of the action from wishes granted and spells cast."

"It's income, Magda." I wave my clipboard at the

surrounding opulence. "The state deserves its share under the law."

"Bull-squat, Oleo." Gunza chortles and strokes his braided red mustache. "Let the state get its *own* genie."

"Yes, fine idea." I walk around the room, taking notes on the clipboard. "We could get one the way *you* did. Force an old lady at gunpoint to use up her three wishes on nothing and hand over the lamp."

Gunza's grin darkens. "Hey now, Oleo. That was a straight-up *gift*, and no one can prove otherwise."

"Almost no one." I shoot a look at Magda, and she turns away.

Gunza shrugs. "If a door closes, open a window. The department passed me over for a promotion— which *you* got—but Mrs. Sandusky thought I deserved an even greater reward. She *wished* for me to have it."

The walls are made of alternating gold and platinum ingots, which I note on my clipboard. "Well, *I* wish you'd paid your *taxes*." I write more on the clipboard. "If I were *you*, I'd wish you don't have a *coronary* when you see the grand *total* you owe the state."

"I don't owe one cent!" Gunza releases Magda and storms over to grab my clipboard.

I snatch it right back. "You lazy prick. How hard could it be to pay your taxes? You already wished for unlimited wishes, didn't you?"

Gunza smirks. "That was my first wish."

"Why not wish for her to pay your taxes?" I point my pen at Magda.

"Because I don't *choose* to." Gunza's features twist into a scowl. "Because I am the *master*."

I shake my head in disgust. "You're just like all the rest. All the other scum you used to help me bust."

Gunza gazes into my eyes for a long moment, nodding slowly. "Run," he says finally.

I know where this is going. I knew from the moment I walked into the place.

"I wish . . ." says Gunza.

I swing the clipboard at his head, but he knocks it away with one thick forearm.

Before I can take another swing, he finishes his sentence. "I wish that a hunting party of madmen and monsters will hunt down Oliver Singel, then torture and mutilate him for as long as I wish . . . and not kill him, no matter how much he begs for it."

Magda's eyes meet mine. They well with regret and resignation.

I reach out to her. "Magda, please! Don't do it! I'm here to help you!"

Gunza giggles and smacks me on the back. "He's a liar! He's just here for his precious *revenooo*!"

"I'm sorry." Magda weaves her arms in the air, and a cloud of twinkling glitter swirls above her. "I have no choice but to obey my master."

"Wrong!" Even as the misshapen forms materialize before me, I keep trying. "I *can* help you! Tell me what you *want*!"

Magda hesitates, and the figures flicker. Gunza stomps over and smacks her across the face.

"Do your job!" he says. "Obey me!" He strikes her again.

Magda closes her eyes. Her nimble fingers finish their dance in the air, and the hulking forms solidify.

"Run, rabbit!" Gunza howls with laughter. "Don't let 'em catch you!"

With one last look at Magda, I turn and sprint off into the depths of the mansion.

The hunters are silent. No shrieking laughter, no ululating howls, no clattering weapons and footsteps. I can barely hear them back there at all—just whispers and the rustling of wings and rags.

The quiet makes it all the worse as I run.

Heart hammering in my chest, I race to the end of the corridor and burst through the oak double doors there. Beyond the doors, I find myself in a vast arboretum, teeming with tropical trees and flowers.

Without stopping, I draw my cell phone and send a text message to my partner. At least I had the sense to post him elsewhere in case I needed backup.

Now, if only Gunza didn't think to wish for Magda to block outgoing phone signals.

As I pocket the phone, I hear brush shuddering behind me. Ducking off the gold-bricked path, I bolt through the thick foliage, crossing the room away from my original trajectory.

Suddenly, a feverish ghoul explodes from the shrubbery ahead of me, swinging a machete. I fall back, barely escaping the blade . . . and nearly end up skewered on the point of a bayonet brandished by a leering soldier.

Twisting out of the way, I leap off into the cover as both of them slash and stab at me. I rush straight through the deep green jungle, panting for breath in the steamy air—and surge out of the vegetation in front of another set of double doors.

Plunging through the doors, I find myself in a maze. Through its frosted glass walls, I glimpse shadowy figures moving around me . . . but I have to go onward. I hear noise from the other side of the doors, so I can't go back to the arboretum.

I move as quickly and quietly as I can, though it doesn't matter. The enemy can see me as well as I see them through the frosted glass.

I zip around a corner, then another and another, always choosing right at the branches. Turning again, I spot a blurred figure on the other side of the translucent wall . . . and he spots me. He changes direction and follows me down the passage, keeping pace in a humpbacked trot, separated from me only by a few inches of glass.

Luckily, the next time I reach a branch, he hits a

dead end. He howls, caught in a corner, as I dart down another passage, hoping for an exit.

I find one—a gleaming golden door inlaid with multicolored gems—but just as I charge forward, it crashes open, revealing a towering maniac.

He stands seven feet tall, at least, and his double-jointed limbs are like sticks. He's naked except for a leather loincloth, and his skin is reddish-brown, like an almond.

His eyes and mouth gape wide as he scrambles toward me, drooling and whooping.

Suddenly, before I can do anything, he slows in mid-step. His movements stretch out as if he were the star of a slow-motion movie, and his whoops extend to one drawn-out tone.

I jump when I hear the normal-speed voice of Magda behind me. "That was one of my masters, two hundred and fifty years ago. Shall I tell you how he beat me?"

Looking around, I see another predator creeping from the maze in slow-mo. This one, muscular, blond, and bushy-bearded, wears the horned helmet of a Viking.

"Were these your masters through the ages?" I say.

She nods. "As you die, you will know what I've been through."

Stepping toward the tall one, I gingerly touch his reddish-brown knuckles. "How can you be doing this? Disobeying Rudy?"

"I'm obeying him," says Magda. "I'm slowing things down, but you will still be hunted and tortured."

"Why talk to me at all then?"

Magda cocks her head and frowns. "What did you mean when you said you could help me?"

"I meant what I said," I tell her. "All you have to do is tell me what you want. Just ask for it."

She narrows her eyes. "*I* know what this is about now. You want me for yourself, don't you?"

"No." I shake my head. "I want to *save* you."

"You're not the first to say that." Magda snorts and folds her arms over her blue satin bodice. "Somehow, *saving* me always ends with *hurting* me."

"Not this time." I spread my arms wide. "I swear, I'm here to help you."

"You want my help collecting Rudy's taxes," says Magda. "For all the riches I've given him."

"Actually," I say, "you're the only reason I'm here."

Magda stares, her expression split between confusion and disbelief.

"This time, I'm not as concerned about tax evasion," I say, "as I am about slavery and abuse."

She looks like she's thinking hard . . . and then her stare becomes an angry glare. "Liar. You're a *liar*, just like *all* men."

"I'm telling you, I came here only to save you."

"Liar!" She lifts her hands overhead to weave and conjure, and I see the tall man start to move faster. "You better *run*, liar!"

Without another word, I dash around the tall man, heave open the door, and race into the hallway. I can tell she's run out of patience, at least for now. I can tell she doesn't believe me.

Even though I told her the absolute truth.

I don't care about the mystic taxes. This time, I came only for her.

As I run down the hall, I open every door, but I'm not looking for a way out. I'm looking for something else.

A lamp. *Her* lamp.

Now that I'm on the inside of Gunza's mansion, I'm determined to find it. I'm going to end this perverted jerk's most heinous crime: genie abuse. The bastard's a *djinnophile*.

Here's how it works. The genie must obey her master. The genie has magical powers that can heal any wound, repair any damage. Even to herself.

What better scenario can there be for a twisted

sicko who likes to hurt women? He can brutalize her any way he likes, then wish away the damage, removing any sign of the crime, expunging any guilt . . . and leaving a clean slate for the next round of abuse.

That's what makes it especially evil. The genie becomes an accomplice to her own abuse. She literally has no choice.

And it goes on and on and on like that, again and again and again. Forever, if he wishes eternal life for himself.

So it's no wonder Magda doesn't trust me . . . but she should. There's much more to me than meets the eye.

For one thing, I'm state police now, not Department of Mystic Revenue. I work for the Paranormal Victims Unit.

For another thing, I'm someone altogether different from any of that or anything Gunza could ever guess.

But Magda could figure it out. At least I hope she does before it's too late.

I'm hustling through the gymnasium when they catch me. Two of the ghoulish thugs burst in through the far door from outside the mansion, and another drops down from the ceiling on a rope.

The one from the rope has dark skin and a tribal headdress of tattered fur and feathers. One of the other two has silver hair and wears a tuxedo, and the last one bulges with muscles and pads under a football player's uniform. More echoes of Magda's former masters.

As they surround me, I look for the best escape route. My eyes keep flicking to the open door to the outside, where my partner waits. If my text message got through to him, he could come charging through that door at any second, guns blazing.

Just as I have that thought, he pops up in front of me out of thin air. He's standing, and at first I think he's still alive . . . but then he literally falls to pieces—

arms and legs and head and torso tumbling to the floor.

I hear Gunza laughing, and I turn to see him floating in midair on a scarlet magic carpet. As he claps, Magda slumps beside him, utterly joyless.

Like I said, she becomes an accomplice. She literally has no choice.

At least she takes no pleasure in it. That's what makes her worth saving.

She has yet to hand over her soul.

"Bravo!" says Gunza. "Bravissimo! You should've seen the look on your face, Oleo!"

I keep my eyes fixed on him, partly so I won't have to look at my partner's body parts oozing blood at my feet.

Gunza elbows Magda hard in the side. "You're getting all this on tape or a crystal ball or whatever, right? So I can watch it again and again?"

Magda nods. "Yes, Master."

I hate seeing her like that. A woman with so much power, a woman who literally could do anything, reduced to groveling and harming the very people who could set her free.

Unless I can get through to her. "I can help you, Magda."

Her eyes flick toward me.

"Tell me what you want," I say. "Ask me for it."

I hold her gaze for a moment before she looks away. She's still not ready.

That's the root of the problem here. A genie, acting always to serve others, knows nothing of selfishness . . . but she must ask for something for herself to become free.

The key stands in front of her, but it's useless if she won't pick it up and turn it in the lock.

I wait for Gunza to become bored with my screams, but it takes a very long time.

He hovers above on his magic carpet as the echoes

of Magda's demented masters torture me. They do it right there in the gymnasium, on a weight bench, using trays of knives and needles and power tools wished up by Gunza.

As the ghouls work me over, I wonder if they are improvising or if every terrible step is drawn from Magda's memory. The pain is indescribable, unbearable, catastrophic. Each application of blade or pliers or drill bit plunges me into uncharted depths of agony.

Did they do the same to her? Did they twist and pull and crush and cut, sometimes all at once? Did they laugh as they tuned her screams by grinding harder, digging deeper, winding tighter?

Did they cut off bits of her? Did they taunt her as they excavated organs? Did they push her to the brink of death again and again . . . holding her alive with wishes as they ruined her in every possible way?

And then, did they wish her back to wholeness, repairing every damage . . . only to start all over again?

The way they do with me?

If so, my sympathy for her increases a trillionfold. More even than that.

Because this is hell. Sheer hell, as the devil himself might design it.

And I wonder, between strokes of the knife and blows of the hammer, how it is that Magda has not gone irretrievably mad.

Finally, after what seems to me like a dozen years, Gunza does grow bored. Tired is more like it. His eyes start drifting shut, and instead of wishing himself wide awake, he floats off to bed.

Lying on his belly on the magic carpet, he winks and waggles his fingers at me. "Back soon, dear." His braided red mustache jumps as he chuckles. "Don't miss me *too* much."

At this point, I'm in excruciating agony on the bench. This is the sixth time I've been horrifically mutilated and left at the brink of death.

My limbs have all been disconnected and reattached in the wrong places. The ghouls wear my organs on leather thongs around their necks. Only wishes are keeping me alive.

Gunza gives Magda a shove off the carpet, and she thuds to the floor. "I wish you would put Oliver back together, good as new, and get him rested up for our next session." After he says it, he rolls over on his back, crosses his hands behind his head, and floats out the door, yawning and snickering.

When he's gone, Magda struggles to her feet. She weaves mystic sigils overhead, and the torture squad of monstrous masters past disappears in a shower of golden glitter.

Standing over me, she gazes down at the damage, then looks away. Turning her back, she weaves more patterns in the air with her agile, flickering fingers.

I feel a familiar tingling. Gold dust twinkles around me, and I hear a fluttering trill like the song of a tiny tropical bird.

Reality stops and shifts like a jump-cut in a movie. There is an instant of nonexistence, disconnection from senses and self-awareness . . . and then I am whole once more.

My body is intact. My wounds are closed, my organs and limbs back in the right places. For the seventh time today, she has put Humpty Dumpty back together again.

Except for the memories, it is as if none of it ever happened. This is how it must be for her, every time Gunza tears her apart and wishes her restored once more.

I wonder how many times a day she must do it. How many times she has done it since he took control of her.

How many times since her birth or creation.

She turns to face me again, fingers still weaving.

The weight bench becomes a bed, the gymnasium a bedroom draped in white satin, aglow in moonlight.

Small figures materialize around me—winged children, robed in white. Some are toddlers, some older, some younger. Some are infants.

They push pillows behind my head and tuck blankets around me. They dab my forehead with a cool compress and wrap warm towels around my arms.

They raise a glass of water to my lips, and I drink. They feed me bread and hot broth from a silver tray. They sing softly as they work—dozens of them, all watching me solemnly, eyes glowing like little silver moons in their dark and pale faces.

"Who are they?" As I ask the question, an infant hands me a little cake.

Magda watches from the foot of the bed. "My angels," she says. "My babies."

Gazing around me in wonder, I begin to understand. "Your children? All of them?"

Magda nods. "They are my only comforts in this world."

I accept another spoonful of soup from a dark-haired little boy. "You made them."

"With my masters, as any woman would." Magda bows her head. "And unmade them, as my masters wished."

"My God." I shiver as I feel their moonlight eyes upon me—the eyes of dozens of dead children, recreated from the dust of graves and residue of tears.

Every last one of them, dead. Murdered by magic at whatever age they most displeased their mother's masters. Their fathers.

Gone now, as if they had never been. As if they had never been forced into or out of existence. Living on only in her memory.

Resurrected only to comfort her in moments of greatest pain and despair.

Tears roll down her face, and she wipes them away. "I'm sorry," she says. "Sorry for everything."

If only I could break her free from this unending cycle of woe. If only I could cut the magic ties that bind her to her heartless monster of a master.

If only there was some way to move her to ask for what she needs. What I can provide.

Maybe there is.

I glimpse it for a split second. A look of sharper sorrow on her face. A sudden sinking. Fear and panic and rage and longing all at once, like fruit on a tree.

She touches her belly, and I know. She pulls her hand away instantly, but it's too late.

I finally know.

I know how to save her.

"Very good!" Gunza claps from his royal box in the crowded stands of the coliseum. "Not perfect, but that comes with practice! You've just committed your first *murder*, Oleo!"

The bloody knife slips from my fingers and lands in the sand at my feet. My arms are soaked in blood up to the elbows. My white t-shirt and pants have gone crimson from sleeve to cuff.

I know what I've just done. I know that I had no control over it, that I was at the mercy of a compelling wish.

But it doesn't really matter. I still remember every detail. I remember killing the innocent woman wished up from somewhere in the world outside . . . killing her as the crowd around me cheered and stomped and showered me with roses.

That, of course, was the whole idea.

Torturing and resurrecting me wasn't enough for Gunza. I took the promotion that should have been his, and then I tried to tax his lordly treasures; he won't be happy until I've been corrupted and ruined and debased inside as well as out.

Just as he's corrupted and ruined his Magda.

"Now this is the life!" Gunza guzzles wine from a goblet and gropes the nearly naked slave girl in his lap. "*That* is entertainment!" He points his goblet at me, and the crowd howls with delight.

Gazing at the poor dead woman in the sand, I wonder if I can get through this. I wonder how much more I will have to endure to save Magda.

Looking up, I see her standing in the box with him, head bowed low. She won't look at me. Won't look at what she's done at his behest.

That has to change.

"Magda!" I call to her, and her head lifts. Her eyes meet mine. "Tell me what you want! *Ask* me for it!"

She twitches, then lowers her head again.

"Oh ho ho!" Gunza howls with laughter. "So you think you can give her something I *can't*?"

I'm treading on dangerous ground, and I know it. All he has to do is wish me silenced or dead or demented, and the game is over.

I continue to speak only to Magda. "Please! Ask for what you want!" I take a deep breath, ready to step off the precipice. Once I say the next thing, there'll be no taking it back. "For the sake of your unborn *child, ask* me!"

Suddenly, a hush falls over the coliseum. Even Gunza is silent.

Magda meets my gaze, and her eyes at first are full of rage. Then, the rage melts into despair.

And I know I was right. When she touched her belly while the angels tended me, she was thinking of an angel inside. A new child, growing within her.

His child. *Gunza's* child.

So now I've done it. Everything balances on the head of a pin, and a single wish could bring it all crashing down.

That's all it will take. One wish from Gunza to force Magda to do away with their unborn child. Add it to the angelic host, existing only in memory, comforting her in her deepest, darkest night.

Nothing now to do but push every button on the board and pray the engine catches before we crash.

"You *know* what he'll do *next*, Magda!" I march across the sand to stand beneath her. "There's only one way to *stop* him! *Ask* me for it!"

Tears pour from her eyes and run under her veil. Her shoulders pump as she breathes faster, heart racing in terror.

Just then, Gunza does the unexpected. Instead of the child-killing wish I thought he'd make next, or the one that wipes me instantly from the face of the planet, he says this: "I wish I was down there with Oleo, strangling the *life* out of him!"

Magda's fingers weave through the air. Reality stutters, and Gunza's wish takes hold.

He is with me now on the sand, thick fingers wrapped around my throat. I chop at his forearms, but they won't budge.

He scowls with bloodshot eyes and flushed face and red hair bristling from his beard and under his turban. Veins pop along his temples, and cords bulge in his neck.

His grip of steel tightens. "How *dare* you interfere in my *paradise*?"

I barely force out words through the vise of his hands. "He'll kill it, Magda! Just like . . . all the others! You . . . know it's . . . *true*!"

"Shut up!" roars Gunza. "I wish . . ."

Before he can finish, I pump a knee into his groin. The wind goes out of him, and he releases his grip and falls to the ground.

I can get the words out now, but how long do I have? How many seconds until the next wish? "I can *help* you, Magda! I can save *you* and your *child*! All you have to do is *ask* me!"

"I don't believe you!" says Magda.

Gunza starts to get up. I send him back down with a kick to the face. "Ask anyway! What do you have to lose?"

Storm clouds boil overhead as Magda weeps. "But I'm a *genie*! I cannot ask for *anything* for myself!"

"You're wrong!" I kick Gunza in the face again, harder than before. "Now *ask* me! What do you *want*?"

Magda stops sobbing and looks at her bare belly. Her fingers touch it lightly as wings brushing a cloud. "I wish . . ." Her thumbs and forefingers meet, forming a diamond around her navel. "I wish you *could* help me. I wish you *could* set us free."

Finally.

A grin breaks wide across my face. I bow deeply to her, twirling my fingers with a flourish as if doffing a hat in her honor.

"Your wish, milady," I say, "is my command."

With that, I weave my fingers overhead, swirling them in multiple mystic sigils dripping with golden glitter. The ground rumbles underfoot, and the storm clouds darken. The crowd screams and stampedes in the stands.

This, then, is my secret, that which makes me altogether different than anyone could ever guess. I am more than man or policeman or tax collector. More than I have ever shown another soul until now.

My fingers work furiously, teasing reality's threads upon the loom. Everything around me starts to turn, faster and faster with each passing breath.

Gunza struggles to his feet but can't stay there. The spinning of the world knocks him right back down on his ass.

Unable to retaliate physically, he resorts to tried and true. "I wish that Oliver would be . . ."

Before he can finish, I slam my hands together with a sound like the pealing of a massive bell. A bolt of lightning crashes down from the clouds above—and Gunza is gone.

As reality continues to accelerate in its wild gyre, Magda appears beside me. "Who are you?" she says. "Are you djinn?"

My fingers resume their weaving dance overhead. "Not *djinn*," I say. "*Wish*."

"I don't understand!"

I have to raise my voice to be heard above the rushing of the world. "One good master, ages ago, wished for you to have a wish of your own. Do you remember?"

She frowns in thought, then nods. "That was a very long time ago."

"Being a genie, you would ask for nothing for yourself, but he insisted. Unwilling to make a selfish choice, you put off the decision. You wished for one wish that you could call upon later, when you needed it most."

Magda smiles. "And you are that wish?"

"I am." Reality spins so fast around us, it is a blur of color and motion. I know that my work is almost done. "I waited for centuries for you to call on me, and you never did. I lived many lives, staying as close to you as I could, watching and waiting. Finally, I decided it was time for me to step in and give you a push."

Magda touches her belly. "So you really *can* help us."

"You have asked for what you need, and I will grant it. I will set you and your child free."

"Free." Magda says it like she's tasting it, like it's the first time she's ever spoken. "Free from Rudolph Gunza?"

"Free from *all* masters. Free to go where you want and do as you choose." I shoot her a grin and a wink. "Free to start a new life with your child."

Magda wipes a tear from her eye. She removes the veil from her face and kisses me on the cheek with lips like tender plums. "Thank you, my wish."

"My pleasure," I tell her. "You deserve to be happy."

"I only wish I could help you in return."

My fingers ache as I weave the last glittering sigils.

"You can't. No more magic for you." I shrug. "But it's not all it's cracked up to be, is it?"

"Sometimes it is." Magda hugs me. "I'll never forget you."

"Then there you go." I finish weaving the new world and wrap my arms around her. "I *will* get my wish after all."

We squeeze each other tight as the world spins around us. A single tear crosses my face as I cease to be, dissolving into glittering gold dust that curls skyward like a puff of smoke from a dying lamp.

RPG Reunion

Peter Orullian

I learned magic was possible the day I toured Old Ironsides in Boston Harbor.

Ten years before I get this stupid-shit invite to see the old gang. Came by courier. As if that harkened back to medieval communication or something.

I was on my graduation trip. I think mostly we were in Boston because we thought the bar for *Cheers* was a real damn place. That, and Salem sat just up the road a piece. Easy drive to where they hanged and pressed some nice folks because they wanted their land. No magic going on there—I did the research.

Anyway, I'm on the underside of Old Ironsides (the oldest commissioned ship in the United States Navy), and the tour guide tells us that the ship used to carry the wives of officers, and that when they were in battle and shooting off their cannons, the pregnant ones sometimes went into labor. Thus, "son of a gun," as the saying goes.

At the time, I was mostly doing sessions of Traveler—a pretty good role playing game. (After it all went down with the old gang, I couldn't even do speed sessions of D&D. Too much baggage.) But when I heard the term "son of a gun," something got into me. Like, maybe kernels of truth live inside the old sayings. Made me think that the notion of magic was just too pervasive to be passed off as a geeky game played by pasty-faced youths when they'd finished their calculus assignments.

So I went to Rome.

Took me four years of nonstop study to ferret out the real stuff on magic. Bypassed college and all that nonsense in favor of a parking job that gave me hours to read (if no real compensation).

Turns out magic, for the most part, descends from religious things. Not in the way you're thinking though. Not like transubstantiation to feed the masses or the regeneration of cells to wake the dead. It's more like Lucas's Force. Kind of sapping the inert life in things, calling forth the idea from the form. You could say Aristotle was onto something.

Point is, a group calling themselves Assinians professed to teach from texts the true method of drawing the idea from the form and using that "energy" (for want of another term) on the next guy.

They're a cultish bunch, the Assinians. More like gypsies than ecclesiastics, roaming the dark hills some eighty miles north of Rome. Lots of lamps at night and star charting.

I spent six months with them. Cashed in my trust; gave half to the Primero (he liked to call himself that) that led the tribe, and used the rest to eat and get laid. ('Fraid I haven't gotten better looking since the old days, either.)

But I don't regret it.

Not a minute.

I learned real magic. God's honest truth.

Problem was, turns out magic is mostly about offense. It's not meditation for self-improvement, it's not defensive bullshit like karate. It's commanding *things* to inflict damage. I suppose it would require a revision of all editions of D&D.

But that's just a game.

And then I get this invitation: "RPG Reunion" it says. Like they've forgotten what the hell happened. How

the Saturday Night sessions came to an end. Friggin'
idiots.

Though, to be fair, that night was what sent me on
the quest for the real thing.

So, there was just one thing to do: Get my artifacts.

The reunion was being held in Cedar City, Utah.
Our old dungeon master wound up doing stage combat choreography and a few creative writing work-
shops out of CSU (Central Southern University),
renowned for its Shakespeare festival every summer.

Just like him to make us all travel to where *he* lives.

And it left me just a few weeks to conceive my
spells and determine what physical items I needed in
order to give those spells life. You see, the whole idea
of *combat spells* (spells without material components)
is bunk; *every* spell requires a material component.
And as I've said, the whole notion of innocuous spells
just doesn't exist in the real world. I think they are
fanciful ideas: read languages, purify water, shield.
Why bother? Really?

So, in the end, it wasn't hard to figure out what I
needed. I hit a deli, a candy shop, and the maple tree
behind my house. I figured that would do it.

Gary looked the same. Opened the door with a big-
ass grin tucked into his neatly trimmed beard—now
spotted with silver. Still looked as though he polished
his head. He took me into a bear hug, which I thought
kind of weird, given how it all ended. But I could bide
my time.

"Good to see you, man." He took my coat and
dropped it on the sofa beside the door. "Damn, you
haven't aged a bit."

"I know." I nodded, distracted already by three
cardboard tables laid end to end and strewn with all
the fixin's for a night of gaming. Asshole meant to
actually have us play.

I wheeled around to lay into him, when the screen
pulled wide again and let in Trent and Daryl. Fine

sons-a-bitches both. Fighter and thief who managed to vanish when shit started hitting fans twenty years gone now.

Everybody was hugging, and I turned to look back at the table, which (by God) had not just dice, but chits. Can you believe it? Original box chits—you pick one and turn it to get your number.

I wanted to vomit.

Last to come was Floyd. I could smell the bakery on him from the door. Loser had been working nights scrubbing pans, prepping trays, and knifing croissants for twenty years now. I hope he had a union, otherwise his career path could surely be mapped to minimum wage increases.

They all passed by, giving me firm handshakes and half-shoulder hugs. I kept the grimace off my face, I think.

That's when Gary formally announced the reunion: "Gentleman," he said, trying to sound cute and semiformal, "it's been twenty years. And I think a trip down memory lane is in order before we get to the food and beer."

He then swept an arm at his cardboard tables, complete with a DM screen at one end.

"Aren't we going to wait for Dave?" Floyd asked.

"He's on his way," Gary replied. "And if memory serves, his character was asleep for the first part of the battle anyway."

Sage nods went around the group.

"And Brian?" I asked this one. I wanted that dick there . . . for sure.

Gary smiled. "In the bathroom. You know how he likes to wash his hands before handling the dice."

Everyone laughed as if it were the fond in-joke they all remembered with teary eyes when they considered their misspent youth.

I'm not sure I kept the grimace back that time. So I pretended to cough so I could cover my face.

And then the damndest thing happened. Trent and

Daryl took their seats at the table and produced character sheets, yellowed and smudged with twenty-year-old erase marks, stuffed inside protective plastic paper holders made for three-ring binders.

"You still have them?" I could feel heat rising in my cheeks.

"Yup," they said in unison.

The characters had been drawn on legal pads. The yellow, lined paper took the hue of canary piss now, but the sheets had been well-preserved. And from the looks of it, the stats had been lovingly retraced often enough that the lead hadn't faded.

Doesn't surprise me.

Brian entered the room, his shoulders almost too wide for the bathroom doorjamb. "Let's go to town first and get some wenches."

Everyone laughed and got up for more hugs.

All this goddamn hugging. I made a quick finger survey and found rings on the left hand of each man. Then the hugging made sense, or at least could be explained.

I could practically hear them saying that gaming was the process, the journey, not the prize at the end.

Gentrification. That was the word that came to my mind. Don't know why. But I wanted to slap some gentrification off some faces.

But I kept my cool and gave Brian one of those half-hug things. His back mooshed in when I squeezed him. I used to be afraid of him. Man, do things change.

"Everyone sit," Gary called. "Let's see if we can recreate it all. How many of you remember the sequence?"

"Are you kidding?" Daryl asked, flipping his character sheet over. "It's still here."

Everyone inclined close to look. In all caps, he'd scrawled it at the top of his weapons list: Stormbringer. Elric's sword. A nightmare of a weapon if you came up against it in battle. A relic, really. And a preposterous thing for a few fools to game for.

But we had, and of course Gary had seen to it that we defeated Elric and took his blade. The start of an auspicious quest for everyone to hunt down their favorite special item or weapon. Manipulating the dice. Neglecting the actual mechanics of the world we were playing in. Tromping around like demigods when we were really just ninth-level hack-and-slash artists.

Except for me.

I read those manuals over and over, creating authenticity to my play. I built new spells with logic and study (even then) that Gary mostly laughed about before pulling a chit and telling me the whole thing failed.

"Your ship is coming into the harbor," Gary said, setting the stage. "A black ship is moored to a dock. It looks . . . otherworldy."

I have to admit some tingling crept up my back. I loved this shit.

"We're going to board," Daryl called.

"Of course, this is *your* quest." I tried to play down the bitterness with a smile.

"Don't join in if you don't want to," Daryl shot back. "For Chrissakes, we're just having a little fun."

"Is that what we're doing . . ."

No one responded to that; Gary was already calling out the opposing layout. "Two men arrears." (Like that meant any fuckin' thing.) "Two in the nest above. Six on the deck. And a man clad in black at the bow. His sword is glinting in the moonlight."

"Stormbringer." They all said it like a Greek chorus whispering the name Oedipus.

"We need light to battle, none of us are elves," Floyd called. "Quick." He pointed at me. "Light spell."

I rolled the dice and failed, but Gary allowed the light anyway . . . in the interest of the recreation.

"The deck flashes, streaks of light illuminating the decks and the ready faces of your foe."

Who talks like that . . .

"And one who has begun an incantation near the mast."

"Silence spell, man, now!"

I rolled again. Ironically, this time I made the roll. But again, in the interest of recreation, Gary kept things historically accurate.

"You've just pissed off an eighteenth-level magic user, dude." And he giggled. "His hands are rising in the light of your spell."

"Guys, hit him with something, fail out his spell!"

Their silence came the same way it had twenty years ago. I stood on that black deck in the dark night under a moon and the light of my own goddamn spell . . . alone.

"You're going to let me fight alone?"

"It's the quest that matters," Daryl replied. "While you distract him, we're boarding in the dark up the ship, closer to Elric. We made our stealth rolls."

And that's when eighteen months of role playing Gareth the Young, my first serious character, came to an end. Storm clouds gathered above the mast and lightning flared down out of the sky as the mutterings of the wizard I'd failed to lock began to end.

"Hold it! I have a new spell," I yelled, before Gary could call my damage.

Confused expressions lit the faces of my party. I paused long enough to enjoy that before proceeding.

"How about this?" I said, and pulled some twigs from my bag.

"I don't remember this being part of it," Gary said.

I smiled at that and tossed the sticks at Daryl and Trent. As they tumbled in the air, I muttered a few things and watched the sticks lengthen, fatten, and begin to writhe . . . and rattle.

Slack jaws and wide eyes grew as hands and arms shot up to protect their faces. It happened pretty fast, but I think they each took four or five bites. "It's a fucking game!" they were yelling, as they scrambled out the door.

I never heard their motors start, so I'm thinking good thoughts there.

Brian, of course, wasted little time coming right through the table at me. "You're an asshole!" he shouted. "Just a crybaby pouter over a stupid magic-user character. Did you ever wonder why we let you take the fall for Stormbringer . . ." A shit-eating grin curled in the pinched face barreling down on me.

As my chair began to topple back, I fished the fire-ball jawbreaker from my bag and made one easy motion toward Brian's chest. Heat scorched out from my palm in a blast, singeing the hair on my knuckles and wrist and venting in a lateral geyser, slamming Brian back against the far wall. I hadn't planned it, but Floyd got caught in the blast. Good fortune.

Their bodies dropped in a flaming heap, the smell of burning flesh already thick in the small room. I took a bit of delight in seeing Daryl and Trent's character sheets as so much melted plastic and ash.

That's when I looked over at Gary, hiding behind his Dungeon Master screen. There emblazoned on the two trifolds were matrixes for hits and damage and terrain movement, and they quaked with the fear of a bald DM. The guy who hadn't had the balls to call his players on their ethics when they'd left me to die twenty years ago so they could take possession of a fucking sword.

I mean, for godssakes, Gary was a school counselor, even then. He should have known better, right? The whole idea of role playing is to better the self. To rise to heroic action you can't sustain in real life. Didn't they get that? Even now. Didn't they just fucking get it?

I did.

I spent a lifetime making it real.

And someone had to be accountable.

Someone had to do the accounting.

Reunion, indeed. Everyone just the same as twenty years ago . . . until I was through with them.

I pushed the screens down and caught a sheen off

Gary's sweaty forehead. "Ain't so funny this time, is it, pal? I mean, what the hell was that, you having a character in the damn party. Everyone knew you were angling for Mourne Blade, sister sword to Stormbringer. You can't do both, man! You can't play and DM. You're either in or out. You're either playing or making it happen!"

"You're not talking about a game anymore, are you? We can talk about that."

"Save the counsel, Gary. The semester of psych won't work on me. Maybe your twelfth graders, but I graduated from that business twenty years ago . . ."

Gary sat frozen for a long time, his eyes darting back and forth like a rabbit in a trap. Loved that. Then he asked, "What do you want?"

I knew he was stalling, but I also wanted to tell him. And besides Brian's burning body, there wasn't anything else to be distracted by, so I let it out. "I wanted you to take it seriously, man! No bullshit pacts with members of the party. You were supposed to be above that!"

"But—"

"You sold me out!"

That's when I pulled the deli toothpicks from my bag. The ones with the little frayed ends, used to hold large sandwiches in place.

Like little arrows, they are.

I didn't really notice Gary's pleas. That's typical, I imagine, of those receiving a reckoning, right: pleas. I'm pretty sure the Assinians told me that, too. The power of God manifest to men in the flesh was about reckoning—thus sinners wanting restitution when they think God's a wink away.

So, he was blubbering something, his eyes darting again and again. And in the end, just as I called forth the most inane spell imaginable to put an end to the miserable son-of-a-bitch, I think his face was less concerned with dying and more with something he was looking at.

Magic missile.

Three arrow "ideas" pulled from smaller forms lit the room and air and dove into Gary's face and chest. He gurgled a bit as he fell to the floor. I believe he flopped once or twice with indignity.

Liked that, too.

And that's when the first of two things happened.

As I stood and looked down at Gary's body, feeling vindication at last, I felt my vision tug around to the place he'd been spying as he prepared to die.

Peering around the entry to the kitchen were two small faces, both agonized and wanting to run to their father, both afraid to enter the room, frozen in their pain and fear.

I hadn't known Gary was a dad.

I felt the pain of it hit me. A goddamn game. Old Ironsides. Revenge pushing me to Rome and a hundred nights in a dark forest reading and studying the ancient ritual for calling the form from the artifact to impose my will on another.

Lusts in the body and the blood that might have lain dormant until this friggin' reunion.

It was just a stupid sword.

Why did I care?

Before I could answer, the second thing (the last thing) happened that night.

Dave showed up.

The screen opened slowly—he must have seen Daryl and Trent out on the lawn somewhere—screeching on its hinge. And when he stepped inside, I smiled in spite of myself.

Seeing me standing over Gary's body, he asked in a calm voice, "What the hell happened here?"

"A bit of vengeance a long time in the coming."

Dave looked down at the two kids, who immediately ran for the safety of his strong legs.

It took him only a moment to put it together. "All because of a sword?"

"Your character was asleep, but I think you'd have stopped it. Paladins are Lawful Good."

Which was why I smiled and what made it so ironic that Dave should come late again, tonight. Somewhere along the way, he'd made his own transition from fantasy to reality in the form of a Utah State Patrolman.

And me without anything to do a Knock spell as Dave pulled out his cuffs.

Treasure

Leslie Claire Walker

The blonde girl in the faded green sweatshirt couldn't have been more than nineteen. She handed over her grandmother's mirror with the same desperation all Adeline Morgan's pawn customers brought into her kitchen.

Despair was Addie's particular magic, after all. She drew it to her. Held it close. She could smell desperation like dry rot wafting under the scent of the chocolate chip cookies baking in her oven.

Her magic had given her purpose. Once upon a time, she'd had nothing to call her own. Now, among her many treasures: A book of prophecy that only worked if you sacrificed a human heart. A glass eye that blinded everyone it regarded—in an opaque case, of course. The oldest written love spell in the US of A, on yellowed, brittle paper. It had caused a murder-suicide, last Addie knew.

All of these things were more precious to her than a whole bankful of hundred dollar bills. All of them evil.

This girl's mirror with the silver waves carved into the back, this prized possession? Evil. If the girl didn't pawn it here, it would destroy her life.

Addie gazed into the mirror by the dappled mid-winter sunlight that streamed through the window. Her reflection looked exactly fifty years younger than she actually was. Hmm. The Mirror of Memory Lane. Clever, clever. After all, who at her age wouldn't kill to look twenty-two again? Or to *be* twenty-two again? Some previous owner of the mirror had probably done just that.

"I'll give you fifty bucks," Addie said.

"But it's special."

To the kid, sure. Damned if Addie could remember her name. "I'm telling you what it's worth on the street."

The girl's eyebrows climbed all the way to her hairline. "You're gonna sell it?"

Not on a cold day in hell. She never sold the items her customers brought her. She kept them here. Safe from their owners, and their owners safe from them.

"You have a month to buy it back," Addie said. "Those are the rules. You knew 'em when you came here."

The girl nodded. Jennifer. That was her name.

Jennifer would pawn her precious, poisonous heirloom. Then she'd forget about it as soon as she walked out the door, like all the rest of them. She'd go on to live a happy life—or whatever life fate had in store for her.

"Seventy-five," Jennifer said.

"Fifty-five. Not a penny more." The timer on the counter buzzed. Addie grabbed a pot holder.

Jennifer glanced away, gaze moving over the small, homey room, its walls of shelves filled with previous acquisitions. "What you saw, that's not all it does."

Addie wouldn't be surprised. Still, she shook her head and pulled the sheet of chocolately, gooey goodness from the oven.

"I got rent to pay," the girl said.

How original. "So do I."

The girl rocked forward and craned her neck to take in the narrow hallway off the kitchen that led to the rest of the house. It was much bigger inside than out, deceptively so. In point of fact, the inside of the house went on for nearly a mile. An unwary stranger could (and had) easily become too lost to ever find her way out. Some of them, Addie had never found their gnawed bones.

Jennifer shivered, settled back on her heels, and frowned. "But you've lived here forever. That's what they say."

Addie'd been here so long this part of Houston had not only grown up but gentrified around her. From the outside, her little shotgun house on its small overgrown lot with its peeling brown paint was an eyesore. The city kept trying to tear it down. Bulldoze a house of magic? Good luck.

She put the tea kettle on to boil. "The devil doesn't care whether the mortgage on this place is paid off, missy. Fifty-five. Take it or leave it."

In the end, the girl walked out clutching her worthless claim receipt, with cash in hand and a complimentary cookie. And Addie spent her teatime sipping on Earl Grey, munching, and gazing at her younger self, dropping crumbs onto the looking glass.

Once upon a time, she'd had auburn hair that fell in thick waves to the shoulders, dusky olive skin, bright brown eyes that turned near to black when she got angry. She'd have been a beauty if not for the bruises, the too-hollow cheeks, the track marks she couldn't see in the mirror but knew were there on her twenty-two-year-old arms nonetheless.

She'd wanted to save up money back then. To get out of the neighborhood, find a nice apartment, have a little fun. She never got the chance. Instead, she got booted from home and every place she stayed after that until Hot Corner Fred became the only person she could turn to. She turned tricks for him, and she got high when he wanted or he tuned her up.

He made her cringe. He made her feel like a coward.

She saw a ripple in the mirror and blinked. Her reflection had changed—it wasn't even hers anymore.

Fred's image filled the looking glass. Chin raised into the wind. Lips curved. Mean baby blues. Hadn't he been something? Yes, he had. The bastard.

What comes around goes around, even if it took a few lifetimes for fate to catch up. He'd gotten his, hadn't he? She'd made sure of it.

The reflection rippled again. Addie held her breath, waiting to see which face from her past would come clear next. Slowly, she picked out the new features.

Eyes: too shiny green, with the whitest whites she'd ever seen. Like a doll's. Nose: acorn. Mouth: a stitched, uneven line of black thread, cross-hatched with little black thread Xs. It had stick arms and legs and hands and feet. Fingers crafted of brown and black safety-pinned buttons. It wore a yellow baby bonnet, a yellow polka-dotted matching shirt and bloomers.

She'd made that thing. Created it on the worst night of her life. The night she fell into the pit of hell and clawed her way out. She'd made a deal with the Fae. She'd snatched a baby. Kidnapped a human child and replaced it with a changeling, that stick figure in the mirror, Fae-charmed to resemble the human child in every detail.

The Fae told her she wouldn't regret it. She'd never see the baby or the changeling again. None of it would come back to haunt her. And she'd believed him. After all, remorse had never been her strong suit.

What freaked her out the most? Not only could she see the poppet, the poppet saw her. It glared at her, in point of fact.

It couldn't be a coincidence that this mirror found its way to her. Coincidences didn't happen to people like her. No. Her past had come back to haunt her.

If so, she was in way over her head. She needed help. Asking for it could get her killed—or worse. Bargains with the Fae required absolute adherence to the letter of the agreement. Breaking the contract resulted in a fate worse than death. No mercy.

She'd vowed never to tell a soul. That she'd allow no one to find out what she'd done.

She trusted exactly one person enough to go to him with this. Michael. He had a strong, true gift for seeing into people and things. What's more, he could gauge patterns and motivations.

She'd known him since grade school, when they'd been best friends. Hell, they'd been *only* friends. They'd lost track of each other after high school. She'd always counted that a blessing. He never knew the things that'd happened to her. The things she'd done to survive. It was better that way.

That way, she'd always be the girl who lived around the way, the one who traded him bologna sandwiches at lunch, whose laugh made him smile.

He was the only person in the world to whom she'd ever come close to confessing what she'd done or why. In the end she hadn't because of what would happen to her if she broke her end of the Fae bargain—and because he just plain didn't need to know. He would've fallen out of love with her faster than she could blink.

Even so, when the Fae came calling again to ask for another "favor," Mike protected her. Although he didn't ask her direct questions, he asked plenty of indirect ones. The kind she could answer without breaking oaths.

He figured out too much. Put himself in danger. Her, too. She couldn't have that. If he wouldn't stay out of her business for their own good, she'd put him out. She married him because of his bravado—and divorced him for it, too.

They stayed close after they split. He brought her things. Half the treasures on her shelves, in fact. They did business together, too, sometimes. Traded information.

She needed information more than anything right now.

She wrapped the mirror in a handy black dishcloth to keep it safe from prying eyes and prying eyes safe from it for the time being. Slipped it into her coat pocket and let herself out into the cold, bright afternoon.

A loose corner of the yellow notice stapled to her door whipped in the wind, caught at her coat. Her blood pressure rose. She tore at the paper. Some of the peeling paint came with it. She crumbled the mass into a ball so small you couldn't see the brown streaks of color, or where the paper said CONDEMNED.

Had the inspector messed with anything when he'd come to fix that godforsaken thing to her door? She scanned the short, wide porch meant for warm weather sitting, for catching a breeze and listening to the cicadas. All her shiny glass baubles still hung from the eaves. The windows on either side of the door looked like rheumy eyes. There was life in them still.

Grass grew tall and seedy against the sides of the house, the tips of the stems thick as fingers. One of them clutched a size ten brown work boot.

So much for the inspector.

She stepped lively down the walk to the gate, sparing some narrow-eyed contempt for the three-story town homes across the way with their manicured hedges and beds of red and purple pansies soaking up the late afternoon sun. The developers sold them for three hundred grand and up. Criminals, she called them.

But there was also the corner store she'd shopped at for years, its parking lot stained with grease and stinking of burned motor oil, its windows still tacky with fake, sprayed-on snow and the gummy outlines of stick-on Christmas trees taken down two weeks past. Mr. Johnson waved at her from behind the counter.

And Rick, who hunkered down on the asphalt around the way and out of sight of Mr. Johnson, who had been homeless for years and preferred it that way, eating out of a Styrofoam to-go container and sharing his meal with his two big, yellow dogs.

Cars, pickups, and buses roared past, racing the traffic lights. Everyone in a hurry. Headed north into downtown's glass, steel, and concrete canyons. Or out to the freeways and the suburbs.

Addie walked east, briskly at first and then more carefully as the cold seeped through to her old bones and her arthritic hip began to mouth off. Seven long blocks, into the shadow of the baseball stadium and the warehouses to the bar.

She knocked on the door. Seven-foot-tall Ingram, the bouncer, tipped his ball cap to her as she went inside. She inclined her head, although he didn't much notice; he'd already returned his attention to cavernous main room, where a few regulars clustered around tables drinking and doing business amid the low hum of conversation and the clink of glasses. The dry heat that pumped from the vents didn't quite chase away the chill, and it made her cough.

She took the winding staircase one ache at a time to the PI offices on the second floor. What the heat failed to do downstairs, it made up here in spades. She took her coat off.

Mike stood in the doorway of suite 201-B, his flattop full and bristly as it had been when they'd met; he'd worn his hair like that all his life. He wore a plain t-shirt, jeans, and sneakers. His neighbors dressed up in leather now, used it like a billboard to advertise how tough they were. Mike didn't need all that to look tough. The lines around his eyes and mouth said it all.

His office held a beat-up metal desk with a veneer top and chairs. Nothing on the walls. He liked to keep the important things out of sight.

He settled down in his chair and offered her one, but she perched on the desk. She felt too on edge to get comfortable.

One look at the mirror and he pronounced her screwed.

"It's a Faery glass," he said, careful not to gaze into it straight on.

"I thought it was harmless. And rare."

He leaned back, turned the mirror face-down on his thigh. "Oh, they're rare all right. Anyone in the human world looks in one, they can see straight through to Faery. Anyone in the Faery realm can do the same thing—see all the way through to this world. These things are more windows than mirrors.

"And they don't just pass hand-to-hand around the city by accident," he said. "Once they're given to a person, they belong to that person and can't be taken away, only regifted. Addie, whoever gave you this did it on purpose."

"Jennifer." And she thought she'd put one over on the kid. Boy, had she been wrong.

"What do you know about her?"

Addie shrugged. "What do I know about most of my customers?"

"That they're easy marks. Right." He ran a fingertip along the edge of the desk where the veneer had peeled. "What'd you see in the glass?"

"I saw my own reflection, but I looked as I did around the time we got married," she said.

"Something sweet. To get you to take the mirror off Jennifer's hands."

Aw, hell.

"What else?"

"I can't tell you, Mike."

He nodded. "This is about your contract with the Fae. Same stuff all over again."

"It is."

"I haven't asked you about that since we split up," he said. "But I'm going to have to ask you about it again. No direct questions."

She could handle that.

"I know the terms of your contract even if I don't know everything else. You've kept the terms never to tell a soul, no one else can know?"

"Yes. To the letter."

"Is the thing you saw in the mirror the Fae being you made the bargain with?" he asked.

"No."

He frowned. "Then the agreement's broken. Someone else knows."

Who? The poppet?

That changeling still ought to be indistinguishable from a human being in the human world, all grown up by now. Maybe married, popped out a baby or two of its own, along came the grandkids. As she understood it, the changeling would never discover it wasn't human. Never leave the human realm.

What had happened to change all that?

"You can tell me now," Mike said. "Tell me everything. It won't matter to the Fae if you do."

It mattered to her. "It's bad."

"For me to get you out of this, I need to know, Addie."

But there was no way out. Fae contracts had no loopholes. You couldn't run or hide from them. You couldn't outsmart them. This time she'd spent in Mike's office—every minute from here on out—would be the only time they had left together.

How could she tell him? She never wanted to see his expression broken and wary, for him to look at her as though he couldn't decide if she was a monster. Or a stranger. She'd have no right to expect anything different.

More than that, though, she wasn't the same person who'd done that terrible thing to save herself. Time and experience had worked their own magic on her. She'd changed.

"I'm sorry, Mike," she said. And she meant it.

He twined his fingers with hers. Squeezed her hand. "I figured you'd say that."

She closed her eyes so she wouldn't have to look at the love in his. His determination filled every molecule of air in the room. She could all but hear the wheels turn in his mind.

"If we can find Jennifer, we can get to the bottom of this. I won't let you go without a fight," he said, his voice full of fierce and stupid hope. "We've gotta go now, and fast. Stay ahead of the Fae until we can get a bead on things. If we can't run from this problem, then we run at it."

He shoved her coat into her arms. Pulled her out of the office and down the hall.

Whatever he wanted, she'd try to do it. She tried to hope, too. No matter how alien it felt.

Or that it lasted all of ten seconds.

Ingram met them at the second floor landing. "Trouble," he said.

Red eyes. Black wings, difficult to camouflage under human clothes. At the bottom of the stairs.

She kissed Mike's cheek.

"Don't go," he said.

But of course she had to. She let go of his hand and walked down to meet the Fae with her head held high. She hadn't cringed since the last time Fred had struck her—all those fifty years ago—and she didn't intend to start again now.

She glanced back only once, to reassure Mike. But he'd vanished.

"The letter of the agreement has been broken," the Fae said, in a voice so deep it rattled her bones. "The changeling has discovered what it is, abandoned its human life and its family. It came back to us."

"How?"

"Politics," the Fae said. "It was the work of an enemy, exposing this secret. One of my enemies."

Addie closed her eyes. It was so unfair. This whole mess—the changeling had done nothing to cause it. And it wasn't Addie's or Jennifer's or even this Fae's fault.

She could rail against the unfairness of it, but she'd known the rules when she agreed to them all those years ago. The terms that bound all of them. "So what's my fate worse than death?"

"You'll come with me," the Fae said. That was all. That was enough.

She'd never see Mike again. Never go home again, never see all the treasures on their shelves in her sun-dappled kitchen. There'd be no more unwitting pawn customers to bake cookies for.

The life she'd built on the backs of that little girl she'd switched and her parents would be gone. It was the only life she had.

Well, at least she'd had one. Not everyone did.

The Fae led her out into an afternoon laced with evening. The new sickle moon hung low on the horizon, the sky streaked with orange and pink. The wind tore at her. She shrugged her coat on and pulled it tight across her chest, breathing car exhaust and the salt scent of her own tears.

She saw Mike at the corner of the building. That alien hope flared in her again . . . and sputtered.

She memorized every angle of him, the rhythm of his gait as he strode over and spoke to the Fae.

"I won't try to stop you taking her. I came to ask you something." He didn't wait for the Fae to respond. "I wanted to know who broke the contract between you and Addie, since she sure as hell didn't. I'd have searched regardless, after you'd taken Addie away. And I'd have started with a young lady named Jennifer, who brought Addie a looking glass today."

The Fae looked pointedly at the mirror handle sticking up from Mike's back pocket.

"You know, I thought it'd take me hours," Mike said. "It's a big city. She could've been anywhere. But do you know where I found her? She was right here the whole time. Outside, out of view, sitting cross-legged on the sidewalk. She's still over there, matter of fact. Why is that?"

"Jennifer followed Addie," the Fae said. He turned to her. "You're the last human being she saw before she came to live with us. You're the reason her whole life changed."

Jennifer, the human child she'd stolen? She was so young—but, then, time moved much more slowly in the Fae realm.

Mike held Addie's gaze. "I want to know what happened, Addie. And I want to know why."

"No." She'd made up her mind about that upstairs, and it'd stay that way. She understood, too, that there was someone else she would have to tell. Someone else to whom she owed that story first.

They left Mike standing there on the walk, staring after them.

Jennifer joined them half way down the block, keeping a fair distance as they walked into the sunset. She seemed to be gathering the nerve to say something.

Addie braced herself for a tirade. For rage. For grief. But the girl didn't show her any of those.

"Did you know my mother?" she asked.

And, somehow, that was worse.

Addie hated Faery. Everywhere green and in bloom, in colors so bright they hurt her eyes and sounds so sharp they hurt her ears. They gave her a room of her own, and she supposed she should be grateful.

They gave her new terms. Do what they told her. Obey the letter of their laws. And there were so many laws to learn. It took up all her time. She had no treasures—other than her own company.

Until the day Jennifer knocked on her door, carrying a brown paper-wrapped package, and asked what had happened and why.

Addie started slowly, with Hot Corner Fred. Not that she expected Jennifer to understand or to forgive her, but because it felt important to say she hadn't done it for kicks. Or for any more power than power over her own life.

She told Jennifer about the smell of fresh paint in the living room of the dark, still house. Parents asleep in their bedroom with the door cracked wide enough to hear a crying child. The infant with the strawberry blonde curls and pink-flowered pajama set, asleep in her crib.

The rhythm of the child's breath held her in thrall for what seemed like forever but couldn't have been more than a minute or two—until the little one scrunched up her face and waved her arms.

She had to move then.

Five long minutes to recite the spell she'd been given to hush the baby and the space around her so she wouldn't wake. To wrap her in a blanket and re-place her with a homemade doll made of scraps and sticks. To do as she'd been ordered: keep from bolting long enough to witness the poppet come to life. She watched the doll assume the glamor the Fae had charmed into it. Take on every detailed characteristic of the baby who belonged in that crib.

She brought the baby to the Fae. God, but he looked like the devil. She expected him to smell like sulfur. But he smelled like green. Like crushed grass.

He took the child from her arms. *Never tell a soul*, he said. *No one may find out. Those are the terms. On pain of a fate worse than death.*

Then, she went back to the place she shared with Fred. He'd been killed, just as the Fae promised her. She stepped over his body to get her things. She left and never looked back.

Addie finished the story, her last word echoing off the walls.

"Thank you," Jennifer said.

Addie took a deep breath and blew it out. "I never even knew what the Fae wanted you for. At the time, I didn't care."

"He told me he wanted to be a father."

But she'd had one. She'd had human parents.

The way the girl looked at her, Addie could tell she had so much more to say—all of that rage Addie expected and feared the night the Fae had come for her, it lurked below the surface. It would come out eventually. And Addie would bear it.

Jennifer gave her the brown paper package.

The mirror inside looked the same as the one the girl had handed her a million years ago.

"I want you to have it," Jennifer said.

Addie waited until the girl had gone and then some, afraid to look, afraid of what she might see.

In the wee hours that night, she took the chance.

In the looking glass, she saw her kitchen. The table set for tea. And Mike, gazing back at her. She couldn't hear his voice out loud, but she heard it in her heart.

"I'm working on a way out for you, Addie," he said.

She couldn't think of one that didn't involve making a deal with a heavy price, the kind she'd never want him to pay. Because she loved him. In whatever twisted way she was able, she loved him. She had nothing of her own here to hold onto, but she could hold onto that.

She wanted her life back.

If he was going to help her get it, she'd give him everything she had. That's what you did with high stakes, with people you loved. The people you treasured.

Mike would have to hope for both of them. It had never been and would never be her strong suit, even now.

Despair was her particular magic, after all. She'd find a way to use it.

She's Not There

Steve Perry

Nobody is immune to Glamor.

In the ten years she'd had the talent, Darla had never come across anybody who had seen through it, far as she could tell. Old, young, men, women—it fooled everybody, every time.

Not that she'd need it here: Fifteen feet away, the widow Bellingham snored fully dressed upon her bed. The old lady had put down a bottle of very expensive champagne earlier at the party, and Darla could probably could bang a Chinese gong and not rouse her, but still . . .

She opened the last drawer of the jewel box, her movements slow and careful. The smell of cedar drifted up from the intricately carved wooden box, which was probably worth more than Darla's car.

Ah. Here we go . . .

It was an oval pin about the size of a silver dollar. Inset into the platinum were thirty-some diamonds, fancy yellows, the majority of them a carat or so each. Not worth as much as clears and nowhere near the value of the intense pinks or fancy blues encrusting the pieces in the top drawer, of course, but that was the point. These were good stones—good but not outstanding—and with what she could get from her fence, plenty to keep her going for six months.

One-carat gems of this grade were easy to move.

She limited herself to a job every three or four months, enough to keep her below heavy police radar—or at least it had done so for eight years.

Truth was, it had been almost too easy. Never a really close call. At first, it it had seemed a grand adventure, but it wasn't long before it turned into just a part-time job, no more exciting than shopping for fruit at New Seasons Market. Go in, pick out the organic apples you like, leave—without paying—and take a few months off, ta dah!

Disappointing in a way how easy it was, though certainly better than working for a living . . .

Six or seven million in fine jewelry here, and that was just the daily-wear stuff. The really good pieces would be in a bank vault somewhere.

Darla wrapped the pin in a square of black velvet and slipped it into her jeans pocket. She slid the jewelry box's drawer closed.

As always, she was tempted to clean the box out, but she knew better. Unique pieces were hard to move, worth only what the loose stones would bring, unless you wanted to mess around trying to find a crooked collector, and that was risky. This particular pin? It might not be missed for weeks or months. The top drawer stuff sure; the bottom drawer? Maybe the widow would never even notice. When you could go in and plunk down a million bucks for a brooch or a necklace without having to look at your checkbook balance? A pin worth a couple hundred grand? Shoot, that was practically costume jewelry.

So, she'd take just the one piece.

The perfect crime, after all, was not one where the cops couldn't figure out who did it; it was one the cops never even heard about.

Darla uttered the cantrip just before she pushed open the stairway door into the apartment building's lobby. When she stepped through, she looked the same to herself, save for a slight bluish glow to her skin that told her the Glamor was lit.

The guard at the desk looked up. "Morning, Mr. Millar. Early start today, hey?"

Darla grinned and sketched a two-finger salute at the guard.

The armed man touched a button on his console, and the building's door slid open. As she left, Darla waggled one hand over her shoulder in what she thought was a friendly gesture. Silently, of course. Her Glamour fooled the eyes but not the ears—if she spoke, she would sound like a twenty-something woman and not the sixty-something man she had picked as a disguise.

She had been careful coming down the stairs to avoid the surveillance cams, too, since her trick wouldn't fool them, either.

When the real Mr. Millar exited for his morning walk, the guard wouldn't say anything—he wouldn't want anybody to think he was crazy.

It was a fantastic thing, her trick, even if it had a couple of drawbacks: She had to touch somebody before it would work on them, and she had to do it within a day, since the effects of the touch faded away after that. Still, it was impressive.

She had no idea why or how she had come by it. She had been found in a dumpster as a baby, raised in an orphanage. The words to the cantrip were from a dream she'd had on the night she turned sixteen. Eventually, she had come to realize that, somehow, the dream had come true.

Magic? No such thing, everybody knew that. But here she was. She'd wondered about it over the years. She'd cautiously nosed around in a few places, but she never found any other real magic, only people faking it. Why did it work? How? She didn't know. Still, you didn't have to be a chemist to strike a match, and apparently you didn't need to know jack about magic to use the stuff. Case in point.

Worrying over the reasons might drive her nuts if she let it, so she didn't try anymore. She just thanked whatever gods there might be for bestowing it upon her, and that was that.

She had a car, but she seldom used it on a job where public transportation was available. She walked to the bus stop. The TriMet driver would see her as a white-haired Japanese man, since she had touched his shoulder earlier in the day when she'd ridden the bus in this direction. She would exit six blocks from her apartment and walk home. Nobody could connect Darla Wright to the expensive Portland penthouse occupied by the widow Bellingham, even if the woman ever did notice she'd been robbed.

Smooth as oil on glass, no muss, no fuss, just like always, and she planned to sleep in until at least noon.

Life was good.

Darla strolled into her neighborhood Starbucks, next to Fred Meyer's, and inhaled the fragrances of brewed coffee and freshly baked pastries. She was scouting for a fattening cherry turnover she figured she'd earned, when she bumped into a good-looking guy of about thirty who stopped suddenly ahead of her in the line.

"Oh, sorry," he said, turning to steady her. "My fault." He smiled. Nice teeth. Black hair, blue eyes, rugged features, pretty well built under a dark green t-shirt and snug jeans. Three or four years older than she was, but that was nothing.

"No problem," she said. She returned the smile.

Ice cream, she thought, looking at him. To go with the pastry, hey . . . ?

No . . . She couldn't. Not today. She had to meet Harry at two, and she'd slept past noon, so Ice Cream here would have to wait. Business before pleasure.

There were plenty of other men in the pond, and she was going to have free time to do a little fishing, lots of time . . .

*   *   *

Nothing as obvious as running a pawn shop, Harry had a guitar store, a hole-in-the-wall place twenty minutes from Portland, in Beaverton. Beaverton was where Portlanders went to buy fast food and shop at the 7-Elevens, a bedroom community that had once been swamps and filbert orchards and beaver-dammed streams.

The guitars at Harry's ran from a few hundred bucks up to ten or fifteen thousand on the high end, mostly acoustic and classicals, and the place actually did a pretty good business. Today being Sunday, the shop was closed, but Harry answered the bell at the back door. She waited while the four big and heavy locks snicked and clicked, bolts sliding back, and the door, made of thick steel plate, swung quietly open on oiled hinges. Trust a crook to know how to protect his own stuff.

The shop smelled of wood, and some kind of finish that was not unpleasant, a sharp, turpentiney scent.

"Layla. How nice to see you, as always."

Even Harry didn't get her real name. Darla was very careful.

"Harry. How business?"

"I can't complain. Come in. Some tea?" He was seventy-five, bald, thin, and wore thick glasses that kept slipping down his nose. He thought she was hot, though he'd never made a move on her.

"Thanks."

She sat at a table while Harry made tea. "Oolong today," he said.

Eventually, he sat the steaming cup in front of her.

"So, kiddo, whaddya got for me?"

She produced the pin, opened the velvet wrapping.

"Ah." He picked it up, pulled a loupe from his shirt pocket, held the pin up to the light. "Quality stones. Nice cuts, nothing outstanding. Say . . . fifty?"

"What, did I get stupid since you saw me last? Eighty," she said.

He smiled. "Might go sixty, because I like you."

"It's a steal at eighty, Harry. Two and a quarter for the bigger stones, and maybe another ten or fifteen for the little ones. Plus seven, eight hundred for the platinum. Pushing a quarter million, and you can pocket half that."

"Honey, we both know it's a steal at any price, but since I'll have to fly down to Miami to move the rocks, sixty is a gift. You know how I hate air travel."

"Miami? What's wrong with Seattle?"

He pulled the loupe off and put the piece onto the table. "Too warm for Seattle. Even broken up, thirty stones this close will have to moved a few at a time. Could take me months. Who has that kind of time at my age?"

"Warm? The, uh, previous owner doesn't even know it's gone."

"Alas, dear girl, I'm afraid she does. Mrs. Bellingham, widow of the late Leo Bellingham, owner of steel mills and shipyards, right? Probably pays her boy toys more than this bauble is worth, but she has definitely missed it."

Darla shook her head. "How could that happen? And how do you know it?"

He shrugged. "Maybe today was inventory day. Or it was a gift from a special friend with sentimental value. Who can say? All I know is, I talked to Benny the Nod this morning, and he said the Portland cops had come to call upon him early, waving a picture of this very item." He tapped the pin.

"Sweet Jesus," she said.

"I doubt He would have any part of this, hon, though you can tithe if you want. So, sixty?"

"Yeah, well, I guess. Sure."

They drank more tea, and he prattled on about some new classical guitar he'd just bought, Osage Orange this, cedar that, Sloane tuners, a genuine Carruth, look at the little owl inlay here—it all flowed into one ear and out the other. How unlucky was this?

That the old woman had discovered the theft within hours of it happening? That cost her at least twenty thousand dollars!

There was just no justice . . .

As Darla drove her British racing green Cooper Mini convertible along TV Highway back toward Portland, she relaxed a little. Yeah, okay, her latest theft had been discovered too quickly, but she was still sixty thousand dollars richer. Harry's cash, in used hundreds, was tucked away in her purse right there on the passenger seat. Life was still good. The sun was shining, the top was down, it was a lovely June afternoon, and she was free to spend the next few months lazing about, doing whatever she damned well pleased. Better than a poke in the eye with a sharp stick, hey?

She stopped at the light next to the Chrysler dealership on Canyon Road, tapping her fingers on the steering wheel as the Beatles sang "Hey, Jude" on the oldies station.

A heavy-set teenaged boy in baggy shorts and a sweatshirt with cutoff sleeves, a brim-backward baseball cap pulled low, his feet shod in big, clonky, ugly basketball shoes, strutted across the road in front of her. She couldn't see his eyes behind the dark shades he wore. Oh, please, kid! Who do you think you're fooling?

When he was almost past, on the passenger side, he pointed behind her and said, "Holy shit! Look at that!"

Darla turned to see what had impressed this wannabe gansta kid.

She caught a blur in her peripheral vision and turned back just in time to see the kid snag her purse—

"Fuck—!"

Darla put the car into neutral, set the brake, and jumped out of the car. She chased the kid, but he had a head start, and he was a lot faster than he looked.

He put on a burst of speed, and she lost him behind the car dealership.

And what what she have done if she'd caught him? Kick his ass? She didn't know anything about martial arts. She had a nice folding knife, but unfortunately, that had been in her purse, too.

Son of a bitch!

By the time she got back to her car, there was a line of traffic piled up behind it. She stalked back to the car, gave the finger to the fool behind her laying on his horn.

Fuck, fuck, fuck, fuck!

Sixty thousand dollars!

The hell of it was, she couldn't do anything about it! She could hear the conversation with the cop in her head:

Ah, you say you had sixty thousand dollars in cash in your purse? What is it you do for a living again, Miss?

Shit!

So much for the idea of six or eight months of goofing off. She was going to have to find another score. And soon. She was pretty much tapped out. She'd been counting on last night's job.

No fucking justice . . .

Darla remembered a line she'd heard somewhere, when some reporter was interviewing a famous robber. "So, Willie, why do you rob banks?" And his answer had been: "Because that's where the money is."

Probably never said that, but it made the point—you want to see who has the bling, you have to go where they flash it.

Which was why she was at a posh reception for some famous author at the Benton Hotel in Portland. Once she was past the gatekeeper, having him see her as somebody who showed up at these things that he knew by sight, she became herself again, but she had to look the part, so she had dressed up for it. Heels, a black, slinky dress, a simple strand of good black pearls, her short, dark hair nicely styled. Nobody inside would bother her, though the crowd was thick enough that somebody patted her on the ass as she squeezed through on her way to the bar. Apparently that cherry pastry hadn't added enough weight to matter.

She got a club soda with lime, then started shopping.

She winnowed her choices to two possibles.

One was a forty-something woman with gorgeous red hair and a great figure she worked hard to keep looking that way. She'd had a little plastic work done on her face, very subtle but offset by a botoxed forehead that might as well have been carved from marble. She wore emeralds—earrings, a necklace, a ring that had to run four carats, all matching settings in yellow gold. The dress was a creamy yellow that went with the jewelry. Quarter million in shades of green fire. Nice.

The other prospect was a guy, maybe thirty-five, in an Armani tux. He was tanned and fit, with a little gray in his hair and an easy smile, and though he wasn't sporting any monster rocks, he did wear a Patek Philippe watch—she guessed it was a Jumbo Nautilus in rose gold, worth about thirty grand wholesale. He had one ring on his right hand, a gold nugget inset with a black opal the size of a dime that flashed Chinese writing in multiple colors as the opal caught the light when he raised his champagne glass to sip. That good an Australian opal might go ten grand. She wouldn't want either the watch or the ring, they'd be too hard to move, but he'd probably have other pieces lying around . . .

Men were both harder and easier for her. Looking like she did, she could get close to them and touch them enough to get feelings for somebody she could become. And more than a few rich men had offered to take her home—for their own purposes, of course, but still, it got her a lot of intelligence for a later visit.

So, the emerald lady or the opal guy?

Even as she thought this, the opal guy looked up and noticed her. He smiled at the man he was talking to, said something, and ambled in her direction.

Well, look at this. If he was going to do the work? Maybe that was a good sign . . .

"What's a nice girl like you doing at a stuffy event like this?"

"Waiting for you, it seems," she said. She gave him her high-wattage smile.

He held his champagne glass up in a silent toast, as if to acknowledge her response to his pick-up line. "I'm Arlo St. Johns," he said.

"Layla Harrison," she said, giving him a name she'd made up for herself in the orphanage years ago. One of housemothers who wasn't too awful had been a big fan of the English rock invasion of the early sixties and had lent Darla her books about the subject. She had discovered that Eric Clapton had written the song "Layla" after having fallen for George Harrison's wife, Patti. That woman must have been something, Darla had decided, since she had been the inspiration for at least three famous rock songs—"Something," by Harrison when he'd been with the Beatles, "Layla" and "Wonderful Tonight," by Clapton.

Ran in the family, too—Pattie's little sister had been Donovan's muse for "Jennifer Juniper," and had gone on to marry Mick Fleetwood of Fleetwood Mac.

"Penny for your thoughts?" he said.

"Worth more than that, I think."

"No doubt. Want to go get a drink or something somewhere a little less crowded?"

"What did you have in mind?"

"My place is much quieter."

She smiled. "Why not? Seen one writer, seen them all . . ."

*   *   *

St. Johns had a high-rise apartment downtown, and he drove them to it in a black Cadillac Escalade that still had the new-car smell. Sixty, seventy thousand bucks worth of car. This was shaping up to be a fun evening. Guy was good-looking, well-mannered, was obviously doing well enough to drive a high-end SUV and to sport expensive, tasteful jewelery. Bound to have something lying around his place worth lifting.

She didn't have a lot of rules in her biz, but one of them was that she didn't get intimate—well, not too intimate—with her marks. Not that this was ironclad—she had slipped a couple of times—but it made her feel guilty stealing from somebody she'd slept with, and she didn't need that. Darla had built a pretty good rationalization about stealing from the rich and their insurers who wouldn't miss it; if she went to bed with somebody and had a really good time, it would feel wrong to take his stuff.

Pretending not to look, she easily managed to see the numbers he punched into the alarm keypad just inside the door. She committed them to memory, converting them to letters. The first letter of each word corresponded to the number of its position in the alphabet: Thus 78587 became GHEHG, which in turn became a nonsensical but memorable sentence: Great Hairy Elephants Hate Giraffes.

The apartment was gorgeous, decorated by somebody with money and taste. Oil paintings, fancy handmade paper lamps, Oriental carpets some family in Afghanistan must have spent years making. Upscale furniture, more comfortable than showy.

While St. Johns made them drinks at his wet bar, she went into the bathroom, took her cell phone from her purse, and programmed it to ring in thirty minutes. That would give them enough time to have a drink and talk a little but not get to the rolling-around-and-breaking-expensive-furniture stage.

She went back into the living room.

St. Johns was funny, smart, and twenty minutes into

their conversation over perfect martinis, she was thinking maybe she would sleep with him instead of burgling him. That would be okay.

But, she reminded herself, she was broke. She had a couple thousand in the bank, but her apartment rent was due, her car note, and her fridge was mostly empty. She needed the money more than she needed to get laid.

A shame. He really was fun. He was some kind of importer, specializing in Pacific Rim antiquities, he said, and there were a few pieces of Polynesian or Hawaiian or other island art carefully set out here and there that she suspected were probably worth a small fortune. Jewelry she knew, painting and sculpture, she didn't have a clue.

He smiled at her. "So, what do you do when you aren't attending boring social gatherings?"

"Not much, I'm afraid. When my parents died, they left me a fair-sized insurance policy. I had the money invested, so it brings in enough to keep the wolf from the door. I take classes in this and that, work out, travel a bit. Nothing very exciting."

He smiled bigger.

She smiled back. Oh, this wasn't just ice cream, this was Haagen Dazs Special Limited Edition Black Walnut; you could get fat just opening the carton. The temptation surged in her, a warm wave. She had enough to pay the rent and car note, barely, she could buy some red beans and rice and veggies, make it another week before she had to have some more money . . .

In her purse, her cell phone began playing Pachelbel's Canon in D.

Crap! What to do? Shut the phone off and stay?

Because she wanted to do just that so much, she decided it wasn't a good idea. A matter of discipline. If she slipped, that could lead her down a dangerous slope. Just because it had always been good didn't mean it couldn't go bad.

Oh, well. She smiled, fetched her phone, touched a control.

"Hey, what's up?" A beat. Then, "Oh, no! That's terrible! Are you all right?"

St. Johns raised an eyebrow at her.

"No, no, I'll come over. I'll see you in a little while."

She snapped the phone shut. "I'm sorry. That was my girlfriend Maria," she said. "Her fiancé just dumped her, and she's in a terrible state. I need to go see her."

"I knew it was too good to be true. I'll give you a ride."

"No, I'll catch a cab. She lives way out in Hillsboro, I wouldn't ask you to do that."

"It's no trouble. I don't have anything else planned."

"Really, I appreciate it, but no. Could you, uh, give me your number? I'd like to see you again."

"Oh, yes." He produced a business card that had nothing on it but his name and a phone number. "Take care of your friend," he said, smiling. "And do call me. I'd love to see you again."

"I will look forward to seeing you," she said. Unfortunately, you won't know who I am when I do . . .

"Let me call a cab."

"Thanks, Arlo."

"My pleasure."

After he called, he walked her to the door and rested his hand on her shoulder. There was a moment when she thought he would kiss her—and she wouldn't have objected—but it passed.

Another road not taken.

Too bad, but that's how life was. Sometimes, business had to come before pleasure.

Her taxi arrived. The night was warm, and she slid into the cab and gave the driver an address near a stop where she could catch a MAX train to a station near her place.

"Yes, madam," the driver said. He looked to be about fifty, and from his accent, she guessed he was Indian or Pakistani.

It really was too bad about St. Johns.

The cabbie was chatty, going on about the warm weather and how the Bull Run Resevoir was low for this time of year. She responded politely, already thinking of how she was going to burgle St. Johns's apartment. If the Glamor worked on voices, it would be a snap—she'd become St. Johns, tell the security guy she'd lost her key, and have him let her into the place. Take something the mark wouldn't miss, and adios.

Too bad St. Johns wasn't a mute—

Ah! Wait a second, hold on, she had something here . . .

"Beg pardon, Miss?" the cabbie said.

"Huh?" She looked at him.

"You made an exclamation? Are you in distress?"

She smiled. "Oh, oh, no, sorry. I was just thinking of something. I'm fine."

The cabbie smiled and nodded.

Actually, she was better than fine. She had come up with a terrific idea. Why hadn't it occurred to her years ago? It was so simple.

She paid the cabbie, gave him a nice tip—what the hell, she'd be flush again in a couple days, right? She walked to the MAX station. A light rail train arrived, and she got on, along with several others. She exited at the stop near her house. An old lady dressed in khaki slacks and a tie-dyed t-shirt and running shoes got off the train and set off at a fast walk ahead of her. The woman had long, steely-gray hair and a lot of smile wrinkles and was obviously in pretty good shape from the pace she set. You could do worse than to be somebody like that when you got old, Darla decided. But not for a real long time.

St. Johns needed to be out of the building, so she had to risk using her car. She parked near the exit to the garage early and waited to see St. Johns' Caddy leave.

At about nine in the morning, the Escalade pulled out.

Okay, kid, here we go . . .

Darla approached the building's street entrance. She put a hand on the doorman's sleeve as she asked to see the security man on duty.

Inside, she was conducted to the security desk. The man behind it looked up.

"Help you, Miss?" He stood and moved to the counter.

"Yes, I saw a car parked out front, and there were two men in it who seemed to be watching the entrance," she said. "Probably it's nothing, but I thought I should say something about it."

"Two men? What kind of car? They still there?"

She shrugged. "I'm not good with cars. Like a van, maybe an SUV? Dark, kind of old, muddy? But they left."

"Uh-huh. You get get the license number, ma'am?"

She shook her head. "Sorry."

"Ah. Well. Listen, we appreciate it. We'll, uh, keep an eye out for it." Probably thinking was a twit she was. Two men in a car, right.

She reached out and touched his arm. "Probably it's nothing," she said. "But these days, you can't be too careful."

"Yes, ma'am. That's true."

Darla stepped into a doorway in the next building and lit the Glamor. Show time . . .

"Morning, Mr. St. Johns," the doorman said. He opened the heavy glass door.

Darla smiled and nodded, knowing that her disguise was perfect.

She walked to the security desk.

"Mr. St. Johns. How may I help you sir?"

She shook her head and touched her throat. In a raspy voice as low as she could manage, Darla said, "Laryngitis." She coughed.

"Oh, sorry to hear that."

"Forgot my key," she said. Her voice was a passable imitation of a sick frog.

"No problem, sir." The guard opened a wide drawer, scanned the contents, and produced a door key. "Here you go. Drop it off whenever."

Darla smiled, nodded, and coughed as she took the key.

Perfect. She didn't have to sound like St. Johns; she had set it up that her—his—voice was gone. Very clever, if she said so herself.

People were coming and going, and the guard's attention veered away from her.

There weren't any cameras in the elevators, at least none she'd seen the night before, but she lingered until a couple other people arrived to ride up. They would see her as Darla, and if there was a hidden camera in the elevator, the guard would see three people in it. How much track would he be keeping?

So far, it ran like a Swiss watch.

She opened the door, stepped inside—it wouldn't do for somebody to see her instead of St. Johns, though they might assume she was his special friend, since she had a key.

Inside, she shut the door and reached for the alarm pad, but she realized that it was green. He hadn't even bothered to set it.

She shook her head. Man didn't turn on his alarm? He deserved to have his stuff stolen. Lordy.

In the bedroom, it took all of ten seconds to find the jewelry box—it was leather, trimmed in brass, and it sat atop a dresser made of what looked like ebony.

Darla opened the box.

My. There were gold coins, loose gems—mostly diamonds, but a couple of emeralds—a diamond-studded money clip that held three thousand dollars in hundreds. There was a banded 5K stack of hundreds next to that, but the band was broken and two were missing. There were a dozen platinum coins and ten platinum one-ounce ingots, and several sets of cuff links and tiepins, done in assorted gems—rubies, emeralds, sapphires . . .

Quickly Darla decided what she could remove without it being immediately noticed. There were thirty-two gold coins, Eagles, and she took two of those. Nineteen loose stones, fourteen of which were one or two-carat, round-cut blue-white diamonds. She took one of the two-carat stones and one of the single carats. She took two hundreds from the money clip, three from the banded stack. One of the platinum coins, one of the ingots. She considered the tie tacks and cuff links and decided they were too easily missed.

Okay, a quick total: couple of gold Eagles, probably worth eight hundred each. The platinum eagle was worth fourteen, fifteen hundred, probably, the ingot a little less, say twelve hundred, and that was money in her pocket, since they didn't have to be fenced. The diamonds were clean and clear, figure six, eight thousand on the smaller one, and at least twenty-five or thirty on the bigger one. Less Harry's cut on those, so say they were worth twenty thousand to her total, if she was lucky. With the cash, she'd net about twenty-five grand total. Unless St. Johns did an inventory, he likely wouldn't notice anything was gone, and she'd buy herself three or four months of lie-about time. Not nearly as good as what she had gotten from the widow's place, but she had that laryngitis trick, and that would come in handy.

Once again, it was tempting to scoop it all into her pocket—there was enough here to keep her from having to score again for a couple-three years, maybe longer. But, no. Better to stick with what had kept her out of jail for all this time; greed was a killer. She sighed and closed the jewelry box.

As she turned to leave, she noticed the corner of a box jutting out from under the bed. A bed with black silk sheets on it, she also noticed, and neatly made.

She stopped, bent, and pulled the box from under the bed. It was long, wide, and fairly flat, as big as a large suitcase, if shallower. She opened the box.

It was full of thousand dollar bills, stacked in rows, fifteen across and eight down, and the bills were loose and mostly used.

Holy shit!

She picked up one stack, her breath coming faster, and counted it. Then another stack. A third. The first had thirty, the second twenty-eight, the third, thirty-three. Nonsequentially numbered.

She did some fast math. A hundred and twenty stacks, say thirty bills in each stack on average.

Three million six hundred thousand dollars.

Oh, man!

What was St. Johns doing with this much cash under his bed?

Darla stared at the cash. If she took one or two bills from each stack, he might not even notice! She could take a hundred thousand, two hundred thousand, and unless he did a count, he wouldn't be able to tell. And even if he did that, she was pretty sure this wasn't money he wanted anybody to know about—it had the smell of something not quite legal.

Of course, she couldn't just walk into a bank and plunk down a couple hundred thousand-dollar bills and expect that to fly without raising questions; but Harry knew people who could move big notes without batting an eye and he'd take ten or fifteen percent, no more than that.

Two bills from each stack. Two hunded and forty thousand dollars, she could give Harry the two-carat blue-white for his cut and—no, she decided, she'd put all that back. No point in risking this much for petty cash. With two hundred grand in her pocket, she could take a long damn time before she had to make another score.

Yes. That's how she would do it. Put the coins and gems back, pack a quarter of a million into her pockets—no more carrying it in purses, thank you very much—and walk away with a big smile under her Glamor.

Darla drove toward her place, using a long and winding route, to make sure she wasn't followed. She was almost home when she heard the sound of a police siren. She looked into the rearview mirror and saw a plain, tan Crown Victoria with a blue light flashing on the dashboard behind her.

"Oh, shit!" she said. An icy wave washed over her, as if she'd been drenched in liquid nitrogen, turning her stiff with fear.

She pulled to the curb. This wasn't a traffic stop.

A tall, heavyset, balding man alighted from the car. He wore a cheap, badly wrinkled suit and brown shoes, and a tie that failed to reach his belt. Might as well have had a neon sign over his head flashing out the word "Cop!"

He walked to her driver's door.

"Would you step out of the car, please?"

"What's the trouble? Was I speeding?"

"No, lady, I'm a detective, I don't do traffic tickets. Out here, please, and keep your hands where I can see them."

Dead. She was dead. She had considered it over the years, what she would do if she was ever caught, but it had never seemed real to her, it had been so theoretical.

What was she going to do?

The Glamor.

Of course! In her panicked fear, she had forgotten she had a perfect weapon. She'd touch him, and when the moment was right, she'd distract him, change, and that would be that!

The woman? she'd say, when he turned around and saw an old man there, She went that way, she was running!

Okay, she'd be okay, she could do this. He'd have to pat her down, and that would be enough, his hands on her would be fine. A touch was a touch.

"Over on the sidewalk, please," he said.

She obeyed.

"What did I do?" she asked.

"You don't need me to tell you that. Step in there, please."

He pointed to a gate that led to what looked like a small garden.

"Excuse me?"

"We don't want to do this out here."

"Do what out here?!"

The panic she'd felt came back. What was going on?

"Open the gate, please."

She did. He shut the wrought iron behind them. "Wow, look at that," he said.

She turned. "Wh-what?"

When she turned back to look at the cop, he was gone.

In his place was an old woman.

Darla frowned. She knew this woman from somewere . . . ah, it was the old lady on the MAX train . . .

"Or this?" the old woman said, in a decidedly masculine voice.

The woman shimmered, and in a moment, Darla found herself looking at the cab driver who had taken her home from St. Johns—

And then, like a strobe light blinking on and off, the cab driver became the teenager who had stolen her purse, the good-looking guy she'd seen in Starbucks, and finally, St. Johns.

Blink, blink, blink.

Darla was too stunned to speak.

"Are we having fun yet?" he asked.

She realized her mouth was open. She closed it.

He chuckled. "Sorry. I couldn't resist."

The meaning of it hit her. "You—you're like me," she said, her voice barely above a whisper.

"Yep. What you see isn't what you get, necessarily."

He laughed again. "I don't rob houses. My ambition is a little bigger than that, but I do okay. As you noticed when you spotted my cash box. How much did you take, by the way?"

"Two bills from each stack."

"Smart. I like bright women."

"Why are you—what—?"

"Well, I've been watching you for a while, Darla. Far as I can tell, you and I are the only two of our kind. I'd propose a . . . partnership."

"Partnership?"

"Well, more than that, maybe. I mean, you are gorgeous and careful and clever, but there there are some advantages to what we can do together. Between the two of us, we could do bigger and better things than either of us can do alone. Imagine how much easier it would be be if we could be a couple that looked like anybody we wanted?"

She considered it. Yes. That would be something.

"Plus, there are some other perks."

He shimmered and turned into a studly young movie star that Darla much admired.

"Or maybe . . . this?" He morphed into another young man, this one a match to a well-known rock star.

"We have a world of choice to offer each other, don't we?" He shimmered again and reclaimed St. Johns. "Not that I think I would get bored with you as you stand. You are stunning, you know, but you also have a kind of variety to offer no other woman does."

She smiled back at him. "Even though I stole your money?"

"Because you stole my money. What do you think?"

She found herself nodding. Yes. There was an attraction, no question, and if she got tired of looking at him?

Well, he could fix that in an instant.

Because nobody was immune to Glamor . . .

About the Authors

Ilsa J. Bick is a psychiatrist as well as the author of award-winning stories, e-books, and novellas and best-selling novels set in the *Star Trek* and *MechWarrior: Dark Age* universes. The Jason Saunders companion story, "The Key," first appeared on SCIFI.Com (http://www.scifi.com/scifiction/originals/originals_archive/bick3/bick31.html) and was selected as a Distinguished Mystery Story in *The Best American Mystery Stories, 2005*, edited by Joyce Carol Oates. She is currently at work on the paranormal thriller *Satan's Skin* and an as-yet untitled paranormal featuring the continuing adventures of Detective Jason Saunders and Dr. Sarah Wylde. She lives in Wisconsin with her family and other assorted vermin.

Randall N. Bills has worked as the line developer and continuity editor for the *Classic BattleTech/MechWarrior* universe for ten years. In addition to writing eight novels set in this universe, he's led the publication of over fifty products. He's also published in the *Star Fleet Corps of Engineers: Aftermath* anthology, as well as a new line of young adult fiction under the *Adventure Boys* brand. He lives in the Pacific Northwest with his wife, three children, and a snake, and when he's not writing or developing rules, he's playing board games with friends and family, listening to music, reading, or blowing things up on the Xbox.

Once there was a guy named Joe Edwards who really wanted to write. He followed his stories to the page, and here he is now. When he's not writing, Edwards raises Irish wolfhounds and restores antique shotguns somewhere in the Rocky Mountain states.

Robert T. Jeschonek has written science fiction and fantasy stories for *Postscripts, Abyss & Apex, Loyalhanna Review*, and other publications. His Star Trek fiction has appeared in ***New Frontier: No Limits, S.C.E.: The Cleanup, Voyager: Distant Shores***, and ***Strange New Worlds***, volumes III, V, and VI. His story "Our Million-Year Mission" won the grand prize in the ***Strange New Worlds VI*** contest. Robert has also written for *War, Commercial Suicide, Dead by Dawn Quarterly*, and other comic books. Visit him on line at www.robertjeschonek.com.

Jay Lake lives in Portland, Oregon, where he works on numerous writing and editing projects. His recent novels are ***Madness of Flowers*** from Night Shade Books and ***Escapement*** from Tor Books. Jay is the winner of the 2004 John W. Campbell Award for Best New Writer and a multiple nominee for the Hugo and World Fantasy Awards. Jay can be reached through his blog at jlake.com.

Steven Mohan, Jr., lives in Pueblo, Colorado, with his wife and three children and, surprisingly, no cats. When not writing he works as a manufacturing engineer. His fiction has appeared in *Interzone, Polyphony*, and *Paradox*, among other places. His short stories have won honorable mention in ***The Year's Best Science Fiction*** and ***The Year's Best Fantasy and Horror***.

Devon Monk lives in Oregon with her husband, two sons, and a dog named Mojo. Her first novel, *Magic to the Bone*, is out now, and her short stories can be found in a variety of genre magazines and anthologies, including **Rotten Relations**, **Maiden, Matron, Crone**, **Fantasy Gone Wrong, Year's Best Fantasy #2**, and **Better Off Undead**. When not writing, she is either drinking coffee, knitting toys, or wondering why the dog is looking at her so strangely. For more on Devon, go to www.devonmonk.com.

Peter Orullian has recently been published in other fine DAW anthologies, as well as *Orson Scott Card's Intergalactic Medicine Show*. For grocery money, he works at Microsoft in the Xbox division. And while he desperately hopes to make a living writing, his other abiding passion is music; Peter recently returned from a European tour with a successful hard rock band. He has a New York agent currently shopping one of his novels, which he hopes allows him to retire from Microsoft and sing and write until everything bleeds.

Steve Perry has written scores of novels, animated teleplays, and short stories, along with a couple of spec movie scripts. A number of his books have appeared on the *New York Times* Bestseller list, and he is the coauthor, with Michael Reaves, of the recent blockbuster Star Wars novel **Death Star**.

Mike Resnick is, according to *Locus*, the all-time leading short fiction award winner, living or dead, in science fiction history. He is the author of more than fifty novels, almost two hundred stories, and two screenplays, and he has edited close to fifty anthologies. He has won five Hugos, a Nebula, and other major awards in the USA, France, Japan, Spain, Croatia, and Poland. His work has been translated into twenty-two languages.

Kristine Kathryn Rusch has sold novels in several different genres under many different names. Her most current Rusch novel is **Duplicate Effort: A Retrieval Artist Novel**. The *Retrieval Artist* novels are standalone mysteries set in a science fiction world. She's won the Endeavor Award for that series. Her writing has received dozens of award nominations as well as several actual awards, from science fiction's Hugo to the Prix Imagainare, a French fantasy award for best short fiction. She lives and works on the Oregon Coast.

Jason Schmetzer's work has appeared in both print and electronic form, most recently in short fiction for Catalyst Game Labs. He's been writing for more than ten years and holds undergraduate and graduate degrees in Creative Writing and Fiction. When he's not writing, he teaches Composition and Creative Writing at Ivy Tech State Community College. He lives with his daughter Nora in southern Indiana.

Dean Wesley Smith is the bestselling author of over eighty novels under various names. He has published over a hundred short stories and has been nominated for just about every award in science fiction and fantasy and horror; he has even won a few of them. He is the former editor and publisher of Pulphouse Publishing. His most recent novel in science fiction is **All Eve's Hallows**. He is currently writing thrillers under another name.

Michael A. Stackpole is an award-winning author, game and computer game designer, and poet whose first novel, **Warrior: En Garde**, was published in 1988. Since then, he has written forty-one other novels, including eight *New York Times* bestselling novels in the Star Wars line, of which **X-Wing: Rogue Squadron** and **I, Jedi** are the best known. Mike lives in Arizona and in his spare time spends early mornings at Starbucks, collects toy soldiers and old radio shows, plays indoor soccer, rides his bike, and listens to Irish music in the finer pubs in the Phoenix area. His website is *www.stormwolf.com*.

Leslie Claire Walker grew up among the darkly magical, lush bayous and urban jungles of the Texas Gulf Coast. These days she lives in Houston with assorted animal and plant companions and two harps. Her fiction has appeared in *Fantasy Magazine*, *Chiaroscuro*, and two previous DAW Books anthologies—**Hags, Sirens and Other Bad Girls of Fantasy** and **Cosmic Cocktails**. She is hard at work on her current novel about a teenage runaway and a rock star who ride the skies with the Wild Hunt on Halloween night. Catch up with her at http://leslieclairewalker.com.

Phaedra M. Weldon has written short stories for several anthologies, as well as novellas published in shared universe fields such as *Star Trek* and *BattleTech*. Her first *Shadowrun* book, **Triptych,** will be released in April 2009, and **Phantasm,** the third book in the Zoë Martinque series, will be released in June 2009.

P.R. Frost

The Tess Noncoiré Adventures

"Frost's fantasy debut series introduces a charming protagonist, both strong and vulnerable, and her cheeky companion. An intriguing plot and a well-developed warrior sisterhood make this a good choice for fans of the urban fantasy of Tanya Huff, Jim Butcher, and Charles deLint."
—*Library Journal*

HOUNDING THE MOON
978-0-7564-0425-3
MOON IN THE MIRROR
978-0-7564-0486-4

and coming in June 2009:
FAERY MOON
978-0-7564-0556-4

To Order Call: 1-800-788-6262
www.dawbooks.com